TASTE OF TORMENT

The Deep In Your Veins Series

Suzanne Wright

The characters and events portrayed in this book are fictitious.
Any similarity to real persons, living or dead, is coincidental and
not intended by the author.

ISBN-13: 978-1495311918
ISBN-10: 1495311910

For all the fans of the series — your support has meant everything to me

CHAPTER ONE

(Sam)

Hearing a throat clear, I slowly turned my head and peered up at the fierce-looking vampire that was standing beside the sofa, glaring down at me. In addition to being my mate, Jared Michaels was my co-commander...and he didn't look happy, which was totally understandable given the circumstances. He had clearly teleported into our apartment using his very impressive vampiric gift, and now I was in seriously deep shit. As Jared's twin brother and fellow vampire, Evan, would say: busted.

I smiled awkwardly, knowing my expression was guilt-ridden. "I wasn't expecting you home just yet."

"Oh, well I can see that." Even scowling, Jared was still unfairly edible. He had a dark, raw masculinity that was so overwhelming it could make a girl feel drunk.

I flashed him an apologetic smile. It had no effect.

"This isn't the first time you've done this, is it?"

Lying would be pointless, considering that our bond would allow him to sense it – a bond that had developed when we were joined through a vampire Binding ceremony five months ago. Binding was so much more than marriage; the powerful bond that formed between the couple could only be broken by death, even if the couple no longer cared for each other. So, in addition to having a brail-like tattoo where a wedding ring might have been, I now also had an extra sense; it was solely focused on Jared, allowing me to know

1

things such as his vitals, his thirst level, and his mood. I didn't need the bond to alert me of his current mood – he was undoubtedly pissed.

Realising that he was waiting impatiently for an answer to his question, I quietly admitted, "No."

He folded his arms across his solid, well-defined chest. "How long has this been going on?"

"Not long."

"Define 'not long'."

I shrugged. "A week, maybe."

"Unfuckingbelievable."

His snappy comment had my snake, Dexter, lifting his head from where he was curled up on the rug. In the beginning, he hadn't liked Jared at all. Thankfully, though, Dexter had gradually warmed up to him as he came to understand that Jared was as equally protective of me as he was. Still, Dexter would bite him in a blink if he thought Jared was any threat to me. That wouldn't be good, given that Dexter's preternatural venom could cause temporary blindness, mental disorientation, and then muscle paralysis. Two bites at one time could also cause excruciating pain followed by death. Sweet.

Wes, who was the Sire of the Grand High Master Vampire Antonio, had the remarkable gift of making his pictures come to life. When Wes drew an image of a snake on my arm, it automatically became a tattoo that could become a live snake. Dexter was a mix of a spitting cobra, a black mamba, a rattlesnake, and a garter snake. Wes had named the hybrid breed 'Strikers' due to how fast they attacked. An amazing thing about them was that they changed colour with their mood. At the moment, Dexter was jet black – which we had learned meant that he was alert and wary.

"I knew you were keeping something from me," continued Jared, not in the least bit daunted by Dexter's shift in mood and the possible danger. There wasn't much that fazed Jared Michaels. "I just couldn't figure out what it was."

"Look, I'm sorry. It won't happen again," I promised.

"I would have thought you had better self-control."

"So I had a moment of weakness. Doesn't everyone?"

"How am I supposed to trust you when you pull shit like this?" A glint of amusement entered his intense hazel eyes, making me inwardly sigh in relief. I'd kind of expected the red tinges to his irises that marked him as a Pagori vampire to start glowing – it was something they did whenever he was angry, thirsty, or horny. Pagoris were the most powerful of the three vampire breeds, having incredible speed and strength. Unfortunately for them, they easily became aggressive and had a very strong bloodlust. "Answer me one thing honestly: did you find it by accident, or did you go looking for it?" My expression must have answered that, because he shook his head sadly.

"I just don't like surprises," I said defensively. Which was why I had searched our entire apartment for my birthday presents. I decided against telling him that I'd also found the other two gifts – it was bad enough that he'd caught me playing with my brand new PlayStation 6, which hadn't yet been released in the human world, complete with the 'Vampire Nation' game.

Jared's shrewd eyes narrowed. "You found the other presents, too, didn't you?"

Crap. "I'm not comfortable with all these questions."

Shaking his head again, he plucked me from the sofa. I instantly wrapped my limbs around him, melting into the kiss that he planted on my mouth. His deliciously spicy, masculine scent swirled around me, making me want to drag him to our bedroom and have my wicked way with him on the king-size bed that we'd moved here from his old apartment.

He pulled back, smiling, and ran a hand through my long, dark hair. "I can't believe I'm going to have to teleport your presents somewhere out of your reach. All you had to do was wait another two weeks."

I pouted. "You don't have to teleport them away. I already promised that it wouldn't happen again."

His smile widened. "Yes, you did. But I'm pretty sure there are loopholes in that promise somewhere."

I sniffed haughtily. "Fine. Be that way."

The randy bastard ground himself against me. "Now you're just making me want to fuck that attitude right out of you."

"Smooth," I teased.

He nuzzled my neck, breathing in deeply. "Unfortunately, being inside you and hearing you scream my name with that husky voice and that British accent will have to wait until later." He had a thing about my accent, but I happened to really like his Californian accent, so happy days. "The guys are probably already at the bar."

Thanks to vampire speed, we would be ready in less than ten minutes to meet with our squad to celebrate the completion of our most recent assignment, which had ended two nights ago. The gated community in which we lived was referred to as The Hollow. It housed vampires and humans, and contained plenty of stores, bars, and also a nightclub. It was situated on an off-the-map Caribbean island, surrounded by a tropical rainforest, and had a man-made beach in the centre for the residents to use. Antonio, his staff, and the legion also had access to the private beach behind his mansion.

Although I had been made a commander on my first night here, it hadn't been the position I'd applied for when I arrived from London. Having been scouted by Antonio's tracker, Sebastian, I had participated in the try-outs for a place in the legion. The majority of people there, including Jared, had thought it completely ridiculous for a female to attend. Although I'd passed each stage and was rare in being a Feeder – a vampire able to absorb and manipulate energy – I was denied a place. It was then that Antonio made me Jared's co-commander. Jared's issue hadn't just been that I was female. No, it was also that I was a Sventé vampire – the weakest of the three breeds.

Although Keja vampires weren't as strong as Pagoris, they were still powerful in that they were hypnotically beautiful. All three breeds had a preternatural allure, but Keja beauty was enchanting enough to bewitch people, ensnaring their prey. Also, like Pagoris, their vampiric gifts were often very substantial. Kejas were identifiable by their fangs and the amber tinges to their irises – tinges that glowed when they were angry, thirsty, or horny.

Sventés, however, couldn't boast of much. Our vampiric gifts were mostly defensive rather than offensive, and we didn't have super strength or a bewitching allure. Still, we were stronger and faster than humans and had incredible agility. We didn't have visible markings – no fangs, no glowing irises – and our bloodlust wasn't overpowering. All of that enabled us to blend well with humans, and therein lay our power. But the other two breeds didn't perceive that as strength. To them, Sventés were inferior in that we were tame and too human-like as opposed to the ultimate predator.

Although Jared overcame his prejudice and wasn't the narrow-minded arsehole he'd once been, the vampire community hadn't been keen on me Binding with him. As Antonio's Heir, Jared was destined to one day hold the position; to rule and protect vampires worldwide. As his mate, I would share that position as ruler. The vampires needed to be secure in the knowledge that their rulers could protect them. As such, having a Sventé as a ruler hadn't been an attractive idea to them.

It was only the fact that I was very powerful as a Feeder – a gift that should technically only run in Pagori lines – that had stopped a riot from occurring. Instead, the guests had spent the week approaching the ceremony testing my patience and strength. Fate had decided it would be funny for me to be weak at the time. Yep, thanks to two vampire scientists, I had been gradually altering while at the same time weakening. No one had known how I was altering or what the bloody hell would happen. We had found out pretty quickly. The sociopathic scientists had been trying to create a hybrid – a mix of all three vampire breeds.

The wackos had also succeeded.

Thanks to them, I was now the only hybrid in the world. In addition to having the Sventé manageable bloodlust, I also had the hypnotic allure of a Keja, and the strength of a Pagori. Nonetheless, I was a Sventé at heart.

A side effect of this hybrid business was the new mercury tinges to my irises – tinges that glowed when, yes you guessed it, I was thirsty, angry, or horny. Jared swore they looked beautiful, but I personally believed he was talking tripe and I rather missed having normal eyes.

Some might think it would be fabulous to be a hybrid, to be so strong. But the very few of us who knew about it were all set on keeping it secret, coming up with bullshit reasons for the new mercury ring to my irises and my sudden increase in power. Everyone believed Antonio's excuses as they had no reason not to; they trusted him. If they knew the truth, they might not be too comfortable with letting me live. After all, if hybrids became a breed in their own right, they would be stronger than the other three, messing with the current dynamics. Pagoris would lose their 'throne', Kejas would be knocked down a notch, and Sventés would be even more vulnerable than before. No one would like that.

Less than ten minutes later, Jared and I were ready to leave. Before going to meet with the squad, Jared unfortunately lived up to his word and teleported my presents out of the apartment and hid them somewhere. It was probably for the best. I was addicted to the 'Vampire Nation' game, so there was a high chance that I would have dug it out and played with it again before my birthday came around.

Finally arriving at our destination, we found six of the squad gathered at the long bar, ordering drinks. Damien, Salem, Butch, Stuart, and Denny were making a huge fuss of David, who had proven to be the most valuable member on this particular assignment – they were like a football team, ecstatic with a player who had 'scored the winning goal'. The youngest of the squad was actually the strongest; David's gift was to produce a psionic boom that could cause such extreme pressure on the skull that it totally overwhelmed the brain and led to a temporary coma.

"It wasn't all me," I heard David say as Jared and I approached. "We're a team. Plus, if it wasn't for Butch, I wouldn't have got close enough to the building to get inside."

That was true. Butch used his ability to negate or deflect anything that came at him to produce a shield and protect David – being so powerful meant that David was always an immediate target. When the others turned to Butch and made the same fuss of him, he smiled and nodded. One thing I had noticed about Butch was that his crooked grins never quite reached his eerily dark eyes. Whether that meant he wasn't good with emotion or that he was simply a sociopath that experienced none, I wasn't sure. Given how creative he could be with his kills, it could very well be the latter. But I didn't have much room to judge.

Noticing Jared and me, they all turned and greeted us with pats on the back. Yeah, they thought of me as one of the boys. I wasn't sure whether to be offended or touched. Even out of work hours, they all called me 'Coach' rather than Sam. Of course, that didn't stop Damien dishing out a compliment purely to annoy Jared.

"Coach, you're looking good." Seeing the murderous glint in Jared's eyes, Damien's dark skin paled slightly, but he was still as amused as always by Jared's degree of possessiveness.

Groaning at Damien, Salem nudged him. "Maybe you should astral project onto the dance floor before you say something else that will endanger your life."

Damien snorted. "No way. The last time I left my body alone with you bastards, I got back to find myself naked with some of Chico's thorns stuck in the cheeks of my ass. My body didn't wake up for, like, three hours." Chico's gift allowed him to release poisonous thorns that caused a victim to temporarily lose consciousness.

"Where is Chico?" I asked. He was usually at the centre of the group, since he was kind of like the 'chief' in a social sense.

Denny flashed me his dimply smile – he had the most adorable baby-face and guiltless blue eyes – and pointed to a spot behind me. "On the dance floor."

Turning, I saw Chico dancing with Jude. The female Sventé had remained at The Hollow after we had helped her get justice on a criminal organisation that had been snatching human babies and selling them to vampire couples. One of those babies had been hers. On becoming a vampire, she had tried hunting the people responsible but hadn't gotten very far all alone.

I noticed that the final three members of the squad – Max, Reuben, and Harvey – were standing near Chico, talking with members of other squads. There were, all in all, ten squads in Antonio's legion. I also noticed that my best friend, Fletcher, was dancing with his boyfriend, Norm – both looked more like they were hyperventilating. Spotting me, they waved. Fletcher also happened to be mine and Jared's personal assistant. And I absolutely loved the camp sod.

The energy in the place and the almost electric atmosphere was affecting Dexter, who was now in his tattoo form once more. I could always sense his mood without even looking at his colouring. Right now, he was feeling energised.

"No Evan?" Stuart asked.

I shook my head. Being Jared's twin and a fellow commander, Evan often joined us to celebrate. Lately, though, he hadn't been his usual playful self and had taken to brooding. He had been in a foul mood since the day after the Binding ceremony when all the guests had left. One of those guests had been a consort of one of the High Masters. As Bran was actually gay but simply too private to announce it publically, his female consorts were nothing but a smokescreen. Evan had been pursuing one of those consorts, Alora.

Evan had actually seen Alora in a vision long before he met her, thanks to Luther whose gift of precognition allowed him to make others have a vision of their own. Evan had been waiting impatiently for her to finally appear in his life. It had been obvious to everyone that she wanted Evan. For whatever reason, however, she had resisted him. I'd asked him about it several times, but he refused to speak of it – even to Jared.

Threading his fingers through mine, Jared pulled me close and gestured to the dance floor. "Come on." I followed him despite that dancing with Jared was never a good thing. Why? Because it was more like foreplay, and no one was as good at foreplay as Jared. Swaying and grinding his body against mine, he fondled and caressed and teased, but none of his touches were invasive. He didn't need to have any part of him inside me to make me so ready for him that the feel of my own clothes was pissing me off.

In no time at all, the entire squad was plastered. Vampires could only get drunk by drinking the blood of intoxicated humans. Some of those intoxicated human females had approached Jared – which was dumb of them really, considering my homicidal tendencies. But Jared never drank from anyone other than me, and vice versa. Despite that I was sober as a judge, I felt drunk from Jared's teasing. Of course he thought that was hilarious and was very pleased with himself. So I bit him.

The thing about Sventé saliva was that it could spark the 'blood donor' to have an orgasm if the vampire drank from them for more than ten seconds. Despite that I was now a hybrid, that hadn't changed. I counted to eight before releasing him, but the damage was done – he was as horny as I was and more than ready to fuck. About bloody time. "I take it you're ready to leave now."

His lopsided smile had me smiling back. "You're a tricky bitch, aren't you? I can respect that." He teleported us both to the living area of our apartment, where we instantly dived on each other, kissing wildly. A few seconds later, we froze. We weren't alone. Breaking apart, we pivoted to find Antonio and Luther sitting on the sofa, blushing and avoiding our eyes.

A blush stained my own cheeks. Like Jared, I was fighting to contain a laugh. "Er…What a pleasant surprise."

"Sorry to intrude," said Antonio with a forced cough, still looking everywhere but at us. "As Luther and I knew you would be returning home soon, we thought we would wait here. Rest assured that we will not be doing that again."

It took everything I had not to laugh. "You can look now." Finally the two Kejas met our eyes, still extremely embarrassed. "Don't take this the wrong way, but why are you here?" Usually when Antonio wanted to speak with us, he simply waited until the daily meetings he held at dusk in one of the conference rooms at his mansion. The fact that it was now approaching dawn made it even stranger for him to come to us.

"This is not about an assignment. It is a personal matter."

I exchanged an uneasy look with Jared.

"Do not be alarmed. It is not bad news." The Latino-looking vampire's huge dark eyes were filled with reassurance. He was a very calming person to be around, which I wouldn't have expected from the ruler of all vampirekind. He was a very elegant, graceful, and collected individual. Luther, his Advisor, was just as elegant. They couldn't have looked more different. Whereas Antonio had dark shoulder-length hair, Luther looked…well, like Gandalf from *Lord of the Rings*.

Jared retrieved two breakfast stools from the kitchen for us, and then gave Antonio a questioning look.

Once we were seated, Antonio took a long breath. "I'll get straight to the point. I have decided to step down from my position as Grand High Master."

My brows flew to my hairline. "Say again?"

"I'm tired, Sam. I have had this position for a very long time, and I'm tired." He sounded it as well.

"You're kidding, right?" asked Jared. I sensed that he was feeling as incredulous as I was.

"I would like to step down and spend more time with the people I care about."

"You mean Lucy, don't you?" I quite liked the brunette. Lucy was one of the humans on the island and was also one of Antonio's vessels – a human who fed him and only him. I'd noticed that Antonio had shed himself of his consorts and vessels until there was now only Lucy.

"In my early years, I was as ambitious as Jared," Antonio told me. "And I fought hard for this position. Then I put everything I had into it, neglecting many of my own needs. At first, I avoided relationships because I wasn't prepared to divide my time and attention. After that, it was because it seemed that I was surrounded by people who were not so much attracted to me but to the idea of being with the Grand High Master."

"Are you planning to Turn her?" Jared's shock was still pulsing in the air.

"Yes. I plan on Turning Lucy and Binding with her. But it means I have done everything the wrong way around – Binding *after* I stepped down rather than before. Ruling without a mate for support can be a very lonely life. I saw that you were headed down that same route, Jared, and I did not want you to make the same mistakes that I have."

I quickly realised something. "You played Cupid, didn't you?"

Antonio tilted his head, stifling a smile. "Perhaps. It is not why I offered you a position here as a commander, Sam. You are here because you deserve to be. But I confess I had hoped that if I forced you and Jared to work together, you would grow close. You seemed to be exactly what he needed, just as he seemed to be what you needed. And I was right, was I not?"

"Sneaky." Jared ran a hand through his hair. "None of this means you have to step down yet."

"No, but I *wish* to. As I said, I'm tired. I wish to retire, to no longer have to worry about the lives of others and to instead concentrate on my own. Do you have any idea how long it has been since I have seen the outside world? Being who I am, my life was always at risk, and I have had to remain on the island. I do not want that anymore, and I do not want it for Lucy. You two are more than capable of ruling. The vampire community has totally accepted both of you, has confidence in your ability to lead and protect them. The question is…are you prepared to take on the responsibility?"

It was more than a mere responsibility and, in truth, I didn't feel at all ready. It was a huge step to take. Yes, I'd known it would happen one day, but I'd envisioned it happening centuries down the line, not now. But how could I place Antonio in a position where he had to remain ruler at the cost of his own happiness? He didn't deserve that. "I'm in."

Jared's shock still hadn't eased in the slightest. I could sense through our bond that beneath that shock was a slither of unease. I would never have guessed that he would ever have any reservations about stepping up when the time came. Yet, that unease was there. With anyone else, I would have said that was perfectly natural. But it didn't fit Jared in this situation.

"I don't like that you're stepping down," he told Antonio. "I think you're easily capable of ruling for a hell of a long time, and I can't imagine you *not* being Grand High Master. But...I committed to being your Heir, knowing this would eventually happen. If this is really what you want, I'll support you." He took my hand. "*We'll* support you."

The smile that spread across Antonio's face was one of relief. "I would like for the Coronation to take place in two months' time, if that works for both of you. This will give me time to tie up any loose ends."

I nodded. "Sure."

"Luther will serve as your Advisor, just as he has served as mine."

The Gandalf lookalike smiled. "It will be an honour."

"Sebastian will serve as your tracker. He will be as loyal to you as he has been to me. And do not forget that you will need to appoint yourselves an Heir at some point. It does not have to be immediately, but you will have to choose one eventually. And choose wisely."

I wasn't what anyone would call 'wise', so that would be where Luther and his advice would come into play.

"The tradition for the Coronation is that only the High Masters and any immediate friends and 'family' attend. The rest of vampirekind will watch via V-Tube." That was basically the vampiric version of YouTube that could be accessed using the V-net, which was the vampiric version of the internet. "In a few days, I will announce the upcoming Coronation. For now, both of you get some rest."

Once both he and Luther had left the apartment, I blew out a long breath and twisted in my seat to face Jared. "Well, that was unexpected."

"And that was an understatement." He scooped me from the stool and brought me to straddle him. "I can sense that you don't feel ready for this yet."

"It's scary," I admitted. There was no judgement in his hazel eyes, only understanding. "I can coach and command a squad of ten, but lead all vampirekind?" In vampire years, I wasn't quite four years old. That wasn't really much experience at this life to have such a high position. "I didn't envision this happening so soon."

He cupped my throat with both hands. "You can lead. You can do anything." He gave me a soft, lingering kiss and slid his hands into my hair. "If you need more time, just say the word and I'll talk to Antonio about it. He'll understand. This isn't showing weakness. It's showing that you're taking this as seriously as you need to take it."

Unbuttoning the top buttons of his shirt, I snaked my hands under Jared's collar and rested them on his broad shoulders. "I can't ask Antonio to wait any longer to step down. Not after seeing how tired he is of all this. He's been on this island for *so* long." Every Grand High Master that had ever been appointed had remained concealed in order to be safe from any assassination attempts. "He deserves to have a life of his own. He hasn't had one for a long time, has he?"

"No." Jared trailed kisses along my jaw. "You're a good person."

"Say again?"

He chuckled at the disbelief in my voice. "Oh you can be merciless, ruthless, and vengeful. And we both know you're downright crazy. But you've got the biggest heart. And it's mine. All mine." His gaze blazed with a possessiveness that made me roll my eyes. Smiling, he gave me a pointed look. "Hey, don't think I haven't seen *your* reaction when another female comes anywhere near *me*. I really thought you were going to drown Joy in the pool that time. It was a shame that you didn't."

Joy had been Jared's consort once-upon-a-time, and she hadn't taken it too well that he'd ended his consort ways for me. When he'd been swimming in what I called 'the bat pool' – it was shaped like a bat with outstretched wings – outside Antonio's mansion last week, she had taken to strutting up and down the side of the pool in the skimpiest bikini imaginable.

Coming upon the scene, I hadn't been a happy bunny. She was constantly trying to get his attention, pathetic though it was. Before I'd even thought about it, my energy whip had been in my hand, I'd wrapped it around her twig-like body, and then plunged her into the pool. It had instantly become clear that anger management classes might be a good idea for me, because I'd kept her under the water for almost a full minute. In my defence…"If she wasn't binging on slut-flakes, there wouldn't be a problem."

What annoyed me more than Joy's antics was the knowledge that she'd once been his consort; that she'd touched him, that she'd had him inside her. I hated it. And she *knew* that I hated it, thought it gave her some kind of power. But it was truly difficult to hate *her* because she was so pathetic it was honestly saddening. It was impossible to feel anything other than pity for this girl who had absolutely no self-respect.

Off that irritating subject…"Are you going to tell me what's bugging you?"

Jared's brows drew together. "What do you mean?"

"You seem uneasy about something."

"I just wasn't expecting this so soon. It's the shock, that's all."

Our bond told me that that wasn't a lie, but I had the feeling there was more to it than that. Choosing to let it go for now, I said nothing. If his sense of unease didn't shift, we'd definitely be revisiting this subject.

He nipped my chin playfully. "There's one thing we'll find really hard about ruling: confining ourselves to The Hollow."

Now that was an extremely good point. I bit my lower lip. "I really don't think I can do it. For one thing, I'll go crazy – or, at least, I'll go crazier than I already am. But for another thing, I like the life we have now. I like being a commander, going on assignments, protecting people, and whipping the living shit out of dickheads."

He laughed. "Yeah, I'd miss that too. So maybe we should make some changes."

"Go against tradition?"

"Face it, baby, we're not much for rules, are we? So we'll come up with new ones. We can't become different people. If we do, we'll run the risk of drifting apart."

That was true. "I'm liking this idea of making up new rules."

Keeping me tight against him, he stood upright and urged me to curl my legs around his waist. "Later. Now I'm going to fuck you until there's not a thought in your head except how hard you want to come."

Sounded like fun.

At dusk, Jared and I headed to Antonio's mansion for the usual meeting that was held for the commanders. Strolling inside the conference room, we found Antonio seated at the head of the table with Sebastian and Luther sitting either side of him. His personal guards and two pit-bulls were standing unobtrusively in the background, as usual. But the other commanders were strangely absent. Instead, there were two vampires that didn't belong inside The Hollow: one male Sventé and one female Sventé. Both were very familiar and a long way from their home in London.

The cute, tiny brunette leaped from her seat, dashed around the table, and was suddenly hugging me so tight that I was worried a rib would crack. Not the most affectionate person in the world, I awkwardly returned the hug, patting her back.

Entertained by my discomfort, Jared smiled. *I take it you know her?* Thanks to Antonio's ability to impart power – thus allowing vampires to develop additional gifts – Jared had three gifts: teleportation, electrokinesis, and telepathy. He wasn't able to read minds, but he could hear any thought that was directed at him. Antonio had once rewarded me with additional power as well, and I'd developed a second gift. But the ability to Merge wasn't a gift I liked to use much as it wasn't exactly comfortable to join your body with someone else's.

Quick warning: the girl is like the energizer bunny, I told Jared. Pulling back, I went to speak, but she beat me to it.

"Oh my God, it feels like it's been years since I last saw you! How are you doing? I'm doing just fine. You look absolutely amazing! I heard through the vampire grapevine that one of your Binding presents was the Keja allure. In my opinion, you didn't need it, but it must be nice having it. Oh and I *love* the mercury ring in your eyes! I'm so sorry that I missed your Binding. My brother will explain why."

Everything had come out in a rush in the sweetest voice filled with excitement and optimism. *See what I mean?* I could easily pick up on Jared's amusement. Ordinarily, someone like Ava would annoy the shit out of me. But there was something very endearing about this female. "I'm great, thanks." I turned to Jared, who was clearly holding back a laugh. "Jared, this is Ava Sanchez. Ava, this is my mate, Jared Michaels."

As I'd expected, Ava had the same response to him that every female did: she went jaw slacked and wide-eyed. I couldn't really blame her. His alluring eyes *demanded* a person's full attention, practically took them hostage. It was impossible not to wonder just how it would feel to run your fingers through his short, tousled chestnut hair, or to skim your hands over his tall, perfectly sculpted body.

Most males would relish and bask in that kind of attention, but Jared hated it. He resented the fact that he got his looks from his deceased twisted mother. Also, it annoyed him that much of the reason females flocked around him was that he was Antonio's Heir. He didn't find being wanted for his looks and position particularly flattering. Although I'd repeatedly told him that he had more to offer than this, he didn't agree. He didn't see himself clearly.

To Ava's credit, she snapped out of her daze quicker than most did. "It's nice to meet you. It was wise of you to choose Sam as your mate – she's the best."

"I can agree with you on that," he replied.

As the pit-bulls, Achilles and Nero, dashed to my side, I gave them a quick stroke before meeting the gaze of the smirking dark-haired male seated next to Sebastian. "Can't say it's particularly a pleasure to see you again, Cristiano."

"Now that's not very nice, is it," he said, amused. The bloke wasn't bad as vampires went. In fact, he was relatively decent and was extremely protective of his sister, Ava. He had actually helped me on a number of occasions back when I'd lived in London. But he was also a taunting prick who lived to annoy people just for the fun of it. He could actually be quite charming, which I had learned the first night I met him when I was still human. As his expression turned nostalgic, I had the distinct feeling that he was remembering that night.

I could sense that Jared was a mixture of suspicious and agitated by the way Cristiano was looking at me with such familiarity. Glaring at Cristiano, Jared spoke to me. *Tell me nothing happened between you two.*

Nothing happened…exactly.

Define 'exactly'.

I'll give you the long version later. The short version is that he once kissed me and he…drank from me. I felt jealousy and anger zoom through Jared, which was understandable since drinking blood was an intimate and sexual act for vampires.

"Why don't you sit down," Antonio suggested with a smile, his eyes warm.

Having exchanged greetings with him, Sebastian, Luther and the guards, Jared and I took seats opposite the two Sventés. Jared draped a possessive arm over the back of my chair, staring hard at Cristiano. Every muscle in Jared's body seemed coiled to strike. Not wanting him so tense, I patted his thigh. It didn't seem to help. He briefly massaged my nape, but didn't otherwise react.

Cristiano gave Jared a respectful nod. "My name's Cristiano Sanchez. Ava is my younger sister. We shared the same Sire as Sam, and we were once all part of the same nest. I took Victor's place as leader of the nest after Sam killed the bastard here at The Hollow." And Victor really had been an absolute bastard.

"Why didn't you attend the Binding?" asked Jared. Most of the vampire community had attended the ceremony, particularly any leaders, Masters, and High Masters.

"It wasn't out of any disrespect. Two other vampires had wanted the position of leader. A voting was held and I was eventually pronounced leader, but there were still some who were sour about it. I knew that if I left the nest before my position had been properly established, one of them would have taken it while I was gone."

"And your position has now been accepted and established?" Jared began gently playing with my hair in a very possessive move.

"Yes." Cristiano's gaze slid back to me and his smirk returned. He probably got a kick out of the fact that he'd once drunk from the Heir's mate.

That was when Jared spoke to him very matter-of-factly. "If you don't stop staring at Sam like that, I'll gut you open right here and I'll truly enjoy it."

Cristiano lost his smirk, and I didn't blame him. Jared had a well-earned reputation as someone who wasn't to be fucked with. Although he could be playful, loyal, and respectful, Jared could also be ruthless, pitiless, and kill without blinking. I'd seen him in battle-mode, watched him destroy other vampires without a lick of conscience. Just his presence alone was enough to intimidate those around him; he exuded confidence, power, and authority.

"Cris, could you please refrain from antagonising these people?" groaned Ava, shooting apologetic glances at everyone. "We need their help, remember."

I arched a brow. "Our help?"

"Cristiano," began Antonio, "tell Jared and Sam why it is that you and your sister are here."

Cristiano straightened, suddenly solemn. "Although I didn't go to your Binding, three of my vampires did. Afterwards, they called me to say that they were going to spend a couple of weeks in New

Zealand with some vampires they had met here and befriended from Quentin Foy's line."

Quentin Foy had been recently appointed High Master vampire over New Zealand, Australia, Indonesia, and all the little surrounding islands after the previous High Master had betrayed Antonio and tried to take over The Hollow.

"The problem is I've heard nothing from them since then." Cristiano shrugged helplessly. "Their mobile phones are all switched off and my psychic connection with them has turned...fuzzy." All Sires have links with their vampires, though they weren't anywhere near as strong as the type of bond that came from Binding with another vampire.

I frowned. "Fuzzy?"

"It's like I'm picking up static. Occasionally I sense their thirst, but that's as good as it gets. All I know for sure is that they're not dead. Something's not right. As you know, Quentin's extremely territorial and rarely grants permission for anyone to step foot on his territory. But getting in touch with him to ask for that permission would be difficult since it's not as if someone like me would ever have a High Master's personal number."

"From what I know about him," began Jared, "Quentin's a luddite. He hates most forms of technology and doesn't use phones."

"That is why they need an escort," Antonio said. "They need someone to take them there, make sure Quentin doesn't feel threatened, and help them find their vampires."

"And you want those escorts to be us." Jared didn't veil his irritation. "With all due respect, Antonio, I think it would be easier to send Sebastian to investigate the matter and find the vampires."

When Sebastian didn't object, I cast a glance at him. Although his peppery black hair was slightly obscuring his expression, I could see that the Keja's penetrating eyes were eager and willing.

"You are right. Sebastian could indeed find them. But I have a bad feeling about this, Jared." Antonio's usual calm expression was anxious. "It could be nothing, but something about it feels wrong. Luther is also uneasy. My instincts have always served me well, and I have learned not to ignore them."

I was curious enough about the situation to want to agree to Antonio's request, despite that Cristiano, who was again smirking at me, would undoubtedly be a pain in my arse. Though he was like this with everyone other than Ava, he'd always taken extreme delight in irritating me for some reason. It wouldn't take much to push me into conjuring my energy whip and slashing his face with it.

As if he sensed my reservations, he said, "You might not like me, Sam, but let's not forget that I saved your life. And I looked out for you during your time with Victor."

Jared looked at me. "Is that true?"

Yes, but I wasn't about to go into the specifics of the situation until Jared and I were alone. I simply nodded.

Jared's gaze drilled into Cristiano. "If you saved Sam's life, then I'm grateful to you for it. So we'll escort you to Quentin's territory and ensure your protection. But you need to understand one thing: whether you helped her or not, if you keep staring and smirking at her, I *will* kill you and I won't fucking care."

Cristiano nodded, again dropping his smirk. Very wise of him.

Antonio relaxed into his chair. "In that case, prepare the squad. You should all leave in an hour."

Ava gave me a small but genuine smile. "Thanks so much. We appreciate it." She really was sweet. I had to wonder how she and Cristiano could possibly be related.

After debriefing the squad, Jared and I made a pit-stop at our apartment to top up on NSTs, wanting to be at full strength. Otherwise known as Nutritive Supplemental Tonics, NSTs were a mix of blood and other vitamins.

The second we arrived in the kitchen, Jared expectedly began interrogating me. "Now that we're alone, you can tell me what the deal is with that guy, Cristiano."

Having retrieved a couple of NSTs from the refrigerator, I handed him one and then leaned against the counter. "I was still human when I met Cristiano. It was back when I was a student in college. My friends and I often went out to the local student bar. Vampires love student bars because most students are eager to have fun, like getting drunk, and aren't fussed about memory gaps – all part of getting rat-arsed, right? So if they wake up feeling weak with a vague recollection of flashing irises or fangs, they're simply going to blame the alcohol or believe their drinks were spiked, just like I had."

I paused to take a long gulp of my honey-flavoured NST. "One night in the bar, I met Cristiano. He laid on the charm, but I'd just come out of a relationship and I wasn't in a kissing-perfect-strangers frame of mind. So he left me alone. But there was this bloke who kept pestering me. He made me feel really uncomfortable and kept trying to kiss my neck. I couldn't shake him off. Then he tried dragging me outside into the alley. That was when Cristiano appeared again. He acted as if he was my boyfriend and he'd been looking for me, and I played along. He got me away from who I just thought was a creepy bastard, which I was totally grateful for. His payment was a kiss."

Jared's growl wasn't a surprise. When I hesitated, he pressed, "Go on."

"Obviously the kiss had just been his way of getting close enough to bite me" – another growl from Jared – "but I was so plastered that the brief sting didn't ring any alarm bells. He explained to me after I was Turned that the vampire who'd harassed me was known for throwing parties that included human 'party favours'. In other words, I'd be laid on a table and the vampires seated around it could simply lean over and drink from me any time they wanted until I was totally drained of blood."

"So he really did save your life." Jared swallowed the last of his Cola-flavoured NST and slung the bottle in the bin. "He said he looked out for you, too."

"He did. So did Ava. You know I escaped from Victor a couple of times. They both played a part in helping me. Of course, each time I was tracked down and brought back to the nest, Victor was beyond pissed. The last time I did it, he almost killed me. But Cristiano managed to calm him down and insisted it would be more beneficial to the nest if Victor stuck to the original plan and allowed me to live and serve him."

Jared stuffed his hands in his pockets. "What I don't get is why Cristiano did all this. I mean, he doesn't strike me as the gallant type."

I fisted a hand in Jared's shirt and pulled him close. "He's not. He took his payment afterwards each time."

"You mean he drank from you more than once?" Jared asked through gritted teeth, placing a hand on the counter either side of me to cage me in. "Not that I can blame him. You taste fucking amazing." He delivered a sensual lick to my neck. "But I hate him for doing it. I hate him for touching you. And I hate him for kissing this mouth I love. Every inch of you is mine."

And those words were as near to romantic as Jared's were ever likely to get. But I didn't care that he was emotionally awkward or that he found it hard to articulate how he felt. He made it clear that he cared for me in other ways; he protected me with a ferocity that I wouldn't have thought possible, would kill or die for me without hesitation. When his attention was on me, it was an undivided attention that was so intense it was both intoxicating and disorientating. It was hard to grasp, to comprehend, that I could really mean that much to someone.

When he swiped his thumb across my bottom lip, I nipped the digit lightly. "There was never anything between us."

"I think he wished there had been. I don't like the way he looks at you."

"You don't like the way any bloke looks at me."

He gave me one of his lopsided grins. "Of course I don't." He gripped my hips possessively and held me flush against him. "I don't like anyone fantasising about this body that's all mine."

I curled my arms around his neck. "Yours? I don't know about that," I said playfully.

His crooked grin turned devilish. "Then I guess I'll have to claim it all over again later so you remember exactly who you belong to."

"I can't see that you have any other choice."

Chuckling, he scooped me up and kissed me hard.

CHAPTER TWO

(Jared)

Exchanging a look with Sam as we stood only one hundred yards away from the caves where Quentin Foy and most of his nest resided, I knew she was thinking the exact same thing that I was: What. The. Fuck?

We had been on his territory for over an hour. Not just us, but the entire squad, Ava and her asshole of a brother, and also Evan – who had appeared as we were ready to leave and insisted on coming. Yet, the presence of fifteen vampires hadn't earned a response. We had initially arrived much farther away, expecting to be approached the very second our presence was sensed. When no one came, we began to advance toward the caves, fully expecting someone to appear at some point. But no one had.

Quentin, like most High Masters, should have guards surrounding his residence to protect him from anyone hoping to challenge him and usurp his position. But there didn't appear to be anyone in sight. Oh sure, that didn't mean that no one was around. There were vampiric gifts impressive enough to allow people to conceal themselves. But it wasn't just that it *looked* deserted. The place was quiet. *Too* quiet.

"I don't like this." Sam was biting her lip, scanning our surroundings once more. "What High Master in their right mind would leave themselves vulnerable this way?"

"Quentin's not exactly popular. It would be downright stupid of him not to have spies at the very least." Seeing that Sam was rubbing the Celtic-looking tattoo that surrounded the base of her third finger, I smiled. It was something she often did when she was confused or anxious, as if the Binding knot gave her strength.

Several times since we returned from our 'honeymoon', I'd been asked how I found life as a Bound male. Over the years, I'd heard some say that being Bound could make a person feel trapped. Back then, I'd supposed that was natural, considering there was no divorce or get-out clause. But being Bound to Sam didn't make me feel trapped or restricted. Instead, I felt centred, more relaxed. I even felt strengthened, which was ironic given that she was my weakness. The power of it all wasn't frightening, it was energising. It meant that she was mine, that she'd always be mine, and that I was connected to her in a way that no one else ever could be. That knowledge was like an anchor. And, yeah, I was possessive enough to feel a bone-deep self-satisfaction about it.

As deeply linked as we now were, I knew and understood Sam much more. Every single layer of her was more intriguing than the last. I liked the idea that the longer the bond existed, the more interconnected we would become. I liked that I would always know where she was – no one could take her and hide her from me again, and God have mercy on anyone who even considered it, because I sure wouldn't. As a matter of fact, neither would Sam, just like she hadn't had mercy on my ex-partner. Magda had also been responsible for Turning both me and Evan against our will. Some women might buy you a shirt or cologne. Sam would kill your ex for you.

Cristiano, who had been sticking a little too close to Sam for my liking, also noticed that she was stroking the knot and he frowned. "What's that?"

She only spared the asshole the briefest glance. "It's a Binding knot."

Ava came from behind Cristiano and bumped him aside so she could get a good look at the brail-like mark. "Aw, that's so nice." She looked at me, her eyes alight with interest. "Do you have one as well?"

I held up my hand to show her, and she smiled widely. Cristiano, however, grunted with boredom. If it hadn't been for the fact that he'd saved Sam's life, I'd be beating him with his own spine right now. Not simply because he seemed to be constantly at her side, but because he looked at her with a longing that made my blood boil. It was a longing that was both emotional and sexual. Oh he was doing his best to conceal it – so much so that Sam hadn't noticed. But *I'd* noticed, and I wanted nothing more than to watch the bastard die…slowly and painfully, if possible.

"The design of your knot matches Sam's," Ava realised.

"Every Bound couple has their own unique design. Sam's will only match mine, and vice versa."

"Aw, how romantic and sweet is that? I want one. But how did it work? I thought vampire skin heals too quickly for us to get tattoos."

"It just appeared there when we exchanged vows," Sam told her, smiling. Her aquamarine eyes met mine, and I knew she was recalling that moment, just as I was. Turning back to Ava, Sam said, "I actually have another tattoo as well. The vampire who gave it to me has the gift of making his pictures come to life." Sam lifted the sleeve of her long-sleeved t-shirt to reveal the black snake twined around her upper arm. When the tattoo wiggled slightly, Ava gasped. "Yeah, Dexter can move around in his tattoo form. He wasn't a fan of Jared at first because the breed is very protective, but he likes him now."

He liked me? Ha. "He tolerates me, but that's pretty much it," I grumbled. He'd stopped hissing at me whenever I touched Sam, which was progress. But he always seemed to wear this cautioning 'I'm watching you' look. It was weird and damn annoying.

Ava clapped her hands a little. "I want one of those as well. Do you think I could get one?"

Standing behind Ava, Salem sighed down at her. "Shouldn't you be at the rear?" His tone was vibrating with impatience.

Ava twisted to look at him. Her little face was scrunched up in confusion as she cocked her head. "Why?" The question was asked with an almost childlike innocence.

A muscle in Salem's jaw ticked. "*Because* something strange is obviously going on and it could be dangerous. It would be better for you to hang back where it's safer."

To my surprise, Ava laughed. Even more surprising, so did Sam.

"You don't need to worry about Ava, Salem." Sam smiled at him. "Don't let that tiny figure and innocent face fool you. She can take care of herself. Not all Sventé vampires have defensive gifts, remember?"

Smiling sweetly, Ava patted his chest. "But it's really nice of you to care." He frowned at the hand patting him, but Ava didn't seem to notice. Twirling back around, she gently nudged Sam. "Isn't he the sweetest thing?"

Sweet? I was pretty sure I'd never heard anyone describe Salem as 'sweet' before.

Damien leaned toward Salem, grinning. "Pretty protective of the little one, aren't you?"

Salem scowled at him. "Shut up."

Actually, it was kind of odd for Salem to give a shit about the safety of anyone other than Sam, the guys, or me. It was also odd that the anticipation of the assignment didn't have him bouncing like a boxer getting ready for a fight the way it normally did — it was quite fitting that his gift was a psychic punch that could knock a person unconscious. The only person who got more of a rush from assignments than him was Butch. However, amusingly enough, Salem appeared to find tiny Ava a bit of a distraction.

Sam's voice blew through my mind like a warm breeze. *Well, I wanted something to take my mind off the Coronation. Seems like this might just do that.*

The Coronation…Now that was something that I didn't want to think about. Thinking about it meant thinking about the vision that I'd had through Luther a very long time ago, back when I'd first been made a commander within the legion. I knew that I'd have to tell Sam about it. Hell, I should have told her before we Bound. But I hadn't because although I knew she was a practical enough person not to let one vision change everything, I'd panicked that it might make her walk away. That was something I wasn't prepared to risk. I'd tell her soon, and if she *did* try to walk away…well, I'd tie her up and keep her captive.

A whoosh of black molecules suddenly appeared, pulling me from my thoughts. A mere second later, Stuart was standing before us. As a Shredder, the squad member had the ability to reduce himself to molecules and reform again at will. "This whole thing is weird."

My words, his mouth. "What did you see?"

"Nothing. I circled the entrance of the caves, but there are no guards anywhere."

Sam shot me a worried look before asking Stuart, "Could you hear any sounds coming from inside?"

"There were noises, voices, coming from the rear of the caves, but I couldn't make out any words. The tone was kind of…flat. Drone, even."

"So people *are* in there but they're ignoring us." Max pulled a face, clearly baffled. "You're right; this whole thing's weird." Ordinarily, it would be Max who lingered around Sam the way Cristiano was doing. In Max's case, it was simply to irritate me as, fortunately for him, he no longer lusted after her. That meant I could let him live, which was good for the squad since Max's gift of causing temporary sensory paralysis made him a valuable member.

"Could they be hiding, hoping we'll leave?" the telekinetic Harvey asked Sam. I noticed that his stance wasn't as cocky as usual – the guy might be a little slow on the uptake, but even he had the sense to be wary right now.

Sam considered that for a moment. "If that was the case, they would be sure to make no sounds at all. Besides, why would they have any reason to hide?"

A puddle of mush appeared beside Stuart and quickly returned to its normal form. One of Denny's animal-mimic abilities was to reduce himself to a soft liquid just like the sea cucumber. "I couldn't get in. The door's sealed so tightly that there are no cracks for me to wiggle through."

"None of this makes any sense, and it's severely pissing me off." Sam turned to Cristiano. "Can you sense your vampires better now that you're closer to them?"

Looking grim, he shook his head. "The connection's still fuzzy."

Chico released a long breath, stroking his Johnny Depp style moustache and goatee. "So I'm thinking we—"

"We'll have to force our way inside," interrupted Evan, glaring at the caves. I had the distinct feeling that he had insisted on coming along so he could blow off some steam and distract himself from thoughts of Alora and whatever the hell had happened between them. Or maybe the problem was what *hadn't* happened between them.

"If we do that, they'll attack instantly," David pointed out, fidgety and nervous.

Butch nodded his agreement. "Considering we have no idea how many are in the caves, it would be a dangerous move." Not that Butch sounded particularly moved by the prospect of danger. In fact, he never seemed to be moved by anything, always appeared deceptively calm, collected, and laidback.

"We'll have to take our chances." Evan's tone was practically lifeless. "It's the only way we can retrieve Cristiano's vampires."

When the squad turned questioning gazes mine and Sam's way, I said, "I'm not comfortable with the idea of invading their home, but I think Evan's right."

Sam nodded. "We have no other option at this point." She turned to the heavily muscled Pagori who was currently tying back his brown shoulder-length hair. Stuart did the same with his own blond curls. "Reuben, I need you to use your gift on Chico, David, and Salem." With a single touch to their shoulders, Reuben's gift of power augmentation had made Chico's poisonous thorns, David's psionic boom, and Salem's psychic punch all fatal. "Don't move quietly – give them plenty of warning that we're approaching the door so that they aren't alarmed. If they still don't open up, we'll have to let ourselves in."

Making no attempts to conceal our presence, we covered the distance to the entrance of the caves. The door was camouflaged to look like part of the mountain in order to fool any humans, but a vampire's enhanced eyesight could easily spot it. When there was still no reaction to our presence, I projected a lightning bolt powerful enough to completely shatter the door. Fanning away floating dirt, I looked to see a downward channel about eight feet deep.

"Not even the noise of someone breaking in has gained a reaction from them." Cristiano shook his head, incredulous.

"Damien, Reuben – I want both of you to wait here and keep watch," I told them. "If you see any movement at all out here, you contact me straight away." They both nodded obediently and took on an alert, aggressive stance. Satisfied, I turned back to the entrance in time to see that Evan had taken the lead and jumped down the channel. He was obviously feeling shitty enough to be careless with his own safety.

Sam looked at me. *We shouldn't have let him come. His head's not in a good place right now.*

I'll talk to him. I swiftly descended only to find myself at the entrance of a tunnel. Evan was waiting there impatiently. At least he hadn't set off on his own. I held his gaze. "Evan, you need to get your shit together."

His eyes flared with anger. "I'm fine."

"No, you're not, and this isn't the time to talk about it. But I swear if you act careless and put Sam and my squad in danger, I'll teleport your ass out of here. Got it?"

He gave me a curt nod and returned his attention to our surroundings. Although it was dark, my vampire night vision allowed me to see the junction further down the extremely long tunnel. Signalling for the others to follow, I moved aside to give them room. One by one, they descended the channel. Before I could give any further directions, Evan began walking, clearly intending to take the lead. Sam and I exchanged an exasperated look but let him be.

We flanked him as he slowly led us through the tunnel. There was no one at all around. No sounds other than our own footsteps. "They *have* to know we're here," I said to Sam.

"It doesn't make any sense that they wouldn't care." As she repeatedly clenched her hands, as if eager to attack a threat we couldn't see, tiny sprinkles of silvery-blue energy dripped from her fingers, peppering the air like fairy dust. Now that she was a hybrid and much stronger, she didn't have to absorb the surrounding energy anymore; it came to her, filled her, waiting for direction. Silvery-blue glimmers of it played around the surface of her body.

We continued down the tunnel, stopping only when we reached the junction. There were no sounds coming from any direction. Sam indicated for Evan to keep moving forward, and we again followed closely behind him. Then I was gagging as a foul stench crept up on me. I wasn't the only one balking.

"It's like rotten fish." Sam's words were muffled by her sleeve as she used it to cover her mouth and nose.

"Jesus," exclaimed Chico, coughing along with the others. "What *is* that?"

Evan suddenly held up his arm, gaining everyone's attention. "Do you guys hear that?"

I did. A voice…but it wasn't *speaking*. It was…moaning?

"Do you think they're all hurt? It would explain why no one's come."

Evan's theory was a decent one, made sense…yet, my gut said no. Every instinct I had told me to get out of there and to get out of there now. I could sense that Sam's anxiety equalled my own. Good, maybe that meant I could talk the crazy bitch out of going any further. Sam never allowed fear to hold her back, she used it as fuel. While that was admirable, it drove me fucking insane because I wanted her safe. Sure she was strong, but she wasn't invincible.

I grabbed her arm, bringing us both to a halt. "We need to leave. This is beyond weird now and has entered the realm of too damn dangerous. We're putting ourselves and everyone here at risk by staying." I expected a snarl or a snort from her, but she instead nodded.

"You're right. This is—"

A long, drawn-out moan pierced the silence. Every single one of us froze in position. A few seconds later, there was another moan; it was filled with pain, hopelessness, and misery. Technically, such a sound should have made me want to run to that person's rescue.

It didn't.

Instead, it made my blood turn to ice. Then there was another sound: scuffling. Someone was coming, but their footsteps were so sluggish that their feet were dragging against the ground as they moved.

I wasn't sure what I expected to see when that person finally rounded the head of the junction, but it wasn't the sight before me. The shirtless vampire was so gaunt, skeletal, and emaciated that it was revolting. His glowing red eyes looked like they had been sucked inward and much of his hair had fallen out. His ribcage was visible, his shoulder blades were sticking out, and he had a greyish, translucent complexion. Basically, he looked like a skeleton with a layer of skin stretched over it. And there was only one thing that made a vampire look like that.

This really wasn't good. "Evan, don't go any closer."

But either my brother was feeling suicidal or he had no idea just how dangerous a starving vampire could be, because he was actually approaching the Pagori. What I wanted to do was order everyone to hold hands and then teleport us all out of there, but I couldn't reach Evan to grab him and there was simply no way I was leaving him behind.

"All of you slowly retreat," I said without moving my gaze from the starving vampire. "We need to get the fuck out of here. Don't take your eyes off him. And whatever you do, unless he leaps at you, don't run." They each followed my commands instantly, except for Evan. He was instead continuing to move forward. "Evan, what the fuck?"

"He's starving, Jared, he needs blood, get over here."

Clearly Evan had never been near a starving vampire before. I had. "Yes, he's starving. That makes him dangerous. He'll attack you."

"Attack me? Look at him, he's practically falling to pieces – he doesn't have the strength to take me on."

That was where my brother was wrong. "You'd be surprised just how strong and fast a vampire can be when it's desperate. Right now, he's desperate. So move your stubborn ass away from him!" I thought he'd keep ignoring me, but instead Evan sighed and took a step backwards. That was when the vampire lunged at him. He knocked Evan to the ground, his mouth latching onto his throat and gulping down his blood so strongly it was sickeningly audible.

Before I could react, one of Sam's powerful energy balls struck the vampire, making him burst into ashes with a scream. Then we were both at Evan's side, helping him from the floor. As I'd expected, the bite was bad. The vampire had almost taken a chunk out of Evan's neck with his overriding thirst. "You okay?"

Evan put pressure against the badly bleeding wound with his hand. "No."

"Well, that explained why no one came." When a vampire went into 'starvation mode', their senses gradually dulled until they were even less acute than human senses. Furthermore, their predatory drives increasingly took over as their need for survival made them operate on an almost animal instinct – losing rationality, reason, and civilisation. That was why they were also unable to focus enough to use their gifts.

I tensed as the ground seemed to rumble beneath us. Worse, it sounded like a freaking stampede was heading our way. Clearly the racket we'd just made and the sound of the vampire's scream had gained us some attention. If that was the rest of the nest coming toward us, we were doomed if we didn't get out of there *now*. I turned, intending to order everyone to hold onto one another so I could teleport us all outside. That was when I noticed that not only was there a big gap between us and the others – who had clearly continued following my order to retreat – but none of them were looking at me. They were staring at the horde of vampires that were charging down the other end of the tunnel, heading for them.

Fuck, we were boxed in.

Having the deadliest gifts, David, Chico, and Salem immediately began attacking the starving vampires approaching them, taking advantage of the distance still between them. At the same time, Harvey used his telekinesis to shove them back again and again. Having faith that they could all handle themselves for now and do what they had been trained to do, I joined Evan and Sam in dealing with the flock of vampires that were fast approaching us.

Sam was attacking with energy balls, energy bolts, and thermal energy beams. Evan was freezing every vampire that came at him – not to ice, but completely immobilising them so that there was no blood-flow, no heartbeat, no breathing, nothing. Mere milliseconds after the vampires were frozen, they exploded into ashes.

I joined the fight; sending charge after charge after charge of electricity from my hands. But there were just so damn many of them that even our combined efforts couldn't keep them completely at bay. Any time a vampire managed to get too close, Sam would slam up her shield, causing the vampire to bounce away. But they weren't deterred; they continued to charge at us. Sam then conjured an energy shield big enough to encompass her, me, and Evan, but the vampires tried crawling over it like ants.

"Bollocks to this," she gritted out. A blast of wind flew out of her palms, sending the vampires zooming through the air until they collided with the wall at the end of the tunnel. She then swiftly tapped into the natural elements, using the earth to quickly build a wall to block the tunnel. "It won't hold them back for long," she warned. She was right; no sooner had the tunnel sealed shut than the wall was being charged at. "Quick, go, go, go!"

Turning, I took in the sight in front of us. Butch had formed a deflecting shield and was using it to protect Salem, David, and Chico as they attacked the starving vampires. Unfortunately the shield wasn't big enough to act as a barrier, and some of the vampires had gotten past it. Denny was shooting yellowy-green ooze out of his thumbs and smallest fingers to engulf and spring them away while Harvey was using his telekinesis to fight off others. But still some vampires had slipped through.

One was currently biting into Stuart's arm, who then quickly exploded into molecules in order to get free. Another had its teeth buried in Max's throat as Cristiano attacked it from behind with a knife that I was guessing he'd conjured – nice gift. Ava was fighting off a third and, damn, could she fight! Sam was right; tiny Ava could take care of herself. Apparently that didn't matter to Salem, because the big guy suddenly turned, looped an arm around her, pulled her back against his chest, and sent a lethal psychic punch hurling at her attacker.

Sam, Evan, and I leaped into action immediately. Sam took Stuart's attacker out of the equation with an energy ball before joining Evan and me at the front of the group. Sam's hands were suddenly like flamethrowers as she set the vampires alight, wincing at their high-pitched screams. My bolts of electricity took care of some of the other vampires that followed while the squad dealt with the rest. Still, there were just too many of the fuckers.

When Harvey telekinetically sent them flying down the tunnels, giving us plenty of space, I hollered, "Everyone hold hands!"

Just then, Sam's wall crumbled behind us. Starving vampires were then charging at us from two directions. Thank fucking God that everyone had immediately done as I'd ordered, because I then managed to teleport us all outside of the caves before the vampires could reach us. Reuben and Damien instantly crowded around Evan, Stuart, Max, and Cristiano, who were all bleeding pretty badly. *Fuck.*

"We need to make sure they're all destroyed." I lifted my hand, and projected an extremely powerful lightning bolt at the entrance. Everything shook and rumbled as the tunnels caved in, crushing and burying alive anything that managed to withstand the impact of the lightning bolt. Breathing a sigh of relief, I grabbed Sam and ran my gaze and hands all over her, taking a full inventory.

"I'm okay."

Her reassurance didn't matter, and nor did the fact that I could sense through our bond that she wasn't in pain. I had to *see* for myself that she was fine. Apparently I was annoying her because she cuffed me over the head, her mercury irises glinting.

"I said I'm okay. But some of these people aren't, so let's get them back to The Hollow now."

CHAPTER THREE

(Sam)

Finding Antonio and Luther on a bench in the botanical gardens, Jared and I relayed to them everything that had happened on Quentin's territory. Their expressions turned grimmer and grimmer as the story went on. The guards were casting each other uneasy glances, and even the dogs looked anxious as if the negativity in the air was affecting them.

"I'm thinking someone trapped all the vampires in the tunnels, and left them there to starve to death," said Jared. "But why? And who would do that? It can't have been an attempt at usurping Quentin or we all would have heard about his replacement by now. The guy would be bragging and claiming his position as the new High Master of Quentin's territory."

Jared made a good point, but there was something else that was bugging me. I cocked my head. "This is what I don't understand. Why, if the vampires were so hungry, hadn't they all turned on each other? If they were thirsty enough to attack all of us like that, so senselessly, why hadn't they fed from each other?"

Antonio leaned forward in his seat; there was a sense of urgency in his manner that hadn't been there before, and apprehension slid through me. "I need to ask you something. And this is very important. In the tunnels, was there an awful smell?"

"Yeah." Jared's elbow brushed against mine as he folded his arms across his chest. "Like rotten fish."

Both Jared and I tensed when Antonio and Luther exchanged a frantic look. They actually paled, which was hard for two extremely pale-skinned vampires to do.

"What, what does that mean?" demanded Jared.

"It means that this was not a case of them starving due to having been trapped there," said Antonio, worry etched into every line of his face. "And it perfectly answers Sam's question."

Jared sighed with impatience. "Antonio, you're losing me here."

"Have you ever heard of 'The Reaper's Call'? It is often abbreviated to 'The Call'." When both Jared and I shook our heads, Antonio explained. "As you know, vampires are immune to illnesses. But like with many species, vampirism has a natural killer designed to keep the population down. Throughout human history, there have always been diseases or viruses that have done much damage to their race. When cures are found for those viruses, others later develop. Some theorise that their purpose is to keep the human population under control, which makes sense. It is the natural way of things, and the same happens for vampires. If it did not, we would outnumber our prey and quickly die out. The Call is not an illness, more like a preternatural poison that travels like a bug. And it *is* a killer."

"There is only an outbreak every few centuries," began Luther. "It seems that it occurs whenever nature feels that the population of vampires needs a 'tweak'. It is a perfectly natural cycle, and this cycle helps maintain a balance in the population. But it does not do so cleanly. The Call works by stopping the vampire from being able to digest anything. Not blood, not food – nothing. As such, the vampire will regurgitate anything it tries to consume and slowly starve to death. A vampire can only survive starvation for four weeks."

Jared rubbed at his nape. I could actually *feel* the crick in his neck. "How does the poison spread?"

Luther took a brief pause before answering with sympathy, "It can only taint its victim by travelling through saliva or blood to open flesh." In other words, a bite would do the trick.

Jared's eyes fell closed and then he was pacing in front of me. "Shit."

Antonio nodded. "Yes…darn."

An ache suddenly struck my chest; I wasn't sure whether it was mine, Jared's, or a combination of both our pain. If Antonio was right, then Evan, Max, and Stuart were now 'tainted'. "Does this mean it's possible that Ava's brother isn't tainted? He was clawed at badly, but not bitten." Currently, all the injured were in the infirmary.

"If he has not been bitten, he is not tainted. Unless, of course, they somehow exchanged blood." I was pretty sure that the latter hadn't happened, so Antonio's news would certainly calm Ava down. The girl was a nervous wreck at the moment, worried she would lose her brother – much like my mate was.

Jared halted. "Okay, so how do we stop it? How do we remove the taint from Evan, Max, and Stuart?"

"You can't." Antonio looked utterly distraught.

"Nothing can stop The Reaper's Call." Luther's voice was sensitivity itself. "As the name suggests, death comes for them. Eventually, it will stop spreading through the vampire population and remain dormant for another few centuries."

Everything Jared was feeling – all the panic, the anger, and the helplessness – hit me so hard that I almost lost my balance. He was vigorously shaking his head, pacing again. "No. No. My brother is *not* going to die, and neither is Stuart or Max." I could sense that he felt he'd failed them all.

Stop tormenting yourself, I told him. *It wasn't your fault.*

He ignored me. "There has to be a way to help them." Pausing in his pacing again, he took a deep breath to steady himself. "If it spreads through bodily fluids, then it's almost like a human virus, right? If we follow that logic, then surely there's an 'antivirus'. There has to be some kind of counteragent."

"If there is, I've never heard of it," said Luther.

"Where did it first originate?"

Luther shrugged. "I have no idea."

"Okay, so who do we talk to? You must know someone who's studied this."

"No one dares get close enough to a tainted vampire to study it."

A string of curses flew out of Jared's mouth.

Aching for Jared, I turned to Antonio. "What now?"

"We need to contain Evan, Stuart, and Max. Although the symptoms may not show for a few days, it is still important to isolate them. It would be safe for them to be contained together as opposed to separately, since they will not attempt to feed from each other. Tainted blood will not appeal to them on any level."

We'll help them somehow, Jared. Again, he ignored me. But I had the feeling that he was simply too trapped by his own panic to focus on anything else.

"We can't afford to allow this to spread any further." Antonio's gaze danced from Jared to me as he asked, "Are you positive that none of the others were bitten?"

I nodded. "Positive." Jared gave him a nod as well.

Luther's brow creased as if something suddenly occurred to him. "Did you see Quentin Foy down in the tunnels?"

"No. But I'm not sure I'd have recognised him anyway." Not when they had all been more like skeletons.

"I have to wonder if Quentin sealed them in there, leaving them to die."

"Why would he do that?" Jared asked.

"Maybe he couldn't find it within himself to destroy them. You know that you would find it difficult to kill any vampires from The Hollow, no matter if they were tainted."

After a short silence, Antonio rose from the bench. "I need to hold a teleconference and alert the High Masters. They need to be aware of the outbreak so they can take precautions with their vampires."

Before he and Luther could walk away, Jared held a hand up to stay them. "Wait, what about Quentin? I mean, if we find out from him when The Call first became an issue in his nest, could we find some way of understanding it better, of fighting it?"

Antonio sighed heavily. "I would like to say yes, but this is something that has been around for a very long time, Jared, and nothing has ever been able to stop it. If there was some way of fighting it, I would imagine that someone would have discovered it by now."

"But not if the only response to the outbreak that vampires have ever made is to kill anyone who became tainted and then hide away, right?"

"Maybe," was all Antonio said, but there was no hope in his voice. "I must get things in motion now." Antonio and Luther hurried away with the guards and dogs, leaving Jared and I alone.

I went to Jared and slid my arms around his waist. He was trembling with fury and hurting so badly, and I felt so helpless. Oh sure I was worried about Evan as well, and the thought of him dying was too much to bear. Similarly, knowing that Stuart and Max were tainted was intensifying the ache still in my chest. But considering that one of the victims was Jared's twin brother, this whole thing had to be a million times worse for him than it was for me.

"I'm not dropping this."

I kissed his throat. "Neither am I."

"We basically have four weeks to find a way to help them. That's the longest they'll last."

I nodded, but I had no clue whatsoever where to start. Apparently, neither did Jared because rather than coming up with some sort of game plan, he just buried his face in the crook of my neck and inhaled deeply. I spoke into his ear. "Come on, let's go home. We'll talk about it there."

He teleported us to the living area of our apartment, but instead of releasing me, he tightened his hold, still vibrating with anger. I soothingly smoothed my hands up and down his back while dabbing kisses on his neck. Bringing his forehead to rest against mine, he rubbed a thumb over my bottom lip. His irises were glowing red, but there wasn't just rage there now. There was also heat and desperation. I knew that look, my body knew that look, and it sent a shiver of need down my spine.

One hand fisted in my hair. "I need you right now." It was a dark rumble.

"You have me."

"I can't go slow," he warned, yanking my head back slightly.

"I don't want you to."

He slammed his mouth down on mine, and I immediately opened for him. The kiss was full of urgency and desperation, as if he thought I could somehow take away his anxiety and pain. Or maybe I was just his escape from it. Tingles of fire were everywhere because his hands were everywhere. Clothes were torn and dumped at our feet. Normally, Jared was the worst tease imaginable. His foreplay could go on for hours, and he'd love every moment of it. But this time there was no finesse, no teasing, no playfulness from either of us.

His hand slid down to the underneath of my thigh and he hooked my leg over his hip, grinding his rock-hard cock against me. An image of me on my knees with his cock in my mouth suddenly flashed in my mind, and I wondered if it had somehow come from him or if the thought was my own. It didn't matter. I dropped to my knees and curled my hand around the root of his dick. Knowing exactly what he liked, I sucked in the energy around me and exhaled a small flame of fire, heating my mouth. I then took him inside, enjoying his groans and moans.

"Fuck, Sam." His fingers tunnelled into my hair and tugged hard as he began pumping his hips, fucking my mouth. "That's it. Keep those lips nice and tight around my cock." As he repeatedly thrust into my mouth, I sucked and licked and swirled my tongue around him. Suddenly he stopped, panting. "Baby, I can't hold out. I'll go out of my fucking mind if I'm not inside you now."

He lifted me into his arms, urged me to curl my legs around his hips, slammed me against the wall, and then drove into me. We both groaned as my muscles clamped tight around him. But he didn't thrust again, didn't bury himself deeper inside me. Instead, he held himself completely still. I could sense him digging deep for control, worried that he was hurting me.

"Baby." The agonised sound was an apology.

"It's okay. You're not hurting me. Now move."

Gripping my hips tightly, he took me at my word and began powering into me. It was deep, it was raw, it was primal, and it was exactly what I wanted just then. His face was a mask of intensity and determination, and he held my eyes with a gaze so piercing and hot it was scorching. "Nothing in the goddamn world beats being in you, feeling you around me, Sam. Not a fucking thing."

I could feel my climax fast approaching. "Jared, I'm not going to last long."

"But you will, baby, because I'm not leaving this body yet." He slowed his movements until every thrust was deliciously yet excruciatingly slow. Curling my hips, he went even deeper with each long, drawn-out thrust. My eyelids drifted shut with the bliss of it all. "Uh-uh, Sam. Eyes open."

Oh he always bloody did this, the sod.

"Come on, open those eyes for me. I want to see them."

But I ignored him. Seriously, what was the point in forcing them open when they'd drift shut again anyway? There was a whoosh of movement and suddenly I was bent over the arm of the sofa and a hand came down hard on my arse. I looked back at him, gaping. "Oh, you little shit."

"Well, if I can't look in your eyes, I might as well look at your ass."

"I am *so* going to—" But then he slammed into me and I no longer gave a crap.

"It really is the most perfect ass, baby." He smoothed his hands over it before cupping it possessively. "Even better, it's mine." Then he was driving into me hard, deep, and fast. My climax soon began creeping up on me again, making my inner muscles flutter around him. This time, he didn't slow down. Instead, his thrusts turned fevered.

Curling his body over mine, he slipped his hands under me to palm and mould my breasts. With his thumbs, he sent shards of electricity into each nipple while at the same time licking my neck. Then one hand again knotted in my hair and yanked, angling my head how he wanted it – a move that might have got him in trouble if I wasn't so close to coming. Without hesitation, he sank his teeth into my neck. The moans he made as he drank from me vibrated against my skin and, oh God, I was going to come. The climax hit me hard, wrenching a scream from me. Jared slammed into me once, twice, and then drove deep as he exploded inside me, half-growling-half-groaning my name.

I wasn't sure how long we stayed there, panting and quivering with the aftershocks, but eventually Jared withdrew from me and then teleported us to the shower. Standing under the spray, he simply held me to him for a little while. It wasn't until we'd finished soaping each other down that he spoke. "How is it that coming inside you makes me calm down and think better?"

I smiled, batting my eyelids. "I'm just special like that."

He chuckled, sucking my bottom lip into his mouth. "You are to me."

When his smile faltered, I knew he was thinking about Evan again. "So what are your thoughts on what to do next?" I sensed that Jared needed to run this show, needed to feel as in control of it as possible. I'd offer my suggestions when necessary, but I'd let him take the lead.

"I'm thinking we need to speak to someone who knows about viruses. Yeah, I know this isn't a virus, but it's something similar. Maybe if we know more about how they work, how antiviruses are developed, we might get an idea of how best to approach this situation."

That wasn't bad as ideas went.

"So we should kidnap a human scientist."

Not such a good idea.

"Obviously we won't let them meet the guys or reveal that we're not human," he continued as we rinsed off the last of the soap from both our bodies. "But we can pick at the scientist's brain for as long as it takes to come up with something."

"Or we could just find and talk to one. The whole 'kidnapping' part could be optional."

As if he realised that his plan was slightly on the dark side, he groaned at himself. "I'm just worried about Evan, Max, and Stuart."

"You won't particularly care if it turns out that Cristiano is tainted as well, will you?"

He shrugged, turning off the spray and stepping out of the shower. "If he is, I'll simply think of it as karma for ogling my mate and constantly giving me smug smirks because he knows how you taste."

Yeah, that had been pretty mean. As we patted each other dry, I said, "Still, it wouldn't be fair to Ava to let her brother die simply because we think he's a dickhead."

After a pause, he inclined his head, conceding that. "I noticed you were right about her – she sure can fight. Who the fuck trained her? Jackie Chan?"

"Her gift is muscle memory. It's a little like having a photographic memory. Whereas someone with a photographic memory can remember in detail anything they've seen, Ava can perfectly replicate any move she's ever seen."

"So all she has to do to learn combat is watch how other people fight and play some Kung Fu movies? Cool gift. Did you notice that Salem—" He cut himself off on hearing a heavy knock on the front door. "It could be someone with news about Evan."

Thanks to vampire speed, we were dressed and at the front door in less than ten seconds. The squad – minus Max and Stuart, of course – Ava, Cristiano, and Fletcher all piled in. Each of them looked a mixture of confused, devastated, and pissed off. So Cristiano *wasn't* tainted then. I would bet that had greatly disappointed Jared, but I wouldn't wish the possible fate of Evan, Max, and Stuart on anyone.

Fletcher pulled me into a hug. "Luv, I'm so glad you're all right. I was with Antonio when he briefed the squad on The Reaper's Call. I swear my heart skipped at least four beats." Like me, Fletcher was

British, and I loved him to bits. But he was also a bloody drama queen – even Norm agreed on that. He addressed both Jared and me as he added, "You must be a bag of nerves right now. I know I am. Poor Evan. And the others of course, but Evan…I've always had a soft spot for him. No doubt you have a plan of action. I'm eager to hear it."

He squeezed himself between David and Damien on the sofa. Reuben had perched himself on one arm of the sofa while Chico perched himself on the arm that Jared had bent me over not so long ago. I had to fight a smile, and I saw that Jared was doing the same.

"Antonio put Evan, Max, and Stuart into a containment cell." Chico traced his goatee. "They're not pleased about it, but they understand."

The containment cells were located beneath the large mansion and made of unbreakable glass. A cell was, therefore, the best place to put Evan, Max, and Stuart, but I still couldn't help balking at the idea of them locked up like that.

"Antonio's news scared the crap out of all of us," continued Chico. "I'd never even heard of The Reaper's Call before. Have you?"

I shook my head. My attention went to Cristiano and Ava, who were clearly devastated to know that their vampires had fallen victim to The Call and died in those tunnels. Ava was cuddling herself while Denny kept a comforting arm over her shoulders. I couldn't help but notice that Salem, who was standing behind them with Cristiano, was scowling at Denny's comforting arm. As if he sensed someone looking at him, Denny turned his head. When he saw the expression on his fellow squad member's face, his eyes widened. Denny looked from Salem to a totally clueless Ava and back again, and then abruptly dropped his arm. Salem simply grunted in what could have been satisfaction. He wasn't an easy one to read.

"Antonio said that you and Jared are planning to search for a way to help them." Ava's voice was surprisingly strong, considering she looked like a small wind could knock her on her arse. "Do you really think you can find one?"

"No other outcome is acceptable," Jared told her. His confidence seemed to reassure her, because she visibly gathered herself and released a cleansing breath.

Leaning against the wall beside Butch, Harvey asked, "Where are you starting your search?"

"Our plan is to learn as much about viruses as we possibly can," replied Jared.

David arched a brow. "It's a virus?"

"No, but it follows the same logic as one. Hopefully we can learn something from a scientist who specializes in viruses."

Salem pursed his lips. "And if we don't?"

"Then we look elsewhere. And we keep looking until we find answers of some kind."

Cristiano suddenly piped up. "Ava and I would like to come with you."

When Jared opened his mouth – most likely to object, just like Salem appeared ready to do – Ava quickly spoke, "You lot must all know how my brother and I are feeling right now. If we help defeat The Call, it will be like getting vengeance for what happened to our vampires. You'd want to do the same in our position."

Jared exhaled heavily. "Fine." Salem didn't look pleased by the decision and was frowning at Ava's back.

"Well then," began Butch, "let's go find ourselves a scientist."

"Wait a minute." We all turned our attention to Fletcher. "Now tell me if I'm overstepping my boundaries here by interfering" – like he really cared about boundaries – "but wouldn't it be much simpler to talk to Bran's Heir?"

I cocked my head. "Bran's Heir?"

"Harry Covington was a doctor during his human life. It's different from a scientist, I know. But surely he'll know something about viruses that could help you." Seeing that everyone was staring at him, wide eyed, Fletcher squirmed under the attention. "What?"

He, a PA, had come up with a better plan than two commanders and a squad from the legion – that was 'what'. "Fletch, have I ever told you how much I love you?"

He gave me a playfully scathing look. "Not often enough, but I try not to take it personally."

Jared, who was filled with a newfound enthusiasm, turned to me. "We might have to return to the whole kidnapping plan. Bran isn't going to want us visiting Covington, knowing we've been in contact with people who are tainted. He won't risk it in case any of us are tainted too."

"Again, though, the kidnapping part can be optional. I say we just ask Antonio if we can join in on the teleconference." Ridiculously, they all looked disappointed that no one would be being kidnapped. Unreal.

CHAPTER FOUR

(Sam)

It took a while for Antonio to finish the teleconference. Once it was over, he asked Bran to remain on the line and then invited Jared and I to sit beside him in front of one of the TVs. Thankfully, Bran granted us some time with his Heir, and soon we were looking at the surprisingly attractive face of Harry Covington. I'd been expecting someone who looked much older. Harry couldn't have been much more than twenty-five when he was Turned.

Clearly anxious for answers, Jared didn't bother with pleasantries. "What can you tell us about viruses?"

Harry looked taken aback by the question but shrugged. "Put simply, they're strands of DNA or RNA covered by a protein coating."

Admittedly, that made no sense whatsoever to me. Science had never been my strong point.

When Jared waved his hand in a 'carry on' gesture, Harry squinted. "This is about The Call, isn't it? You think it's like a virus."

"It seems to be similar."

"That's what I thought in the beginning. I was wrong."

I arched a brow. "You've been in contact with people who were tainted?"

"No, but I've researched it. As you can imagine, it intrigued the medic in me. It's in my nature to want to treat something, to cure it. I've done my best to understand The Call over the centuries. What I've learned isn't good."

Beside me, Antonio softly cursed.

Gritting his teeth, Jared urged, "Go on."

"My opinion is that it's entirely different from a virus. You see, viruses aren't alive, but nor are they dead. They exist somewhere in between. In effect, they're parasites. Without a host or a group of host cells, they can't thrive or survive. The Call, however, is very much alive."

That didn't sound good. "What do you mean by 'alive'?"

"Not alive as you or I know it. It isn't a biological organism. In fact, it's not at all tangible. The Call could be described as incorporeal venom. It travels into the blood, contaminating it, polluting it. It is nothing you could see, nothing you could fight, because it has no physical properties. It doesn't attach itself to cells, doesn't use us as a host – it simply 'visits' us, doing a circuit through our blood and tainting our system as it does so. That's why it wouldn't be possible to treat The Call in the same way that humans treat a virus."

And there went Jared's optimism. He scrubbed a hand over his face. "In other words, there's no point in looking for a counteragent."

"No."

"So, we're fucked."

Harry's eyes slid away. "Well…"

Jared straightened in his seat. "What?"

"There is someone who might be able to help your vampires. She wouldn't be able to come up with some kind of counteragent, but it's possible that she could help the tainted."

"Who?" Jared and Antonio asked in unison.

"Her name is Paige West, and she's a Keja vampire who is part of my line. Her gift…She can heal, but she's not a healer."

Frowning, I shook my head. "I'm not following."

"Her gift is actually offensive. If you were to harm her, she could take her pain or her injury and give it to you, and it would be three times worse when revisited onto you. Her gift is more about inflicting pain and avenging herself than about healing."

Well. Call me odd, but I found that gift kind of intriguing. It was pretty much a karma-like gift, and I was a big believer in tit for tat.

"And she can do that for others?" asked Jared.

"Yes, she can take their pain or injury, but she must have someone to give it to. Without that, the hurt will almost instantly return to the person it came from. I imagine it would work on tainted vampires. But I can't be sure."

"We'll take our chances." Jared shrugged. "At this point, we have nothing to lose anyway."

And if there was even the slightest chance that she could help

Evan, Max, and Stuart, then Paige West was now my new best friend. "Where do we find her?"

Harry gave us a grim smile. "That's the tricky part. Nobody actually knows where Paige is."

Well, crap.

"She doesn't particularly enjoy this life and has cut herself off from all vampirekind?" asked Antonio. It wasn't an uncommon thing.

"No. It was, in fact, her decision to Turn. Her Sire sent her on an assignment – I'm not sure exactly what it was – but instead of coming back with the information he wanted, she killed the vampire who had the information. After that, she disappeared, along with the information, and no one has been able to find her."

Well great. Just great.

"Surely her Sire has a vague idea of her location," insisted Jared.

"Possibly, but I'm not certain."

Antonio tilted his head. "Who is her Sire?"

"His name is Robert Langley. I can give you his contact details." After consulting his smartphone, he rattled off an address and a cell number. Jared entered it all into his cell phone while Antonio scribbled it down onto a piece of paper. "Warning, Robert's not the most pleasant of people."

"That's okay." Jared smiled, looking a little evil, to be honest. "Neither am I."

Antonio briefly bowed his head at Harry. "You have been a huge help, Covington. I appreciate it."

Jared nodded. "Yeah, thanks."

"Don't thank me yet. Even if you find Paige, it won't be easy to convince her to help you because she clearly wishes to be left alone."

Jared's evil smile widened. "Don't worry about us finding a way to make Paige cooperate. We can be very persuasive."

Ending the call, Antonio swerved in his seat to fully face Jared and me. "I've never heard of Paige West. Perhaps that is because she has isolated herself from our kind. In any case, I will have Sebastian locate her. He is the best tracker there is."

"He is," agreed Jared. "And I appreciate having his help. But I won't rely on him. Not with this. Finding her is too important. This woman might be our only chance of saving the guys. Sam and I should still go see Robert Langley, find out what he knows about her."

Understanding that Jared needed to feel that he was actively helping, I clasped his hand and gave it a supportive squeeze. "Then we leave at dusk."

"Yes, it is important for you both to rest first." Antonio sighed. "I can only speculate on how exhausted you must both be – physically and emotionally – after this evening's events."

"I'd like to briefly speak with Evan before we head home." Jared massaged the palm of my hand with his thumb. "He'll be glad to hear Harry's news."

Antonio grimaced. "Would it be wise to give him false hope? For all we know, Paige West's gift will not help with The Call."

"It *has* to," stated Jared. "There are only three people in this world I care about – Sam, Evan, and you. I absolutely refuse to lose any of you."

My chest was literally aching with the echoes of his pain that were running through me. I leaned against him, wishing I could help and hating that I couldn't. His arm closed around me, keeping me there. I wanted to assure him that he wouldn't lose any of us, that we'd find some way to help Evan. But we'd never been up against anything like this before. Since meeting, Jared and I had had our fair share of trials and dealt with some really freaky scenarios, but nothing like this. How did you go about fighting something that you couldn't see, that had no physical properties and no counteragent?

"I think it would also be best to delay the Coronation until after The Call is once again dormant." Antonio's expression begged us to understand. "For one thing, it is imperative that this matter is dealt with immediately. Also, most of vampirekind is now on lockdown, intent on staying out of The Call's reach. We would therefore have no witnesses, no celebration. And I very much doubt a Prelate would risk travelling here to perform the ceremony. I haven't yet announced my intention to step down, so there will be no one to disappoint."

"I agree." I frowned as something suddenly struck me. "One thing, though. Is it really possible to remain out of The Call's reach by hiding? I mean, Quentin's nest was underground and yet it struck them. Is it possible that it tainted someone before them? That the tainted vampire then took it to the nest with him?"

"Only Quentin can answer that question. None of the other High Masters know where he is. It's possible that he did in fact die in the tunnels."

I hoped not, or it meant that his answers had died with him. If there were more tainted vampires out there, it was important that we found and contained them.

There was a brief knock, and then Luther entered the room. "Please tell me you have good news."

Sebastian followed Luther inside. "Yes, I need something to give me hope."

Antonio filled them both in on our conversation with Harry Covington.

Luther looked slightly optimistic by the end of it. "Let us pray that this woman can help us."

"We have to find her first." And convince her to help. If I had to resort to Jared's new solution to everything and kidnap her, I'd do it in a heartbeat.

"Leave that to me." Sebastian's voice was full of determination. "There is no place the Keja can hide where I will not find her."

"Sam and I will be doing our own investigations too," Jared informed him. "Between all of us, we should be able to find Paige West in time to help the guys."

Luther gave him an encouraging smile. "I have faith in you all, and so will Evan, Max, and Stuart." He lightly touched me on the shoulder. But then he stiffened and a gasp flew out of him as his eyes took on a faraway quality that meant one thing – he was having a vision. Oh, this was never good. When Luther finally snapped out of it, his gaze ran along everyone in the room, who were all now standing.

Most likely in response to the sheer fright on his Advisor's face, Antonio tensed. "What is it, Luther?"

"Please don't talk in riddles," I begged him. He had a habit of being very vague with his warnings, and it drove me bloody mental.

Luther inhaled deeply. "They will come for her. Paige West, they will come for her."

"Who? Who will come?" demanded Antonio.

"There were so many of them in the vision. So many. If you bring her here, they will do whatever it takes to get to her." He looked at me then. Oh bloody wonderful. "And it could mean that you are forced to make a very difficult decision, Sam. A decision no one should have to make."

Well fuck a duck. I massaged my temples. "I don't suppose you're going to tell me what that decision is, are you?"

"I wish I could. But as you know, sometimes a vision can be just a *feeling*, a *knowing*. I could feel the weight of a painful, frightening decision bearing on you – a decision that affects so many, that your safety rests on."

Jared, who was feeling kind of numb as if he didn't really know how to feel about all this, spoke. "So what you're saying is that if we bring Paige West here, there's a distinct possibility that things will go tits up and Sam could be harmed?"

"Yes."

Sebastian sighed. "The question is: are we willing to risk all that happening in order to save the lives of Evan, Max, and Stuart?"

Cursing a blue streak that had everybody's eyes widening, Jared dropped back down into his seat and buried his face in his hands. So many emotions were flickering through him so quickly that I couldn't even identify what they were.

"We will give you both some time alone." With that, Antonio led the others out of the room.

I sat beside Jared, placing a supportive hand on his back. "We have to do this, Jared. We have to help Evan, Max, and Stuart."

He lifted his head, gazing at me with eyes that were filled with so much turmoil that it hurt to maintain eye contact. "I can't risk you. Do you understand that? I *can't* risk you." Then he was on his feet, pacing.

"But we can't risk them, either. You know this." But he wasn't listening. He was deep in his own mind, lost in his own thoughts. I rose from my seat and grabbed his arm to halt him. "We can't ignore this. They'll die, Jared."

"I know," he gritted out. "And I hate being in a position where I actually have to fucking choose between you and my twin brother. But baby, nothing in this world could make me risk you. I just fucking can't." He locked a hand in my hair and roughly pulled me close.

I tucked my head into the crook of his neck and slipped my arms around him. "You're not choosing. *I'm* choosing."

"No." The word was filled with agony yet resoluteness. His overprotectiveness often tended to piss me off, but this was so much more than overprotectiveness – this was a bone-deep, all-consuming fear of losing me. I could feel the echoes of it. An ache started to build in my temples from the pressure of it.

"Jared—"

He pulled back to cradle my face. "You just don't get it. You never have. You are essential to me. I told you the night of our Binding ceremony: I need you here with me, always, no matter fucking what." His expression said, 'And you'd agreed'. Yes, I had.

"But—"

"Did you see the look on Luther's face when he mentioned that decision you'll have to make?"

Yes. He'd looked stricken, wrecked. And it had put the bloody shits up me.

"He said your safety rests on it." I opened my mouth to speak, but Jared shook his head and stepped away. "You might be prepared to risk yourself, Sam, but I'm not. Not for you, not for anyone." His eyes, expression, and tone were adamant – he wasn't budging on this.

Anyone else might have accepted their fate and backed down, but that wasn't who I was. "I don't expect you to like my decision to help them. I don't even expect you to respect it. But I'm asking you to understand it. Evan's been a great friend to me, like a brother, and I adore him. Max and Stuart are part of our squad, I care for them, and it's my responsibility to protect them."

Jared simply shrugged, seemingly unmoved. "They'll understand." Annoyingly, they would. In fact, they would insist that we didn't even try to find Paige West. They would put me before themselves, the plonkers. I couldn't let them do that.

My words were quiet, pained. "I can't let them die."

"And I can't let you be hurt."

"I love you for caring as much as you do, Jared, I do. But this is Evan, Max, and Stuart we're talking about."

He smiled a little. "Trying to put me on a guilt trip, baby? It's not going to work. I know how you think."

I took a deep breath. "Okay, let's look at it this way: Luther said the whole 'me being faced with a decision' thing *could* happen, not that it definitely would."

He shot me an 'oh for God's sake' look. Of course he did. I was clutching at straws, and we both knew it.

"His vision means we've got a heads-up. It means we know we need to be even more vigilant and careful than usual. That puts us a step ahead."

He shook his head, incredulous. In fact, he looked like he was considering throttling me. "You're just not getting it. Maybe that's my fault. Maybe it's because I don't tell you I love you often enough. Baby, you're the only 'good' thing that I've ever had. There's simply no fucking way I'm letting anything at all happen to you. No. Way."

"Jared, please just—"

"Put yourself in my position, Sam."

Oh the bastard just had to say that, didn't he?

"If Luther had been talking about *me* just then, would you have been so eager to go track down Paige West?" When I didn't answer, he gave a soft, humourless laugh. "Didn't think so."

But there was another way to look at it. "If Luther *had* been talking about you, would you have wanted to sit back and let Evan, Max, and Stuart die just because I was worried and scared of losing you?" He wouldn't even meet my eyes, let alone respond. "Didn't think so."

A muscle in his jaw ticked. "You won't talk me in circles, Sam. You won't get your own way this time."

"You think I *want* to risk myself? Now that we're Bound, we're interconnected so tightly that if I die, you die. Even the thought of you dying makes me feel ill."

"Then you know exactly how I'm feeling. To risk ourselves is to risk each other – neither of us wants to do that. This conversation is pointless."

I counted to five in my head, seeking patience. It didn't work. "You're twisting what I'm saying. My point is that you can count on me being on high alert and having a distinct sense of self-preservation simply in order to keep you alive."

His smile was rueful. "Touching, but *I will not risk you*."

"And I will not risk them."

There was still no hint of compromise in his expression at all. "Stalemate, baby."

"What if we get other people to track Paige down for us?" Maybe if I agreed to sit in the background a little, it would settle his nerves.

He snorted. "Nice try, but it won't make any difference, and you know it. Luther said that Paige West coming here would be the catalyst. It's not going to matter who brings her."

"So we're just going to sit back and watch Evan, Max, and Stuart die?"

"Hell, no. I'm not giving up on them. But I'm not bringing Paige West to The Hollow, and that's final."

We couldn't even take Evan, Max, and Stuart to see her instead. They needed to remain contained. "How about a compromise?" I held up a hand to halt any attempts he might make to object. "Just hear me out. We spend the next few weeks trying to find some way of helping them. We'll track Quentin Foy down as well; ask him how The Call suddenly struck his nest. During that time, we'll have Sebastian locate Paige West. If we don't find a counteragent or some other solution in those few weeks, we approach Paige then. That's a reasonable deal, Jared."

He sighed tiredly, shaking his head. "You never give up, do you?"

"You like that I never give up."

"In other circumstances, yes, I do."

I closed the distance that he'd created between us and fisted a hand in his t-shirt. I kept my tone gentle, sensitive, cajoling. "At least agree to Sebastian tracking her down. What harm could that do?"

It was a long moment before he answered. "Fine. But I won't agree to her coming here."

So bloody stubborn. I wanted to argue that further, but I knew he wasn't going to budge on this. Not now. Maybe if in a few weeks' time we hadn't found another possible way of helping Evan, Max, and Stuart, then maybe Jared would relent. I just had to hope that we did find an alternative to involving Paige West. If not, it was quite possible that we were all fucked.

(Jared)

When I set off with Sam to see the guys in the containment cell, I hadn't expected to find them playing poker – acting like nothing was wrong. But maybe that was how they were coping with the situation. Spotting Sam and I standing on the other side of the glass, they all paused in their game and approached us. They looked completely normal, healthy. I might have wondered if they had been immune to The Call if it wasn't for the fact that their bite marks were oozing rather than healing. Soon enough, their symptoms would begin and I'd be looking at three skeleton-like vampires if I didn't find some answers fast.

"I don't suppose you have anything good to tell us." Max didn't appear optimistic. Neither did Evan or Stuart.

I told them about the teleconference with Harry Covington, but neatly avoided the subject of Paige West. When I sensed Sam's discomfort, I quickly spoke in her mind. *Don't mention Luther's vision. Antonio was right – it would only give them false hope, and they won't support your case to bring her here anyway.*

Her almost imperceptible nod was begrudging.

Satisfied, I continued. "We're going to search for Quentin Foy, ask how his nest became tainted. Maybe he has answers as to when The Call first struck. If it didn't surface inside those tunnels, it means others outside the nest might be tainted. If that's the situation, we need to know before it has any chance of spreading."

Evan nodded. "But we're kidding ourselves if we think we can fight The Call, Jared."

My expression hardened. "You don't know that for sure."

"Yes, I do."

"Evan's right," said Stuart. "This thing has been around for centuries. No one was able to get rid of it, and – as far as I know – no one was ever immune to it."

Sam scowled at them. "If you expect us to just sit back on our arses and let this drop, you can think again."

Evan smiled sadly. "I just don't want you both exhausting yourselves, searching for something that doesn't exist. I know how you are, Jared. You'll start feeling guilty that your efforts are fruitless. I'll bet you're already blaming yourself for what happened down there."

He'd always been able to see right through me. "I shouldn't have let you come with us. I knew your head wasn't in a good place, I knew you'd be reckless, but I let you go anyway."

"You couldn't possibly have known what lay in wait for us down there. If it's anyone's fault that I'm tainted, it's mine. I didn't listen to you in those tunnels. I threw myself into a dangerous situation, and I even put myself in the lead. You told me to back away from that vampire, you warned me that he'd attack, but I ignored you."

"You're not responsible for what happened to Stuart and me either," Max adamantly stated to Jared. Stuart nodded his agreement. "You trained us well, and you kept us behind you in those tunnels because you thought we'd be safer that way. Even when you heard the first horde of vampires coming, you tried to get us to leave instead of asking us to face them with you."

"Shit like this happens," said Stuart, shrugging. "I knew when I joined the legion that my immortality would be fragile. Every time I left for an assignment, I was conscious that it could be my last. It's no one's fault that we got hurt. If you can find a way to help us fight The Call, great. But if you can't, it doesn't make you responsible for what will happen to us." He smiled widely. "Just know that my replacement in the squad will have big shoes to fill."

I couldn't imagine replacing any of them. Sensing Sam's anguish, I took her hand in mine and squeezed it lightly. "We'll do what we can." Evan's expression was begging me to let it go. "If it was me in there, if the situation was reversed, what would you do?"

Evan answered without missing a beat. "Search high and low for a way to fix this fucking mess."

"Then don't expect me to do anything different."

"Do you want us to contact Alora about what's happening?" Sam asked carefully.

Grinding his jaw, Evan replied, "No."

"She cares about you, Evan." Sensing Evan's scepticism, she quickly added, "It was written all over her face at the Binding ceremony. I don't know why she resisted staying here with you, and I'm not asking – that's your business. But if it was Alora who was tainted, wouldn't you want to know about it?"

"Yes, I would. But I don't want her to see me like this."

"It's possible that she'll find out from Bran," I pointed out.

"If she turns up at The Hollow, you don't let her down here." Evan's voice was harsh. "Not for any reason."

I understood why he was so set on this: if he was going to slowly wither until he eventually died, Evan wanted Alora to remember him as he was before. In his position, I would have wanted the same thing. But..."You're not going to die."

Evan ignored that. "Promise me you won't let her down here."

I nodded. "I promise."

Evan looked at Sam then, brow arched expectantly.

After a brief hesitation, she spoke. "I promise."

Satisfied, Evan gave a slight smile. "Now get out of here. We've got a poker game to play, and I was winning until you both showed up."

Max snorted at Evan. "You *think* you're winning – there's a difference."

Bantering, the guys returned to the table at the centre of the room and went back to their game. And I hated the thought that that could have been the last rational conversation I'd ever again have with my twin brother.

CHAPTER FIVE

(Sam)

Frustrated, I slammed the thick book on my office desk. From his seat at his own desk, Jared arched a quizzical brow, smiling in amusement. I just shook my head. His smile widened, but he said nothing and returned to...well, whatever the hell he was reading.

Five days had gone by of researching The Call by reading books, surfing the V-Net, and consulting various knowledgeable vampires by teleconference. But none of the information had proven to be any more informative than what Antonio and Luther had been. We had explored every possible idea and examined every possible theory in our search for a counteragent, but our efforts had so far come to nothing.

Furthermore, there was no trace of Quentin Foy anywhere, so we were no closer to finding out if there were more tainted vampires on the loose or not. Another squad within the legion had searched the borders of Quentin's tunnels and also the nearest towns, but no tainted vampires had been found.

According to Sebastian, who regularly kept in contact by cell phone, Robert Langley hadn't been much help with the Paige West situation. Sebastian sadly didn't believe he was close to finding her yet. Jared was still refusing to even consider bringing her to The Hollow, but I was just thankful that he had at least conceded that there was no harm in Sebastian attempting to locate her.

Conscious that we had been badly neglecting our usual duties, Jared and I had given the squad the rest of the night off and then retreated to our office. Although the squad were in top shape and had amazing control of their gifts, we still worked with them each week Monday through to Friday in order to ensure that things stayed that way. Unfortunately, recent events had messed with that schedule – not to mention the morale of the squad. Still, to their credit, they hadn't slacked off.

Unable to concentrate on the work matters in front of me, I'd again read through many of the huge, old, musty-smelling books that contained information on The Call on the off-chance that I'd missed something. But it quickly became apparent that I hadn't. So I'd inhaled another whirlwind's worth of dust for nothing.

And now I was utterly pissed.

A knock was quickly followed by the entrance of Fletcher. He hardly ever waited for a 'come in'. Humming to himself, he placed an NST and some crisps on first Jared's desk and then mine. Busy reading, Jared merely gave Fletcher a nod of thanks. It still made Fletcher melt on the spot. Yes, my PA had a thing for my mate. Who didn't?

Being an Empath, Fletcher instantly picked up on my mood and shot me an 'Are you all right?' look over the rim of his glasses. I forced a smile and nodded, but he didn't seem convinced. No doubt he'd quiz me later, I thought as I watched him leave the office.

I glanced at Jared to see that he was still reading. You would think he would be just as pissed as me, given his brother's condition. But no. For the past five days, Jared had been nothing but positive and optimistic. Maybe refusing to accept the possibility that Evan might die was his way of facing it, of dealing with it, and avoid falling apart.

My way of dealing with it? I didn't have one.

With a groan, I let my head flop down onto the desk. My forehead met the oak with a thud. Ow.

There was a sigh that – annoyingly – had a trace of amusement in it. "Come here, baby."

"No." I was quite comfortable where I was.

"Why?" I could hear the smile in his voice.

"I don't need a reason."

"Come on, come to me."

"I'm busy."

"You're going to end up with a red mark on your head."

"So will you if you don't shut the fuck up."

He chuckled. "That's my girl. Now come over here."

I finally lifted my head. "What do you want?"

"To hold you. I've missed you." He gave me a meaningful look that I easily interpreted. It was fair to say that I had been snappy and impatient with everyone, even him, for the past few days. Rather than taking the let's-face-this-together approach and allowing us to be each other's strength, I had emotionally pulled away. It was in my nature to deal with things alone, to disappear into my own head while I worked it out. I was a 'thinker', my dad had always said. I'd silently ponder over things, explore the matter in my mind, rather than confide in anyone. It was a good thing, really, since my parents hadn't exactly been interested in anything I was thinking or feeling. My conception had been an accident, a bad accident, and they had never let me forget it.

But retreating into my own head wasn't fair to Jared, was it? Not now that we were Bound.

What made me feel even guiltier was that he hadn't complained, hadn't even commented on it, despite that he must have wanted me with him one hundred percent right now. He'd given me that time, that space. But that time was apparently over. With a heavy exhale, I rose from my seat and went to him.

He swivelled his chair to face me and gripped my hips, pulling me to stand between his legs. "Hey," he said gently.

Resting my hands on his shoulders, I bit my lower lip. "I'm sorry."

Slipping his hands under my t-shirt, he pressed them against my back to pull me closer. "So you're done?" No judgmental words or looks; only total understanding – now I felt even guiltier. "I know you're worried about the guys. I wouldn't expect anything different. But you're letting the stress of it all get the better of you." Again there was no judgement there. "I hate seeing you like this."

I understood, since – likewise – I'd hated seeing him an absolute wreck after the wacko brothers had kidnapped me.

He squeezed my hip gently. "You don't have to go it alone when shit happens, Sam. Not anymore. I'm here."

"It's like a mental reflex, but I'll work on it."

"Good, because I want my mate back. I miss her. I miss her giving me attitude, and teasing me, and cursing me to hell and back."

My smile mirrored his. "And she's missed you."

"That's an extremely good thing because I plan to—" He paused at the knock on the door. "Yes?"

"Antonio is here to see you," announced Fletcher. There was an odd note to his voice that made me frown.

Jared rose to his feet. "Let him in."

Antonio breezed into the room with his guards and pit-bulls in tow. He also had two unfamiliar Kejas with him. "Sam, Jared...I would like you to meet Eloise Montana and Fredrick Collins." Really? Because he didn't sound as if he'd *like* us to meet them at all. In fact, he didn't appear pleased about their presence either. "Fredrick is also one of my vampires."

"I'm the first vampire he ever sired," added Collins, cocky and self-satisfied by that fact.

I hadn't met many vampires that had been sired by Antonio, so I was instantly curious about him. The impeccably neat Collins was average height, had short mousey hair, watchful beady eyes, and looked like he'd be right at home in a corner office. And I didn't like him. It was an immediate feeling that I couldn't explain. Every instinct I had severely disliked this bloke. His gaze ran over both Jared and I studiously. Something not holy on the side of the angels glinted in those eyes as he focused on Jared.

Moving my attention to the smartly dressed Eloise, I saw that the tall, slim female was staring at Jared and smiling. People stared at him like that all the time, but there was something in her eyes that told me this wasn't the first time they had met.

Running a hand over her long mane of coal-black hair, she practically purred, "It's good to see you again, Jared."

Yep, I was right.

Antonio's brow puckered. "Oh. I did not realise that you two had already met."

Without moving her eyes from Jared, she told Antonio, "We met briefly when I came to attend a gathering here many years ago. Despite the meeting being brief, it was certainly memorable."

In other words, you bonked her.

Um...yeah. He sounded loathed to admit it. *It was just the one time and was nothing but a quick fuck. In fact, I was wasted that night. Remember, baby, it was only ever the Heir they wanted.*

I mentally rolled my eyes, exasperated that he persisted in believing that his status and his looks were all that women thought he had to offer. But this wasn't the time to have that conversation again.

"It's an honour to meet the Heir." There was a bitter edge to Collins' words. Ah, jealousy. "You must be very proud to have been selected for the position."

Eloise slid her gaze to me. Distaste glinted in those eyes. "You must be the famous Svente everyone's been talking non-stop about."

"You have me at a disadvantage," I told her. "You've heard much about me, but I've never before heard anything about you."

Jared cocked his head at Collins, still ignoring Eloise – wise decision. "I can say the same about you, Collins. It's odd that I've never heard of Antonio's first-born. In fact, in all the time I've been here, you've never once visited. Not even for the Binding ceremony."

Collins flushed. "It wasn't possible. I have…commitments." The bloke didn't even visit his own Sire? A Sire who anyone would be lucky to have? What a prick. I'd have been proud to have a Sire like Antonio.

Seemingly uncomfortable and also a little pissed off, Antonio spoke to Collins. "I think it is time that you told them why you and Eloise are here." Something in his tone had the hairs on the back of my neck raising.

Collins, someone who clearly had an overinflated sense of self-importance, straightened his posture. "Eloise and I work together as representatives within the Prelature."

The Prelature was the office of the Prelates – a body of vampire ministers that had the authority to perform and administer various rites such as Bindings and Coronations. These ministers also had the authority to enforce order, and they had 'representatives' who were simply paper pushers that dealt with any cases put forth to the Prelature. It was therefore useful in that it could deal with small squabbles or issues, alleviating Antonio's workload. It existed outside of all forms of authority in order to be totally neutral, and was older than even the concept of the Grand High Master. Of course, most vampires sought out Antonio in times of trouble, but there were some who preferred to stick to the 'old ways' and turned to the Prelature.

The Prelature didn't deliver death sentences or imprison anyone, and it didn't deal in corporeal punishment. In fact, the Prelates disapproved of such things, but they weren't always lenient. The Prelature's punishments came in the form of official reprimands (simply public warnings), exile (banishing vampires from their nests), monetary fines (even so far as taking away *all* the vampire's belongings; for those who had spent their very long lives accumulating wealth, this hurt), or even dismissal of their positions in cases of gross negligence.

As Eloise shot me a smug smirk, unease slithered up my spine.

"There have been complaints," Collins informed me.

"Complaints?"

"A member of your squad has made complaints about you, Commander Parker."

Nothing he said or did could have shocked me more. Not a single thing. Not even if he had stripped off his clothes and done the Macarena dance on my desk in a G-string. Maybe I should have felt hurt, devastated, and betrayed by Collins' news. But I didn't feel any of those things because *no way* would I ever believe in a million sodding years that one of the squad would do that. "Bollocks."

"It is but the truth," Eloise seemed to take delight in saying.

"What game are you playing?"

Collins lifted his chin. "I realise this must be difficult for you, Commander Parker. But this particular member voiced a number of serious concerns. They didn't feel they could go to Antonio with this matter as they feared he would not be impartial, being as fond of you as he so clearly is."

"Concerns? Like what?"

"That you work them too hard and for very long hours. That you use unorthodox methods to train them – methods that involve subjecting them to pain. That you take them on more dangerous assignments than any other squad is taken on by their commanders. That you have harmed, and even killed, many humans on your assignments. That you used the squad in order to help avenge another vampire, which we all know is *not* an assignment. That you absorb their energy in order to use their gifts for yourself – that is exploitation at its worst."

I just stood there, dumbstruck. I had no words. And that didn't happen often.

Jared bristled. "Tell me you're not serious."

Collins' tone was grave. "On the contrary, I'm very serious, Commander Michaels. So is this matter – it is not just one complaint, it is a whole list of them."

Oh it was a 'list' all right: it was a list of things that had been twisted into sounding dark and cruel. Yes I worked the squad hard, but I didn't work them any harder or longer than other commanders did their own squads. It was true that I sometimes hurt the squad during training, but only as part of helping them develop better reflexes. Besides, when you were training with people who had such violent gifts, there was going to be some pain whether everyone liked it or not.

It was also true that I had taken them on many dangerous assignments, but that was because Antonio often chose us to deal with such matters. Yes, I had killed during assignments, but I had never killed an innocent. It was also accurate that we had helped Jude avenge what had happened to her, but that had only been insofar as allowing her to come along while we dealt with the matter – we would have crushed that criminal operation in any case. And, yes, I had absorbed each member of the squad's energy at one time or another to use their gifts, but it was only during training so that I could help them learn to better use and control those gifts.

Yet, all those things had been twisted in such a way as to make me indeed sound exploitative and cruel. What bugged me was that whoever had made these supposed 'complaints' had to have had inside knowledge of how I worked in order for them to have any knowledge to twist. Other than Evan, Antonio, Sebastian, or Luther, I never let people observe training sessions. The only people outside of the squad that I had taken on assignments were Jude, Ava, and Cristiano. None of them would have any reason to do this. But I didn't believe for even one second that any member of my squad had anything at all to do with it. "Who *really* made these complaints?"

Collins was the image of snootiness. "As I told you, it was a member of your squad."

Jared narrowed his eyes. "Oh yeah? Then who?"

"They wish to remain anonymous."

I snickered. "Well of course they do."

"I heard that two of your squad members are currently tainted. It is very sad, and I was quite surprised. Frankly, I would have expected better from the Heir, his mate, and their personal squad."

Oh, the little fucker.

"Fredrick, that is enough," snapped Antonio.

"I have a valid point. These people should be powerful enough to protect and lead all vampirekind one day, yet they could not even lead and protect their own squad. Commander Parker is supposed to be particularly powerful, and yet two of her squad are now dying. My investigations show her to be hot-headed and reckless. One only needs to listen to tales of what occurred during the week of the Binding ceremony to know that. I believe two vampires went to the event and never returned."

"If you're talking about the woman who Turned me and came here with her consort, they almost had Sam killed." Jared's tone was dark and menacing, vibrating with a barely controlled rage. "No one was going to let them leave here alive."

Collins straightened his tie. "The Prelature does not condone violence. You may perceive it to be excusable, but her first-born, who reported her disappearance, would not agree with you. The fact remains that Commander Parker is reckless. And that is not the only problem. Show them, Eloise."

Still smiling smugly, Eloise dug out a newspaper from her briefcase and handed it to Jared. Her irises were glowing amber with lust, and all I wanted to do was bitch slap her. Jared didn't even look at her as he took the British newspaper that was opened on a particular page.

Oh bugger. My stomach sank as I saw the photo of Jared and me, strolling around in London. It was one of the places we had visited during our 'honeymoon'. The headline of the article was 'New Lead in Missing Person's Case'. There was then a detailed account of the day I had disappeared and an appeal from the police for more information.

"If the police try to identify Jared," began Eloise, "imagine their reaction when they find a missing person's report from nineteen years ago that shows he hasn't aged."

Jared snorted contemptuously. "They'll just think it must be someone else. They certainly aren't going to scream, 'Shit, he's a vampire!'" *And I strongly doubt my mother bothered filing a report about me*, he told me. *She only ever cared about Evan.*

"Perhaps," allowed Collins. "But that isn't the point."

"What about me? I'm on that photo too. You're not calling *me* reckless."

Collins ground his teeth before speaking. "The squad member was clear that you are an extremely good trainer and that they have no issues whatsoever with you or your techniques." He sounded annoyed by that.

"What is it you intend to do?" It was more of a dare by Jared – a clear 'just fucking try to harm her in any way and I'll kill you'.

"Eloise and I intend to spend the next few months observing Commander Parker."

I double-blinked. "Say again?"

"We will observe you as you train your squad. Observe you as you work. When we are done, we will make a report recommending whether or not we believe you should be allowed to keep your position as a commander."

Jared gawked. "You can't do this! You don't have the authority to pull this shit!"

Collins looked sincerely affronted. "I can and I do, Commander Michaels. I am a representative of the Prelature. Even the Heir's mate is not immune to its authority. It operates outside any other vampiric laws."

Scrubbing a hand down his face, Jared inhaled deeply. "I don't believe this."

"Believe it. Now, I'd like to meet your squad."

I arched a brow. "And why is that?"

"Eloise and I need to interview each of them separately and ask them some questions about you and how they feel about having you as their commander."

I shrugged one shoulder. "That's fine." He and the Keja bitch seemed surprised; clearly they had expected me object. "Why would I have an issue with it? There's nothing negative for you to find. Come on, they're probably in the basketball court."

With Jared hot on my heels, I rounded the desk, and exited the office. Collins, Eloise, Antonio, the guards, and the pit-bulls all followed closely behind us as we led the way to the court. I buried my rage as best I could, determined to keep a hold on my temper, but it wasn't easy. If it hadn't been for Jared's warm presence beside me, it might not have worked.

I had been right about the squad being at the basketball court. Jude, Ava, and Cristiano were also there. Hearing us approach, they turned as a unit, suddenly alert – and probably hoping we were there to give them some good news.

"Everyone, this is Fredrick Collins and Eloise Montana," announced Antonio reluctantly. He looked totally defeated. "They are representatives of the Prelature and they are here to investigate Sam and judge her suitability as a commander." Ignoring the gasps, curses, and mutters, he continued, "They will explain everything."

"It is a pleasure to meet you all." Smiling widely, Collins stepped forward, seeming both awed and excited. He made me think of someone who was in the presence of their favourite rock band. "Eloise and I would like to take each of you aside and ask you some questions."

Chico's expression was hard. "Yeah? Fuck that."

Collins seemed taken aback. Prick. That was called 'loyalty'. It strangely hadn't seemed to occur to him that they might be a little pissed off by all this.

"We're not talking to either of you." Salem turned to me, gesturing at the newcomers. "Coach, what the hell is going on?"

"Oh do elaborate, Mr Collins," I said with a smile. There was no chance I was giving explanations for him.

He clearly didn't want to answer – probably because he didn't want to be the focus of the squad's anger. "A number of complaints were made about Commander Parker."

David gaped. "Made by who?"

"One of you, of course."

Harvey shook his head madly, slashing a hand through the air. "No fucking way."

"None of us would do that!" maintained Denny.

"It is so," said Collins shakily. "The complainant wishes to remain anonymous, so I will not be revealing their name."

"It is protocol for us to interview each of you." Eloise went to Collins' side. "We need to get a distinct picture of what it is like to have Samantha Parker as a commander."

Butch snorted. "Then I'll draw you one."

Collins licked his lips nervously. Who wouldn't be nervous having a gang of powerful pissed off vampires rounding on you? "As Eloise said, this is purely protocol."

"No, it's bullshit," snapped Damien.

"Total and utter bullshit," agreed Reuben, so wound up he was close to crushing the basketball he was holding. I had the feeling he was imagining that it was Collins' head.

"I'm not having any part of it," declared Denny, wearing a mutinous look.

Realising that the squad was close to attacking the representatives, I sighed. "It's fine, talk to them."

Chico looked at me like I was simple. "You're kidding me, right?"

"We've got nothing to hide, have we?" It wasn't a question from me, it was a confident statement. "There's obviously been some kind of misunderstanding. The sooner we get it cleared up, the better. We've got more important things going on right now."

After a long silence, Chico ground out, "Fine." He pointed hard at Collins. "But then you stay the fuck away from me. You got that?"

Still somewhat nervous, Collins gestured at Eloise, who gave Jared a secret smile as she past him. "If you could follow Eloise, she will take you to the mansion where we intend to…Great, thank you." Grumbling and scowling, each of them practically stomped after her. Seeing that Ava, Cristiano, and Jude – who were clearly seriously pissed – hadn't moved, Collins turned to them. "I'm sorry, are you all members of the…?" He let his sentence trail off when Salem came up behind Ava and glared down at Collins. The bloke swallowed hard and forced a smile, taking a step backwards.

Ava peered up at Salem. "Aw, it's my hero again." His sudden scowl didn't seem to bother her in the least. "You really are too sweet."

Salem growled but, again, Ava didn't appear to be affected. "Be good," he told her gruffly before joining the rest of the squad.

It was hilarious watching big, bad Salem turn protective and possessive of small, bubbly Ava. I would never have expected the two to match, but just maybe Ava was what Salem needed. He was too serious and work-focused. Ava's personality wouldn't allow for that. Oddly, though, despite that Salem behaved so protectively, he was also very distant with her and brushed off her attempts to talk more intimately with him.

Jared went to follow Collins. "I'll come too." He was seemingly just as worried about the squad being alone with Prick Number One and Prick Number Two as I was.

Collins' eyes briefly glistened with anger. "Actually, I'm going to need time alone with them. They might feel pressured or intimidated if you are nearby." His tone was pleasant, but his eyes were cold. "You don't have a problem with that, do you, Gerald?"

I gave the bloke a sad smile that said, 'Oh you really don't wanna play like that with Jared'. My mate had been raised by someone who played mind games, which meant three things. One, Jared could spot those games a mile away. Two, he had absolutely no tolerance for them. And three, he knew exactly how to handle people who played them.

"Why would it be a problem?" Jared looked sincerely confused –

it was a total slap down, an implication that for Collins to be a problem, Jared would have to actually care. Translation: 'You're not important enough for me to give a flying fuck what you do.' For someone who clearly thought they were extremely important, it had to have chafed. Collins' face turned crimson with both embarrassment and anger as he marched away.

A gaping Jude approached with Ava and Cristiano. "Tell me I imagined all that."

I sighed. "I wish I could." As Antonio appeared beside me, I asked him, "All right, what's the deal with these two? Please tell me it's some kind of sick joke." His grim expression confirmed that it wasn't.

Cristiano, who came to my other side and shot me a brief look of concern, asked Antonio, "Seriously, is all this for real?"

"I'm afraid it is," replied Antonio sadly.

"But you don't believe there's been a complaint," Jared detected, pulling me close to him and, in effect, away from Cristiano.

"If there has, I do not believe it has come from the squad."

"Then who?" Ava asked Antonio.

"As the Heir's mate, Sam will always have enemies. If these people cannot harm her physically, they will hurt her in other ways."

That would have happened in any case. I had a talent for offending people. "I'm pretty sure the answer is no, but I have to ask if there's any chance you can put this crap to an end?"

"I am sorry, Sam, but for the Prelature to be impartial, it has to be immune to all authority. One of my predecessors once tried to challenge it, and that did not end well. If I was to interfere, it would look bad for you – as though you are not confident that their decision will clear your name. Fredrick would certainly see it as such."

"Not to be a bitch, Antonio…but what possessed you to choose him as your first-born?"

"I Turned him centuries ago when he came to me with evidence of not only the existence of vampires, but of my being one. Back then, people were much more superstitious and they often staked perfectly innocent humans who were simply ill. Collins promised to withhold the evidence if I Turned him. He was not a bad person…just very misguided, very unhappy because he did not feel that he fit amongst his own kind. I had felt the same during my human life. I truly believe that becoming a vampire helped me as a person.

"But Collins...he felt short-changed because his gift is not very substantial and the Keja hypnotic beauty could not make people 'love' him. It was not enough that women desired him. He wanted them to adore him, need him, and be obsessed with him." Antonio shook his head. "Nothing was ever good enough for him. Nothing ever fulfilled him. Some vampires within the nest that I was part of back then were similar to him, and they all left as a group. I did not hear from Collins again until I was made Grand High Master. He came here, liked what he saw, and asked to stay. But when it became apparent that he expected to be made Heir simply because he was the first vampire I ever Turned, I made it very clear that things did not work that way. Offended and angry, he left. This is the first time I have heard from him since then."

After a short pause, Jared spoke. "Would he make something like this up out of jealousy? I mean, would he try to get to me by using Sam just because I have the position he wants?"

Antonio pursed his lips as he considered that. "Collins can be slimy and vindictive, but I'm not sure he would do something like this as he is a stickler for rules. I will contact the Prelature and find out if this is an authentic complaint. In the meantime, be careful, Sam. Do not give them anything to use against you. You are a fantastic commander – we all know that. You do not need to act any differently than you normally do. But...try not to kill Collins or Eloise, that's all."

"I can't make any promises." I went to head back to the Command Centre.

Jared's hand engulfed mine. "No more work." There were then familiar flutters in my stomach as he teleported us away. We reappeared on a narrow path in the rainforest. He shrugged. "You wanted to take Dexter for a walk – or a slither, whatever."

This wasn't about Dexter, though. This was Jared trying to keep my mind occupied on things other than the black cloud hanging over us. I could sense that he was just as angry as I was, but he was doing his best to put it aside so he could calm and comfort me. I squeezed his hand. "Thanks." Knowing Dexter was currently twined around my waist, I peeled up my t-shirt and said, "Novo." The Latin word for 'change' was enough to make the four-inch long tattoo become a live one and a half foot long snake. His colouring was presently pearl-white, indicating that he was excited. Of course he was excited – he loved being in the rainforest, hunting for food.

Dexter's tongue briefly flicked my chin, and then his intelligent and very observant gaze landed on Jared. Dexter shot him what could only be described as a 'mind how you step' look. Jared simply rolled his eyes. Dexter then slinked down my body and began slithering along the ground.

"I can't believe all this is really happening."

Wrapping an arm around my shoulders, Jared pulled me close to his side as we walked along the narrow path in the same direction that Dexter was heading. "You know the squad aren't behind this, don't you?"

"Of course I do. But it doesn't mean this whole thing isn't pissing me off." Considering that I would soon be ruling all vampirekind alongside Jared, I'd be losing the position of commander anyway. But the point at play was that if Collins' report recommended that I be wiped of my position, I would no longer have the support of the Prelature. Without that, no Prelate would be prepared to perform the Coronation. As such, there would be no ascension. In addition, people might once again be wary of me if the Prelature ruled that I wasn't fit enough to lead my squad and that I exploited them.

If Antonio had announced his decision to step down, I might have wondered if this 'complaint' was someone's way of ensuring I didn't take his place. But only a handful of people knew of Antonio's intention. Plus, it was believed that I had the support and acceptance of all vampirekind anyway.

Another important question would be: "Who would do this?"

"Like Antonio said, you'll have enemies; people who are jealous of what you have and of how powerful you are."

"Like Joy?" She had openly flirted with Jared in front of everyone earlier. That was why it had been so hilarious when Denny wrapped her in yellowy-green ooze. It was sweet in a Denny way.

"She's a bitch, baby, I know that. But I'm not sure if she'd go this far to piss you off. To be honest, I don't think her imagination's good enough to come up with something like this."

Valid point. "But it has to be someone from The Hollow – someone who knows how I work. Joy's sneaky enough to do a little spying."

He conceded that with a tilt of his head. "Maybe we should

consider Dickhead, too."

That made no sense to me. "Sure, he likes to poke at you and he finds some dark amusement in the fact that he drank from me in the past—"

"There's nothing amusing about it."

"—but he's not so much of a prick that he would try to make me lose my job. What possible motivation could he have to do it?"

"Maybe he's bitter about us. He wants you badly, baby. You don't see it, just like you never see when anyone wants you, but it's true."

I rolled my eyes. "Whatever. Hey, what about Magda's first-born? According to Collins, they reported that she never returned home and they aren't too happy about it."

"But how would that vampire know enough about you and how you train the squad to twist it all?"

I groaned, totally bamboozled. "I hate this."

He kissed my temple – his touch gentle despite the anger that occasionally seeped to the surface. "Don't worry, baby, I'll find out who did this. And then I'll kill them."

I snorted. "Not if I get there first." And I had every intention of doing so. "What worries me about having someone hovering over me is that they might pick up on the hybrid thing."

Jared shook his head. "That won't happen purely because no one would ever believe it was possible. Besides, Antonio came up with good excuses for why you're more powerful and stuff. Don't worry about that. In fact, don't worry about any of it right now. We're spending some time together – you and me. Let's shove this shit aside for a while and move on to a lighter but extremely important subject: Have you come up with any new rules for us to put into place after the Coronation?"

Despite my mood, I actually smiled.

"Come on, baby. Don't go retreating into that head of yours again. I know what's happening is fucked up on so many levels, but you're stronger than this. And I'm here."

Still feeling bad for having held back from him before, I relented. "I'm still working on the rules, but I've come up with a few. I'm thinking that the whole consort thing should be banned from The Hollow."

He laughed – a sound I hadn't heard in a while. "I really shouldn't be surprised, should I?"

"Don't get me wrong; I'm not saying flings or one-night stands shouldn't be allowed or that anyone has to be celibate. If the males here want to get randy, that's fine. But if they want to make things exclusive, they can give the females the respect of calling them 'girlfriends', and vice versa."

Still laughing, he nodded. "Sounds fair."

Surprised, I looked up at him. "Yeah? I was expecting you to defend the concept of consorts, considering you once had some."

He shrugged. "Vampires having consorts has always been the norm. And if you spend a long time with people who consider it the norm, it's easy for you to do the same. That was why I never really saw the whole thing the way you did. Plus, those women had been using me; I didn't see why it couldn't work both ways. But looking back, I can see it was kind of...seedy. We can't stop all vampires from having consorts, but we can at least ban it from happening in The Hollow."

"That's not to say I'll force all the vampires who are currently consorts to leave The Hollow, but they'll have to find another way of fitting in."

"That's fair."

"Although...it wouldn't be so bad if Joy left."

"She'll probably do it of her own accord after the Coronation. The last thing she'll want is to directly serve us."

I hoped he was right – not just for my sake, but for Joy's. There was a high chance I'd severely hurt her if she kept pushing me.

"Enough about her." He kissed my hair. "Don't let her get to you."

I barked a laugh. "Says the bloke whose mood turns homicidal whenever he's around a particular Sventé by the name of—" I laughed again when he clapped a hand over my mouth.

"Don't even say the fucker's name," growled Jared. "Whenever he looks at you, I can tell he's trying to picture you naked."

When he released my mouth, I said, "Joy *knows* what you look like naked, as does Eloise, so I'd say I've got the shittier end of the deal here."

He twirled me so that I was facing him and then plastered me against him. "But they don't matter to me. You're what matters." He slid a hand under my hair to cup my nape as his mouth landed on mine. He sucked and bit my bottom lip, toying with my mouth and coaxing me to open for him. Then his tongue swept inside, teasing mine. "I love how you taste. Everywhere."

I nipped his bottom lip and then licked over it to soothe the sting. "When we get back home, you can prove it. And then maybe I'll return the favour. Be aware that this time, *you'll* be the one coming first – no matter how much you tease me."

His devilish, lopsided grin surfaced. "Hmm, I accept your challenge."

Laughing, I kissed him again.

CHAPTER SIX

(Jared)

My gut twisted at the sight of Evan's hollowed cheeks and sickly complexion. Lying on one of the mattresses in the cell, he looked exhausted and full of utter despair. Max was gagging in the far corner of the room while Stuart watched with eyes that were disturbingly vacant. It was always the same – within an hour of drinking an NST, they would be vomiting, totally unable to digest it, totally unable to quench what had to now be an overriding thirst.

They had been tainted for almost two weeks now, and I had come here each and every evening to visit. I knew that I was just torturing myself by witnessing as my brother increasingly deteriorated like this. I knew this wasn't helping me. But how could I stay away from my own twin, especially at a time like this? How could I not visit him, despite that neither of us derived any comfort from me being there?

I didn't want him to feel alone. Being away from him at a time like this made me feel guilty, like I was abandoning him, even if that didn't make an awful lot of sense. Right now, though, he wouldn't even *look* at me. I wasn't sure if he was pretending that I wasn't here or if he was simply hoping that if he ignored me, I'd leave. Maybe he didn't like that I was seeing him like this. While I understood that, it couldn't keep me away. Not from my twin brother.

I wished I was there to give them some good news, but the truth was that neither Sam nor I had found anything that could help. I'd *forced* myself not to even think of giving up, and to remain hopeful. For a while it had worked. But I could feel my original optimism beginning to fizzle away, leaving me with only pain, fear, and anger – all of which I had buried so deep that Sam couldn't pick up on them through our bond.

Hiding my pain and fear was a childhood habit that had stayed with me. My narcissistic mother had practically fed on those things, so I'd done my best to deprive her of them. I hadn't wanted the twisted bitch to see just how much she could hurt me. As a kid, it had been my way of fighting back. And it was the ultimate form of revenge if your foe got kicks out of any pain that they could cause you. Really, it was no wonder I was pretty fucked up.

For Sam, I had been doing my best to snap out of that habit of burying everything deep. She wasn't my mother; she wouldn't use my emotions against me. She wasn't someone who I needed to protect myself from. For once in my fucked up life, I'd allowed myself to *need* someone. And I *did* need Sam. Hell, without her, my optimism might have disappeared altogether. But I couldn't share my deeper emotions on this subject with her, couldn't lean on her this time. We were too at odds on what we believed was best to do in this situation, and I didn't want to give more weight to her solution of involving Paige West by revealing that my optimism was beginning to dwindle.

Still, although I hadn't felt able to totally confide in her, Sam had been the anchor that had enabled me to stay focused and keep from losing my shit. She probably didn't know it, but she was the only thing that was keeping me relatively sane throughout all this chaos – or as sane as I could ever hope to be.

Hearing soft footsteps, I knew it was Antonio. I didn't look away from Evan though. I stood there willing him to meet my eyes, willing him to see my determination to help him – as if that determination alone could encourage Evan to fight, to not give up. But no, my brother was refusing to acknowledge me. And it fucking hurt.

Reaching my side, Antonio sighed sadly at the sight behind the glass wall. "It is difficult to remain positive when confronted with the effects of The Call."

Translation: 'Stop coming here before you lose all hope'.

"It's hard to stay away. I feel like I should be here for him. I *want* to be. I want to help him."

"Maybe you can."

At those words, my head whipped around to face Antonio. "What do you mean?"

"Quentin Foy – he has been found. Harvey's idea to put a bounty on Quentin's head offering a reward for his whereabouts was a good one; it made finding him much faster. I truly have no idea if anything he tells you could help with this but—"

"In all honesty, I'm not hopeful that he can help." That wasn't something I'd told Sam, though. "But I can't leave any corner unexplored."

Antonio gave a nod of understanding. "Then get Sam and the squad together." He held out a small sheet of paper on which an address was scribbled. "This is where you will find Quentin Foy." Antonio squeezed my shoulder. "Best of luck."

I immediately teleported to the arena. Understanding that I'd needed to see Evan, Sam had agreed to begin the training session without me. She and the squad paused when I arrived, clearly intrigued by the urgency in my manner. I held up the sheet of paper. "Time to speak with Foy. He's still in New Zealand and—"

"You're going on an assignment?" Collins called out from the spectator seats.

It took extreme effort to stop grinding my teeth. Since arriving, Collins and Eloise had insisted on sitting in on every training session, whether it was in the arena or in the rainforest. Collins always took notes the entire time, but he was never silent. No. He always had lists of queries, he repeatedly questioned Sam's decisions, and he even criticised her techniques.

I *felt* as fury whizzed through Sam each and every time – it was the same fury that filled me. But her responses were always brisk, formal, and business-like. It was true that she didn't have much patience when it came to assholes and could happily whip the living shit out of them, but Sam was also very controlled when she needed to be. Feeders *had* to be controlled or the energy would overwhelm them. I was literally in awe of how she had managed to hold back from hurting the interfering bastards, because I personally was so very close to snapping.

Whenever she sensed that my own control was slipping, Sam would immediately calm me; reminding me telepathically how important it was not to give the assholes anything to report that could be used against her.

As Collins began descending the steps, I finally replied to his question. "Yes, we are."

"Is that such a good idea, Jared?" An indecently dressed Eloise trailed after Collins. She said my name like it was an endearment, said it with enough familiarity to have Sam's blood boiling as it was a constant reminder that she and I knew each other intimately – even though I could hardly remember that night. "You and Commander

Parker have been seen in public. We do not want more photographs of you going around. It would be best if you both laid low for a while."

"I'm not letting the squad do this alone," I stated firmly. My tone left no room for negotiation.

Eloise came closer – *too* close. "Then perhaps, Jared, you should go without Commander Parker. The appeal was for information about her." I was always 'Jared', and it was spoken in such a warm tone. By contrast, Sam was always 'Commander Parker', and the words were pure frost. It was designed to annoy Sam, and it did.

But it also annoyed the shit out of me. I stepped away from Eloise. "Not a fucking chance."

Unfortunately, she wasn't deterred by my irritability. "But Jared, you—"

Sam, cool and business-like, interrupted, "Let's remember that you and Mr Collins are here to *observe*, not to give advice." Eloise clenched her fists but said nothing.

"Ava and Cristiano will want to talk to Quentin," David pointed out, dismissing the presence of Eloise and Collins. He was right; the siblings would want to find out what had happened to the vampires from their nest.

"We'll take them with us," I said.

"You cannot." At Collins' words, everyone slowly spun on their heel as one to look at him with their brows arched. The sight might have been funny under other circumstances. Clearly nervous – most likely because the entire squad was sneering at him – he stammered, "I-it is against p-protocol as they are not part o-of the squad."

Sam made a contemplative sound. "You are right, Mr Collins. I suppose this means that you have changed your mind and that both you and Miss Montana will be staying behind? After all, neither of you are part of the squad, are you?"

Collins and Eloise exchanged a frustrated look. They understood the message – if Ava and Cristiano didn't go, neither did they. He lifted a shoulder. "I suppose there are circumstances in which allowances can be made." How freaking kind of him.

"Yes," Eloise begrudgingly agreed through her teeth.

Sam joined her hands, faking a smile of pure delight. "Excellent. Glad that's all cleared up."

As she intended, her enthusiasm nettled Eloise, who then turned to me so fast that her hair swished around her face. Tossing it over her shoulder, she snapped, "Jared, I have to once again object to Commander Parker accompanying you. There has been a public appeal for information about her—"

"In London," Sam inserted pleasantly, holding up her index finger. "We'll be in New Zealand."

"—which means it is important that she maintains a low profile for a while. I have to stress the importance of her remaining concealed."

"And I have to stress that I don't give a fuck."

Sam shot me a smile that told me I was *so* getting lucky later.

Quentin Foy was a tall, thin vampire with wise eyes. He was also damn fast. The second we burst into his hotel room and he spotted me, he sped through the suite so quickly that he actually managed to dodge Sam's whip as it attempted to trap him. But there was no avoiding Harvey's gift. He telekinetically dragged Quentin to an armchair, and – a trick that Sam had recently taught him – then used his gift to actually pin Quentin in place.

As Quentin's eyes swallowed the sight of me, Sam, David, Denny, Butch, Harvey, Salem, Ava, Dickhead, and – unfortunately – Collins and Eloise surrounding him in a semi-circle, he looked ready to hyperventilate. Who could blame him?

"We're not here to kill you." I took a non-threatening step forward. Sam mirrored my move so that we presented a united front.

Unconvinced, Quentin snorted. "Right. That's why Antonio put a bounty on my head. Where are my vampires?"

"If you mean the ones in the neighbouring suite, they're perfectly fine. Other than having been shot with poisonous thorns to make them sleep for a while, that is. Three of my squad members are watching over them." Chico, Reuben, and Damien were under strict orders not to hurt them unless it was totally necessary.

"Is it typical for your commanders to request for some of you to disable a suspect's companions like that?" Collins asked Salem. His response was a growl that made Collins edge away from him and involuntarily bump into Butch, who snarled at him.

Admirably ignoring the prick's presence, Sam spoke to Quentin. "Antonio put a price on your head so that you would be found – and found fast. That's all." Her tone was reassuring but grave. "We have questions that only you can answer."

Quentin's expression went from panicked to wary. "Questions?"

"About the nest of tainted vampires you left behind in your tunnels," I explained.

He sighed heavily, suddenly looking defeated. "You killed them," he surmised. He didn't sound judgemental, just sad.

I might have felt bad if Evan, Max, and Stuart weren't now dying after being attacked by them. "We had no choice. If you agree to answer our questions and don't try to run again, we can free you from the telekinetic hold. Your choice." When Quentin nodded his agreement, I signalled at Harvey to release him.

Once he did so, Quentin rolled his shoulders and shifted in the seat. "Thank you."

Hearing the sound of paper flicking, I turned my head to see that Collins was scribbling his observations down in a notepad. "Was the telekinetic hold uncomfortable?" Collins then asked Quentin. Un-fucking-real. The guy just stared at Collins blankly. I had yet to meet anyone who hadn't taken an instant dislike to the asshole. Coming up behind Collins, Eloise gave Quentin an encouraging smile, urging him to answer the question. He didn't.

"Why didn't you kill your tainted vampires yourself?" Sam asked Quentin, still ignoring her 'observers'. I honestly didn't know how she did it. "Don't get me wrong, I can understand why you would find that hard – it would be the very last thing I'd want to do in your shoes. But if you were going to give up on them, why not save them weeks of suffering?"

"I didn't trap them there to die," snapped Quentin, offended. "I didn't give up on them. I left them there hoping I could find some sort of cure that I could take back to save them."

I arched a brow when he didn't elaborate. "And?"

His shoulders fell; he was the image of hopelessness. "And nothing. What everybody says is true – you can't stop The Call."

That was not what I'd hoped to hear. More of the little optimism I had left began to fizzle away.

"When did your vampires become tainted?" At least Sam was staying focused. Right then, my spirits were plummeting so fast I could hardly think straight. Most likely sensing that, she reached out and briefly clasped my hand. The energy clinging to her skin buzzed against mine. It was strangely comforting. Using that to centre myself, I swiftly pushed down the dark feelings of anger, pain, and fear that were trying to surface. The last thing I wanted was for Sam to sense them.

"One of my vampires came home with a huge bite," said Quentin. "He said that he was attacked by another vampire in a town that was miles away from our own. His opinion was that his attacker had been a newborn vampire who was a little undernourished; he'd felt guilty for killing him. We didn't think it was anything odd as many newborns are kept isolated and weak by their Sires while they get their bloodlust and gift under control."

He was right about that. It had happened to Sam. "So you just figured that it had been a newborn who escaped his nest?"

"Yes," replied Quentin. "But my friend's bite wouldn't heal. It just kept getting worse. I didn't know enough about The Call to realise that it was a symptom. It wasn't until he and some of the others started vomiting that I realised what was happening. By then, it was too late. He'd fed from many vampires within the nest, and they'd fed from others, who'd fed from others, and so and so on – the taint had already spread amongst the nest." His eyes took on a faraway quality. I knew his mind was back in those tunnels.

"That was when you left?" Sam gently prodded when he failed to continue.

Quentin's gaze met hers, once again focused. "Yes, the few of us who hadn't fed from any of the tainted vampires then left and sealed them inside, hoping to find a cure to bring back to them."

Ava stepped forward. "Did three Sventés escape the tunnels with you?" Salem reached out and tugged her back to his side in a protective move.

Quentin shook his head. "No, I'm sorry."

She squeezed her eyes tightly shut and bowed her head. Salem began rubbing her back at the same time that Cristiano curled an arm around her shoulders. The two males then took to scowling at each other. It was something they did a lot since, according to Sam, Cristiano was very protective of his sister and had never liked other guys being around her.

Returning my attention to Quentin, I said, "It would have been helpful if you had alerted people that The Call had surfaced."

"I couldn't risk it. I was worried that people would come and destroy my nest before I'd had a chance to search for some way to save them. Yes, I know history says that there's no way to fight The Call, but I didn't want to accept that. I *couldn't.*"

That was something I understood all too well. I was still pissed that he hadn't told anyone, but I could admit to myself that I might have done the same in his position. "This vampire who was the first to become tainted...Did he tell you the exact place that the supposed 'newborn' attacked him?"

"If you're wondering if there are more tainted vampires out there, the answer is yes. I've had some people hunting for them in that area, but they haven't been easy to find."

Sam frowned. "How can they be difficult to find? I mean, they're not exactly inconspicuous. Surely the taint should be widespread in that area by now if some are loose in society."

"Not if the bitten vampires realise they're tainted in the early stages and then isolate or kill themselves. It is what many tainted vampires have done throughout history to prevent The Call from doing too much damage to the population – and, of course, because they feared attacking those they cared for. My people have found the occasional lone one roaming in that area, but there haven't been many. Each one they found has been destroyed."

Well that was good news...Just not the good news that I'd wanted.

His astute gaze landed on me. "Some from The Hollow are tainted," he guessed. "Antonio?"

I shook my head. "No, he's fine. But I can't say the same for my twin brother or some of my squad."

Quentin's face softened. "I'm sorry. I understand your pain. My sister was tainted. Trust me when I say that if there was a cure out there, I would have found it. If I were you, I'd end their suffering now."

"I can't," I choked out.

"You're not prepared to give up. It does you credit. But there really isn't anything you can do to save them."

"You cannot fight The Call." Collins' voice had me gritting my teeth again.

Butch's lopsided grin slowly surfaced as he again glared at the prick. "You'd be surprised what we can do." Such simple words, and yet they carried a dark threat that made Collins audibly gulp and

Eloise back away slightly. Yeah, Butch unnerved everyone.

"Give us the exact location where the tainted vampires are loose," Sam said to Quentin. "We can have a squad from the legion help your people hunt them down."

He nodded. "I would appreciate the extra help."

"If you need a place to stay for a—"

Quentin shook his head. "Thank you. Really. But I won't rest until The Call is dormant once more."

Because that was the only form of revenge for him, I understood. It was the same reason that Ava and Dickhead had stuck around. I knew that if Evan was ever to be killed by anyone or anything, no revenge would ever be good enough for me.

"Do you have the authority to make such a decision, Commander Parker?" Eloise perched a hand on her hip. "You're a commander" – *for now*, she didn't say but it was clear in her voice – "but you do not command the entire legion. Surely such a decision should be for Antonio, and Antonio alone, to make." I knew that Eloise truly wasn't concerned about that; she simply wanted to slap down Sam in front of everyone, undermine her authority and embarrass her.

Sam cocked her head. "*This* makes you happy? Really?" She shook her head, like she pitied Eloise. Her posture almost regal, Sam gave the bitch her back. "Thanks for being so forthcoming, Quentin." After all, he could have given us the silent treatment for destroying his nest and his home. "Help will be with you soon." The dismissal of Eloise's 'concern' had the woman turning an amusing shade of purple.

When we returned to The Hollow, Sam and I found Antonio and Luther in one of the parlour rooms, where we recounted the night's events. They didn't seem surprised that we hadn't obtained a lot of helpful information, but they were saddened by it. At Sam's suggestion, Antonio agreed to arrange for one of the squads to aid Quentin in locating any loose tainted vampires – rolling his eyes at our tale of Eloise's behaviour.

"No doubt she and Collins will come to see me soon enough to complain about it." Then he revealed something that neither Sam nor I wanted to hear. "According to the vampires I spoke to from the Prelature, the complaint made about you, Sam, is in fact authentic. I still do not believe that it was made by anyone from your squad. But someone made it. No doubt Collins is enjoying the idea of hurting you, Jared, by upsetting your mate. But he truly believes that the complaint was made by someone from the squad."

"What about Eloise?" Sam asked from her seat on the sofa facing theirs. "I mean, I know all she and Jared did was bonk on one occasion" – Luther stifled a chuckle – "but it wouldn't be the first time that someone got a little jealous about my relationship with him."

Sprawled beside her, I ran a hand through her hair. "If I wasn't the Heir, they wouldn't give a shit, baby."

How many times do I have to tell you that you underestimate your own worth?

I didn't respond. She'd said this to me over and over, and had also told me that I was wrong in thinking that women had always thought I had no more than a high position and a pretty face to offer. It didn't matter anyway, because the only person I cared about having anything to offer was Sam. If she was under the illusion that I was all those things, that could only be good.

"But it's obvious that Eloise would like to put me on a drip of bleach," continued Sam. "And she's clearly enjoying all of this. Could she be behind it somehow? Surely she could have made it look like an authentic complaint."

Antonio pursed his lips. "It's possible. But I have the feeling that there is more to this." He paused and exhaled a heavy breath. "On another note, Alora has been in touch."

Sam and I both looked at each other and groaned. We didn't need more complications.

"She wishes to come here. She heard from Bran what has happened to Evan, and she wants to see him."

"You can't let her." I shook my head. "Evan made us promise not to let her see him the way he is now."

"I thought as much, but I was not sure." After a pause, Antonio added, "She was a mess when I spoke to her by teleconference."

Luther nodded. "Distraught."

I wasn't feeling particularly sympathetic toward her right then. "Yeah, well, she had her chance to be with him and she fucked it up. Maybe if she hadn't, he wouldn't have insisted on going on the assignment and he wouldn't be dying."

Sam gave me a pointed look. "Jared, no one's to blame for what happened to him. Not Alora, not Evan, not you – no one."

Antonio sighed. "What occurred between Alora and Evan...As

she told me in confidence, I cannot repeat the details. But I will say that she had good reason to hold back from him. I would not have entertained her request to see him if that was not true. I care for Evan, and I do not want people around him who would wish to hurt him emotionally or physically. You know that."

"She simply wants the chance to help find a way to save him," Luther said carefully, obviously very much aware I wasn't in the best mood.

Oh hell, no. "Don't even suggest bringing her in on this. Evan made us promise."

"He made you promise not to let her *see* him." Antonio held up his index finger. "But he did not make you promise not to let her help you."

Sam tilted her head slightly. "That's true."

I twisted to face her, demanding, "Tell me you're *not* considering this."

"I know if it was the other way around and I was her—"

"You would never have let me down the way she let Evan down." For a second, Sam looked surprised by my confidence in her. She even looked touched by it. But that didn't stop her from continuing to put forward her case, just as I'd known it wouldn't. Sam never gave up on anything. I admired it even as it annoyed the shit out of me.

"People make mistakes." Her voice was soft, low. "We've both made our fair share. We've hurt each other. But we've always fixed those mistakes. She wants to fix hers; she wants to help."

I snorted. "Her gift is to communicate with animals – that's not going to help us fight The Call."

"No," agreed Luther. "But you understand the *need* to feel as though you are helping, even though it is possible that you cannot."

"Alora can do that without coming here."

Sam shook her head at me. "You are so bloody stubborn."

Was she kidding? "Baby, three words: pot, kettle, black."

"I'm not stubborn, I'm tenacious – it's a gift and a curse."

"It's a pain in my ass, *that's* what it is. Like earlier when I said—"

"Why are you bringing up old shit? You're always doing it. Like a plunger."

I scrubbed a hand over my face. "I can't have this conversation."

"Thinking has never been your strong point, has it?" She looked at Antonio then. "The pressure gets to him every time."

You'll pay for this. I had to battle a smile. She didn't bother to hide hers.

If you mean you're going to tie me to the bed again and make me come over and over until I can't think straight...come and give it to me.

I did. You swallowed it, remember?

Ooh, good one.

Antonio rose from his seat. "I must go now to arrange for a squad to join Quentin Foy's hunting party. Think on the Alora matter a little more."

Not interested in having that conversation again, I simply took Sam's hand in mine and teleported us...to the bottom of the pool – for maybe the third time this week. The subsequent bitch slap wasn't a surprise.

CHAPTER SEVEN

(Sam)

It was the sound of a moan that woke me the next evening. A moan filled with desperation, need, and bliss. I quickly realised that it had come from me. A talented tongue lashed my clit, making another moan slip out. Without opening my eyes, I reached down and threaded my fingers through Jared's hair, tugging hard. He growled and began what could only be described as a sensual assault – flicking my clit with the tip of his tongue, fluttering that tongue through my folds, swirling it inside me, and stabbing me over and over with it. Then he was licking, nibbling, suckling, and sipping. God, he was good.

Soon enough, I came hard. But he didn't stop. He continued his assault until he'd pushed me into another orgasm. Still, though, he didn't stop. I tried to wriggle away. "No, I want you inside me."

"Give me one more," he demanded. I hadn't thought it was possible to come again, but when he zapped my clit with his thumb I was gone. "Good girl."

While I lay there being racked by aftershocks, he trailed the tip of his tongue up my body, tracing the dips and hollows. Then his mouth latched onto a taut nipple. Nope, he wasn't done teasing me yet – typical. I wasn't sure whether I was pleased or annoyed…Maybe a bit of both.

He sucked hard and raked my nipple with his teeth the way I liked it. He gave the other breast the same attention, not stopping until I was squirming and moaning once more. "Jared—" I gasped as I was roughly flipped onto my stomach. Looking back at him over my shoulder, I scowled. "Oi!"

He just smiled, licking along my spine. I knew that impish look – it meant that the teasing still wasn't over. Just as he had to my front, he traced the dips and hollows of my back with his tongue, occasionally pausing to deliver a sharp nip.

"The downside to you healing instantly is that I can't mark you." He licked the curve of my shoulder. "I want you all marked up." His teeth sank into my shoulder just as two fingers plunged inside me. Swallow. Thrust. Swallow. Thrust – the rhythm was driving me insane. Just when I was ready to start cursing him, he withdrew his fingers and his teeth, and flipped me onto my back. He loomed over me, his face a mask of utter resolve. One hand scrunched in my hair while the other gripped my hip.

I smiled into piercing hazel eyes that were huge pools of need. "Good evening."

Jared's sensual mouth curved. "Happy birthday, baby." Then he slammed home, wrenching a gasp out of me; I was so wet that he was balls-deep in just one thrust. We both groaned as my muscles clamped around him. He didn't give me a moment to adjust, and I hadn't wanted him to. Instead, he tightened his grip on my hip and began ruthlessly pounding into me. "You feel so fucking good, Sam."

Locking my limbs around him, I scratched at his back and arched to meet his thrusts. Each one was hard, fast, and powerful; making me feel totally and utterly taken. His pace was relentless and frantic, building the friction inside me. But I wanted more of him.

Reading my body well, he hooked my legs over his shoulders and shifted his angle, going even deeper. "I need your mouth," he growled, curling over me.

I reached up to meet his kiss. It was as dominant and possessive and drugging as always. I drew his tongue into my mouth and sucked on it, smiling at the throaty groan that escaped him.

"Bite me."

I raked my teeth over his shoulder and then bit down, drinking deep and loving the masculine, spicy taste of his blood. He upped his speed as the effects of my Svente saliva fed the tension building in him – I could actually *feel* his orgasm approaching, and it was speeding along my own.

"Come with me," he breathed. Then he groaned as he buried his face in the crook of my neck and bit down hard. With each gulp of blood that he swallowed, my body wound that much tighter until after only mere seconds I exploded around him with a scream. His teeth sank deeper as my body milked him, shoving him into his own climax.

Finally his teeth released my neck and he delivered a sensual lick to the swiftly healing bite. "I don't know how it is that you make me come so hard, but I'm not complaining."

I chuckled. "Right back at you, Michaels."

He let my legs fall from his shoulders and nipped my bottom lip. "As you already found your gifts, I don't have any birthday surprises for you," he grumbled.

"That's okay. I don't like surprises. So, um, did you teleport the gifts back here?" I asked casually. He wasn't fooled.

Shaking his head, he sighed as he slid out of me and rolled us onto our sides. "You can't wait to get back to that game, can you?"

"It's addictive!"

"I thought you might like it…since it features lots of violence, gore, and combat."

"My character has more depth than that, you know," I snapped playfully.

"Hmm. I guess I should let you get back to your game before you seriously hurt me."

I clapped a little. "Yay!" I literally shoved him away as I jumped out of bed and dashed into the bathroom. A few minutes later, clean and feeling refreshed, I rushed into the living area. His throaty laugh followed me. As I'd expected, the PlayStation 6 was waiting there nicely, along with a stack of Stephen King books and the box that I knew contained a gorgeous pair of diamond earrings. But there was something else, too: it was small-ish, rectangular, and gift-wrapped. Sensing Jared behind me, I turned and arched a questioning brow. He just smiled mischievously and lounged on the sofa.

Well. I normally detested surprises, but I was strangely excited as I retrieved the gift from the table. It was roughly the size of a DVD…or a video game, I quickly realised. I tore off the wrapping paper. Then I could only gawk. No, this seriously couldn't be what it seemed. It just wasn't possible. The gift was in fact a video game, but it wasn't one I'd ever seen before. It was called 'The Hollow'…and it was actually a game based on The Hollow. Fascinated and stunned, I gave Jared a 'what the fuck?' look.

His smile widened. "I wanted to get you something that you would never have guessed in a million years; something unique. I had a team of people working on this, including vampires whose gift is technology-based. As you can see, you have the option of playing as different people within The Hollow – including me, you, and members of the squad. They each have the gifts, strengths, and weaknesses in the game that they do in real life. Even Dexter's in it. There are lots of potential assignments and mysteries. The special effects are absolutely amazing. You could even think of this game as a method of training in—" He grunted as I suddenly dived on him. "Does this mean you like it?"

Straddling him, I kissed him hard. "I bloody love it. I noticed that one of the 'baddies' in the game is Magda. This means I get to kill her over and over again, doesn't it?" At his nod, I was so touched I almost cried. "This is the sweetest, most thoughtful thing that anyone has ever given me." He laughed, and I wrapped my arms around him. "Thank you."

When I finally pulled back, he slid a hand under my hair and squeezed my nape as he tugged my face to his. He sucked my bottom lip into his mouth, coaxing a contented sigh from me. Then his tongue boldly swept inside, stroking mine, as his hands slid down my back to cup my arse. Releasing my mouth, he just stared at me…like he was drinking me in, like it was perfectly normal and acceptable to stare at someone. And it always annoyed me.

"Stop it or I'll let Dexter spit venom in your eyes and temporarily blind you."

He smiled, running his fingers through my hair. "No you won't. Is it really so bad that I like to look at you? Like to look at you knowing you're mine and that I've tasted every single inch of you?"

"Yes, it is. Now, can we play this game or what?"

"I'm not going to be able to pull you away from it without a fight, am I?"

"Nope."

He just rolled his eyes. "Antonio has a birthday meal planned for you later. That means you can play the game until then. I have a feeling that the squad will want to play it too."

Jared had been right. When the squad – along with Jude – came to wish me a happy birthday and each gave me a present, they joined me in playing the game. It was so well thought out. The first level was the try-outs. The second level featured a number of training sessions in the arena. Then each level thereafter was an assignment with a different 'baddy' each time. And of course things got harder and harder as the game went on. It even had bonus levels such as paintballing and swimming in the bat pool.

The players were so life-like that it was almost freaky. The structure of The Hollow was picture perfect – even the surrounding rainforest was amazingly identical to the one here. The squad took turns at playing as other people, boasting that they had better control of that person's gift than they did. That caused some arguments.

Even Antonio and Luther had a turn when they came to pay me a visit. I would never have guessed that they were so competitive if I hadn't seen it for myself. Some of the curses that flew from their mouths had even my eyes widening. Fletcher and Norm also had a turn – Fletcher played me, delighted to be able to use an energy whip.

Of course they all asked if Jared could have one made for them, even Antonio and Luther. But Jared refused, telling them that he wanted me to have something that nobody else had. Fletcher and Norm thought that was extremely sweet. Everybody else whined about it. I couldn't blame them – it was even more addictive than 'Vampire Nation'. So addictive that I played it until my eyes hurt, and I actually moaned when I realised that it was time to attend the birthday meal that Antonio had organised.

Forcing myself not to be an ungrateful bitch, I came away from the game, and changed into a little black dress that Fletcher had given me as a birthday gift. "Ready to go?" I asked Jared as I exited the en-suite bathroom.

His hands landed on my hips as his gaze explored every inch of me. "If it wasn't your birthday meal, I'd say skip it so I could roll this dress up and bury myself inside you." He nuzzled my neck, inhaling deeply.

I smiled, skimming my hands down his chest, and wishing the shirt wasn't in the way. "You can do that later."

"You can bet your sweet little ass I will." He dropped a kiss on my mouth. "Come on, everyone will be waiting." To my surprise, Jared didn't teleport us to Antonio's huge parlour room. Instead, he took us to…the beach. A strangely empty beach.

I frowned. "Where is—" He twirled me around, and I gasped at the sight ahead of us.

"You look amazing," Jared whispered into my ear as he started to lead me across the sand. No, what I could see ahead of us was 'amazing'. Several tables were set up on the sand, all with white table cloths, lanterns, champagne glasses, and flowery centre pieces. I loved the beach at night, loved the way the moonlight played off the water. That was clearly why they had done this for me. God, I was spoiled rotten by these people and I probably didn't deserve it.

With the exception of one table, all the others were seated with guests. On the first table sat Antonio, Lucy, Luther, and – *groan* – Collins and Eloise. On the second were Fletcher, Norm, Ava, and Cristiano. The third seated Butch, Salem, David, and Denny, while the fourth seated Chico, Jude, Harvey, Damien, and Reuben. My heart squeezed as I thought of the three people who couldn't be here.

Everybody stood, smiling, as Jared and I went to the empty table in the centre. "Oh my God," I said a little breathlessly. "I can't believe you all did this."

Fletcher looked at me like I was daft. "Of course we did this; we love you."

"We wanted to make your evening special." Antonio smiled. "I hope we manage to do so."

I found myself wishing I was better at receiving things because I wasn't sure what to say. "Thanks…It's really amazing." That seemed to satisfy everyone, because they all grinned and sat down.

Most likely sensing my relief, Jared laughed silently as he sat opposite me and laced his fingers through mine. "Neither of us is good at the whole expressing gratitude thing, are we?"

I shook my head. "Luckily they like us in spite of it."

"You're wearing your earrings," he observed, leaning forward to gently finger one.

"Once again, thank you for them." See, I could do gratitude sometimes.

"You're welcome. I'm just relieved you like them. You're not really a jewellery person. In fact, you're pretty hard to buy for. And you're even harder to surprise, since you insist on hunting your gifts down – I swear you've got a nose like a bloodhound."

I chuckled, feeling ridiculously happy. A twinge of guilt immediately followed the feeling – here I was celebrating when Evan, Max, and Stuart were stuck in a cell, dying.

Jared squeezed my hand. "Hey," he said gently. Of course he'd known where my thoughts had taken me. "They'd want you to celebrate your birthday."

He was right, they would. That was exactly what I needed to hear. I was about to flash Jared a smile of thanks, but then his face morphed into a scowl as his eyes focused on something over my shoulder. Confused, I turned to track his gaze. Ah...Ava and Cristiano were approaching us.

Wearing her usual cheery smile, she bent and planted a kiss on my cheek. Being courteous for a change, I stood and awkwardly accepted the hug she gave me. I wondered if I'd ever be much good at physical displays of affection...Probably not.

"Happy birthday!" She handed me a gift-wrapped box. "Don't open it yet. Wait until you're alone." Leaning in closer, she added in a whisper, "Well, wait until you're alone with Jared." Her cheeky grin made me laugh. "This is from me *and* Cris, by the way...Although it was me who picked it out. He'd blush if he knew what it was." Well that certainly had me intrigued.

"We just want to wish you a happy birthday," Cristiano said, his voice uncharacteristically rough. "You look beautiful." When Jared growled, he held up his hands in a gesture of innocence, though his smug smirk was there. "It was just an observation."

"There you are," drawled a familiar and very unwelcome voice. Then the bony form of Joy was lounging all over Cristiano. In Fletcher's words, Jared's old consort was a cross between a whippet and a witch. I'd honestly never seen anyone so thin. My brows arched in surprise at the way she was petting Cristiano. Ava rolled her eyes while he sighed tiredly and tried to shift away from Joy. She just moved with him.

After licking her lips at Jared, Joy gave me a sickly sweet smile. "Happy birthday." She had said it in the same tone as someone would say, 'I hate you.' "Hope you're having a good time. Did Jared get you anything nice? I'm surprised he let you out of the apartment. When it was my birthday, he never let me out of the bed."

How could I not pity her when this kind of crap gave her a kick? "Aw, such a precious little brat, aren't you?"

Her smile faltered slightly. "Black is very slimming on you – good thinking, wearing that. Curves don't look good on everyone."

Groan. "As for you...I see you're still a fan of the, um, starved look." Honestly, if she swallowed a sprout, she'd look pregnant.

Jared, Ava, and Cristiano chuckled quietly.

"Such a joker," Joy spat bitterly.

"I was actually deadly serious, but sure."

"Personally, I wouldn't be so happy if the guy I was Bound to would never be totally satisfied with me. Jared likes a little variety in his sexual diet. Even three consorts couldn't keep him completely satisfied. Maybe right now he's happy enough with just you, but that will change. Once the novelty wears off, his interest will wane."

I was really supposed to believe that? Snort. I gave her a pitying look. "Jealousy isn't attractive, you know. You don't wear it well."

Jared, who I could sense was totally riled, went to say something to the bitch. But then Denny – my very own personal saviour – appeared at her side and held up his index finger. A sting suddenly appeared at the tip, making Joy gasp.

"Two things can happen," began Denny. "You could walk away of your own accord, or I could stab you with this and drag you away. I wouldn't recommend the latter. It itches like crazy, and you'll have an oozing spot tomorrow. So, what will it be?"

Joy shot me an ugly scowl, shoved away from Cristiano, and then marched off.

I sent Denny a smile. "You know I adore you, right?" He laughed and returned to his table.

Cristiano gestured at Joy's retreating form. "I think she thought she'd find an ally in me."

Confused, I asked, "Why would she think that?"

Cristiano frowned, apparently surprised by my question. Then he looked at Jared, arching a quizzical brow.

"She doesn't see it," Jared explained with a sigh.

Ava blinked rapidly, looking just as surprised as her brother. "Really? But he always—" She stopped as Cristiano took her arm and began to literally drag her back to their table. Wearing her cheery smile again, she waved at me. "Enjoy your meal! And happy birthday again!" I noticed that Salem followed the cute little thing with his eyes as she moved. She presented him with a bright, flirty smile to which he grunted. For whatever reason, she seemed to find that hilarious.

Sitting once again, I asked Jared, "What did you mean when you said, 'She doesn't see it'? See what?"

"That Dickhead wants you, of course." He rolled his eyes, taking my hand and tracing over the Binding knot. "I think he's right. I think Joy thought he'd be as jealous as she is about us and then they could be buddies who together made our lives miserable." He pinned my gaze with his. "You know Joy was talking shit, don't you? You're all I want."

Now it was my turn to roll my eyes. "If I thought you wanted anyone else, I'd plonk your bare arse on a cactus."

He winced. "Fair enough. Okay, no more talk about other people. I think we should talk about how great I am and how hot you are for me." I burst out laughing. "You know it's true."

"It's true. Want to know just how hot I am for you? Or should I say how 'wet' I am for you?"

His eyes narrowed at my impish smile. He leaned forward and feathered his lips over mine, asking quietly, "You're not wearing any underwear, are you?" When my smile widened, he groaned. "You can't do this to me." I just laughed again. "Come here. I want to feel you."

"Oh no," I chuckled, dodging the hand that reached for my leg under the table. "Too many people are around, and I'm unfortunately the focus of attention. You'll just have to wait until we get home."

He shook his head, looking pained. "It's going to be a long-ass night."

It was, but it was also a great night. The meal was delicious and the atmosphere was so jovial that it was almost effervescent, making energy cling to my skin and sprinkle from my fingers like fairy dust. Jared sucked chocolate sauce from my finger at one point just for an excuse to taste my energy-coated skin – according to him, my skin fizzed like sherbet or honeycomb whenever energy clung to it like that.

Eloise spent most of the night scowling and sneering at me from her seat, but that just made things even more fun. Collins was more interested in trying to get pally with the squad, but they only seemed interested in growling or snarling at him. Surely he'd worked out by now that they pretty much despised him. Could he not take a hint or something?

Antonio made a toast, once again wishing me a happy birthday, after which everybody then asked me to make a speech. Ha. As if. They simply laughed at my refusal, knowing that I wasn't much of a public speaker.

When people asked for music, Fletcher – always prepared – plugged his iPod into a set of speakers. Everyone danced on a kind of makeshift dance-floor on the sand. Considering Fletcher's taste in music, it was no surprise when 'YMCA' came on, or 'Oops Upside

Your Head' – he actually dragged Luther onto the dance-floor and taught him the moves. As usual, I never danced to the slow songs, although it wasn't for the lack of trying on Jared's part to get me up there.

It was when he left me alone for a moment to go and speak to Antonio that a soft voice spoke. "Hi, Sam."

Looking up, I found Antonio's future mate smiling down at me. "Lucy…Hi. Sit down."

Her expression was grateful and, if I wasn't mistaken, contained a hint of relief. "Thanks." She perched herself gingerly on the chair, as if ready to bolt at any moment. Whether she suspected I would send her on her merry way soon or she was just edgy because she knew that Jared would be back at any moment, I wasn't sure. Many people found him intimidating. "I wanted to say happy birthday. I love that dress."

"I can't take the credit – Fletcher picked it out." Knowing I was a bit of a tomboy, he always selected dresses for me. "But I get the feeling that you haven't come to chat about my dress."

Her smile turned sheepish. "Um, Antonio told you that he plans to Turn me soon, didn't he?"

"He did, yes. Are you having second thoughts?"

"I'm not having second thoughts about Turning, but I know a lot about the different breeds of vampire and, well…" Her voice lowered. "If I'm honest, being a Keja doesn't appeal to me. The bloodlust isn't as strong as that of Pagoris, but it's strong enough that it would take the best part of a year for me to have it under control. I'm not keen on being isolated for that length of time. But Sventés…well, you guys are more human-like. It takes you less time to gain control."

I could see where this was going. "You're wondering if I'll Turn you?"

Biting her lip, she nodded. "I'd rather be a Sventé."

There were a number of potential issues with her request. "Have you spoken to Antonio about this? If I'm honest, I don't think he's going to want any vampire other than him to Turn you." It would be hard for him to know that she had a blood-link with another vampire. I certainly hadn't liked knowing Jared was linked to Magda but ding dong the witch was now dead.

"I know it might offend him. That was why I wanted to ask you first. It's not worth even bringing it up to him if it's not something you would be prepared to do – I'll have offended him for no reason. Have you Turned anyone before?"

"No. Until I came to The Hollow, I hadn't been living the kind of life that I'd happily bring someone else into." The biggest issue at play here, however, was that I was no longer a Sventé. I was a hybrid. And anyone I Turned would become like me. That was if it even worked. For all I knew, I wasn't able to Turn anyone, considering my new genetic status wasn't natural for vampires. But that wasn't something I could reveal to Lucy.

Aside from all that…"Really, though, I've never wanted to Turn someone, and I'm not sure that I ever will. The idea has just never appealed to me. It's a big responsibility to begin a line…a little like beginning a family." Ruling alongside Jared would bring me enough responsibilities. "And my being linked to someone else would most likely drive Jared mental."

Lucy gave me a half smile, though she was clearly disappointed. "I understand."

"If I were you, I wouldn't talk to anyone else about your reservations. It's something that you and Antonio need to work out between yourselves. He'd never force you to be a Keja if he thought that it would make you unhappy. Trust him to do what's right for you. And trust me when I say that communication is really important if you're going to be Bound to someone."

"You're right." Seeing that Jared was returning, Lucy quickly stood. "Thanks, Sam. I really appreciate you hearing me out. And thanks for the advice." Then she was gone. Hmm. Clearly Jared *did* intimidate her.

Frowning, Jared tipped his head in the direction of a quickly retreating Lucy. "What was all that about?"

"Girl stuff."

He abruptly pulled me out of my seat and into his arms, grinning. "In other words, mind my own business?"

"Something like that." Noticing that his irises were glowing red, I narrowed my eyes. "Why do I have the feeling that your thoughts have turned X-rated?"

His grin turned devilish as one hand slowly glided down the bare skin of my back that was revealed by the dress. "You know…I've always wanted to fuck you on the beach." He ground the hard bulge in his pants against me.

Intriguing, but…"It's not happening while there are witnesses."

"No, it's not. No one gets to see this body but me. It's all mine. But it will happen soon." He tugged on my bottom lip with his teeth. Taking advantage of my gasp, he swept his tongue into my mouth. The kiss was slow and leisurely, teasing me and coaxing me into wanting more. It worked. "Let's go home."

I had no objections, although…"It would be rude to leave my own birthday meal early."

"Why? We did the same thing at the after-party of our Binding ceremony. Plus, everybody's eaten and most of them are—" He cut himself off and released a low growl as something behind me caught his attention.

I swivelled my head…and groaned at the sight of Collins and Eloise heading for us. "My evening is now complete."

As they stopped beside us, Collins smiled at me, though it was forced. "Happy birthday, Commander Parker."

"Thank you." I was surprised I didn't shudder. Even if he hadn't been making my life so hard, the slimy sod still would have made me feel uncomfortable.

Collins' smile faded as he looked at Jared. He gave him the tiniest nod. "Commander Michaels." He'd somehow made that sound like a profanity.

"Collins." And Jared had done the same.

Eloise raked her gaze over Jared, standing a little too close to him for comfort as she played with her hair – something she did often. "Hmm, you're looking very smart tonight, Jared. Weren't you wearing that shirt the night we first met?"

What a little bitch. I *knew* that he hadn't worn it then because I was the one who'd bought him that shirt. Obviously she was looking to piss me off on my own birthday and potentially ruin the night – surprise, surprise. Sadly, it was working.

Most likely sensing that, Jared kissed my forehead and soothingly caressed my back. He tossed Eloise an annoyed glance. "Since my memory of that night is pretty vague, I really couldn't say." Well that made me smile…particularly as it looked like steam might come out of her ears at any moment.

Collins held his hand out to me. "Perhaps you could join me for a dance, Commander Parker."

Jared answered for me. "Not even in an alternate dimension."

I had to wonder if the bloke was suicidal – seriously, who asked to dance with another person's mate when said person hated them? And why was there such calculation in Collins' beady eyes? Had Eloise asked him to separate Jared and me so that she could talk to him alone? It seemed more likely to be that than for Collins to be in a suicidal mood.

"I didn't ask you, I asked *Commander Parker*." Collins raised an imperious brow at Jared. "Do you always make her decisions for her?"

Apparently he was in a suicidal mood. Before Jared slit his throat, I quickly intervened. *Jared, he'd love to get a rise from you. Don't give him the satisfaction.*

Jared said, with all seriousness in the same tone that someone might use to ask if he took sugar in his coffee, "Actually, no. She only likes being bossed around when she's in bed and totally naked."

As Collins stood there with his mouth bopping open and closed, I buried my face into Jared's chest and let out a silent laugh. The bloke was a total prude, and Jared knew it.

Jared leaned in closer to him, speaking quietly. "Personally, I blame the Fifty Shades trilogy. Don't get me wrong, using the tie and the silver balls on her was a lot of fun. But, frankly, the leather crop and the cane make me a little uncomfortable. Still, if that's what makes her happy…" He let the sentence trail, shrugging.

I risked a glance at Collins to see that his cheeks had turned crimson. Eloise was curling her upper lip at me, the picture of bitterness.

Clearly uncomfortable and itching to get away, Collins said, "Oh, I think Antonio's signalling for me to return to the table."

"Shame," sighed Jared. "Well, I guess you better go."

He couldn't seem to get away fast enough. After shooting me one last snarl and flicking her mane over her shoulder in a dismissive gesture, Eloise followed him.

Peeking up at Jared, I smiled. "He really has no idea who he's messing with, does he?" Thinking he could outwit Jared was just plain dumb. "I almost feel sorry for him."

Jared just shrugged. "I'm not interested in him. I'm interested in finding out what Ava bought you. Her mischievous smile has me intrigued."

Same here. "All right, let's go."

"But if there's a crop in there, it's going to be a hard limit for me – just so you know."

I could only laugh at the prat.

CHAPTER EIGHT

(Sam)

Some people seemed to have a talent for making you want to strip them naked, lather them in fish guts, and throw them into a pool full of hungry piranhas. Fredrick Collins was one of those people. Sitting at my office desk with Dexter curled up on the table beside my laptop, I pointedly ignored Collins as he hovered over me while I again surfed the V-Net for information on The Call.

When I'd agreed to fully cooperate with him, I hadn't realised just how much of a pain in the arse he was going to be. Every training session, he watched and took notes the whole time. Every session, he was full of questions, despite that he didn't need to know the answers to most of those questions. And every session, he repeatedly attempted to undermine me and persisted in criticising me. For someone who was there to 'observe', he had an awful lot to bloody say for himself. For God's sake, he even criticised the clothes I wore – suggesting that a tank top was revealing and, therefore, would tease and distract the squad. Was he having a laugh?

It hurt – really hurt – to refrain from whipping the living crap out of both him and Eloise, but I had promised myself that I would be on my best behaviour. The fact was that having people so closely 'observe' the sessions and see how the squad worked was actually dangerous; it was information that could be used against us if it ended up in the wrong hands. Although he and Eloise had signed a confidentiality agreement in blood to the effect that they would never share it with anyone other than those within the Prelature, neither Jared nor I was reassured by that.

As such, we had secretly instructed the squad to not use their full strength, to not allow Collins and Eloise to see just all of what they could do and just how well they could truly do it. We had also reduced training hours and given the squad longer breaks, thus giving

Collins and Eloise less to 'observe' and write about.

But a big issue was that Collins didn't just observe training. He regularly examined my office, he watched over me as I worked at my desk, he asked to read my reports, and he also liked to witness my interactions with other commanders. In other words, he had become my shadow. And it was getting to the point where I was ready to smash his face into a wall. Or maybe I could just let Dexter bite him. Strongly linked to my emotions, Dexter could sense what Collins made me feel, and my snake was utterly pissed whenever he was around. In fact, he had hissed at Collins three times in the past half hour. He perceived him as a threat, and Dexter liked to eliminate threats. It was *so* very tempting to let him.

Although she didn't hang around me like a bad smell, Eloise was just as much of an annoyance as Collins. She accused me of stupid crap like being too firm with the squad, though other times she would complain that I was being too lenient. She also accused me of being 'too friendly' with the squad, though it was clear she was insinuating that I was flirtatious – and wasn't that the pot calling the kettle black. She even went as far as to imply that I was flirting with the squad to make Jared jealous, obviously attempting to create tension between us. It hadn't worked, of course, which seemed to be irritating the crap out of her. Good.

When she wasn't with Collins, she was lounging near the bat pool like she was on bloody holiday or something. When she *was* with Collins, she divided that time between nit-picking at me and staring lustfully at Jared...making me want to rag out every strand of that mane she seemed to love. She persisted in wearing low-cut tops and cut-off shorts. Collins had suggested a number of times that she change into 'more appropriate clothing', but his suggestions had been ignored.

She flirted so much with Jared that even Joy was pissed with her. I'd actually come across them arguing a few evenings' ago. Joy had ripped her a new one and then winked at me conspiratorially. When I'd mentioned it to Jared, he'd informed me that Joy particularly hated Eloise as Joy had been his consort during the time that he had bonked the bitch. In Joy's weird little mind, Eloise had made Jared cheat on her. Her weird little mind also saw me as the lesser evil in this case. Well, whatever.

One thing Jared was extremely good at was sussing out a person's strengths and weaknesses. He had pointed out that both Collins and Eloise had one very big fault: they thought that they were untouchable. So silly of them. If they continued as they were, they would quickly learn that things didn't work that way…because I made sure they didn't.

Leaving my side – *finally* – Collins popped his head out of the door. "Fletcher, could you please fetch me a—"

"I work for Sam and Jared. Unless the request comes from them, the answer is no."

I smiled. Oh God, I loved Fletcher. He was just as pissed off with Collins as everyone else was. The bloke was truly talented at alienating people and making enemies.

Collins stuttered, "Y-yes, but—"

"After all, what kind of assistant would I be if I spent my time doing things for others? There's a NST dispensing machine in the corner of the hallway." Judging by the clicking sounds, Fletcher had immediately gone back to typing. Disssssss*missed*.

Sighing in disappointment, Collins perched himself on the edge of my desk again. "I've yet to see the squad's personal files."

Was he high? Incredulous, I asked, "Why *would* you see their files?"

"I need every scrap of information to complete my report."

"But that doesn't include their files." And he had some nerve to ask for them.

He gave me an impatient look. "I'm here to observe you as their commander."

"Appreciated," I said slowly, like I was dealing with a small child, "but their personal files have no bearing on that." He was just being a nosy bastard because he was freakily obsessed with the squad.

"On the contrary, I need to see that you keep the files updated – that you properly record the squad's progress." His snippy tone earned him a hiss from Dexter. As usual, Collins flinched at the sound.

"Well you'll just have to take my word for it when I say that I do." Planning to head back to the arena now that lunch break was over, I switched off my laptop and spread out my arm beside Dexter. Without hesitation, he began to curl himself around it.

Collins folded his arms, glaring down at me disdainfully. Pompous prick. "You have to cooperate with this investigation, Commander

Parker."

"I have, and I will continue to do so. But I will not disclose *personal* information about anyone without their expressed permission. Now, if the squad agree to you seeing their files – well, that's different." As Dexter finished winding himself around my arm, I said, "Novo," returning him to his tattoo form. Only then did I move my attention back to Collins. "Ask them. If they agree, I'll make their files available." But hell would freeze over before the squad would agree to that, and he knew it.

"I could always call my superiors and have them—"

"Do what you feel you need to do, Mr Collins. But don't ever think that threatening me with anyone or anything will get you what you want. Your big, bad displays of authority are wasted on me. As you yourself said, I'm 'reckless'."

He flushed. "I would recommend that you do not make an enemy of me, Commander Parker." His cautioning tone was severe, almost threatening. "As your observer here, it is in my hands whether or not you keep your position."

I leaned forward. "Yeah? Well observe me pretend to give a rat's arse." With that, I stood and made my way around the desk, my head held high. Exiting the office, I waved briefly at Fletcher – who, clearly having heard the conversation, was keeled over with laughter – and advanced down the hallway. Unfortunately, Collins shadowed me as per bloody usual.

"Where are you going?" he asked, remaining slightly behind me.

"Lunch time is over. I'm returning to the arena."

"What about Commander Michaels?"

"He'll be meeting me there." Jared had wanted to pay Evan a brief visit. It was something he did *too* often in my opinion, and each time he came out of there he was even more devastated than the last time. A part of me wanted to tell him to stop going to the cell and doing this to himself, but I understood why he did it. I also understood that the reason he went without me was that he didn't believe he deserved my support. He was blaming himself to some degree, and nothing anyone said would shift his opinion on that.

"It was strange that he didn't have lunch with you this evening."

"Was it?" I kept my tone bored, ignoring what was clearly a prompt for information on what Jared had been doing.

"Usually you're both joined at the hip." His voice was sharp, almost bitter.

"No need to be jealous, Mr Collins."

He spluttered. "I am not jealous! Quite frankly, Commander Parker, you are not someone who I could permanently tolerate on a daily basis. You're simply too aggravating."

"Why, thank you. But I wasn't implying that you want *me*, I was implying that you have a little thing for Jared." In truth, the only emotions he ever felt around Jared were jealousy, bitterness, and hatred. There was never desire there, but I liked to needle him. Tit for tat, right?

"I beg your pardon!"

"Don't worry, you're not the only one who wants him. And I can totally understand."

"I do *not* want your mate! I do not even enjoy his company. And if you must know, I am one hundred percent heterosexual."

Without turning to look at him, I wagged a finger. "Now, now, there's really no need to lie."

"I am *not* lying," he stated through his teeth, his temper rising.

"Sure you are."

"How dare you! That is a very—"

I stopped dead and twirled to face him, almost causing him to crash into me. "Oh, so you don't like it when someone makes incorrect judgements about you? *Join the fucking club.*"

He didn't say another word as he followed me inside the arena, which was a very good decision on his part. Inside, Jared and the squad were waiting. A scantily dressed Eloise was already seated in the spectators' area. Strangely, she was also completely still. Only her eyes were moving, and they were gleaming with panic. Realisation hit me, and I sighed at Harvey, shaking my head.

Shrugging, he released her of his gift. "It was just a demonstration. They're both constantly asking for them." No, it was his way of cheesing her off. The squad was getting sick of Collins and Eloise watching them like it was a show and they were performing seals.

Jared smiled at me, but his eyes were troubled, bruised. "Hey. You ready?"

You sure you're up for this? If you need some time alone after seeing Evan, go home and I'll be up in a little while.

Thanks, baby, but I'd rather be with you. Plus, I need to keep my mind on something else.

Accepting his wishes despite my reservations, I switched my attention to the squad. Having worked on their physical stamina earlier, we intended to now work on their gifts. As usual, they enthusiastically rose to every challenge, but they cleverly faked limitations or difficulties that they didn't have, ensuring that the information that went to the Prelature wasn't accurate enough to be used against us.

As usual, Collins repeatedly interrupted the session to ask questions such as, "Is it really important that they always suck in their surrounding energy?", "Are they punished if they do not do it?", and "Do they enjoy doing these exercises despite that they can harm each other?" His most annoying question came at the end of the session: "Are they rewarded when they overcome their weaknesses, or is this the strongest that the squad will ever get?"

"This squad is not weak, Mr Collins. The members are simply stronger in some areas than they are in others." He flushed.

"I can't help but notice that your questions are becoming more and more about the squad and how *they* feel rather than about Sam's actions," observed Jared. He was right.

Collins shifted nervously in his seat. "Naturally it is important how they feel. It tells me whether or not they enjoy having Commander Parker as a commander."

"But you already asked us that question during our interview," Chico pointed out. "So you already know the answer to that."

Butch nodded. "Commander Michaels is right. You're a little too interested in us."

"Maybe he wishes he was part of the squad," mused Damien. His expression said 'like that would ever happen'.

That gave me an idea. "Is that true, Mr Collins?" I gave the arsehole a delighted smile. "Oh, why didn't you say something sooner? Come on down here."

Collins froze. "Excuse me?"

"You can spend five minutes with the squad before they leave the arena. Come on, there's no better way of understanding what it's like to be part of the legion than up close and personal. It'll be fun."

(Jared)

I really did love this woman. By the end of the five minutes, Collins had been psychically slapped at least twenty times, was lathered in yellowy-green ooze from head to toe, had over a dozen thorns sticking out of his ass – luckily for him, Reuben had lessened the strength of Chico's gift and so the thorns only caused him discomfort – and then Denny had farted skunk-like musk at him. To top it all off, Collins had a personal encounter with the ceiling thanks to Harvey's gift.

Wheezing, a pale Collins staggered toward the exit. "It's all right. I'm okay." He put a hand to his stomach and swallowed hard. "I think I'll go lay down for a while."

David gave him a falsely sympathetic smile. "Yeah, I think that might be for the best."

"Eloise, could you carry my things? I'm unable to do it myself." Collins showed her his ooze-covered hands.

Eloise did as he'd asked, shooting me another inviting smile as she past. "Maybe I'll see you later, Jared. I'll be at the pool if you need me for anything. *Any*thing." That was getting real old.

Unlike Sam, I wasn't convinced that Eloise wanted me as desperately as she and her body language implied. In fact, I'd been told by another commander that Eloise had been amusing herself with a few of the guards – and all at once. Nor did I believe that she was under the illusion that I'd ever cheat on Sam. She never invested any real effort in trying to get my attention. Sleazy smiles, flirty comments, and walking around half naked were *nothing* compared to the type of things that Joy had been known to do.

I personally believed that Eloise simply did all that to rile Sam, maybe in the hope of making Sam snap and do something that wouldn't look so good in the report, or maybe simply because Eloise was – as I'd soon come to realise – jealous of Sam. Jealous of how powerful she was, of how people looked up to her, and of how they respected her. Flirting with Sam's mate was guaranteed to anger her. Possessiveness took on a whole new meaning when two people were Bound – probably because of the protectiveness the couple had of the bond and the instinctive need to eradicate any threat to it.

Eloise was undoubtedly frustrated that Sam wasn't responding violently to her taunts. Sam knew that I'd never betray her, and she knew that I'd never leave her. Not just because of how deeply the bond connected us and just how much it allowed her to see, but because I never let her forget it. Of course, someone as fickle and selfish as Eloise wouldn't understand that and wouldn't expect Sam to hold back. Nor would she expect that Sam would put her position and her squad before her own wants.

It seemed that people had a habit of underestimating my blunt, crazy, homicidal ray of sunshine. More fool them. I'd been guilty of that at one time, but it wasn't a mistake I'd repeated. I didn't doubt that Collins and Eloise would soon learn that they had stupidly underestimated her in many ways. She could be impulsive, sure, but she could also bide her time when need be.

"Now that they're gone, I can tell you what happened yesterday evening." Chico double-checked that Collins and Eloise were gone before he spoke again. "When you went home after training, we all headed to the basketball court for a while. Collins turned up, wanting to play, like we were all good friends – the cheeky fucker. Anyway, I told him no. That I only played with people I trusted. He said that his presence here at The Hollow should prove his loyalty to us."

Reuben shook his head in disbelief. "He really thinks that investigating the complaints that have been made against you is good for us, Coach – that he's helping and protecting us from potential harm and exploitation."

Harvey smirked. "Butch cleverly took advantage of that."

We all turned to Butch, who shrugged and smiled crookedly. "I told him that if he was really loyal to the squad, he'd reveal which one of us apparently made the complaints."

I stiffened. "And did he?"

"At first, he said the complaints were made anonymously," replied Butch. "But I reminded him that he'd already told us the first night he came here that he knew their name and that he was respecting their wish to remain anonymous. We were just about to walk away from him when he blurted out their name."

There was a long moment of complete silence before Sam asked, "Who?" Butch didn't respond.

Damien sighed, rubbing the back of his neck. "Max."

Sam shook her head. "I don't believe that."

"Good, because neither do we," stated Salem. "Max is a convenient person to blame it on, since he isn't in any state to defend himself."

"Do you think Collins might be blaming someone who can't object because he believes it's his way of protecting the person who supposedly made the complaints?" asked David.

"I don't know." I turned to Reuben. "I agree that Collins truly believes he's helping here. He honestly thinks these complaints are genuine."

Chico looked at Sam cautiously. "You know that none of us would ever do that, Coach, don't you?"

"We respect you, and we look up to you," began Damien. "Hell, we owe what we've become to *you*." I wasn't offended that I wasn't being given equal credit. Sam *had* helped them dramatically in the sense that they'd had no idea of the things they could do with their gifts until she came along. Without her, they may never have learned to use their gifts to their full potential, may never have attained such control over them.

"You don't need to try to convince me of that," Sam assured them, rolling her eyes. "I have never – not even for one second – believed any of you would do this. If I wasn't confident in your loyalty to me, Jared, and each other, I wouldn't have you with me on assignments, watching my back, would I?" That clearly settled them.

"We just wanted to be sure." David gave her a half-smile. "No one could blame you for wondering."

"Well I don't 'wonder'. We'll find out who's behind all this and we'll deal with it. Until then, we need to keep handling Collins and Eloise the same as we have been doing since they arrived: give them nothing to whine about or use against any of us."

"It occurred to me," began Harvey, "that if someone came up with a plan like this, it might not be to make you lose your job or to discredit you. That might not be the true goal."

Sam's brow furrowed. "What do you mean?"

"Coach, this is eating up your time and attention. It's restricting, too; you need to constantly be on your best behaviour, and you can't afford to push us hard during training. In short, this whole 'case' that's been made against you is distracting you from researching a way to fight The Call. Maybe that's the goal."

I cocked my head. "I never thought of it like that." At Sam's sceptical look, I added, "Don't get me wrong, I think Collins does truly think this is a real complaint and he would like to see you lose your position purely because he's an asshole. But it's still possible that the motivation behind the complaint isn't what we thought it was."

Sam twisted her lips. "Okay, so let's say that's true and someone wants to keep me distracted...Why? Why would they want me to find it even more difficult to fight The Call than it already is? Why would they hamper our attempts to find a counteragent?"

Harvey shrugged. "I didn't say I had all the answers. My brain is good with strategies, but that's pretty much it." Yes, by his own admission, he lacked common sense.

"It could be that someone is hoping that The Call spreads around The Hollow, killing many of its inhabitants." Chico waved his hand. "This place will always have people trying to take over it. It's happened too many times to count."

"Yeah," said Damien. "And if Evan, Max, and Stuart were to die – which won't fucking happen – it would mentally weaken us all, wouldn't it? Weaken us enough to put us all in a shit state of mind."

And look what had happened to Evan when he'd been in a bad state of mind.

Sam slowly paced up and down. "To sum up, it's *possible* that someone wants me distracted, wants us all mentally weak and off-balance, and wants to stop us from battling The Call – and possibly because they fully intend to leap on that in order to invade The Hollow. But surely if there was going to be an attack, Luther would have foreseen it."

"Luther doesn't foresee everything, though." David shrugged. "If he did, Evan, Max, and Stuart wouldn't be in a cell right now."

Luther did say that a lot of people would turn up for Paige West, I reminded her.

Yeah, for Paige. Not for control of The Hollow.

It's neither here nor there anyway because there's absolutely no way that she will come here.

Sam rolled her eyes at me but didn't push me on the subject this time, thank God. It caused disputes between us every time, and I was sick of having the same argument over and over. Nothing in the world would make me risk her. I just fucking couldn't. But she didn't seem to get just how much she meant to me. To her, I was being stubborn and unreasonable. To me, I was putting Sam before anything else and determined to keep her safe.

Sure, a part of me felt bad for refusing to bring Paige West here when she could potentially save Evan, Max, and Stuart. But how the hell could I do that, knowing something bad could happen to Sam, to the thing that mattered to me more than anything?

When I'd gone to see the guys earlier, I'd spoken to Evan telepathically even though he didn't appear to be in a rational enough state of mind to understand me. All three of them had badly deteriorated and looked fucking awful – almost as bad as their attackers had. It was a reminder that time was running out. I'd told Evan a little about Paige West, told him about Luther's vision, and begged him to understand why I couldn't bring Paige here. Begged him to understand that I just couldn't be without Sam. I'd told him that if the situation was reversed, I wouldn't have wanted him to sacrifice Alora and his life with her just for me. It was true. If he had understood my words, he hadn't let on.

Once Sam and I were finished talking to the squad, I teleported us both home. Sam took three steps toward the kitchen area and abruptly halted. So attuned to her that I sensed her outrage, I stiffened. "What's wrong?" Then she was strangely zooming through the entire apartment at vampire velocity before returning to me.

Clenching and unclenching her fists, she ordered through her teeth, "Teleport me to the bat pool."

"Baby, what's—"

"*Now*, Jared."

Not liking her tone whatsoever, I shot her a reprimanding look. Right now, I'd humour her, but…"I'll spank your ass for that later." Taking her hand, I teleported us out of there.

The second we appeared beside the pool, Sam twirled as her shrewd eyes searched her surroundings. Her gaze landed on something – no, some*one* – and she made a hissing sound that would have made Dexter proud. Before I had the chance to calm Sam down and stop her from doing anything that she would later regret, she was stomping over to an unsuspecting Eloise. *Well, shit.* "Sam—"

"What the fuck do you think you're playing at?"

Startled, Eloise lifted her head from where she was lying on a sun lounger – all vampires enjoyed moonlight bathing. "Excuse me?"

Hands on her hips, Sam glared down at her. "You were inside my apartment!"

That sure surprised me.

Eloise blanched. "I don't know what—"

Sam laughed, but it wasn't a pleasant sound. "Sweetheart, did you really think that if enough time went past for your scent to fade, I wouldn't have known you'd been there? You can't hide an energy signature. Feeders like me are *all* about energy. And your energy signature was all over my fucking apartment! What I want to know is what you were doing in there."

Eloise desperately looked around for some form of help. That was when I noticed that we were no longer alone. Antonio, Luther, and Antonio's personal guards all stood near the patio doors, clearly baffled.

"Well?" demanded Sam.

"I-I, um, I was looking for Jared."

"You know what? I don't believe you."

"Why?"

Sam chuckled, regarding Eloise with mock pity. "Because you're lying, silly. After all, it's not like you were going to find him in my set of drawers – and you had a good root through them, didn't you?"

Her eyes danced from side to side. "I was, um..."

"I'll tell you why you did it. You did it...because you thought you could. No other reason. Just like Collins, you have a strong sense of entitlement purely because you're a representative. Well, let me be very clear: you can pester me during my work hours and invade my office, but my personal time and my apartment are out of bounds. So unless you want to know just how 'reckless' I can be, I suggest you quickly learn to respect my personal boundaries."

Despite being a nervous wreck, Eloise maintained, "You can't hurt me."

"Sweetheart, why would I waste energy hurting you when it would be much more effective to chop off that mane of yours?"

Eloise let out a gasp as her hand flew to her hair. "You wouldn't." Oh but Sam would, and Eloise knew it.

"I advise you not to test me on that. Now piss off."

I'd honestly never seen the woman move so fast.

Antonio came and put a hand on Sam's shoulder. "I must apologise on Eloise's behalf. Her behaviour is truly unacceptable, and I shall have a conversation with her about it later."

Sam waved a hand. "I wouldn't bother yourself with the whole thing, Antonio. Let her dig her own grave."

"If you are not too busy, could I speak with you both for a

moment?" Without waiting for a response, he gestured for us to follow him and Luther through the patio doors. Exchanging a look with Sam, I shrugged and took her hand. We trailed behind them down the eternally long hallway, not stopping until they reached one of his parlour rooms. With his hand on the doorknob, Antonio said, "There's someone here to see you both."

When he opened it wide, Sam and I stepped inside. Almost instantly, we froze. I wasn't in the fucking mood for this. I groaned at Antonio. "Why is *she* here?"

"I think you should listen to what she has to say." He motioned at the empty sofa that was positioned opposite an identical one on which a nervous redhead sat gingerly.

I was ready to object when Sam squeezed my hand and tugged. *Let's just hear her out. There's no harm in that.*

Fine, but two minutes is the most I'm staying here.

Alora smiled nervously as we took a seat opposite her. Antonio sat beside her and took her hand in his. Luther sat at her other side. After a moment of silence, she cleared her throat. "I know you don't want me here—"

"So why are you here?" I snapped. I winced when Sam pinched my arm.

Tears shimmered in Alora's eyes. "Because it's Evan," she said simply – there was a confusing amount of adoration in her voice.

"You love him," whispered Sam. She nodded.

In my opinion, her actions said something totally different. "Then why did you reject him?"

Alora seemed bewildered. "I didn't reject him. I just...I couldn't give him what he wanted."

Cryptic shit. I hated cryptic shit. "What does that mean?"

"He didn't tell you?" When I shook my head, she straightened in her seat as if bracing herself for impact. "I'm Bound to someone else."

I could only gape at her. "What the fuck?"

She averted her gaze, seemingly embarrassed. "Please understand I was only nineteen years old. What's more, I was no more than eighteen months old in vampire years and I didn't truly understand just how serious a Binding actually was."

I looked down at the third finger of her left hand and saw a bulky emerald ring that no doubt covered a Binding knot.

"I bought every lie that Gregory ever told me. I agreed to Bind with him after only being with him for three months. It wasn't until after the Binding that things changed, *he* changed." She sounded as angry with herself as she was with him.

"He hurt you," Sam guessed.

"In about as many ways as a person can hurt another."

"Does Bran know?" I asked.

"Yes. Bran saved me from him. It's a long story, but he got me away and he kept me as his 'consort' to give me added protection. I think you know why he really keeps female consorts. The arrangement worked well for both of us, in that sense."

I considered that for a minute. "So your loyalty to Bran kept you with him? Bran refuses to let you leave him?"

"No. Bran would let me leave if I wanted to do so. In fact, he doesn't think there's any safer place for me to be than here, with Evan. But Gregory wants me back. Because we're Bound, he knows exactly where I am at all times. But he's not powerful enough to take on a High Master vampire and he's not stupid enough to try. But it means that I've always felt trapped, knowing that if I left Bran, Gregory would be able to take me back to him. I hate him, *hate* him, but I'm stuck with him."

"I take it you didn't tell Evan in the beginning."

"No. I just felt so ashamed of myself. Ashamed for being so gullible as to Bind with someone I hardly knew. But at the time, it had felt right."

I couldn't really vilify her for Binding with someone after only knowing them for a short time. Not when Sam and I hadn't known each other for long.

"I understand," said Sam. "It felt right for me and Jared, even though we hadn't been together long."

"Yes, and it would have continued to feel right for me if Gregory had really been the person that he pretended to be. But he's a far cry from it. He's violent and he's abusive, and I didn't want Evan to be responsible for keeping me safe. I didn't want him in any form of danger. So I gave him a bunch of excuses as to why I couldn't be with him, but they never deterred him. I don't think I've ever met anyone so persistent," she added endearingly. Her face fell as she continued. "When he asked me on the night of your Binding ceremony to stay here with him permanently, I finally told him about

Gregory." She gave me a sad smile. "Imagine how well you would have taken it if you found out that Sam was Bound to someone else."

I would have wanted to hunt down and kill the fucker...but to do that would have been to kill Sam too, because she wouldn't have survived the severing of the bond. Fuck, no wonder Evan's head had been in a shitty place. "So you didn't reject him?"

"No. It was actually the other way around. I asked if he could handle being with someone who he could never Bind with, someone who would always be tied to somebody else – even though I despised that somebody else. He didn't answer me. He just...walked away." Tears began to trail down her face and she brushed them away with her thumbs. "Then when it was time for me to leave the next evening, he didn't come. Not to ask me to stay or even to say goodbye."

Sam puffed out a long breath. "Alora, I'm so sorry."

"Yeah, me too. Evan doesn't want me and he's never going to want me – I don't blame him. In his position, I'm not sure if I could handle it either. It would be agonising to know that he was Bound to someone else, to know that I'd never have that same bond with him. But I still want to help him. Maybe I can't. But I need to try. I need to do *something*. If you were me, Sam, if Jared had made it clear that he didn't want you, could you still have sat back and ignored the fact that he was dying?"

Sam snorted. "I would have done whatever I could to help, whether he wanted me to or not."

I might have smiled at that if I wasn't so pissed with how things had worked out – or, more specifically, how they *hadn't* worked out – for my brother. I mean, really, could the situation be any more fucked up? I ran a hand through my hair, sighing heavily. "Where is Gregory?"

Alora dabbed her wet cheeks with the tissue that Antonio handed to her. "Canada."

"He doesn't try to contact you?"

She shook her head. "He's too scared of Bran. Please don't ask me to go back home. I need to do something."

I was silent as I thought on that. "I won't ask you to leave," I eventually said. How could I expect her to do that when she was clearly in as much agony as Evan was over the whole thing? "But I'll be honest, Alora, I don't see how you can help. None of us have been able to come up with a solution. I have one condition, though. If you stay, you can't try to see Evan."

"I'm guessing he made it clear that he didn't want me here. It's okay." Another sad, wobbly smile.

"That's not what I mean. Evan just doesn't want you to see him *like that.*"

"Nice of you to try and spare my feelings, but I know he doesn't want me around."

"I wouldn't be too sure of that." My words didn't seem to affect her.

After a short silence, Antonio smiled. "I'm glad that is settled. I will have someone escort you to the Guest House, Alora." He called out a name, and one of the guards stationed outside the parlour stepped inside. "Please take this young lady to the room that I instructed to be readied for her. Thank you."

Alora rose from her seat and flashed both Sam and me a grateful yet sorrowful smile. "Thanks for letting me stay, and for understanding why I need to be here."

When the door closed behind her, Antonio looked warily from me to Sam. Oh shit, now what? "One more thing before you both leave: I have news from Sebastian. He has located Paige West."

So not what I wanted to hear.

CHAPTER NINE

(Sam)

A whole hour. We spent a whole hour arguing over whether or not we should risk bringing Paige West to The Hollow. But we were still at stalemate, because neither of us was willing to back down. Jared had eventually walked away – a gesture that the conversation was over. He was now lying in the hammock on our balcony, totally silent.

And I bloody hated it.

The last thing that I wanted was to be at odds with Jared. Knowing that Evan, Max, and Stuart could die, seeing the pain on Alora's face...All of that had brought with it an acute awareness of just how easily everything could end. How easily the people important to you could be taken away, just like that. I'd experienced it with a boyfriend that my Sire had killed – Bryce had been murdered in front of my very eyes. The pain of that loss had never left me, and nor had the memory of the look in his eyes just before Victor killed him. Even the *thought* of anything happening to Jared was ten times worse than having lost Bryce. The frightening fact was that it could just as easily have been Jared who was hurt in the tunnels. The very idea made ice-cold fear shudder through me. There was truly no such thing as immortality.

At any other time, I might have stormed after Jared if he walked away mid-argument. But although it looked as though he had petulantly walked off in a huff and was now sulking, I was connected to him on a level so deep that I knew it was much more than that. An all-consuming fear was tormenting him, haunting him, clawing at him. But there was more – pain and rage were bubbling and sizzling inside him...and he was desperately trying to hide it all from me. That realisation had stopped me dead in my tracks.

It was then that, having tapped fully into our bond, I'd realised something else. By fighting so hard with Jared on the subject of Paige West for the last few weeks, I'd caused him to pull back. Watching his twin deteriorate had swamped him with dark emotions, and by arguing with him, I'd more or less left him to deal with it all by himself. I'd made him feel that I wouldn't support him purely because I disagreed with his decision about Paige. He thought that I'd tell him it was his own fault that he was feeling this way.

In sum, I'd made him feel totally alone.

Shit.

Jared didn't function as others did. I knew that being raised by a narcissistic mother who emotionally and physically abused him had made him shut down in many ways. I knew that he didn't share his pain with others because, in Evan's words, emotions had always gotten Jared in deep shit. I also knew that, as a result, unless you literally dragged it out of him, Jared would bury it all deep. But I hadn't expected him to do that with me, I'd thought we'd gotten past that. I was wrong. He'd buried the extent of his pain as deep as he possibly could. Oh I'd felt echoes of his pain and fear and anger through the bond at times, but I hadn't realised the extent of it until now. All that optimism he'd shown had been his smokescreen.

I'd worked so hard since we got together to help him defeat this psychological impulse to hide his pain. I'd actually been making progress, but I'd clearly gone back a step because by not being there for him through all this, I'd made him retreat. He'd once described me as his refuge. Well I clearly hadn't been that this time.

Maybe some would say that he needed to buck up and deal with his shit like an adult. But he'd become emotionally independent at a young age, was used to taking care of himself and not needing anyone. He'd let himself need me, and I'd gone and let him down. First by mentally retreating from him, and then by being pissed with him rather than being understanding. He hadn't sulked, he'd just withdrawn. That, for me, was even worse than being cursed at or given the silent treatment.

Determined to ensure he didn't feel alone any longer, I went out onto the balcony. To anyone else, he might have appeared totally relaxed lounging in the hammock, watching the waves lap against the shore. But I knew better. I could feel his turmoil, and it caused a hollow ache in my chest.

I stood beside him, but he didn't say anything. He didn't look at me or acknowledge my presence in any way. Yes, he was trying to irritate me by ignoring me like this. But he wasn't being a hurtful prat. This was actually one of his sneaky little avoidance tactics; he was hoping that if he annoyed me, I would walk away and then we wouldn't get back to arguing.

"I don't want to fight again," I assured him softly. "I'm done with that."

His gaze flicked to me, examining my face. Then he effortlessly dragged me on top of him with one arm without even slightly unbalancing the hammock. Sad hazel eyes stared into mine as he brushed stray strands of hair away from my face. "Good. Neither do I." That was one great thing about Jared. He didn't brood endlessly or expect a dramatic apology before backing down. He'd easily accept a peace offering and happily move past the dispute.

"I just...I don't want to watch them die, Jared."

"Me neither, but I'm not going to change my mind."

"I'm not here to ask you to. Like I said, I'm done with bickering." His answering kiss was so gentle that it was more of a whispering of his lips over mine. "Please tell me you have some kind of plan because I'm all out of ideas."

He sighed, returning his gaze to the ocean. "So am I, baby."

And he hated himself for it, I could sense. He was literally wading in guilt. "Stop it, Jared. You did your research on The Call, you consulted several people, you surfed the V-Net, you spoke with Quentin Foy – you've literally done all you can to try to find a way to help them." Apart from one thing, and I would bet my life that having me hound him about not letting Paige West come here had made him feel even guiltier. Crap. "Nobody blames you. And everyone who knows about Paige understands why you don't want her here."

His eyes darted back to mine. Wariness and doubt was swirling in their depths. "Even you?"

"Even me."

"You'll really stop fighting me on this?"

"What you need is for me to be here for you, and I haven't. First I disappeared into my head. Then I fought you instead of being more understanding. But like you said, I'm stubborn – I can get so set on one path that I almost develop tunnel vision."

The pad of his thumb breezed over my bottom lip. "We're both guilty of that." He exhaled heavily, looking like someone with the weight of the world on his shoulders. "It's possible that she couldn't have helped anyway. Covington said that he couldn't be sure. I could have brought her here and put you in danger for nothing." Again his thumb stroked my bottom lip. I bit the digit gently. He smiled, but it was strained. "Even if it *had* worked, Evan would have kicked our asses for taking the risk."

"Exactly – you have nothing to feel guilty for because he would sooner reprimand you for taking risks than blame you for being careful."

Scrunching his hands in my hair, he tugged so that my forehead rested on his. "I miss him," he whispered. "We can't help him, can we?"

"It's not looking good," I admitted.

"A part of me wonders if I should just end his life now. It *isn't* a life. He's suffering, he's in pain, and he's lost most of who he is. But I just can't. I still have a small bit of hope that I'll find something that will help him, and I won't stop trying. But I have to make peace with the fact that I might not be able to do anything, don't I?"

"*We* have to make peace with that," I corrected, knowing that without that peace, the guilt would swallow us whole. "Stop shouldering all this. You told me I didn't have to go through shit alone anymore. Well, same here." I buried my face in the crook of his neck and snuggled into him the way he liked it. His arms closed tightly around me. "We should have had this conversation sooner. I would *never* have told you that it's your own fault that you're hurting. I wouldn't use your emotions against you like that; I'm not your mother." I lifted my head to meet his gaze. "I *always* want to know how you feel, even if it's about a subject that we're at odds on. Got it?"

"Got it." Cupping my chin, he kissed me gently. "You're the only reason I haven't totally lost it. You're my only weakness...but you're my strength, too."

"Right back at you, Michaels."

He chuckled softly. "Stay here with me for a while."

So I did. It wasn't until dawn that he teleported us both to bed where he proceeded to make me come over and over. When he finally slid inside me, he kept every thrust slow and sensual, refusing to release my eyes. It was so fucking intimate, it was scary. As he exploded deep inside me, he gave me those three little words that he didn't often say, being the emotionally awkward person that he was. Unsurprisingly, I fell asleep with a huge smile on my face.

I was still smiling when I woke up at dusk...although that might have been because the sneaky sod was suckling on a nipple. Once again, he teased me half to death – he even used the fur-lined cuffs and chocolate body spread that Ava had bought me for my birthday – before making me come repeatedly. It was hard and fierce this time, and it was what we both needed.

Having washed, dressed, and downed a few NSTs while munching on toast, we were just about to teleport to the arena when there was a knock at the front door. Opening it, I found Antonio, Luther, and – of course – the guards and pit-bulls.

Antonio's mouth curled into a slight smile. "Notice that we *knocked* this time."

Luther's smile matched his. "It avoids any further awkward situations."

Had they turned up fifteen minutes earlier, they would have interrupted something that no amount of knocking would have stopped. I gestured for them both to sit on the sofa, extremely curious about their early visit. The dogs came for a brief stroke before settling at Antonio's feet while the guards lurked in the background.

No sooner had Luther sat down beside Antonio than Jared rounded on them. "If you're here to talk about Paige West and get me to change my mind—"

Antonio raised his hand, palm out. "Be assured that that is not why I am here. I respect your decision. After all, it would devastate me to place Lucy in any form of danger, so I understand. And I do not want Sam in danger any more than you do. I am here because Quentin has been in contact."

I tensed immediately; his tone had suggested that this really wasn't good. "Oh God, what now?"

"As you know, he has been tracking stray tainted vampires. Following different clues, he eventually tracked them to a small village located within a rainforest that housed vampires and humans. He believes that this is where The Call originally surfaced."

Well that was one question answered.

"We have two problems."

"Only two?" I said dryly. Jared snorted in amusement.

"Firstly, the tainted vampires have slaughtered almost the entire village." His tone was sad, regretful. "The vampires who are not dead are tainted."

Oh bloody wonderful. "And secondly...?" I prompted.

"Quentin's intention would obviously be to kill all of the tainted. Unfortunately, these deaths have not only come to our attention. Others have also gone to investigate. A human military team was sent to deal with the matter."

"Fuck," Jared bit out.

"Quite." Antonio sighed. "In Quentin's opinion, these humans know they are dealing with vampires, going by their weapons and equipment. They are most likely part of the government agency that investigates things like this. From what he has seen from their other belongings, he suspects that this group of people has been posing as a team of medical volunteers inside the rainforest and that they responded to the many rumours of the suspicious locals. Many such rumours are ripe there."

"Other humans might have dismissed them," Jared pondered, "but a government agency that believes in our existence would be interested in following any lead."

"Yes."

"Did the military team wipe out the tainted vampires?"

Antonio's expression hardened. "The humans did not attempt to kill them. They attempted to sedate and capture them."

Jared gawked. "Are they fucking brainless?"

"It would seem so. In a few cases, the humans succeeded in confining them to small, iron-barred cells. The Pagoris, however, were able to break out. They savaged many of the military team, but another team simply came at the orders of whoever is 'running the show', as Quentin put it."

Jared folded his arms. "I'm guessing Quentin fears trying to attack the remaining tainted vampires, since it would risk exposing himself, his vampires, and Commander Rodney's squad to the humans."

"Indeed." Antonio's mouth twisted as his expression morphed into one of anger. "But he did it anyway."

Another gawk from Jared. "Please tell me you're kidding."

"I wish I was. The humans were able to capture a small number of Quentin's vampires and also some of Rodney's squad; they are all now being held in the military vehicles. The humans have not yet left the area because they want to capture more vampires first. That cannot be allowed to happen. Those humans cannot be allowed to keep any of the vampires that they are holding – not the tainted or the untainted."

No they bloody well couldn't.

"This whole thing just keeps getting better and better," Jared muttered sardonically, running a hand through his hair.

"This particular assignment will be extremely difficult because you will have two purposes. Number one, all of the tainted vampires *must* be destroyed. Number two, each and every one of the vampires that have been captured by the humans need to be freed."

"What about the humans?" I asked. "Do we let them live?" I didn't relish the idea of killing them for simply being curious and downright stupid, but there weren't a lot of options.

"This is where it gets tricky. The secret of our existence needs to be preserved at all costs, but it is clear that this agency already knew of our existence prior to the attack on the village. They most likely have other evidence somewhere. From what Quentin has told me, they do not seem to know enough about vampires to suggest that they have ever captured one before. That, at least, is good news."

"Killing them wouldn't really fulfil a purpose, then, would it?" I shrugged. "They already know our secret. Even if we kill them, others from the agency will know, so it achieves nothing."

Antonio nodded. "Exactly. We can do one of two things: kill them all to deliver a message to their superiors that coming at us will only end in death, or we could free the vampires without being seen and deliver a different type of message. A message that although we are powerful, we are not senseless killers and we are only interested in our own."

"The latter might be for the best," Luther offered.

"I agree." I stuffed my hands into the pockets of my combat pants. "If they see us as evil beings, they might become set on finding and destroying us all. Right now, they're just curious. *Stupidly* curious."

"Quite right. It is imperative that every last tainted vampire is destroyed," stressed Antonio, his gaze intense. "If not, The Call will continue to spread and soon enough we will have another situation like this on our hands. I know it feels wrong, in a sense, to kill them.

But we have tried to find some way of helping them and we have had no success. And there are so very many of them. The best thing we can do for them is end their suffering." Antonio's gaze danced from me to Jared. "I would like to send you, your squad, and another six squads along with their commanders. I am not taking any chances this time."

"Ava and Cristiano will insist on going," Luther pointed out.

It was clear that the idea troubled Antonio, but he shrugged. "It would be unfair to request that they remain behind when they wish to avenge what has happened to their friends. We all know a little about the need for vengeance. If they wish to take the risk of being attacked and tainted, we must respect that." Turning his attention back to Jared and me, he spoke. "I want you and your squad to concentrate on freeing the vampires that have been captured."

I rolled my eyes. "You mean you don't want us fighting the tainted again because some of us were bitten last time."

"True. But my decision is also based on the fact that your squad is, by far, the stealthiest. All your practice on the tactical field has helped tremendously with that. You have members that can get in and out of places without being seen. You also have members that are deadly enough to kill a tainted vampire without even touching them – both of you included. You are, without a doubt, the best people to deal with this side of the assignment."

Jared nodded. "Where *exactly* are they within the rainforest? I don't want to waste time searching."

Antonio handed him a slip of paper. "According to one of Quentin's vampires who has the ability to teleport, these exact coordinates will take you one hundred feet from the humans' camp." Once Jared had tucked the paper into the pocket of his jeans, Antonio added, "He and Quentin will be waiting for you there."

"You should leave as soon as possible." Luther's anxiety was obvious in every line of his face. "We are not sure how much longer the humans will wait around."

In total agreement with that, I slipped my hand in Jared's and he immediately teleported us both to the arena. Since we had only minutes ago tanked ourselves with NSTs, we didn't need to make a pit-stop at our apartment.

As usual, the squad was patiently waiting for us in the arena. Thankfully, nobody was late because we didn't have time to hang around, and we still needed to find Ava and Cristiano to give them the option of coming along. We quickly briefed the squad on the situation. It was no surprise when they began cursing at the news of the humans being involved, but they were raring to go. No doubt feelings of helplessness had been plaguing them just as they had been plaguing myself and Jared. This assignment meant that they were doing *something*.

"Ava and Cristiano will want in," said Denny. "After seeing Ava so distraught when she heard the vampires from her nest were dead, I don't think it would be fair to leave her or her brother out of it." Salem didn't appear happy about that, but he said nothing.

"We plan to take them," I told Denny. "I don't suppose anyone knows where they are?"

"They're with Jude and Alora in the canteen," Chico said. Alora and Jude had immediately 'clicked' – probably because they both knew what it was like to live without someone that meant everything to them. I knew from Chico that Jude had tracked down her baby just to check on her. The little girl had been adopted by a really nice human family, so at least Jude had that knowledge as comfort – however little comfort that may be.

"When do we leave?"

Frowning at that, everyone spun to look at the beady-eyed male who was tucking his notepad and pen into his coat, ready to go.

"*You're* not going anywhere," I firmly stated to both Collins and a half-naked Eloise, who was licking her lips as she eyed Jared. No shame. She had absolutely no shame.

Collins lifted his chin. "Our purpose here—"

"Seems to be purely to be a pain in our asses," finished Damien. Collins flushed, shrinking under the disapproval of the squad.

"Haven't we been through this once before?" Eloise huffed, bored. "We must accompany you on assignments in order to accurately complete our report. We did so last time, and we will do so this time."

I really didn't have the patience to deal with either of them right now. I took a calming, steadying breath. It didn't help much. "We allowed you both to come with us when we spoke to Quentin Foy because there was minimal danger involved. This assignment is totally the opposite."

"Which supports the complaint that you take your squad on very risky missions," Collins said with a smug grin.

"I was just about to say the same thing." Eloise was wearing a similar smirk.

I could only shake my head at them. "It's pathetic that you think we have time for this crap." With that, I gave them both my back and marched out of the arena with Jared at my side. Everybody followed as we made our way to the canteen. Unfortunately, that included Collins and Eloise. *I won't set them on fire. I won't set them on fire. I won't, I won't.* But I'd dream about it.

Collins hurried to my side, breathless as he attempted to match my pace. "Commander Parker, it is important that I—"

"Back off, Collins," Jared ground out. "We're not taking you or your colleague on this assignment. Deal with it."

The bloke honestly looked like he was chewing on a bee or something. "I will be forced to contact my superiors—"

I smiled. "Good idea. Tell them I said 'hi'."

He gasped in outrage. "Commander Parker!"

Ignoring his rant, I entered the canteen. The purpose in my strides made Ava, Cristiano, Jude, and Alora instantly tense.

Cristiano stood. "What's happening?" I swiftly gave them a rundown on everything.

"I'm coming," both Ava and Cristiano declared in unison. Salem scowled at her for that, but Ava gave him a cute smile and patted his chest.

"I'm coming, too," stated Jude, rising from her seat. When Chico went to object, she added, "It's possible that a human will spot one of you. Wouldn't it be a lot easier to wipe their memory than kill them?" Jude's gift would enable us to do that. She was only able to delete twenty minutes worth of memory, but that would be enough.

Alora got to her feet. "I want to come too. Like I said, I need to do *something*." When I hesitated to respond, she said, "You'll be surprised what a substantial gift communicating with animals can be – they can tell us things that we wouldn't otherwise know. It helped when The Hollow was attacked by Bennington and his supporters."

Jared sighed. "Your mind isn't in the best state, Alora. I don't need someone there who's going to take unnecessary risks. Been there. Done that."

"I won't. I promise." She softly chuckled, though there wasn't much humour there. "Believe me when I say that I want to live, and I won't be leaving this life without kicking and screaming."

After a brief silence, Jared spoke again. "Any rashness from you and you'll be teleported out of there. And I mean that. I hesitated with Evan. I won't make the same mistake again. Got it?"

Alora saluted him. "Got it."

"If these people are all going, there is absolutely no reason why Eloise and I cannot be taken along." Collins' superior, haughty, I-get-to-do-whatever-I-want-and-you-will-obey-me tone grated on every nerve I had.

"Oh there's an extremely good reason," I told him in a menacing voice, invading his personal space. The snooty tosser immediately backed up. "As you repeatedly state, you're both observers here. Everyone on this assignment will be expected to protect themselves and the people around them. Passive people will simply get hurt. And if you think I'll be held responsible for anything that happens to you or Aphrodite here, you're very wrong. Besides, I only take along people who I trust to watch my back and the backs of those around me. I certainly don't trust either of you, which means *you're staying behind*. As Jared said, deal with it."

Collins looked ready to explode, but then he sniffed arrogantly and adjusted his tie. "Fine. I must warn you that I'll be making a note of this in my report."

"Ooh, a note? I'm trembling in my trainers. Note *that* as well."

Laughing, Jared gripped my hand. Taking his cue, everyone grabbed hold of one another and he teleported us all out of there, happily leaving behind a flushed Collins and a snarling Eloise.

CHAPTER TEN

(Sam)

Quentin and the bald, stocky vampire beside him jerked back in surprise as we all appeared in front of where they were crouched low in the rainforest. Quentin seemed a mixture of relieved and invigorated at the sight of us. After we had all exchanged nods of greeting, he gestured to the bloke with him. "This is one of my vampires, Gio."

Jared was immediately all business. "What are we dealing with?"

Quentin pointed to the camp that was set up a hundred feet away. Our vampire enhanced vision meant that we could see it quite clearly. "From what we've been able to gather, there are approximately sixty-eight to seventy humans remaining in total – almost all of those are roaming the village and the surrounding area, hunting vampires. The rest of the humans are based in this area. I didn't want to launch an attack until I had your back up."

"Actually, there won't be an attack. We have a new plan." I relayed our conversation with Antonio. "As such, the new objective is to kill every last tainted vampire *but* to allow the humans to live."

Quentin looked extremely disappointed, which was no surprise given that these humans had sedated and captured some of his vampires. "What about the captives? One of them is my brother. I want him out of there."

"We'll deal with the vampires that are being held captive," Jared told him, perfectly understanding Quentin's distress. "Is your brother tainted?"

"No, but the others are."

"Then we'll get your brother out," I assured him. "But the tainted will be destroyed – only the untainted prisoners will be freed, I'm sorry."

Sad but resigned, Quentin nodded. "I understand."

"In order to free them, we plan to not be seen or heard by the humans. Providing the other humans don't make their way back to camp, there's no reason that it shouldn't be possible."

Quentin frowned thoughtfully. "I'm assuming it would help if we distracted the roaming humans and led them even further away?"

"Yes." Jared glanced at the camp. "If the other humans return, everything could go to shit. Disable them if you need to, but do not attack them."

"One of my vampires can induce sleep, and another can cause hallucinations – those gifts in particular would help here."

Resolve blazing in his eyes, Cristiano spoke. "I want to go with Quentin." He needed his revenge, I understood.

"Me too," declared Ava.

When Salem growled, I shook my head at him and spoke quietly. "It's her choice. She and her brother need this. It's the only reason they've come." His response was a grunt.

Jared spoke to Quentin. "While some of you concentrate on distracting the humans and leading them away, the rest of you need to silently hunt every tainted vampire before the humans can gain possession of them."

Chico rubbed at his nape. "I'm surprised they aren't senselessly attacking."

Quentin grumbled, "They're hiding – their primal instinct for survival has taken over; with no rational thoughts, instincts are all they have now. Once you've freed my brother, I'd like it if you could bring him here. Gio will be waiting for you once he's teleported me to the others."

I gave him a nod. "Good luck hunting."

Quentin grinned as he stood. "Good luck creeping."

"You all take care," said Ava, her gaze lingering on Salem. Cristiano just nodded at us.

"You too," I said simply. Once Quentin, Gio, Cristiano, and Ava teleported away, I turned to the others. "Damien, I want to know where every single guard in this camp is situated." Stuart would have been a great help here; I keenly felt his absence. "Denny, we need to know exactly how many humans are in that tent and what kind of weapons they have."

"*And* exactly how many vampires are being held in the vehicle," added Jared. "I don't want to teleport in there without being prepared. The second the tainted know they have company they'll most likely cause a racket. We don't need that."

Denny swiftly but silently advanced fifty feet through the forest before reducing himself to a puddle of goo and quickly slid toward the camp. Damien stilled and bowed his head, and I knew he had gone astral travelling to gather the information we needed.

"I was expecting to find myself in the middle of a war zone." Chico scanned his surroundings warily. "The place is quiet." He shot an anxious look at Jude, who was crouched beside him.

"Yeah," agreed Butch, "*unnaturally quiet*. Even worse than when we went to the tunnels."

Harvey swatted at a mosquito. "This kind of reminds me of our tactical training field. You know, being an abandoned village that's deathly silent."

Jared's mouth twisted. "Then think of this as what we've practiced a million times during training – moving quickly but silently, and remaining out of sight."

Alora hugged herself, rubbing her upper arms. "I hope Ava will be okay."

Jude seemed just as anxious. "She's just so tiny."

"Ava can take care of herself, believe me." Feeling Dexter's cautiousness, I almost smiled. His constant presence was a comfort, even when he was in tattoo form.

Suddenly Damien's head lifted and he took a long breath.

"You okay?" Reuben asked him.

"Yeah, fine." Damien turned to me and Jared. "There are fourteen guards in total. Six are patrolling the camp. Four are guarding the tent. And another four are guarding the vehicle containing the cages. Every last one of them is vigilant. They clearly know it's in their best interests to be alert. They know what they're dealing with."

Jared cocked his head. "Vigilant and nervous, or vigilant and confident?" There was a distinct difference. One meant that they might easily panic and that their 'flight' instinct would make them hesitate. The other meant that they were psychologically prepared and wouldn't hesitate to act.

"The patrollers and the ones guarding the vehicle look alert but spooked. The others are pretty confident – even seem a little high on adrenaline."

Jared went to speak again but was distracted as a puddle of goo slithering toward us. It quickly reformed into Denny.

He shook himself a little. "There are five humans inside the tent. They're definitely military, and they're armed with shit that I didn't even know existed."

Damien nodded. "The guards – particularly the patrollers – are well-armed too. I don't even know what it is they're carrying. I did identify smoke bombs and tranquiliser guns, though."

"Nineteen humans in total, then." I pursed my lips. "Not too high a number."

"How about inside the vehicle?" Jared asked Denny.

"There are ten captives," replied Denny. "There are four of Quentin's vampires in there – only one is untainted, and he's out cold. I'm assuming he's Quentin's brother. The other six are from Commander Rodney's squad and, thankfully, they're just injured and knocked out."

His face a mask of absolute determination, Jared spoke. "Okay. First we need to disable the six patrollers. Chico, Salem, David – that's where you guys come in. I don't want Reuben to strengthen your gifts while you deal with the humans. All I need is for them to be out cold for a while. Afterwards, you hide the patrollers in the trees." Without hesitation, they slinked away – splitting up and heading in different direction to target the guards.

"It's weird being on an assignment that doesn't involve torturing anyone," commented Butch after a full minute of silence. Typical. It was looking more and more like the sociopath theory might be accurate.

Harvey snickered. "Yeah. It's always cool watching Coach frighten the shit out of people with her whip. Sexy as hell, too. Ow!" He scowled at Jared for cuffing him over the head.

Reuben shook his head at Harvey. "It wouldn't be so bad if you did that purely to irritate Commander Michaels like Max and Damien do" – Damien smiled at that – "but no, you do it because you don't have the sense to keep your mouth zipped. It's seriously worrying." Denny, Jude, and Alora chuckled quietly.

Just then, Chico, Salem, and David returned. Chico dusted his hands. "Done. We hid in the same spot so it'll be easier to keep watch over them."

Satisfied, I nodded. "Then let's move on to the next stage of the plan: getting to the captives. Chico, I need the humans guarding the vehicle out of the equation – I don't want them responding to any noises they hear inside it. But don't move until I give my signal."

"Sure thing, Coach."

"What about the humans guarding the tent and the people inside it?" David asked me.

"Providing they remain where they are, there's no need for us to even so much as breathe in their direction." I could only hope that things ran that smoothly. "Chico, Harvey, Jude, Alora – keep watch over them. If any of them head toward the vehicle or they realise that the patrollers are down, telepath Jared straight away. If too many of them head for us, then I'll need Chico to put them asleep for a while. Harvey, you use your telekinesis to help hold them back and give Chico time to target them all."

"What about us?" Reuben gestured from him to Damien.

"I need you both to keep an eye on the unconscious patrollers. If they look to be waking, contact Jared immediately."

"My gift can help here," said Alora. "I can ask the local wildlife to give me warnings if more humans approach and to keep them distracted for us. They'll act as my eyes and ears."

"That would help a great deal." Jared pointed from David to Salem. "I need you both to act swiftly once I teleport you and Sam inside that vehicle. We don't want the tainted having a chance to react to our presence. That means we destroy them as quickly as possible. In order for you to do that, you'll need Reuben to strengthen your gifts."

As soon as Reuben had done his thing, I spoke. "Chico, the second you've disabled the humans guarding the vehicle, telepath Jared." He saluted me. "Now everyone move into position." Everybody other than David and Salem silently slunk away, seeming to almost melt into their surroundings.

Fidgeting as usual, David shuddered. "Is it me, or does this just seem too easy?"

Jared's brow furrowed. "You think it's a trap?"

David shook his head. "It just feels like...I don't know...like fate's being a little too helpful. And that's always odd."

Salem shrugged. "Don't forget, we're dealing with humans here. It's bound to be easier."

"I guess you're right."

Jared nudged me. "Chico just contacted me. The guards are out cold."

"Then we move." As Jared teleported us inside the vehicle, the smell of rotten fish hit me so hard I felt dizzy, but I didn't have time to even balk. Instantly, we targeted the tainted. I took out one with an energy ball to the chest, Salem destroyed one with his lethal psychic punch, and David delivered a psionic boom to the third vampire's brain. Like that, they were all ashes. It was clear that Jared was disappointed not to be able to kill one, but his gift of electrokinesis could be pretty noisy and we couldn't risk him alerting anyone.

Salem assessed the mess of broken cages and the small puddles of blood. "You can see where some of the vampires escaped and attacked."

Jared's face scrunched up in distaste. "According to Antonio, the tainted Pagoris got free and killed many of the humans. Come on, let's get these guys out of here."

He tugged on the door of the cage that was holding one of Rodney's squad. The sedated Keja didn't even stir. Due to the strength of the lock, it took the combined efforts of Jared and me to break open the cage. David and Salem worked as a team to free three of the others while Jared and I helped the remaining two. None of the injured woke, though a few of them made low moaning sounds that seemed more like yells in the silence of the vehicle. Thankfully, there was no contact from any of our squad, so that had to mean that the humans hadn't heard anything.

After teleporting Quentin's brother to Gio, Jared moved Rodney's squad members in two trips; placing them with Butch, Reuben, and Damien. In the meantime, Salem, David, and I concentrated on destroying any evidence in the vehicle. Sure it was fair to note that the humans clearly already had some, but why give them more?

No sooner had a tingle of apprehension crept up on me through my bond with Jared than he appeared before me, his expression dark and anxious. I stiffened. "What's wrong?"

He grabbed my arm. "We have to get out of here *now*."

"What? Why?"

"Apparently the animals alerted Alora that humans are approaching; they sent her pictures of them coming from every direction."

Fucking fabulous. "They know we're here?"

"No. Chico said someone in the tent was talking over a radio a few minutes ago but he hadn't been able to make out what was said. Now he's thinking that the humans had ordered all their hunters to return to camp. I don't know if they're planning to leave or what, but we need to move because I don't have any intention of getting shot by a tranquiliser. I told Chico to take the others to where Butch, Reuben, and Damien are waiting with Rodney's squad members so I can teleport them all in one swoop. I'm going to teleport you three back to The Hollow first and then go back for—"

"No. I won't leave until my squad is *out*. Besides, I have a little more evidence here to get rid of. Teleport to the others and take them back first."

He growled, "Fuck, Sam."

"Do it. We don't have time to argue."

"Pain in my goddamn Pagori ass," he muttered before disappearing.

Thirty seconds later, we'd destroyed the last of the evidence. I turned to David and Salem. "Come on. Staying in the vehicle won't be the best idea."

"Where are we going?" asked David, following me as I quietly scampered to the double doors at the back of the vehicle.

"The trees," guessed Salem, knowing exactly how my mind worked. Rainforest trees were good for hiding in.

"Yes." Carefully and quietly I swung the door open...and was knocked flat on my back as a skeletal, grotesque-looking Keja dived on me and clamped his teeth around my throat. *Well, fuck.* I didn't even have time to defend myself before it burst into ashes, thanks to either David or Salem – I wasn't sure. They were both at my side at the exact same time that Jared teleported in front of me, clearly having felt my pain through the bond.

He blanched. "Oh, fuck no."

It was my own bloody fault. I'd had everyone concentrating so hard on the humans, trusting Quentin and the others to deal with all the tainted vampires. I should have known better than to take it for granted that we were completely safe from them. Jared immediately dragged me against him and took me to The Hollow. It was lucky that David and Salem were holding onto me or Jared might have absentmindedly left them behind in his haste to get me home.

Arriving in the infirmary, Jared laid me down on one of the beds.

"No, baby, no – this can't be fucking happening." He clasped his hands behind his head, staring down at me in pure disbelief.

A good-natured Keja who liked to act as a nurse – apparently letting go of her human profession had been hard – rushed over with a towel. Salem snatched it from her and pressed it firmly against the bite wound on my throat. Following that, he immediately called Antonio using the infirmary phone. The rest of the squad – who had clearly arrived there with Rodney's injured squad members and were supportively remaining at their side – surrounded my bed. They cursed, growled, gawked, and hit me with questions that I was too distracted to answer. Fuck, the bite was itching like crazy and it was taking everything I had not to scratch it. Was it supposed to itch? I didn't recall Evan, Max, or Stuart reporting that.

The nurse, Mary Jane, repeatedly tried to squeeze through the boys to reach me, but they weren't budging. I internally shrugged. It wasn't like there was anything she could do to help me anyway.

David swallowed hard. "Coach…Shit, I feel like I tempted fate."

"This is no one's fault but my own for concentrating too much on the humans."

He knotted his hands in his tousled hair. "We should have sensed that vampire out there."

"If we hadn't already been surrounded by the scent of rotten fish, we would have done."

"You just wouldn't let me teleport you home, would you?" Jared took to pacing beside my bed, which was why people were giving him a wide berth. This was what Jared did whenever I got hurt. Took it out on me. Yes, it was unfair. But logic never prevailed over his panic and fear. I was used to it at this point. "You just had to wait until the others were safe."

"Yes, I did. And I'd make the same decision again." That was clearly the wrong thing to say, despite that it was the truth, because everyone looked ready to explode at me. "You can lecture me about it later." I went to sit up, but Jared pushed me back down.

"No, don't move."

"Why? Lying here isn't going to make any difference. And it's not like there's anything anyone can do. The only thing to do now is—"

Jared's eyes flared with rage, his irises glowing like lasers. "*Don't* ask me to lock you up in a fucking cell!"

"You want me to attack people and let the taint spread, is that it?"

"And you'd be perfectly fine with confining me in a glass cage, would you?"

"Well of course not," I snapped. "But what else do you expect me to—" I double-blinked as there was a whizz of movement through the doors and suddenly Antonio was beside me. Clearly he'd used vampire momentum to get here.

He looked distraught. "Sam, how did this happen?"

"How do you think it happened?" Jared snorted. "She did what she always does. She put herself in the line of fire. If she had just let me teleport her out of there when I suggested it, she—"

"I've told you, *you can lecture me later*." I returned my attention to Antonio. "I need to know something. Will Jared become tainted too because of our bond?"

"No." Antonio sighed, his voice low and filled with regret. "But he will gradually deteriorate and weaken as you do. Then when you die, he will die also."

Fuck, fuck, fuckety, fuck.

"Let me take a look at the bite." Antonio gently eased back the towel. The combination of horror, repugnance, and confusion in his expression made my stomach plummet. "David, I need a wet pad to clean the wound."

In vampire speed, David was back with the pad. "Here."

"Thank you." Each gentle dab only made the wound itchier. It was driving me bloody mental and I had to ball my fists to keep from clawing at it. When Antonio was done, he gasped. David's mouth fell open. The others had similar reactions.

Oh God, now what?

"What's wrong?" Jared cupped my chin, turned my head, and leaned over to get a good look. "It's almost fully healed," he said incredulously.

"But not in a good way," warned Antonio.

I frowned. "How can it be bad if I'm healed?"

Antonio's gaze darted from me to Jared. "This is something we need to discuss in private."

So this was related to my hybrid status, then. Well there was no way he could clear the room, since the injured were being tended to here.

"Then we talk alone," Jared stated. Understanding, Antonio held onto my hand while Jared lifted me into his arms. Then suddenly we were in our apartment and Jared was positioning me on the sofa.

I tried to sit up, but he urged me to lie back down. Huffing, I humoured him.

"Now what did you mean?" Jared asked Antonio, keeping his hand on my shoulder.

"Do you remember how swiftly Sam healed during her duel with Magda? She had gaping holes in her shoulders—"

"Thanks for the reminder," I grumbled.

"You shut up," Jared said, but his tone was surprisingly gentle despite the anger surging through him.

"My point is that she healed unnaturally fast, which we all attribute to her being a hybrid. Vampires have accelerated healing, but if our injuries are quite severe, we can take hours to fully heal. In the case of The Call, the bite marks worsen. They do not heal at all. As you can see, Sam's wound has closed. But the teeth marks remain, and they look ugly and angry."

"Ugly?" I echoed. "Someone get me a mirror. I want to know what all the fuss is about." Truthfully, I wasn't as calm as I sounded. But if I was to express my panic, it would feed Jared's fear and make him ten times worse. When no one moved, I pressed, "A mirror!"

Cursing, Jared disappeared into the bedroom. He was back at my side in a blink with my handheld mirror. At the same time, there was a knock at the door.

"That will be my guards. I lost them in my haste to get to Sam." It turned out that Antonio was right. The guards entered with Luther and the pit-bulls in tow.

Jared arched a brow at Luther. "You didn't foresee this happening?" The Advisor had been known to keep things to himself for fear of altering a person's path too much.

Grim, Luther shook his head. "Believe me, this is not something that I would have kept from you. In fact, I would have locked her away myself to keep her safe."

Any other time, I might have scowled at him for that comment. But I was too busy panicking about the bite mark on my throat. Dear God, it looked disgusting. Just as Antonio had said, the mark was in fact seriously ugly. Although the skin had healed, it was in a weird zigzag fashion, like someone had done a really bad stitching job. Furthermore, the patch of skin around it was blotchy and a blazing red. "All right," I said shakily, placing the mirror on the coffee table.

"What does this mean?"

"I can only speculate, because I have never seen this happen before." Antonio sighed. "But it seems to me that although the skin has strangely closed, your system is tainted."

That was my guess as well. I swallowed hard. "You know what needs to be done."

"We're not locking her up," Jared quickly and vehemently stated.

Luther laid a supportive hand on Jared's shoulder. "I hate to agree with her, Jared, I truly hate it. I do not like the idea of her caged any more than you do. But it is important that she is isolated."

He shook off Luther's hand and stepped away. Denial was pasted all over his face. "She can't pass it on unless she bites someone."

"She might lose rationality quicker than the others did," Antonio cautioned in a sensitive tone. "She's a hybrid, Jared. We have no idea how she will react to The Call. But we do know that she will not survive it," he added in a low voice that was loaded with anguish. The resolve in Jared's expression didn't even slightly lessen.

"Can you give us a few minutes alone?" I asked Antonio and Luther.

Antonio nodded. "Certainly. I will make the appropriate preparations." In other words, he'd ready me a cell.

Once Jared and I were alone, I sat up and appealed to him with a look. "I know it's hard for you to do this. But I don't want to hurt someone. I don't want to taint someone. Please don't put me in a position where I might do that. It's bad enough that I know you're going to die because of me."

He snickered, but his anger was gone now. There was only a sense of defeat. "You think I'd want to live without you? You think I even could, whether we were Bound or not?"

A lump of emotion suddenly clogged my throat and my eyes filled. "I'm so sorry."

He crouched down in front of me and tucked my hair behind my ear. "We knew when we Bound in that ceremony that it would mean we depended on each other to live. I don't regret it, and I'd make that commitment all over again."

"Then you're a dumb prat."

He swiped my tears away with the pads of his thumbs. "And you're a crazy bitch."

I gently curled my hands around his wrists. "You have to let them confine me, Jared."

"Sam, don't—"

"I need to be sure that I can't hurt anyone. I'd have to go in it sooner or later anyway. It might as well be sooner." Shuddering at the prickly itch tormenting me, I released his wrist and went to rake my nails over the skin. Jared snatched my hand and kissed my palm.

"Don't scratch it. I can *feel* how much it's driving you crazy."

My guess was that it would get worse the longer I was tainted. "Take me to the cell. Please."

Squeezing his eyes shut, he rested his forehead against mine. "Baby..." His panic, fear, and devastation were zooming through me, swarming me, stealing my breath. There was even an element of guilt there – typical.

"You're not at fault," I insisted. It didn't seem to make any difference.

After a series of deep breaths, he rose to his feet and stared down at me through tormented eyes. I thought he'd scoop me up and take me to the cells. Instead, he retrieved his cell phone from the table and punched in some keys. Seconds later, he was speaking in a defeated yet resigned voice. "Call Sebastian. Tell him to bring Paige West here."

Oh.

CHAPTER ELEVEN

(Jared)

Standing outside the glass cell, having that impenetrable barrier between Sam and I that even my gift of teleporting couldn't breach, felt so damn wrong that my stomach was twisting painfully. The idea that I couldn't reach her if I wanted to was like a lead weight in my gut, because I already knew that feeling. It brought back all the fear and panic from the time the Trent brothers had taken her from me – as if I wasn't panicking enough right now.

She just sat on the mattress with her head resting against the glass and her legs pulled up to her chest with one arm wrapped around them. Her aquamarine eyes were holding mine and pleading with me. Not to help her, but to stop feeling guilty. Maybe she was right and it was dumb to blame myself for this. But if I had just ignored her stupid insistence on waiting for the squad to be out of there before leaving, she'd be fine right now. Of course I knew deep down that putting the squad's safety before her own was what any commander would have done. Hell, I'd have done it. But I was still angry at both of us.

I had agreed to isolate Sam from everyone while I dealt with Paige West – whenever the hell she arrived – because I knew that Sam needed the peace of mind that she couldn't harm anyone. Midway through the process of becoming a hybrid, there had been an incident when she had lost all sense of rationality and dived on me, latching onto my throat – much like a newborn vampire would. That loss of control, that knowledge that she had hurt me, had never sat well with her. If she did it again now, she wouldn't just hurt someone, she would taint them. So, yeah, I definitely understood why she didn't want to take any chances here. Still, if I hadn't known that confining her like this was only a temporary measure, I probably wouldn't have agreed to it.

Movement in the cell beside hers caught my attention: Evan was staggering across the room with the most agonising look on his face. How must it feel to literally starve, to feel as your body withered away? How must it feel to sense you were beginning to lose reason and rationality? Max and Stuart looked in much the same agony. There was nothing left of *them* there. They were all just shells now. Droning, skeletal, starving shells. It was fucking…Shit, there were no words to describe what it felt like to see the two people that I loved most in the world dying.

I wanted to hit something, smash something, wanted to rage at fate – it truly was a bitch. Instead, I placed the palm of my hand against the glass of Sam's cell. Reaching over, she splayed her hand over mine. I hated that I couldn't touch her when it was the one thing I needed right then, hated that I couldn't comfort her. Whether Sam would admit it aloud or not, she was scared. "You'll be out of there soon," I promised her. "Paige's gift will heal you."

Her smile was sad. "I hope you're right."

I *had* to be right, otherwise I'd agreed for that female to be brought to The Hollow – thus chancing Luther's vision coming true – for no damn good reason at all. But Paige coming here didn't have to mean that the vision *would* become reality, I mused. The things Luther foresaw didn't always happen, as I knew perfectly well. If we took precautions by getting the female out of here as quickly as possible, we could prevent anything more from happening. It was hardly likely that she would want to stick around here for long anyway, not if she was so set on being away from the rest of her kind.

Hearing voices, I glanced at the door. Not only was Antonio, Luther, and the guards here, but also the squad, Jude, Ava, Cristiano, and – oh shit – Alora. Evan was going to have my balls for this if – no, *when* – Paige healed him. As Alora caught sight of Evan, her now horrified eyes instantly watered and she slapped a hand over her mouth. How much she cared for him was flashing on her face like a neon sign. Evan briefly glanced at the crowd, but there was no sign of recognition in his eyes.

Antonio gave me a sympathetic smile. "Sebastian has arrived with Miss West and who seems to be a friend of hers. Apparently Miss West refused to leave without her. They are waiting for you in the piano room. You should know that she has no idea why she has been brought here. Sebastian worried that if he told her what we wanted from her, she would put up a huge fight. He merely told her that she had been sent for by you and he assured her that she would come to no harm whatsoever."

Dropping my hand from the glass, I told Sam, "I'll be back soon."

She nodded, giving me a half-smile.

Leaving her felt wrong, but I forced myself to step away from the cell. I was just about to teleport out of there when I noticed that Cristiano had separated himself from the crowd and was leaning against the back wall; the expression on his face stopped me short. He wasn't looking at me, but at Sam. Like the others, he was clearly distressed and angered by what had happened to her. But there was so much more to be seen on his face: pain, anguish, yearning, and utter despair. Slowly, I walked over to him. "That's why you never went to the Binding ceremony. You love her, don't you?"

My voice seemed to snap him out of whatever zone he had been in. His gaze met mine. As my words filtered through, he sighed and returned his eyes to Sam. "I accepted a long time ago that I'd never have her. Victor hadn't allowed me or anyone else to touch her. But even if he had, she'd never looked at me that way. Not once. Not even the night I kissed her when she was human. But just because I accepted that I'd never have her didn't mean I could watch her Bind with someone else."

Oddly, I felt a twinge of sympathy for him. I wasn't a particularly sympathetic person, but I knew that if *I'd* had to see Sam with someone else, it would have destroyed me.

"Do you know what's strange? The fact that I've drank from her actually makes it worse. I know *exactly* what I'm missing." His eyes returned to me. "So as much as you think I'm smug that I've tasted her, you couldn't be more wrong. It would be a hell of a lot easier if I didn't know what I *could* have had if things had been different." He swallowed hard. "You make sure you save her. I'd rather watch her with someone else than watch her die."

"So would I." And that proved just how important she was to me, because I wasn't the self-sacrificing type. Without another word to anyone, I teleported to the ground floor of the mansion and appeared outside the piano room. Opening the double doors wide, I strode inside. In addition to Sebastian and three guards were too dark-haired females, but that was where the similarities ended for the two women. One was tall and lithe with blazing green eyes while the other was short and curvy with brown doe eyes.

The tall brunette stood slightly in front of the other female – a protective move. I recalled what Antonio had said about Paige refusing to leave her friend behind, which suggested that the protective vampire was Paige West. I thought the 'keep the fuck back' body language was kind of odd. Did she think I wanted her friend for some reason?

"You're the Heir," Paige realised. Her protective stance didn't ease. In fact, it turned aggressive, but she made no move toward me.

"I am."

"Well if you're going to hurt me, let's go," she dared tauntingly.

"So you can give your injury to me? No thanks. In any case, I have no intention of harming you…or your friend, if that's your worry."

Her eyes narrowed suspiciously. "Then why did you have someone track us down?"

"Not both of you, just you. I need your healing skills."

She blinked in surprise. "I'm not a healer."

"But your gift *does* heal, in a sense, doesn't it?"

"Yes," she eventually allowed.

"That's why you've been brought here."

She was silent for a moment. "You just want me to heal someone for you? That's it?" Her tone was sceptical.

"Not just one, there are four."

She snickered. "And then you'll hand me over to my Sire or, worse, execute me for whatever it is that he's accused me of doing so that people will hunt me down."

"I have no interest in anything that has happened between you or your Sire."

"You're the Heir. It's part of your job to ensure that justice is found."

"Right now, I'm not talking to you as the Heir. I'm talking to you as someone whose mate is so badly hurt, she's dying." Her friend gasped. "If you can heal her injury and that of the others, your crimes – whatever they are – will be instantly pardoned."

Paige cocked her head, assessing me carefully. "If I heal them, you'll let us leave? *Both* of us?"

"Yes. You have my word on that."

Still seeming suspicious, she let her gaze dance from me to Sebastian and back again. After a moment of silence, she gave a curt nod. "Okay. I'll help them. But Imani stays with me – I don't want her leaving my side."

"Fine."

My disinterest in separating them appeared to surprise Paige. It also made her relax her stance slightly. "Good. I guess you better take me to them then so we can get this over with."

I couldn't have agreed more. The quicker I got everyone healed, the quicker I could get both of these females out of The Hollow before any shit had the chance to hit the fan. Sebastian gently took Paige's arm, who quickly clasped Imani's hand, and teleported them away. I immediately followed, appearing outside the row of cells beneath the mansion. Paige was regarding the crowd of people warily while gripping Imani's hand tightly.

"Everyone, move side," I ordered. Obediently, the crowd parted, which then allowed Paige a clear view of what was inside the cells.

She gaped. "You said they were *injured.*"

I jiggled my head. "I may have downplayed the matter slightly."

"Slightly? These people are tainted with The Call! I can't help them."

"Sure you can. If you take away their injury and their pain, you should automatically take away the taint."

"They'll attack me the second I go near them. Thanks, but I kind of like being alive."

I pointed to the three droning males. "See the guy chewing on his mattress? That's my twin brother, Evan. It's kind of hard to tell that we're even related when he looks like that, huh? The other two are members of my squad, Max and Stuart." Maybe if I made her see them as people, it would help. I walked to where Sam still sat; her aquamarine eyes glimmering with a contradictory mixture of sadness and hope. "And this is my mate, Sam."

"I've heard about her," Imani said softly. "You were Bound recently, weren't you?"

"Yes."

"And if she dies, you die too," mused Paige. The implication that it was only my own ass I was bothered about saving was clear in her voice.

"That's right, I do, but it's her life I'm more interested in saving."

Paige rested her hands on her hips, blowing out a long breath. "Look, I'm sorry that they're all sick, okay. I really am. But I can't—"

"We have ways of holding them still so that they can't hurt you," I quickly assured her. "All you need to do is touch them."

"I could be tainted!"

"*Only* if they bite you. They won't be able to do that because they'll be unconscious. And even if they do bite you, you can simply pass that injury back to them." I took a step toward her, too frantic with worry to keep calm any longer. "Maybe you're right and you can't help them, I don't know. But you have nothing to lose by trying. I have *everything* to lose by you not trying."

"You really love her," whispered Imani, sounding shocked.

Yeah it probably was surprising to see that the big, bad Heir who they had undoubtedly heard plenty of dark shit about actually felt something for another person. "More than anything," I confirmed.

Imani tugged on Paige's hand. "Help them."

Paige was quiet for a minute, seemingly torn. I was pretty sure that everyone was holding their breath. "I have a condition."

Okay, I could negotiate. "What condition is that?"

"You give Imani and me refuge in The Hollow. Permanently."

My eyes closed as desolation hit me. If I agreed to her condition, Luther's vision could come into effect. Through the bond, I felt Sam's anxiety.

"We've been hiding for a long time," continued Paige. "We want to *live* again."

While that was understandable, she truly had no idea what she was asking. Of course I could explain Luther's vision, but that would likely make Paige demand to leave immediately – especially since she seemed to be so protective of her friend. She was scared of something, and she looked ready to bolt any second.

"It is your choice, Jared," said Antonio. But it wasn't really a choice at all. There was no way I could turn Paige down. I'd exhausted every other avenue – she was the only chance we had left to save Sam and the guys.

I sighed inwardly, turning to the crowd. "Harvey, I'll need you to hold the guys into position while David and Salem put them to sleep." Swallowing hard, I told Paige, "I'll grant you refuge if you heal the four of them."

When Paige hesitated, Antonio spoke. "Jared would never back out of a vow."

After an encouraging look from Imani, Paige nodded. "I'll need someone to transfer the taint to."

Ava clasped her hands together. "Ooh, can we use Collins?" She truly looked excited by the prospect. Salem snickered.

"Unfortunately, no," replied Antonio. "I have prisoners that have been here for some time who can take on the taint."

"You haven't executed them?" Paige asked him.

Antonio's smile was a little on the evil side. "Why would I do that when it would make their punishment be over quickly?"

"Ah." There was a wealth of nervousness in that sound. Paige cleared her throat. "Do you have four prisoners?"

"One will not be enough?"

"When I pass on an injury, it's three times worse. In this case, it'll mean the taint will be three times more advanced when the vampire gets it. He'll have to be killed instantly."

"Well then, it is lucky I have four."

I could see that she wanted to ask just how many he did have, but she bit her tongue.

Antonio pressed his hand on the imprint that was situated on the glass door of the cell. The door made a hissing sound as it unlocked, but Antonio didn't open it immediately. "Everyone ready?"

Rolling his shoulders and clearly eager, Harvey said, "Oh yeah." Salem and David simply nodded.

The second Antonio opened the door wide, the three tainted vampires charged. Harvey stepped inside and used his telekinesis to send all three vampires crashing into the back of the cell. While he held them in place, Salem and David then used their gifts to knock each of them unconscious.

"Harvey, don't lose your grip on them." I wasn't taking any chances. Squeezing past him, I walked into the cell. Paige, Imani, and Antonio came in behind me, and were shortly followed by two guards, who were dragging in an unconscious captive. They placed him beneath where Evan was pinned to the wall. I looked at Paige, who was holding her nose. Yeah, the stench was bad. "Ready?"

She answered by walking to Evan and reaching out to lay her hand on the oozing bite mark, balking at the repugnant sight.

When her hand froze in mid-air, I assured her, "Even if he wakes up, he won't be able to move."

Apparently those words satisfied her, because some of the tension left her body and she placed her hand on his throat. What happened next was one of the weirdest things I'd ever seen. It was like something was rippling under her skin, circling her lower arm as it ran from her hand to her elbow. That was when she pulled her hand away and gripped the leg of the unconscious vampire at her feet. The rippling happened again, this time going from her elbow down to her hand and to the now tainted vampire...And it had all happened in a matter of seconds. In a blink, he went from normal to being even more gaunt and skeletal than Evan had been. His eyes snapped open – no rationality there at all – but before he could move, I obliterated him into ashes with a bolt of lightning.

Paige's eyes widened. "Wow. And I thought my gift was awesome." Taking the tissue Antonio offered her, she wiped the disgusting ooze from her hand.

Darting to Evan's side, I could only gawk as I marvelled over the fact that, yep, the bite was gone and the taint had left him. Except for the dark circles under his eyes, he looked totally normal. A lump formed in my throat. Fuck, I'd missed the shithead.

"Is he healed?" Antonio's voice was dripping with anxiousness.

"Yes, some-the-fuck-how, he's okay." Everyone cheered, and I saw Paige flush under the praise that was subsequently thrown at her from the people outside the cell. Knowing that the psychic hit he'd taken to the head would mean Evan would be out cold for a while, I contemplated asking Paige to touch his head and attempt to take away the effects of the hit. But that would mean dragging in a fully aware prisoner to then take on the effects of it – the longer we messed around, the longer Sam would be tainted.

Seemingly reading my mind, Antonio said, "He will be fine in the infirmary until he wakes." Of course I could teleport him there, but I didn't want to leave until Sam was okay.

"I will take him," offered Sebastian as he entered the cell. Flashing Paige a thankful smile, he scooped up Evan and disappeared. The guards then dragged in another two prisoners. Just as with Evan, Paige healed both Max and Stuart by transferring the taint to the unconscious captives, who I then quickly disposed of using my gift.

Afterwards, Sebastian teleported both Max and Stuart to the infirmary.

That was when we exited the cell and moved to Sam's door. She was on her feet now and was leaning against the back wall as if to reassure Paige that she was no threat.

"Sam has only been tainted for a few hours," Antonio told Paige as he unlocked the cell door. "She is still completely rational."

Tell her that if she feels more comfortable with Harvey pinning me in place, it's fine, Sam told me.

"She said that she's happy for Harvey to hold her still using his gift, if you'd prefer that. I won't have anyone knock her unconscious, but I'll agree to her being held in place."

Paige tilted her head. "You can talk to her through your bond?"

"I'm telepathic." Panic flashed across her face. I quickly added, "But I can only read thoughts that are directed at me." She seemed relieved by that, which made me wonder what she was hiding. "Would you rather Sam was held still?"

Paige bit her lip and glimpsed briefly at her friend. I sensed that she was more worried about Imani's safety than her own. There was clearly a story behind that, but it simply wasn't important to me right then. All that mattered was getting Sam healed.

"If it's all the same to you," began Paige, "I'd rather Harvey did his thing."

Hesitantly, Harvey came forward, looking awkward. "You sure you're okay with this, Coach?" It was actually kind of nice that he didn't want to use his gift on her. She nodded and smiled encouragingly at him. As soon as Antonio opened the door, Harvey used his gift to keep her pinned to the wall.

I then entered the cell. "Hey, baby." I wanted nothing more than to drag her to me, but that would have to wait a minute.

"They're all okay? Evan, Max, and Stuart?"

I smiled. "All three of them are now healed and in the infirmary, where they'll stay until they wake up." I moved aside to allow the guards to drop an unconscious prisoner at her feet. "Now it's your turn."

Sam switched her attention to Paige, who was gaping at her bite mark.

"It healed." Yep, Paige was totally freaked out.

"The skin healed, but I'm still tainted," said Sam.

145

"But…how?" Finally Paige met her eyes.

Sam shrugged. "*How* can a Sventé vampire be a Feeder? *How* can a gift as offensive as yours actually do something as amazing as save a person from something that nothing and no one has ever been able to fight? Some things just *are*."

After an encouraging nudge from Imani, Paige stepped forward and went to place her hand on the wound. But then she was gaping again. "Um…you have a snake tattoo wriggling toward the bite mark." No doubt Dexter was downright pissed to know that Sam was tainted by The Call. It wasn't something that he could protect her from.

"Long story cut short," began Sam, "Dexter is my…protector. He can become a live snake at my command. He can't hurt you as a tattoo, so don't worry."

Nodding at that, Paige finally touched the wound. The same thing happened as before…apart from one thing. At the same time as the rippling started to travel up Paige's lower arm, energy began to cling to the surface of Sam's entire body – it was almost like a protective blanket. Then those silvery-blue trickles all shot to the bite wound, and a light flashed beneath Paige's hand just as there was a loud crackle.

Paige stumbled backwards, shaking her hand. Not taking her eyes from Sam, she transferred the taint to the unconscious vampire. Only when I'd destroyed the now tainted captive did she speak. "What was that about?" Again she shook her hand. She didn't seem worried or afraid, just fascinated. "It was like getting a minor electric shock."

Genuinely baffled, Sam replied vaguely, "Working with energy always brings surprises. Harvey, can you release me now?"

"Oh, sure. Sorry, Coach."

As she sagged, I pulled Sam to me and held her tight. People piled in the room, surrounding her, telling her that they were glad she was fine and even making jokes – *jokes*, really? Despite that she was healed, I couldn't find any humour whatsoever in this situation. I didn't pay any attention to them; I only had eyes for Sam. "Thank fuck you're okay."

She looked at Paige, who was regarding everyone warily. "Paige…Thanks. You don't need to worry. No one here will hurt you. After what you've done for us, I'll never let them."

Chico turned to Paige. "You healed four people who are important to me. I owe you for that. The last thing you have to worry about is being harmed here. You and your friend have our protection."

Paige swallowed hard, looking on the verge of tears. It had clearly been a long time since she had felt safe. "Thanks."

I pressed my forehead to Sam's. "I need to be alone with you." Ignoring the questions coming from the others, I took us to our apartment. Okay, that was kind of selfish but I'd always be that way where Sam was concerned. I brushed her hair aside to frame her face with my hands. "I don't know what will happen now that Paige is here, but I don't want to think about it yet."

"Me neither. I need to shower. I can still smell rotten fish on my skin from when that vampire dived on me." If the taint had progressed, the same stench would have been wafting from her.

Cupping her ass, I lifted her, and she wrapped her legs around me. Licking and nibbling on her mouth, I carried her to the bathroom. When she went to undress herself, I shook my head. "Let me take care of you."

What I wanted most was to be buried inside her, wanted to fuck her hard and release all that fear and anger. But she came first, and the last thing she needed was that. So instead, I slowly stripped her naked, placed her under the spray, and gently soaped her body. I had to bite back a groan when she started to return the favour, sliding her soft hands everywhere she could reach. When she went to touch my cock, I gripped her wrist. "Baby, you may have noticed I'm hard as a fucking rock right now. It's already hard enough to hold back. I can't have you touching me."

"Why, exactly, are you holding back?"

"I don't have the control to go slow, to be careful with you."

She kissed my chest. "Where did you get the strange idea that I need you to be slow and careful?" Her free hand shot out and curled around my cock – sneaky bitch. Her strokes were firm, sure, and bold. When I wrapped my hand around hers, halting her movements, she sank her teeth hard into my pectoral.

Groaning, I knotted my hand in her hair, intending to yank her away and stop her feeding. Instead, I found myself pressing her closer to me, encouraging her to take more. I was on the verge of coming, thanks to her Sventé saliva, when she suddenly stopped.

There was no fucking way I could resist her then. I took her mouth, dominated it, plundered it, loving that it was mine.

I tugged her hand off my cock, backed her against the tiled wall, kicked her legs open wider, and then dropped to my knees. Her whole body jerked as I parted her folds with my thumbs and blew on her clit. "I love how responsive you are." I began toying with her clit, alternating between suckling on it, flicking it with my tongue, and lightly nibbling on it. Then I tilted my head and slid my tongue between her folds. "Let me hear you, Sam." The entire time I ate her out, she groaned and moaned and whimpered. Of course she also cursed me to hell and back for keeping her hanging on the edge.

"Enough," she croaked, trembling.

"It's never enough, baby." I got to my feet, slipped my arms underneath her thighs, and elevated her high. Then I dropped her hard on my cock, making her cry out. Fuck, the feel of her muscles pulsing around me was almost too much. "Is that what you wanted?" I ground out.

She groaned in assent and squirmed, tempting me to move. Keeping her legs balanced in the crook of my elbows, I slowly withdrew before slamming back inside, going deeper this time. But it wasn't deep enough. "I want you to take it all, Sam." Once more I slowly pulled out and then, with one smooth, fierce stroke, buried myself balls-deep inside her. "That's it." I flexed my hips, making sure I was as deep as I could get. Her face was scrunched up in either pleasure or pain, I couldn't tell. "Too deep? Does it hurt?"

She nodded. "But not in a bad way."

"Good because I need to be deep inside you right now." I needed to know, *feel*, that she was okay.

"Good because I need you there."

I hitched in a breath. It wasn't often that Sam ever claimed to need anything. "I'm here. And I'm going to fuck you hard. So hard. And you're going to love it. And you're going to explode all over my cock and wring me dry." Then I was mercilessly punching my cock in and out of her. Her irises were glowing mercury with arousal – so fucking beautiful.

She grappled at the wall for purchase, and tried arching into my thrusts, but I had her pinned exactly as I wanted her. There was only one other thing I wanted. I bit into the juncture of her neck and shoulder, groaning as her blood flowed onto my tongue. The syrupy punch to it was too damn good. I drank deep as I pounded into her, groaning again when I felt her teeth sink into my shoulder. *Fuck.* My pace became frantic, violent, as she completely overwhelmed every one of my senses. "Come, Sam," I ordered roughly. "Milk me." She screamed around my shoulder as she came; her muscles tightened and rippled around my cock, wringing every last drop of come out of me, like her body was determined to have it all.

It was a few minutes before I could speak again. "Shit, I needed that."

Panting, she breathed, "Me as well."

As I dried her body with a towel, she remained pliant against me. I couldn't help but smile since Sam being pliant wasn't a regular occurrence. She was still limp as a noodle when I positioned her on the bed and came to rest next to her, my head propped on my hand. "You okay?"

Her eyes fluttered open. They were pleasure-drunk but also...baffled. "You really would do anything for me, wouldn't you?"

"You're only beginning to realise this now?" I gently ran my finger from the hollow of her throat down between her breasts and further down to circle her belly button. "You should already know that." My hand splayed possessively over her stomach. "You should feel it here. In your gut."

"I really didn't think that you would bring Paige here. Not when it was possible that it would bring trouble to The Hollow and everyone here."

She thought that I'd ever let her die for any reason? I shook my head, gazing at her with mock sympathy. "I love this place, and I care about some of the people in it, and I consider it my responsibility to keep everyone who resides here safe. But you come before everything and everyone."

Her brow furrowed as her expression suddenly turned vulnerable. I knew why it was so hard for her to comprehend. No one had ever put Sam first. Not her parents, who had been more interested in running the family business than caring for her. Not her Sire, who had killed someone she cared for and then used her in every sense of the word. Not her nest, who had stood by and watched as she was used that way. Granted, many of them feared Victor and a few of them *had* tried to help her, but it hadn't been enough. So even though she could feel how important she was to me, she still couldn't understand it. She didn't realise what lengths I'd go to in order to keep her or to protect her.

She snuggled into me and pressed a soft kiss to my chest. "I really am sorry that I put your life in danger."

I cupped her face, brushing the pad of my thumb along her cheekbone. "Baby, you don't need to apologise for that. You did your job; you looked out for our squad. I was never angry that my life was threatened. I was only angry that something had happened to you. It wasn't your fault – I shouldn't have blamed you."

"But you could have died." Her voice was low, pained.

"I was more worried about you." Confusion flashed across her face. See? She just couldn't quite grasp that someone would put her first, that they would find her so vital and necessary to them. Making a mental note to try to tell her I loved her more often, I kissed her mouth softly. "Sleep, baby. You're exhausted."

"Only if you don't let me sleep too long. We need to make sure that Evan has the chance to speak to Alora before she leaves."

"I'll wake you up in a couple of hours."

She closed her eyes. "Stay here with me."

Her plea squeezed my chest. As much as she had tried to hide it, she had been terrified when she'd been bitten – more terrified for me than for herself. I knew from experience that coming extremely close to death had a way of making you realise just exactly how much you had to lose, just exactly what was important and just how important it truly was. It could shake you and your equilibrium in a way that not much else could. And she was shaken. I rested my head on the pillow and practically enveloped her body with mine. "I'll be right here."

She drifted to sleep with a smile on her face, and – just like I'd done the time she'd been unconscious after killing her Sire – I stayed where I was and watched her sleep.

CHAPTER TWELVE

(Jared)

When I arrived at the infirmary a few hours later, it was to find that it was empty apart from a still unconscious Evan and Mary Jane. She explained that Max and Stuart had already woken over an hour ago and had gone to their apartments to wash and change. A little worried that Evan hadn't yet woken, I settled on the chair beside his bed, intending to wait until he did. Mary Jane wanted to linger so she could tend to him when he woke – purely because she liked to fuss over people. But as I knew I'd need to speak to Evan privately, I asked her to leave. Besides, he was healed now, so her help was no longer required.

It was over half an hour later that his eyes finally flickered open. Relief breezed through me. "Hey, shithead."

Tired eyes landed on me and his mouth slowly curved into an amused grin. "Hey, asshole." He looked totally drained and hung-over, but that was a hell of a lot better than how he'd looked a few hours ago.

"Here." I handed him an orange-flavoured NST. He chugged it down. "Take it easy." Evan being Evan, he didn't listen. "I'd hug you, but you still stink."

He chuckled. His voice slightly hoarse, he said, "You found a counteragent?"

"You don't remember what happened?"

He shook his head. "I don't remember much. But I remember the thirst. I remember the hollow feeling in the pit of my stomach." He gave me the empty bottle and then gratefully took another NST. He drank that one a little slower. "It's strange…I feel thirsty, *really* thirsty, but I don't have awful hunger pangs or anything. Shouldn't my system want to make up for lost time?"

"Mary Jane put you, Max, and Stuart on a drip of pure blood for the first hour after you were healed when you were all unconscious."

"That explains it then. But it doesn't explain how I'm healed, or how I ended up unconscious in the first place."

"I didn't find a counteragent. I found someone who, sort of, has the ability to heal." I told him about Paige West, including the part about Luther's vision – it turned out that Evan didn't remember the time I had telepathically told him about it all while he was ill. I also told him about the assignment and about how Sam had been bitten. His eyebrows rose higher and higher as the story went on. "I'm sorry I never brought Paige here sooner, but—"

Evan raised a hand. "Don't be. You were protecting your mate. I'd never want anything to happen to Sam either. She's like my sister. I'm glad she's okay." His face pulled into a frown. "It's kind of odd that her bite wound healed by itself, huh."

"Antonio thinks it's because she's now a hybrid. Her skin heals unbelievably fast – maybe even so fast that it began to heal before The Call had the chance to fully taint her system and fuck up its healing abilities."

"Is the ugly mark still there?"

"No, it disappeared once Paige removed the taint from her body." I rubbed my nape as I continued, uncomfortable, "On a whole other subject…There's something you should know. Alora's here."

Evan blinked. "Alora? Why?"

"When she heard you were tainted, she came here."

Incredibly perceptive, Evan narrowed his eyes as he said accusingly, "You broke your promise, didn't you? You let her see me like that?"

"Alora cares about you, Evan. She wouldn't have come on an assignment and endangered her life if she—"

"You let her go on an assignment?" He gaped, clearly horrified and pissed.

Damn, I was just digging a deeper hole for myself here. I pushed on. "Even though she believes you'll never want her, she came here and asked for permission to stay for a while to help find a way to save you." I let that sink in for a minute. "She told us everything, Evan. To be honest, I was a bit of a bastard to her in the beginning because I thought she'd rejected you."

He averted his gaze. "It was me who rejected her. It was a shock, you know. What she told me…I'd never have seen that coming."

"Me neither."

He blew out a long breath. "I guess that because I saw her in the vision, I always took it for granted that she'd be mine. That once I finally found her, everything would fall into place, you know? It never occurred to me that there would be other obstacles. And as obstacles go, this one's a bitch."

"Was it only shock that made you reject her or is she right and you really don't want her?"

He ran a hand through his unkempt hair. "We'd never have what you and Sam have."

I leaned forward in my seat. "Evan, I love being Bound to Sam. If you want the truth, it's the extra security that someone as fucked up as me needs. But we were still happy before the Binding, and we would have continued to be happy if we hadn't done it."

He met my eyes then. "But could you have been happy with her knowing that someone else was Bound to her? That she belonged to someone else?"

"I won't lie, it would have been fucking torture if she was Bound to another guy. But it wouldn't have kept me away from her. Nothing could." It was the truth. "You're thinking that Alora belongs to that prick because they're Bound, but that's not how it works. Someone can only belong to you if they allow it. We know that better than most. Our mother never saw people as people – they were objects for her to own, use, and manipulate. But we never let her own us. We rejected her, just as Alora rejected that prick."

"I can't even kill him. If I killed him, she'd die." His laugh was hollow. "Hell, Jared, her fucking life-force is tied to someone else's. I don't know how to even begin to deal with that."

"I get that but, like I said before, she doesn't belong to him. She made an error of judgement when she was young and she's been paying for it ever since in a truly big way. Do you think she likes being joined to someone she despises? Or did you get so wrapped up in your pain that you forgot about hers?" His silence spoke for him. "If you're prepared to let this keep you from Alora, then maybe you were wrong and you guys aren't meant to be together after all." Evan opened his mouth as though to object, but then he snapped it shut. "Maybe you just made yourself think she'd be yours because you saw her in that vision through Luther. Maybe you had that vision for no good reason at all."

Evan tilted his head. "You've never told me about the vision that you had through Luther."

I stiffened. "You never told me about yours until Alora finally arrived here."

He winced. "I didn't want you to spoil it."

"How would I have spoiled it?"

"By laughing about how I was being faithful to someone I hadn't even met yet."

That actually hurt. "I'm not *that* much of a bastard, Evan. Just because I hadn't really seen the point of relationships back then didn't mean I thought everyone else was dumb for wanting one. I knew you didn't function like I did, and I didn't want you to. I envied the fact that you weren't fucked up about women and relationships despite our childhood. But I was glad for it, too."

His smile was a little sad. "Oh I'm messed up in my own special way, trust me on that. But you went through a hell of a lot worse than I did. That kind of shit makes its mark. And don't think I didn't notice that you totally evaded the subject of your own vision, by the way."

Yeah, well, that wasn't something I had any intention of touching on. If I was going to talk about it, then Sam deserved to be the first to know. "That's not important at the moment. We're talking about *you*. About your future. Are you really going to fuck it up?" The stubborn shithead said nothing. "She only came here to help find a way to save you," I reminded him. "You're fine now, which means she'll be leaving very soon unless you stop her."

It was clear how much the idea pained him. "She's probably already gone."

A smile slowly surfaced on my face. "Sam's keeping her occupied."

"Of course she is," he said dryly, smiling. "You're a pair of interfering little shits, you know."

"Yeah, I know." I stood. "Come on. I'll take you back to your place so you can shower and change, because you really do reek. Then I'll take you to Alora."

He sighed. "I hurt her badly."

"So make it up to her. She cares about you, and you care about—" The doors suddenly opened and the entire squad piled into the room. Every one of them was so jovial and keyed up that they looked like a kid in Disneyworld.

Stuart grinned at Evan. "You're awake. In case you didn't already know, you look like shit."

Max was also grinning. "Yeah, like a tornado survivor or something."

Evan snorted. "You guys don't look like spring chickens either, you know. Glad you're both healed, too."

So was I but, not really good with emotional stuff, I simply said, "Yeah, it's good to see that you're okay."

Max exhaled heavily as he turned to me. His expression was serious now. "I wanted to talk to you about something. The guys told me about that asshole, Collins. I've already told Sam, but I want you to know too that the fucker's lying – I did not make any kind of complaint about her."

"None of us believes that you did."

He looked taken aback. "Not even you? I mean, I know you don't like me. And you're still paranoid that I want Sam."

"I'm actually not." It was true. Sure, I could be possessive and jealous and overreact when someone touched or flirted with her. But I knew when someone *wanted* her and when someone was just trying to fuck with me for their own damn entertainment. The latter applied to Max. "I've known for a while that you don't want her anymore. You even told me that, remember?"

"Yeah, but I wasn't sure if you believed me."

"Well, I did." I snickered. "If I thought you really had said that shit to the Prelature out of bitterness and some kind of 'if you can't have her than no one can', I wouldn't have asked Paige to heal you. I'd have let you die and not given a shit." Max tipped his head, accepting that.

"Okay, I'm feeling left out here," said Evan. "Who the hell is Collins?"

"I'll explain everything before I take you to Alora." When Evan grimaced, I added, "You'll regret it forever if you don't at least talk to her. Even if it's just to say goodbye."

After a moment, Evan nodded and got to his feet. I grabbed his arm, ready to teleport us away, when Chico suddenly spoke.

"Wait, the main reason we're here is to invite you both to the party we're having tonight." He gave us a pointed look. "I'll expect to see you there. If anything deserves to be celebrated, it's the fact that everyone's alive and well."

I couldn't argue with that. "I'll be there."

"Me too," said Evan. Only then did the squad leave the room, still giddy and even boyish in their excitement to be a whole squad once again.

I then teleported Evan to his apartment where he showered and changed into fresh clothes. As we both drank some NSTs, I told him all about Collins and Eloise. Evan's face increasingly darkened until he looked ready to pounce on someone. Yeah, Collins and Eloise seemed to have that effect on everyone.

"I'm surprised by – and kind of in awe of – Sam's restraint." Evan chucked all the empty NST bottles into the garbage can.

"So is everyone else." Tapping into my bond with Sam, I found her exact location and teleported both Evan and I there. This particular room was the only one inside Antonio's mansion that had a tall glass aviary in the centre which was framed by a narrow stream. Inside the aviary were trees, plants, and animals such as rabbits, guinea pigs, canaries, and other species of birds. It was a place Antonio often came when he needed to relax and think.

Sam, Alora, Antonio, Luther, Sebastian, and – God help us – Collins were gathered around the aviary. Talking about him to Evan had gotten me all wound up, and now it was taking everything I had not to punch the smarmy bastard.

"Evan, it is great to see you well again." Antonio hugged Evan, giving him a paternal smile. "You have been sorely missed."

Sebastian lightly slapped Evan's back, smiling widely. "Yes, it's good to have you back."

Luther's expression was grim. "I wish I had foreseen what would happen to you, Evan. If I had—"

Evan raised his hand to halt Luther's words. "You can't foresee everything. And look, I'm fine now."

"Stop hogging my sort-of-brother-in-law," Sam playfully griped before giving him a brief hug. "I didn't think I'd ever be glad to see that cocky smirk again." Evan laughed, returning the hug.

The second Evan and Alora locked eyes, everything in the room seemed to still. It was a pivotal moment, because it could go either way – particularly since I still had no idea what Evan intended to do about the situation. He went to speak, but then Collins stepped forward.

"It's a pleasure to finally meet you, Evan."

Evan automatically shook the hand he offered. "And who are you?"

"My name is Fredrick Collins."

Snatching back his hand, Evan glared at him. "I can't say it's a pleasure for me."

Collins started but recovered quickly, forcing a shaky smile as he stepped back. "Yes, well, it's good to see that you're well. I must admit that I didn't believe there was a way to fight The Call. The counteragent must indeed be a substantial one." It was a hint for more information. No one had told Collins about Paige West – she had requested her involvement be kept secret from outsiders, not wanting her Sire to hear of her location. 'Not knowing' was clearing killing Collins.

Evan didn't take the bait. Instead, he switched his attention back to Alora. His face softened. "Can we talk?"

Her smile was wobbly. "Sure." When he held out a hand and she took it, he flashed her a smile and led her out of the room. Hopefully that smile meant good things, because if anyone deserved happiness, it was Evan.

Satisfied, Sam smiled at me. "I have to admit I wasn't sure if he'd come to see her. Whatever you said to him clearly worked." She kissed my cheek. "You did good."

I slipped my arm around her shoulders. "They'll sort it out." Or, at least, I hoped they would. I looked at Antonio. "How did the humans take it when they realised all their captives were gone?"

Antonio's mouth twitched into a smile. "According to Quentin, the whole thing was quite humorous. When they caught the vampires, the humans had thought themselves very clever. To have the captives taken from under their very noses like that...it was a wake-up call; it told them that they truly had no idea what they were dealing with and it was best to leave well alone."

"It's doubtful that they will give up on trying to catch and contain some of our kind," said Sebastian. "But they will have received our message loud and clear."

Antonio nodded, still smiling. "They were certainly very fast as they packed up and left, or so I'm told."

It would have been fun to watch. "And all the tainted vampires?"

"Quentin assures me that every last one has been destroyed. There were no other casualties, so all the untainted vampires returned home safely. It was only Sam who was hurt."

For a second, as I recalled the moment she'd been bitten, the cocktail of dark emotions came back to me. I contracted my arm around her, incredibly thankful that she was okay.

Collins twisted his lips as he looked at her. "At least your recklessness only got yourself hurt this time, Commander Park—" He gurgled as my hand fisted in the collar of his shirt and I slammed him against the wall.

"Hurt? She could have fucking died! And that was because she put everyone else's safety before her own. That's the kind of person she is. Me? Not so much. I'm selfish enough to care more about her safety than anyone else's. Do you know what that means for you? It means that if you keep pushing like this, I'll push back. Know what else?" I placed my face close to his; he froze and his eyes widened. "You won't even see it coming."

"You cannot threaten me," he said shakily.

"Oh I can. And I just did. You're making the mistake of thinking that working for the Prelature gives you some kind of immunity; that you can do and say what the fuck you like. *No one* will keep you safe from me if you keep spouting bullshit like that about Sam."

He audibly gulped. "Release me." It was more of a plea than a demand.

"But this is fun."

Sam sighed tiredly. "Let him go, Jared. I'm sure he'd like to jot the incident down in his little notepad. Just remember to preface it with your aggravating, insensitive, callous, very disrespectful – not to mention totally unprofessional – comment, Mr Collins."

Sneering, I reluctantly released the mouthy prick and moved away.

Fixing his tie and shirt, a trembling Collins cleared his throat. "I'll let this one slide." Because he knew Sam was right. He'd crossed a line, and my reaction was completely justified.

"Good of you," muttered Sam.

He practically scrambled to the door. As he reached it, I spoke again. "You should know one other thing. Max isn't very happy to hear what you said about him. But I'm sure you'll find out for yourself just how unhappy he is soon enough." Collins licked his lips nervously and scurried out.

Sam shook her head incredulously. "It's almost like he *wants* to get hurt."

"I can't guarantee he'll leave here in one piece," I told Antonio. "If I don't kill him, it's possible that someone else will since it's not just me he's managed to piss off."

Antonio glanced at the door, sighing. It had to be disheartening to know that one of his vampires – his first-born, for that matter – was such a damn asshole. And no doubt it was hard for him to see Collins behave this way toward people Antonio cared for – particularly knowing it could very well get Collins badly hurt. A part of Antonio had to feel torn about the whole thing. "If something bad should happen to him while he is here, it will be safe to say that he dug his own grave."

Fully aware that talking anymore about the asshole would only worsen my mood, I quickly changed the subject. "Where are Paige and Imani?" It would be nice to hear that they had changed their mind and decided to leave – however selfish of me that might be – but I wasn't optimistic about it.

"They are in the Guest House, resting. It is sad that Paige's presence here could lead to something awful, but there is no denying that she did us the greatest service. It would be dishonourable to treat her badly."

I knew that comment was for my benefit. "I don't intend to treat her with anything but respect. I'm not pleased she's staying, but she saved Sam and the guys. I'll always be thankful to her for that." Of course I hated the fact that Paige being at The Hollow could bring danger to Sam, but she would have died without Paige's help anyway.

Sam frowned. "Was it just me who noticed that she seems kind of paranoid that we want Imani?"

I began toying with Sam's hair, twining a long, silky strand around my finger. "No, I noticed that too. It's odd how overprotective Paige is of her. I'm beginning to wonder if the girl needs protecting from something or someone."

"When I first found Paige," began Sebastian, "she panicked and immediately ordered Imani to run. I'd say Imani is in fact in some sort of danger. But if there is some kind of secret, Paige is hardly likely to tell us what it is when she's as wary of us as she is right now."

"True," said Antonio. "I am sure Paige will explain eventually, as I'm assuming she will hope that we will be added protection for

Imani if that is indeed what the girl needs."

"On another note, do you think there are still some tainted vampires out there?" I asked Antonio.

"I held a teleconference with the High Masters a few hours ago," he replied. "They confirmed that they have tracked down all the tainted vampires from their nest and also those in their vicinity, and that they have destroyed them all. As such, I am hoping there are no more."

I ran my gaze along Antonio, Luther, and Sebastian. "Do you think The Call will go dormant again now that all the tainted are dead? I mean, how much damage to the population does it usually do before it stops?"

Luther delicately shrugged one shoulder. "It differs each time."

"And that could either be because all the tainted were destroyed or because The Call was *ready* to go dormant again," added Sebastian. "It's reasonable to assume that it is the first. That would be my guess."

"We have another very big issue." Luther suddenly looked troubled. "Collins and Eloise will no doubt spread the news of how Sam, Evan, Max, and Stuart have been healed. In addition, Quentin is quite aware that Evan was tainted, so he will get quite a shock when he realises Evan is alive and well. Others will want to know how they were saved. We need to have some sort of story ready."

"Do not worry," said Antonio. "I will think of something." And I had no doubt that he would come up with something good, just as he had when explaining the changes that Sam had undergone. "Now that the tainted have been dealt with, I will soon be making the announcement about the upcoming Coronation. I will schedule the Coronation for in three weeks' time. By then, if there are any more tainted vampires, it will be apparent."

"Are you making the announcement by teleconference?" Sam's nervousness wasn't obvious in her voice, but I could *feel* it. Who wouldn't be nervous about ruling all of their own kind?

"Yes. I would like you both to be there."

I nodded my agreement. "When are you planning to do it?"

"Friday evening."

So that gave Sam and me five evenings before everything changed for us forever.

"For now, set aside your worries, and enjoy your evening. I hear the squad are throwing a party." Antonio smiled. "We have all been invited, so we may make an appearance."

"Then maybe we'll see you there." I took Sam's hand in mine. "Just be aware that when the squad throws a party, they *really* party."

CHAPTER THIRTEEN

(Sam)

Jared couldn't have been more right. Although the party was supposed to be taking place in Chico's apartment, the entire apartment block – which housed all ten squads of the legion – was celebrating and partying hard. Music was blasting, food and NSTs were being passed around, and intoxicated humans were lounging in almost every room.

Jared and I made our way up to Chico's apartment, which proved to be packed with people. Exchanging nods and smiles with everyone, we shouldered our way through the crowd until we found the squad. All ten of them were gathered in the kitchen, laughing at a story that Fletcher was telling them. As Jared and I walked in, the squad turned as one and endowed us with huge grins and back-pats. Of course Max kissed me smack on the mouth just to piss Jared off. Predictably, Jared shoved Max across the room. Everyone, including Max, thought that it was hilarious.

"I'm so glad you came!" squealed Ava as she wrapped her arms around me. I realised then that Cristiano, Norm, Jude, Paige, and Imani were also there. It was certainly a surprise to see the latter two. "And I'm so glad you're healed! When I heard you'd been bitten and then saw you in that cell, I was in tears."

Yeah, I remembered seeing Ava so distressed. Touched, I smiled. "I'm fine now, thanks to Paige." I shot the female a grateful smile. Her answering one was awkward and shaky.

"She and Imani didn't want to come to the party," Ava whispered, "but Butch and Stuart dragged them here. As far as the boys are all concerned, those girls are the best things since sliced bread."

Yes, it did look as though the squad was determined to make the new additions part of our group. Paige and Imani would find it incredibly hard to resist them since Butch and Stuart weren't the type to take 'no' for an answer.

"My darlin' girl," drawled Fletcher, pulling me away from Ava and into a huge hug. "I swear I had palpations when I found out you were tainted." He pulled back and pointed hard at me. "Don't you ever do that to me again! My heart couldn't take it a second time."

Rolling his eyes at his boyfriend's dramatics, Norm pushed him aside and kissed my cheek. "I could make fun of him, but in all honesty, we were both bawling like babies when we heard what had happened to you."

"You should know better than to think I'd ever let her die," interrupted Jared, snorting. Both Fletcher and Norm melted at the sight of him. Oh for the love of all that was holy!

When Jared smiled at someone over my shoulder, I turned to see Evan and Alora coming over. He flashed me a wide smile. "Thanks for being an interfering bitch and keeping Alora so busy that she couldn't leave until I'd talked to her."

"I was hoping that Jared would talk some sense into you. Does this mean that you're keeping her here?"

Evan tugged Alora close. "How could I not?" She blushed, leaning into him.

Hearing a throat clear, I swerved to see Cristiano. This time, there was no smug smirk. I was surprised at how…awkward he seemed. Cristiano was nothing if not terribly sure of himself.

"It's good to see you…healed."

"Thanks," I said simply, waiting for his seemingly ever-present smug smirk to surface. It didn't come. I wasn't sure whether to be suspicious or simply glad.

"It was a shock hearing that you'd been bitten, seeing you hurt. I suppose I've always thought of you as invincible after the amount of duels I witnessed you have for Victor." Gruffly, he added, "Just be more careful in future."

That had my brows flying up. I was expecting Jared to call him a dickhead and tell him to fuck off for giving me a warning like that. But although Jared slid an arm around me in a very possessive gesture, he didn't curse at Cristiano or order him to bugger off. In fact, Jared nodded at him in greeting. Cristiano even returned the nod. They were practicing civility? What had I missed? *Have you two reached a truce or something?* I asked Jared.

He kissed my temple. *Nope. I've just decided to let him live. For now.*

Jude came forward, her expression oddly calculating. "I, um, just wanted to ask…would it be so bad if I slit Eloise's throat?" She was totally serious. Jude did love her knife and would latch onto any excuse to use it.

Before I could answer, Chico came up behind her and began pulling her away. "Jude, remember that talk we had about…" His voice faded as he moved away and the music overrode his words. I wasn't sure if I wanted to know what that 'talk' had been about.

Antonio, Luther, and Sebastian turned up later on…and just in time to see Stuart, Max, Evan, and I being perched on the other squad member's shoulders and paraded around while people cheered. I wasn't impressed, nor was I happy that Jared didn't rescue me. Instead, he actually laughed. Plonker. I shot him a look that swore revenge but he just laughed harder.

When Denny and Damien finally finished their circuit around the apartment and returned me to Jared, he gripped my hips and slid me down his body until my feet met the floor. He easily dodged my bitch slap and pinned my hands behind my back. "Come on, baby, how could I not celebrate that you're healthy and safe?"

Well, when he put it like that…"You're still a plonker."

Laughing again, he mashed his mouth with mine and sucked on my bottom lip before giving it a sharp nip. "I'll make it up to you later."

And he did.

Ignoring the 'oh for God's sake' sigh that came from my left, I concentrated hard on the very important matter in front of me. Jared knew that I needed to focus, so he could sigh all he wanted. I blocked him out, blocked out everything around me, as I put every ounce of my concentration into dealing with the enemy in front of me. Almost –

"As much as I'm glad that you love my gift, we have to go. The squad will be waiting."

"Fine," I grumbled, saving my progress and switching off the game console. Jared just shook his head at me, smiling. I shrugged a shoulder defensively. "Okay, so I get a little too engrossed in the game."

He snorted. "That's the understatement of the year, but whatever.

Think Max and Stuart are definitely ready to return to training?"

"They've had enough time off." We had given the entire squad three evenings off training, allowing Max and Stuart to fully recover from the exhaustion that had been riding them and giving the boys some time together. According to Antonio, 'reconnecting' would be good for them and for morale. It had also given me a nice break from my annoying shadow. Unbelievably, Collins had turned up at the squad's party, expecting entry. Butch had opened Chico's apartment door, looked at Collins blankly, and then allowed it to swing shut in his face. Ava had been delighted by it and had hugged Butch in gratitude. Salem hadn't liked that.

I'd talked a little with Paige and Imani over the past few evenings, slowly getting to know them. Although Paige was pretty guarded, she was no longer suspicious of me. She wasn't yet comfortable with everyone else, though. Imani was quiet among a crowd, but she was very chatty at other times – especially around Butch. She was pretty much the only person I knew who thought he was normal. I found both females to be very nice and fun, albeit cagey, people. I still had no clue as to why they still expected to be betrayed by everyone sooner or later, or what it was they were so afraid of. Paige had looked on the verge of telling me a few times, but she had quickly snapped her mouth closed. Winning her trust would obviously take time.

Abandoning my contemplations about Paige and Imani, I took the hand that Jared held out to me. A second later, we were stood in the arena. The entire squad was waiting there, laughing and joking – clearly excited to be training as a whole squad once more. The sight tightened my chest, making me smile. Training hadn't been the same without them all there together. Unfortunately, Collins and Eloise were also present, sitting in the spectators' area.

As usual, Eloise was practically half-naked. "You look good this evening, Jared," she called out, close to purring. She licked her lips as she ran her gaze over him. Her eyes then moved to me and she grimaced. "Rough night?" The insinuation that I looked like shit was clear.

"I'd quite like to kill her," I told Jared with all seriousness.

His mouth twitched in amusement. "But you know better than to let her get to you. We both know that she's been baiting you since the second she arrived."

I did know that. Admittedly, it hadn't occurred to me in the beginning. But the more she persisted in pushing my buttons, the more I'd come to suspect that she was hoping I would do enough to fuck up the result of the Prelature's investigation. It could simply be out of spite because I had Jared. But I sincerely doubted it, because she had never pursued him in the past – why bother now if she had originally been satisfied with a one-night stand?

As Antonio had pointed out, I would always have enemies because I had a position of power, so Eloise's behaviour could even be down to that. Or it could be something else, something darker…Unfortunately, I was beginning to think it was the latter.

As Collins descended the steps and made a beeline for me, I inwardly groaned. Presenting him with a bright but totally false smile, I said, "Yes, Mr Collins?" He began ranting, pointing his finger as he towered over me…but no words came out. My confusion lasted only a few seconds. I sighed at Max, who shrugged. "How long has he been like this?"

"Since he tried to join us for breakfast earlier like we were all chums. He actually tried to play volleyball with us on the beach last night, too. That's *our* time, Coach, and he's got no right to bug us then." Yeah, I could understand how Max felt. I'd been just as pissed when Eloise went to my apartment.

Butch came to Max's side. "He's right. That dick's got some fucking nerve, Coach."

Max briefly sneered at Collins. "After everything he's done and what he accused me of, he should be grateful I only took away his ability to speak."

I hadn't been there when he confronted Collins the previous night about his claim that Max had contacted the Prelature about me. But apparently the little prick had told Max that he had only alleged it was him to protect the identity of the real complainant. He'd even apologised to Max, but his apology hadn't been accepted. Collins had made himself an enemy for life in Max. If the entire squad didn't already despise Collins, they would do so now purely because to go against one of them was to go against all of them.

"You're right, Max. He deserved this, and he's lucky he got off so lightly. But now that it's time for training, I'm going to need you to give him his voice back – sadly."

The entire squad groaned in both disappointment and frustration.

Mumbling under his breath, Max waved his hand at Collins.

"...Parker you have no control over your own...Oh." Collins paused, clearing his throat with a cough.

When he opened his mouth to speak again, I could tell another rant was coming. I raised my hand. "I don't have time to listen to your grievances, Mr Collins. I have a squad to train."

"Yes, well, a particular member of your squad—"

"Got mightily pissed off when you approached him during his own time," I finished. "If you had expected him to react any differently, you only have yourself to blame. The squad has been quite clear since the very beginning that they do not want your company. Had Max targeted you during training hours, I would have reprimanded him. But he didn't. It's not his fault that you can't take a hint now, is it?" Collins said nothing. What *could* he say? I was right, and he was very much aware of that. "Now, is there anything else?"

His usual snooty look reappeared and he straightened to his full height. "Yes, as it happens," he snapped. "I wish to know if there is a particular reason why you have not yet made use of the tactical field since Eloise and I came here."

The tactical field was located within the rainforest and was more like a small abandoned village, only the buildings were made of plywood and obviously it wasn't normal to have drums and piles of tires lying around. We usually trained there once or twice a week, and we sometimes played paintball there as well. It had been a Binding present from Evan, and I bloody loved it. That was the reason why I hadn't used it since Collins and Eloise had arrived. It was a special place to me that I had no intention of sharing with them. "I use it when I need to, Mr Collins."

My vague answer clearly irritated him. "It is important that I observe all your training methods, *Commander Parker.* I noticed that the squad have not ceased calling you 'Coach', despite that I have repeatedly suggested that you should order them to refer to you with the appropriate title. Allowing them to give you a 'pet' name undermines your level of authority."

Pet name? What-bloody-ever. "I happen to disagree with you. Now if you don't mind, I have a squad to train, and you're delaying the session."

"I would appreciate it if you would move the session to the tactical field."

And I would have appreciated it if he'd sod off home, but we didn't always get what we wanted. "Sorry to disappoint you, but that will not be happening."

He lifted his chin. "Then I will be forced to note your failure to cooperate with my request. I will also note that you persist in wearing vests, revealing more skin than necessary."

"Yes, I'm sure the squad are drooling at the sight of my arms and shoulders. Maybe you should be a little more concerned with how very little your colleague is wearing, Mr Collins." Turning away from him in a sure sign of dismissal, I switched my attention to the squad. Max and Stuart turned amusingly giddy, clearly having missed working with everyone.

Having been fully debriefed on our 'plan', Max and Stuart were sure to fake weaknesses that they didn't have during the session, and they didn't question the longer breaks that they were now getting. They also took advantage of their recent encounter with death by faking tiredness and claiming to need a rest here and there. Although I knew it was for the best, it was still pissing me off because not only did it interfere with their training, but it meant that I couldn't push them harder. And I *needed* to push them harder. Paige's presence could cause a battle of some kind, and I needed the squad fully prepared. Of course they were more than capable of protecting themselves and each other during battle without additional training, but I wanted to be sure that they were at their best.

Expectedly, Collins spent the entire time asking questions and criticising my every move to the point of nit-picking. In addition, he complained for the millionth time that I swore too much (so?) and made a sound of disapproval each time that I did. He also complained that bringing Dexter from his tattoo form was distracting the squad – that was the whole point: to teach them to perform while distracted, because that was what they would need to do in a battle. Furthermore, he complained that when I divided the squad for sparring, I pitted them against members who they were quite vulnerable to gift-wise – well, duh, how else were they going to learn to rely on more than just their gifts to survive in a battle? The bloke was utterly clueless.

Eloise also gave her penny's worth: I was condescending, I was too impatient, and I lacked room for error – all of which was simply to piss me off. But I didn't rise to her bait because I knew it greatly annoyed her. Maybe that was why at the end of the session, when the squad had left and I'd just returned Dexter to his tattoo form while Collins babbled at me about something or other, she reached out to touch Jared. In a split second, a dark combination of rage, jealousy, possessiveness, and a need to *hurt* whipped through me so fast and hard that I almost swayed. I wanted nothing more than to grab the bitch and throw her across the arena. But I didn't.

However, something else happened.

Just as her fingers went to touch Jared, a cold draft sliced through the air, raising the hairs on my arms. We all stiffened as the icy breeze built and built until, suddenly, a silvery-blue wind of pure energy formed around Eloise. What happened next was even more shocking. Like it was a vacuum, the whirlwind literally spat her across the wide space, causing her to collide into the far wall. What the fuck? The silvery-blue energy wind then instantly disintegrated like mist.

Jared's head whipped around to face me. *How did you do that?*

I blinked. *I didn't.* Or, at least, I hadn't meant to do it. That counted, right? I kept my face carefully blank, not letting Collins or Eloise see my confusion.

Coughing and dusting herself off, Eloise rose to her feet. "You bitch!" She marched toward me, and I half-expected the wind of energy to appear again. It didn't. Not even as she closed in on me. So I did the smart thing. Rather than attack her, and thus give her what she wanted, I called, "Novo." Like that, a jet black Dexter was draped over my shoulders again. He hissed at Eloise, his scales turning red, and she stopped dead in her tracks. She was perfectly aware that he would attack her without hesitation if she attempted to harm me in any way.

Eyes wide, she pointed at me, shaking. "You just—"

"What had you expected would happen?" Jared's voice was calm, bored even. "Sam and I are Bound. You tried to touch me – and we all know that it was a flirtatious move on your part. Bound couples have gone to war over each other. You're lucky that all Sam did was send you on a little trip across the arena."

Eloise swerved to face a gaping Collins. "Do something! She attacked me!"

Outraged, Collins went to speak, but Jared beat him to it.

"No, she didn't. She defended our bond." Folding his arms across his chest, Jared glanced at Collins. "You know how it works. Your colleague's behaviour is considered a threat to the bond. She wanted a reaction. She got one."

Collins clenched his fists. "It was a most violent reaction that could have left Eloise seriously hurt! My report—"

"Note it all down if you must," I told Collins, somehow still masking my shock at what had just occurred. "But you'll need to also note her provocative behaviour."

Eloise curled her upper lip. "*All I did was try to touch him!*" Dexter hissed at her again, making her flinch.

"Ah, but it wouldn't have been an innocent touch," I pointed out. "Flirting with a Bound male is as good as signing your death warrant."

"That is no excuse for your actions, Commander Parker!" maintained Collins. "And I believe it is quite clear that you do not deserve that title!" His raised voice earned him a hiss from Dexter.

"The session is over," rumbled Jared, scowling, "so there are no more notes for you to take. I suggest you both go."

"The session may be over," allowed Collins as he marched toward the door, "but *this* is not." He strode out of the building with an outraged, complaining Eloise in tow.

Once they were gone, Jared turned to me. "How did that happen?"

"I honestly have no idea."

He inhaled deeply. "Then I think we need to have a chat with Antonio."

So we did. Well, *Jared* did. I just sat next to him on the sofa in the parlour room opposite Antonio and Luther, who hadn't said a word. I was still in shock, and I was also shitting myself. My gift had gone haywire once before, and I didn't like the idea that it could be happening again.

Sensing my unease, Jared shackled my wrist with his hand and massaged my pulse point comfortingly with his thumb. I hadn't returned Dexter to his tattoo form, wanting to calm his overprotective state first. Plus, he strangely had a way of relaxing me. Curled up beside me, he was currently a brilliant blue, indicating that he had calmed and was pretty content. Well, at least one of us was.

Antonio looked at me. "I cannot say I'm surprised this has happened."

I blinked rapidly. "Say again?"

"You are an expressive person, Sam. But you have spent the past few weeks bottling up your emotions, despite how hard Collins and Eloise have tested your patience. Anybody who strangles their emotions will eventually get to a stage where they 'explode'. A vampire's gift is tied to their emotions. As such, it was truly only a matter of time before your gift…had an outburst, shall we say."

One of Jared's brows slid up. "You're saying that happened because she's stressed? Her gift had a tantrum?"

"Taking into account recent events, I would imagine that Sam is a bubbling cauldron of various emotions, for want of a better phrase. Her gift of absorbing and harnessing energy is strongly linked to her emotions. As such, the energy inside her will be bubbling just the same. Pent up emotions will manifest themselves some way or another. They eventually find an outlet."

"All right, I can accept that my gift ran riot because I've been keeping a lid on my feelings. But I've never formed a whirlwind of energy before. It was huge, and it was bloody powerful." I'd always been able to call on the natural element of air, but that was totally different from actually forming a whirlwind of energy.

Jared shook his head in wonder. "I swear it was almost like it was alive."

"Just as every human produces energy, every vampire produces preternatural energy," said Luther. "Preternatural energy is the fuel that fires vampiric gifts. The preternatural energy that Sam now produces is hybrid energy. It is powerful, and it calls to the surrounding energy like a magnet. The two energies mingle together inside of her, creating one hell of a cocktail, and strengthening her gift. Have you ever seen a mixture of chemical substances bubbling inside a corked bottle?"

Jared nodded in understanding. "The cork came off."

"I would say so, yes."

I massaged my temples. "I blame the brothers."

Jared gave my wrist a squeeze. "I should have made their deaths more painful."

I went to assure him that their deaths had been satisfyingly painful enough, but then the doors were barged open and in marched Eloise and Collins. Oh bloody great.

(Jared)

They truly couldn't have picked a worse time to piss around. Now that I fully understood the toll these assholes had taken on Sam, I didn't have the patience to deal with their shit. And of course Collins and Eloise had shit to dish out. What was new?

Eloise stomped towards where each of us had risen to our feet. She snarled at Sam before addressing Antonio, her head held high. "Your *commander* attacked me! I expect her to be reprimanded!"

"Oh you do, do you?" drawled Antonio. His tone was menacing enough to make Eloise take a cautious step backwards. It wasn't often that Antonio was anything other than cool and collected, but right now he was clearly on the verge of snapping.

Dexter hissed from his place on the sofa, his scales now red once more. Clearly only just noticing him, Collins jerked away and involuntarily bumped into Eloise.

She went to snap at him but then gripped his arm instead and urged him toward Antonio. "Fredrick witnessed the whole thing. Go on, tell him, Fredrick."

Clearing his throat, Collins nodded. "I did indeed witness Commander Parker attack my colleague, and I will be reporting this incident to the Prelature. I will also be reporting that she has hindered my investigation several times. It is quite clear that she does not deserve her position, and I will be making that clear in my report."

Sam gave a humorous laugh. "Mr Collins, I've cooperated with you even though your investigation is way too intrusive for my liking." Her tone was business-like and brisk. "I've answered your questions, I've let you watch my training sessions, and I've let you shadow me. But I will not allow you to bully me, and that is exactly what you have repeatedly attempted to do. You have thrown your authority around, expecting me to hop, skip, and jump at your say-so." She took a step toward him, wearing that haughty, all-knowing, school teacher look that always made me want to fuck her within an inch of her life. "As such, you should know that I'll be making an official complaint about both of you."

Collins gaped. "Excuse me?"

And this was where he would learn that Sam wasn't to be fucked

172

with. And I had a front seat. Smiling, I folded my arms over my chest and watched my mate at work.

"I have witnesses to attest to the fact that Miss Montana dresses inappropriately, spends much of her working hours at the pool – oh and I have photographic evidence to support this, should you wish to see it – and persistently makes inappropriate comments to Jared. Had she been a male and Jared been a woman in that situation, it would most likely be classed as sexual harassment. Worse, Jared is Bound to another. That bond is considered very sacred, is it not? She shows no respect for it, which is a very serious thing, as you are both fully aware."

Pausing, she shot Eloise a withering look that actually made her cower. Turning her attention back to Collins, Sam continued. "As Jared pointed out earlier, vampires have gone to war in the past in order to protect such a bond. It is instinctive for us to vigorously defend it, even if violent measures are needed. Even knowing this, she behaves inappropriately, which puts both of you in danger – it can certainly be counted as *reckless* among many other things. We all know how you feel about recklessness, Mr Collins. She also invaded my home on one occasion, which is not at all tolerable. And let's not forget that she's been sleeping with some of the guards when she is here to *work*. All of that, I think you will agree, is totally unprofessional behaviour."

Collins just stood, dumbfounded, and looking at Sam as if seeing her for the first time. I noticed that Antonio and Luther were as equally amused as I was. Eloise, on the other hand, was staring at Sam; her eyes glimmered with a mixture of horror, shock, and fury.

Eventually Collins gathered himself. "W-well your complaints are indeed s-serious," he allowed. Eloise gasped, glowering at him. "But I must point out that these only apply to Eloise." It was typical that the slimy piece of shit would only be interested in saving his own skin, happy to hand his colleague out to dry.

Sam smiled. "Oh I've got a number of complaints that I can make against you."

His expression turned wary. It definitely should. "I know that you have felt shadowed, Commander Parker, but protocol states that I stay here as an observer."

"But bothering my squad during their free time isn't protocol, is it? Asking them personal questions and requesting to see their personal files isn't protocol either. You also publically revealed the identity of the complainant when, according to you, they wished to remain anonymous. That not only went against protocol, it placed them in danger – after all, the rest of the squad would not have reacted well to such betrayal, had they believed any betrayal had taken place. As it turned out, you purposely accused the wrong person; that, in and of itself, is appalling. And let's not also forget that you interrupted a training session by participating."

His face flushed with outrage. I half-expected him to stomp his foot. "You invited me to participate!"

"But you're here in a professional capacity, Mr Collins. You should have declined. As you have repeatedly stated, protocol says that you stay here as an *observer*. There's also the fact that you persistently ask my PA to do things for you. That interrupts his work and, therefore, interferes with the quality of it. You're also very rude to the Heir – again, many witnesses can attest to this. As if all that isn't bad enough" – she took a step closer to him – "you're sleeping with an old consort of Jared's."

The others all gasped in shock. I'd been a little surprised myself when Sam told me a week ago.

Sam grinned. "Yes, Daniela told me all about this very unprofessional behaviour. Unlike Joy, she's not jealous of my relationship with Jared, and she's loyal to the people in The Hollow. You ask her a lot of questions about Jared, don't you? Personal questions related to his past, his behaviour throughout the years, his relationship with me, and even his strengths and weaknesses. You've been using her to get information. No woman likes to be used, Mr Collins. So you can bet your arse that any answer she gave you was a load of shite."

Purple – that was the only word to describe how he looked right then. "I have no interest in Commander Michaels."

"No, you have interest in the position of Heir. And he has that. And you just hate him for it, don't you? You want to find something that you can use to make some kind of case against him to the Prelature, perhaps something that could cause him to lose his position." She shook her head very slowly, her gaze drilling into him. "It's not going to happen."

He took a long, steadying breath. "What is it you want?"

Sam arched a brow. "Say again?"

"What is it you want from me? You want me to write a report in your favour?"

"Are you trying to bribe me, Mr Collins?" She gave him a mockingly reprimanding look. "Tut, tut, tut. This just keeps getting worse, doesn't it? No, I'm afraid you don't get to wangle your way out of this. My complaints will lead to you being shadowed on your next case, right? Then you'll know exactly how it's felt for me." When he just gaped at her, she cocked her head. "Didn't anyone ever mention my vengeful streak to you? I'm a believer in tit for tat."

Proud of her, I came up behind Sam and curled an arm around her shoulder to run my finger along her collarbone. "In other words, Collins...you're fucked." The Prelature took complaints against its representatives very seriously. I wouldn't be surprised if Sam's complaints had him fired. One thing was for sure: his report wouldn't be recognised as well-founded. In fact, particularly given the testimonies of the squad, the complaints against Sam would be branded as groundless and then instantly dismissed.

Collins tilted his head as he regarded Sam. "I underestimated you." She just smiled.

"It happens a lot," I told him. "People see her temper and overlook her intelligence. They're always sorry for it."

"Jared's good at sussing out a person's weaknesses," said Sam, talking to both Collins and Eloise now, "and he quite rightly pointed out yours. You both thought you were immune to authority, untouchable. And you went on a power trip. Wrong move. You basically set your own trap." And rather than constantly rise to their taunting behaviour over the past few weeks, she sat back and allowed them to unknowingly spring that trap.

I shrugged at them. "At least she didn't whip the shit out of you – be grateful, because it hurts like a son of a bitch."

"Collins, I think it would be a good idea for you and Eloise to leave tomorrow." When they went to object, Antonio added, "You have caused quite enough damage – to the people here, and to yourselves." Guided by Luther, a glum Collins and a cursing Eloise left the room. Antonio gave Sam an approving nod, smiling in amusement. "I hope I never end up on the wrong side of you. Do not forget that the announcement about the Coronation will be made on Friday evening."

Like we could forget something like that. It only gave Sam and me tonight and tomorrow evening before everything changed. Once it was officially declared that Antonio's rule was reaching an end, he would then begin relinquishing his authority little by little, deferring matters to us.

Seemingly satisfied by my nod, he followed after the others with the guards trailing behind him.

Sam released a cleansing sigh. "I've been waiting to say that shit for a *long* time." She held her arm out to Dexter, who began to curl himself around it. "It was worth biding my time just to see the looks on their faces just then."

"It *would* have been if it wasn't for the emotional toll it took on you and your gift."

She waved her hand dismissively. "Watching a whirlwind sling her around was fun." Now that Dexter's entire body was twined around her arm, she said, "Novo." He returned to his tattoo form, which began a slow slither upwards. She smiled at me. "Let's go home. Apparently I need to give all my bottled up emotions an outlet; killing Magda all over again on the PlayStation will make me feel better."

I smiled back, in the best mood after just watching her slap-down Collins and Eloise. "Sure thing, my homicidal psycho."

CHAPTER FOURTEEN

(Sam)

S tanding in front of the mirror, I tugged on the sleeves of my white shirt and scowled at my reflection. Many people looked good in suits – smart, sophisticated, and elegant. I was not one of those people. Instead, I looked like a kid playing 'dress up'. Jeans, combat pants, tank tops, t-shirts – that was more my style...which was exactly why Fletcher had turned up at my apartment with this stuff. When I tugged at the sleeves again, he gently slapped at my hand.

"Stop fussing. You look fabulous."

I snorted. "I don't mind occasionally wearing a dress, but a suit? This just isn't me."

"Luv, I know you feel uncomfortable, but you can't wear casual clothes tomorrow night while Antonio announces to the High Masters that you and Jared will soon be replacing him."

I'd told Fletcher about the upcoming announcement yesterday evening, making him swear to keep it to himself until after it had been officially made by Antonio.

"You like the black high heels though, don't you? Admit it."

In truth, I quite liked them, but I was feeling too put-out to admit it. Going for aloof, I sniffed. "They're all right."

His smug expression said that he was seeing right through my act. "Shame Collins left last night."

Surprised by his words, I pulled a face. "Is it?"

"I was planning to put hair remover in his NST."

I laughed. "I don't think he would have drunk it anyway. Not after you put laxatives in the last one you gave him."

Fletcher smiled impishly. "The poor sod had about ten seconds between when a cramp struck him and when a shit actually popped out. Who would have thought he could run so fast? But when you've gotta go, you've gotta go."

"I think I preferred it when you put a blob of hair in Eloise's sandwich."

His smile widened. "Took her at least fifteen minutes to realise it was a chunk of her own precious hair."

Watching her balk and choke had been fun for everyone. "Right, I better get changed. Jared will be here any minute now to take me to the arena." No doubt the squad would be just as joyous to not have 'observers' anymore while they trained.

Fletcher rooted through my wardrobe and pulled out a t-shirt and combat pants. "Where is that hunk of yours?"

When he plonked the clothes in my arms, I huffed indignantly. "I do know how to pick out clothes."

He waved his hand dismissively. "Oh chillax and get ready."

Rolling my eyes, I began to dress. "Bossy little sod, aren't you?"

"Bossy? Not at all. I just know what you should be doing, wearing, and thinking." Taking my new – and very boring – clothes, Fletcher hung them up in my wardrobe. "So, how do you feel about being made co-leader of our kind?"

I shrugged nonchalantly. "I knew the day would come eventually."

"That doesn't answer my question."

I shot him an impatient look. "You're an Empath; you know exactly how I'm feeling."

"I can sense that you're nervous. But you're also worried. Something's bugging you."

Finally dressed, I sighed. "Jared's keeping something from me."

Fletcher perched himself on the edge of my bed. "What kind of 'something'?"

"I don't know. I don't think it's anything *really* bad, but whatever it is, it's eating at him."

"Have you asked him about it?"

"Yeah. He did a typical Jared thing and shut down." But I wasn't pissed off with him. Just disappointed and concerned.

"Luv, you know how guarded he can be," Fletcher gently reminded me.

"But we've been working on that. Both of us have, because we're both as bad as each other in that sense. Sometimes he buries his emotions so deep that I don't have a prayer of understanding what's going on in that head of his. This time, though, it's different."

"Different how?"

"He's not hiding his emotions or being cagey. He just won't tell me what the problem is. It's like he's torn about it – he wants me to know, yet he doesn't." I retrieved a hair-tie from my bedside cabinet and scooped my hair up into a ponytail. "I haven't poked him about it because so much has been going on – his twin brother was dying, Collins and Eloise showed up and insisted on making our lives hell, I was bitten, and he's also got the pressure of knowing that Antonio will have us replace him soon. I didn't want to add to any of that pressure, so I kept quiet. But now that everything's mostly okay, I'm tempted to ask him about it. He probably won't tell me without a little pressure anyway."

Fletcher was quiet for a minute, and I could tell his little mind was working away. "Maybe you should at least wait until after the announcement has been made. There's a possibility that it's something that could cause a little dispute between you, and you don't want to be at odds with him at a time like this."

That was a good point. "I just don't like that something's playing on his mind. And, yeah, it's irritating me that I don't know what it is. But mostly, I'm worried about him. He's been through enough these past few weeks." How he hadn't snapped, considering his total lack of patience, I wasn't sure.

"Then be here for him now. Don't push him at a time when he needs you. You know you're the only person he lets himself need; the only person who he wholeheartedly trusts. This is a time when you should be at each other's side, presenting a united front and facing all these changes together and all that stuff."

Why did he have to be right?

"You can spare the poor sod a little more time, can't you?"

"Fine," I grumbled.

Fletcher smiled, reaching over to pat my hand. "That's my girl."

At that moment, Jared appeared beside me. *Speak of the randy devil...*

As usual, Fletcher melted at the sight of him. With a dreamy sigh, he got to his feet. "Don't mind me. I'll let myself out." He gave me a look that said *Remember what I told you.* "See you later." In vampire speed, he was gone from the apartment.

Jared held out his hand. "Ready?"

Smiling, I took his hand. "Yep." In a blink, we were at the arena. The squad was filing inside, talking loudly and laughing.

When Max glanced around the spectator area and found it empty, he turned to me. "They've seriously gone?"

"They left last night," I confirmed. The entire squad whooped at that. I felt like whooping along with them. I'd missed being able to work without having someone hovering over me, noting every itty bitty thing that I did and criticising my every move. Knowing that my shadow was gone and that the bitch of the century was no longer around to flirt with Jared, I couldn't help smiling. Life was good.

"I heard that they'd left," began Denny, "but I didn't believe it. I couldn't think of anything that would make them up and go like that."

When Jared and I exchanged a smile, Reuben narrowed his eyes. "What did you do, Coach?"

"Are they still alive?" asked David.

Affronted, I huffed. It would take more than annoying behaviour to make me lose my cool enough to kill someone. "Yes, they're still alive."

"Damn," muttered Damien. The others looked equally disappointed.

"Tell me you at least maimed them or something," pleaded Stuart. Beside him, Harvey seemed hopeful.

Jared chuckled. "It was tempting, but no, they're both still in one piece."

Chico stroked his goatee. "Then how did you get them to leave?"

I joined my hands behind my back. "Let's just say that since the case will undoubtedly be dropped, there was no reason for them to stick around and observe us any longer."

"Which means we can work you as hard as we need to," said Jared, grinning impishly. "So let's move on quickly from the subject of those assholes because they've wasted enough of our time as it is." The squad nodded, their expressions now determined. "Sam and I expect you to give your all tonight. Anything less is unacceptable, because there is absolutely no excuse in the world why you can't give it to us after how average your recent training sessions have been."

To their credit, they appeared to welcome the challenge as opposed to feel disheartened by it. But then, no doubt holding back for so long had been frustrating – a little like driving a Porsche but only being able to travel at thirty miles per hour.

From the very first minute of the training session, Jared and I worked the squad hard. We *had* to. It was imperative that they were at their best, because the worry that lay in the back of my mind was that if something happened to me, Jared would instantly die too, and then the squad would be alone. As such, smack bam in the middle of a particular training exercise, I interrupted with, "Did you hear that outside?" The false panic that I'd injected into my voice had them all tensing, instantly alert. "It sounded like...an explosion." Wide-eyed, they listened intently.

Jared frowned. *Baby, what are you doing?*

Trust me. When the squad heard nothing and their unease melted into confusion, they glanced at each other questioningly.

"Coach, I didn't hear anything," said Butch.

"That's because there was no explosion. But imagine if there was. Imagine if, while you lot are training or lounging around or playing basketball, you suddenly hear that The Hollow's defences have been breached. Worse, a battle is now ensuing. Furthermore, Jared and I have been captured and quite possibly killed. What do you do?"

Shocked by my abrupt change in exercise, they didn't move or speak. Interrupting their exercises for any reason wasn't something that I usually did. But I was doing it to make a point.

"The last time the walls were attacked, we knew in advance thanks to a vision from Luther, and we were well prepared. But Luther doesn't foresee everything. And if you think that the next vampires who attack – and vampires *will* eventually attack this place again one day – will do so while you're alert and ready, you've got another thing coming. They'll want to use the element of surprise and catch you off-guard. They'll try to remove Antonio, Jared, and me from the equation first – not only because we're powerful, but because it would affect everyone's morale in a huge way and instil utter fear in you all. So, I'll say it again: let's imagine this place has been infiltrated, that you don't have commanders now, that you need to rely on each other...what do you do?"

As I'd expected, they each cast glances at Chico, naturally looking to him for leadership. Noticing that, he straightened to his full height, accepting the responsibility. "That's where I come in."

Jared folded his arms across his chest. "And what is it that you'll do, Chico?" Understanding how my mind worked, Jared now knew exactly what the purpose of all this was. "You're now responsible for your squad's safety and you have to lead them into battle, it's now down to you to guide them."

"I'd pair us up, just like how Coach told us to pair up during the last battle. Salem with Reuben, me with Damien, Stuart with Denny, David with Butch, and Max with Harvey. That way, everyone has someone looking out for them whose gift complements theirs in some way." The rest of the squad nodded, seemingly pleased with the plan.

"You wouldn't decide to simply charge into the battle as a whole to compensate for not having us with you?" I asked, pursing my lips.

"No, because we'll already be shaken by you guys not being there. The worst thing to do would be to deviate from what we've been trained to do. We'd stick to what we know."

I smiled. "Excellent answer." I spoke to them all then. "We're your commanders and we're powerful, but we're not invincible. If something were to happen to us, you will still be expected to fight alongside the other squads. You cannot afford to dwell or to have a moment of doubt. You need to turn any emotions you feel into fuel, and you need to protect this place and the people within it."

"I know what it's like to suddenly find yourself without a commander," said Jared, beginning to slowly pace. "It happened to the squad I joined when I was first accepted into the legion. It's scary. It's a shock to your system. It can shake your confidence. And that's exactly what your enemy would be counting on in that situation. No other commander would try to lead you because they wouldn't know enough about you and your capabilities. It would mean that you guys were on your own."

Unease snaked around the entire squad as they cast each other nervous glances.

"But that doesn't have to be a bad thing," continued Jared. "You know each other inside out. You know each other's strengths and weaknesses. You know who the best strategist is, who is the fastest, who is the stealthiest, and who is physically the strongest – you know all of this information, and you can take advantage of it."

"We're going to try something a little different now." Tapping into the energy of the earth, I built a large wall near the far end of the arena. Following that, I added a few ledges to the rear of it before springing to the top and perching myself on the edge. Jared joined me. "I want you to imagine that this wall is the entrance of a building.

Commander Michaels and I have been captured and you suspect that we are being kept behind it. For all you lot know, we could in fact be dead—"

"Until we knew for sure, we wouldn't assume that you were dead," growled Chico. "We'd do our damn best to get into that building." The others all nodded, looking resolute.

I couldn't help be touched by that. "The problem is that it's well guarded. The other issue is that you're being pursued from behind. Wouldn't it be best to concentrate on keeping yourselves safe?"

"You wouldn't leave us behind, and we wouldn't leave you behind," Salem firmly stated, and I knew he was referring to the assignment that had led to me being tainted.

"Exactly," said Denny.

"So, then, what next?" Jared asked Chico.

"Next, I'd do what you guys would do: I'd split the squad into two. Five of us would work on getting into the building while the other five covers us. I know it would mean deviating from pairing up, but that particular situation would call for it."

Pleased, Jared gave him a nod of respect. "How exactly would you split the squad?"

"I'd have Harvey, Reuben, Damien, David, and Butch cover Salem, Max, Denny, Stuart, and me."

I smiled. "Good thinking, Chico. I'm going to ask you all to split up just like that now."

Brows drawn together in confusion, they obediently divided into two groups.

"Chico, you and the four who you believe would be the best choice to invade this building are going to try to do exactly that."

"Are you and Commander Michaels going to fend us off?" asked Stuart, getting into position in the middle of the arena with the rest of his team.

"No. Harvey, Reuben, Damien, David, and Butch are going to do that. I agree with you, Chico – they make a good defensive team. Now it's up to you to get past them in order to save your commanders, assuming we're still alive, that is. If any of you receive what would be classed as a 'fatal' hit if Reuben hadn't weakened your gifts for the training session, you'll be expected to sit in the spectators' area. Harvey, I'm making you leader of your team." He grinned at that and pulled his members aside.

As both teams engaged in a huddle, Jared and I jumped down from the wall and sat in the front row of spectator seats. The commanders had now been removed from the equation, and the squad had to think for themselves.

From where they stood in the centre of the arena, Chico's team made the first move. Chico aimed a spray of thorns at Butch, who was covering David, the strongest link, at the top of the wall. They both ducked by squatting on one of the ledges that I'd added to the rear of the wall. Instead of retaliating, David psychically 'zapped' Max before he had the chance to rob their senses, taking him out. But it was no more than a minute later that a psychic hit from Salem removed Butch from Harvey's team. Salem had obviously thought that he would then have a clear shot at David, but he'd greatly underestimated him. David did very well at using the building as cover. Jared and I had trained him never to rely on Butch, to be prepared to protect himself if the need arose, and he had clearly listened extremely well.

Each time anyone from Chico's team came near the wall, Reuben would dash from behind it – the bloke was seriously fast – and attack, simultaneously weakening their gift. At that point, Harvey would send their 'attackers' flying away; never attacking from the same spot twice. Damien worked at diverting the attention of Chico's team by making them target his astral self while he kept his physical body safe behind the wall. This then gave David a chance to eliminate those who were distracted by Damien. In no time at all, David had gotten rid of Salem and Stuart. Denny eventually snatched Reuben with his yellowy-green ooze, chucking him aside. That then left Harvey, Damien, and David against Chico, Stuart, and Denny.

Stuart repeatedly did his best to get near the wall in particle form, but Harvey always managed to send those particles swishing away. Apparently determined to get rid of Harvey, Denny took a massive chance: able to leap high distances like a copepod, he abruptly jumped to the top of the wall, where Harvey was currently situated. He wrapped himself around Harvey, and took him to the ground – eliminating them both from the exercise, but giving his own team a better chance.

Chico made a quick dash for the wall, shooting thorns at Damien's astral self. David managed to psychically hit Chico before he could reach them, taking him out. But Stuart, still in particle form, took advantage of David being distracted by Chico and literally swished around the wall, reaching Damien before he had the chance to return to his body. Despite that there was only one of Chico's team 'alive', all of them still cheered and made a huge fuss of Stuart.

I was truly impressed. They had done a lot better than I'd been expecting. They hadn't had to work so hard in a while, and this was the first time that they had been instructed to act without any guidance from Jared or me. They had rose to the challenge, met it head-on, and given it everything they had. A commander couldn't ask for more.

When Jared and I re-joined them, they instantly quieted and turned to face us. Each one of them looked extremely pleased with themselves, despite that technically only one of them had 'survived'. "The one thing I love about this squad is that it functions like a well-oiled machine." They almost flushed at my praise. "If in a situation like this you do exactly as Chico said and you stick to what you know, you'll continue to function this way and you will survive." I let a mean smile surface on my face. "And you'll get revenge for Jared and me."

Denny's smile matched mine. "Coach, I can assure you that if, by some fluke, someone managed to kill you, they wouldn't live to tell the tale. That's a promise."

Seeing their fierce expressions, I believed them. I just had to hope that it wouldn't come to that.

(Jared)

Click. Clack. Click. Clack. Click. Clack.

The noise was driving me fucking insane. After a long evening of training, I had retreated to the 'bat pool' for a little down time while Sam went to one of the cafés with Fletcher. All I'd wanted was to have some time to myself, a little peace and quiet, in the hope of relaxing my hyped-up mind. Despite that I was excited about ascending, I was still nervous at the knowledge that Antonio would be making the announcement tomorrow night. It also served to remind me that my time was running out – I'd need to tell Sam about the vision soon. I could delay it until after the announcement, but it wouldn't be fair to go through with the Coronation without telling her.

As I'd swum length after length, the tension had begun to leave my body, and my thoughts had stopped running wild. But that had quickly changed when Joy appeared ten minutes ago. She had taken to strutting up and down the side of the pool in a pair of stilettos and not much else. I'd hoped that ignoring her would make her leave, but no such luck. She hadn't broken stride or ceased to attempt to draw me into conversation. I'd give it five more minutes, I decided. If after that she still —

"This again?" a bored and very familiar husky voice asked.

I peered up to see Sam approaching with her head cocked to one side, regarding Joy like she was a freaky yet morbidly intriguing bug. She halted parallel to where I was afloat, but she didn't move her eyes from Joy.

Fletcher sidled up to Sam, gawking at the sight of Joy. "I take back what I said about her looking like an Azkaban escapee. Right now, she's making me think of a washed up Playboy Bunny who's surviving on a diet of paint chips and crack cocaine."

It was actually a pretty accurate description. Sure, Joy had the Keja hypnotic allure. But dark emotions like hatred and bitterness had a way of distorting a person's beauty, even making them look haggard and gaunt.

"I can't see why it should bother you so much, Sam." Joy did a slow strut toward her, hands on her hips...or where her hips *should* be. "Unless, of course, you see me as a threat to your bond with Jared...?"

Wearing a deadpan expression, Sam replied in a flat, toneless voice, "Yes, that's what it is."

"Or maybe you're just jealous." Joy smirked at Sam as she stopped in front of her. "Jealous because you know that I've had your mate. That I've touched every inch of him. That I've had him inside me."

Scratching her forehead, Sam sighed. "Joy, you might think that gives you some kind of edge, given that your IQ matches that of a vole and your brain works on a different frequency than the rest of us. But, honestly, I actually pity you. Yes, you shook the sheets with Jared a number of times in the past. But come on, it doesn't make you special because let's face it, he was a bit of a slut."

Frowning, I whined, "Hey!" Fletcher gave me a look that said *Well you were*. I opened my mouth to object, but instead I exhaled a resigned sigh. "Yeah, okay."

Joy was too focused on Sam to even register that I'd spoken. Her chuckle contained no trace of humour. "Don't worry; I know that I was only ever a piece of ass to him. I know he doesn't care about me the way I care about him. But I also know that he'll never be satisfied with just one woman. He needs more than—"

"Yes, so you've said before," said Sam tiredly. "And I'm sure he'll go running off to you when he realises this. But until that happens, I can let you both live. So why not run along."

Joy straightened her shoulders. "I'm not scared of you." Could the woman possibly get any dumber?

A smile slowly spread across Sam's face. "But you're scared that I'll Merge with you again, aren't you?"

Fear briefly flickered in Joy's eyes. When Joy had once attacked Sam, my mate had retaliated by launching herself at her...only to instead accidentally Merge her body with Joy's and completely take her over. It had left Joy drained and disorientated, not to mention pissed that she'd lost control of her own body to Sam.

Not wanting Sam to have to listen to any more of this shit, I teleported to the sun lounger that I'd claimed, retrieved my towel, and patted myself dry as I came to stand behind her. But my gaze was on Joy. "I'd tell you that I'm not going to leave Sam, but this is something you're already well aware of. Deep down, you know nothing that you or anyone else does will ever tempt me away from her."

Joy's face hardened. "You need more."

"I have what I need." It was true.

"We were happy until she came here. You didn't love me, I know that. I even know that you love her. But it doesn't change the fact that she'll never be enough." She shrugged her shoulders. "It's not like you would be the only Bound male who has a consort on the side, is it?"

Fletcher tilted his head. "And you would honestly be happy to be someone's dirty little secret?"

It was clear on her face that no, she wouldn't be. I knew exactly why she wouldn't let that be an issue. "You don't want *me*, Joy. You want to be the Heir's consort again. That's all it is. It was the only reason that you ever wanted me."

Her eyes flared. "No. I care for you."

"Then can't you be happy for him?" asked Sam.

Joy snorted. "Are you really telling me that *you* would be happy for him if the situation was reversed?"

"Oh there's no denying that I would want to skin you alive and make a rug out of your flesh, but I'd stay away and let him live his life. I certainly wouldn't be so pathetic as to hang around him the way you do, trying to lure him back to me."

"How is it pathetic to remind him of what he's missing?"

"Don't you have any pride at all?" Fletcher asked Joy, shaking his head in amazement.

Her eyes alight with hatred, she sneered at him. "Says the one who prances around like a fairy."

Fletcher seemed more amused than offended. "I'm more of a woman than you'll ever be."

Sam chuckled. "He's got a point, Joy."

A flush of pure anger crept up her neck and face. "It might not be me that Jared comes to when he finally realises what he really needs, but he *will* turn away from you at some point. You'd be a fool to doubt that." Then, in vampire speed, she disappeared.

Fletcher swerved to look at me. "The crank truly believes that, doesn't she?"

Chuckling again, Sam answered for me. "Of course she does. I know it seems weird, but think about it from her neurotic point of view. Jared didn't just have her as a consort; he had two others as well. Joy probably wasn't too happy about it. Then there's the fact that, even with three consorts, he still bonked other females when the mood struck him. Her mind had two choices: believe that she wasn't what he needed because she lacked somehow and he didn't care at all for her, or believe that he was simply someone who needed more than one woman and it didn't reflect on her whatsoever, that he might even care for her. She convinced herself of the latter, because it suited her to believe that. It made the situation not hurt so much."

"So seeing him Bound and committed to someone else threatens her illusion," deduced Fletcher. "If she accepted that you're all he needs, she'd have to accept that what she's always believed in the cause of emotional self-preservation is untrue."

Sam nodded. "And who would want to accept that the person they care about has never cared about them? It would certainly piss me the fuck off."

It would piss me off, too. I'd want to know what the fucking point was in finding and caring for this person so much if they would never feel the same. To then have that person leave me for someone else and be so happy with them – happy enough to join with them for life – would be the final twist of the knife. Wanting to fend off the dark feelings threatening to surface at just the idea of that, I slipped my arm around Sam to pull her close. Okay, so I could feel a teensy bit sorry for Joy, just as I did for Cristiano. But I still believed that my being Heir was what interested Joy the most.

Fletcher shrugged, as if to shake off the matter. "Well, it's been a long night. I'm off to find Norm." He gave Sam a brief hug, offered me a shy wave, and then left us alone.

Sam raised her gaze to mine. "Did the swim help? I know something's on your mind, but I'm not going to ask what it is. Tell me in your own time...just don't take too long."

Appreciating that she wasn't pushing, I kissed her gently. "We'll talk about it soon," I promised. "You know, you've impressed me. My holding back is annoying the shit out of you – I can sense it. Usually when I piss you off in some way, you retaliate with that whip of yours. But you've contained yourself."

She placed her hands on my chest. Her smile dripped with pity. "Aw, Jared, whatever made you think I was going to contain myself?" She shoved hard – so hard that I went zooming backwards and landed in the pool.

Kicking to the surface, I coughed up the mouthful of water that had clogged my throat and glowered at my mate. Appearing rather self-satisfied, she folded her arms. I shook my head at her. "You know you're a bitch, right?"

She smiled. "It's part of why you love me."

I had to smile back. She was right, it was.

CHAPTER FIFTEEN

(Sam)

Just as I had yesterday evening, I fiddled with the sleeves of my white shirt as I stood in my bedroom, scowling at my reflection in the mirror. Just as he had yesterday evening, Fletcher slapped at my hands. "Oi," I whined.

"Stop fussing before you rip the bloody sleeves at the hem."

"*You* stop fussing before I clock you over the head." If I could help it, I'd never wear a suit again.

Jared entered the bedroom, totally edible in a grey shirt and black trousers. Unsurprisingly, Fletcher gawked in admiration, and I didn't blame him. The sod could pull off just about any look. I was totally envious.

Jared's brows rose. "Wow, you look—"

"*Don't,*" I bit out.

He sighed. "I was going to—"

"Give me a false compliment because you know I feel awkward," I finished.

He shot me an impatient stare. "Actually, it wouldn't have been a false one. You look—"

"*Don't.*"

He threw his hands up in a gesture of exasperation. "Here I am pushing past my difficulty with giving compliments, and you're shutting me down. You're never going to learn to accept one, are you?"

"Then why keep doing it?"

He grunted, sliding his arm around my waist and pulling me against him. "You ready?" When I nodded, he added, "I don't just mean physically." He gently tapped my temple. "I mean, are you mentally ready for this?"

Having the uncharacteristic need to fidget and keep my hands

190

busy, I adjusted his collar and smoothed my hands over the arms of his shirt. "About as ready as I can be." But there was a nervous tremor to my voice.

Cupping my chin, he lifted my head so that he could meet my eyes. His own eyes were shining with adoration and reassurance. "You'll be fine." He dropped a kiss on my mouth and then went to say more, but stopped at the knock on the door. Fletcher dashed out of the room to answer it, and quickly returned with Evan and Alora.

Alora smiled at me. "Hey, you look—"

"I wouldn't bother if I were you," mumbled Fletcher. "She'll only accuse you of lying to try and make her feel better."

Knowing me well, Evan didn't comment on my appearance. "Nervous?"

"Of course I'm not," I said with a forced smile. But, as I said, he knew me well; he wasn't buying my act. But rather than make a big thing out of it, he simply offered me a supportive smile.

Jared tightened his hold on me as he asked Evan, "What brings you guys here?"

"Just wanted to check on you both and, you know...do that whole 'moral support' thing."

I rolled my eyes. "You mean Alora made you come."

Evan's expression was pure innocence. "No, I *do* have a sensitive side, you know." Then it was Alora's turn to roll her eyes. "Off the subject, I've just met that Covington guy who had recommended you find Paige West. He's here with Bran and Paige's Sire, Robert Langley."

I didn't like the sound of that. Bran was a regular visitor, but the others weren't. "Have they asked about Paige?"

"Langley was asking where she was, but Antonio just said that she healed the tainted vampires and then left. Bran wasn't interested. He only came here to see Alora. She invited him."

"I wanted to tell him that I would be leaving his line and why," she explained. "After everything he's done for me, it would have been insensitive not to do it face-to-face."

True. "And he's okay with it?"

"Yep." Evan grinned. "He even offered us his best wishes for the future."

Fletcher gently tapped his watch. "Time's-a-ticking, people."

I took a deep breath. "Then let's go." Before I vomited with nerves. "See you three later." They each gave us a smile just before Jared teleported us both to the mansion.

Standing outside the room in which the teleconference would take place, he took both my hands in his and searched my eyes. "You sure you're okay about this?"

I knew that if I said no, he would teleport me straight back home – no hesitation, no judgemental comments, and no temper tantrum. He would put me before what Antonio wanted and even before what he himself wanted. And that was what gave me the strength to nod and reply, "I'm fine. Let's do this."

Flashing me a smile filled with pride, he dropped a kiss on my mouth. Then, keeping one of my hands in his, he opened the door and led me inside. From their spot in the corner, Antonio's personal guards gave us a nod. Sitting at the long table were Antonio, Luther, Sebastian, Bran, Covington, and a male who I presumed was Robert Langley. Each of them immediately rose to their feet.

Antonio smiled widely. "Punctual, as always. Sam, Jared, you know Bran and Harry Covington." He then gestured to the unfamiliar balding, podgy Keja. "This is Robert Langley, Paige West's Sire."

Scowling, Langley simply grunted at us.

Covington shook Jared's hand and then mine. "It's a pleasure to meet you both in person."

"Likewise," I replied.

Bran's mouth curved ever so slightly at the sight of Jared, who he had a clear soft spot for. "It will be an honour to follow you. *Both* of you."

I hadn't been expecting that. "Thanks." Sebastian and Luther must have picked up on my nerves because they gave me a reassuring smile. No amount of smiles would calm me at a time like this, but I appreciated their efforts.

Antonio gestured for us to take a seat. "As Bran is here, it makes sense for him to sit in on the teleconference, considering he is one of the High Masters. Covington, Langley, you may both stay if you wish."

"I'd love to," said Covington. Langley gave a grunt of affirmation.

Seemingly satisfied, Antonio swerved to face the wall which displayed several T.V. monitors. He pressed a button on the platinum remote control in his hand. With that, each of the screens switched on, and we were then looking at the faces of all of the High Masters. "Good evening." They each returned his greeting. "As you can see, I'm joined by Jared, Sam, Luther, Sebastian, Bran, his Heir Harry Covington, and one of Covington's vampires, Robert Langley." The rest of us then exchanged greetings with the High Masters, who all looked extremely curious. "I am calling because I have an announcement to make."

Here we go. I had to hope that Antonio was right and I truly had won them all over, or this could be bad. Jared's reaction would be creatively violent if someone even hinted at me not being suitable for the position.

"In three weeks' time," Antonio continued, "I intend to step down from my position as Grand High Master."

He gave everyone a moment to absorb that, and I watched as surprise and a hint of sadness entered their gazes. Everyone liked and respected Antonio. I, too, was sad that he was stepping down. It would be weird not to have his guidance.

"At that point, Jared and Sam will replace me. I am confident that you will all support this and that you will follow them as you have followed me."

I hadn't been so confident, but it appeared that Antonio was right. They were now all smiling at Jared and me, and nodding supportively. Well, that was a relief. One of the High Masters began to speak, but not a word registered in my brain because a shard of pain lanced through my forehead. But it wasn't really my pain; it was coming from Jared. *What is it?*

He rubbed at his temples. *Something's wrong. I've got over a dozen voices shouting at me all at once.*

Saying what?

He took a moment to concentrate, and then his face paled and his eyes widened.

Jared, what's –

The door behind us suddenly burst open, and strange vampires rushed into the room surrounding us in under the time it took to blink. Instinctively, I slammed up my shield, sheltering both Jared and me. But I couldn't shield the others. Couldn't because Luther and Sebastian were now contained in some kind of jelly-like bubble, Antonio's guards were a clump of ashes, Bran was being held in a chokehold by Langley, and – so much worse – Covington had a curved, jagged-edged knife pressed to Antonio's throat. In addition, over a dozen vampires were boxing us all in. *Well, fuck.*

"Move, and your Grand High Master is dead," rumbled Covington. Going by the way the knife in his hand glowed, it was enchanted in some way. His once kind face was now a mask of callousness.

Jared narrowed his eyes. "You wouldn't."

"Wouldn't I?" Covington gave an almost imperceptible nod to Langley, who instantly snapped Bran's neck. A millisecond later, the High Master was nothing but ashes.

I gasped, too stunned to speak. I understood his message – he didn't give a shit about his own mentor, so he wasn't going to care about ours.

"You fucking bastards," growled Jared, itching to attack but knowing that he couldn't. I was feeling just as pissed and helpless.

Sebastian and Luther hurled some obscenities as they struggled to pierce the bubble containing them, but Covington and Langley just laughed. The sound of absolute mayhem suddenly reached me over their maniacal laughs. Something was going on outside…something bad. I wanted to run to the window that overlooked The Hollow, but I didn't dare move, didn't dare take my attention off Covington.

What the fuck's going on? I asked Jared.

The Hollow's been infiltrated, Jared told me, enraged. *I don't know how bad it is yet. But according to Evan, a quarter of the legion is missing from the fight. Alora's checking with the animals to find out if the missing squads are in the rainforest.*

Shit, shit, shit, shit, shit! I wasn't someone who stood back while everyone endangered their lives. And I hated the idea that my squad was out there fighting without us leading them. But right now, I couldn't afford to fucking move. This crazy fucker obviously wanted to die because I was going to kill him for even *touching* Antonio.

The High Masters all began shouting in outrage. Covington quickly spoke. "Before you all jump on your white horses and come here to defend these people, you might want to know what *exactly* you'll be defending. You might want to know the truth about why the Heir's mate is so powerful."

Oh, shit. Jared stiffened beside me. Each of the High Masters quieted, *willing* to listen. Well that really wasn't good. It suggested that maybe they had suspected that I was something 'more' all along.

The door behind us opened again, but I resisted the urge to look, wanting to keep Covington in my sights. The click-clack of heels – *two* sets of heels, I instantly realised – was soon followed by the appearance of a strange female Pagori and that bloody bitch Eloise. There were more footsteps and then more strange male vampires came in. Worse, the males had Paige and Imani with them. Imani was crying while Paige fruitlessly struggled like crazy to get free.

Langley walked right up to Paige, grabbed her by the throat, and smiled evilly. "Eloise assured me that you and Imani were here, but I wasn't so sure. I missed you." She spat in his face. Nice move. But that move earned her a slap.

Half-naked as usual, Eloise sidled up to Covington while smirking at me.

"I'm going to kill you," I told her simply.

Her smirk faltered slightly. "No, Sam. You're the one who's going to die tonight. You'll soon be a lump of ashes just like Bran, Collins, and all the other vampires that are now dying."

I wondered whether it was Eloise or Covington who had killed Collins. It made sense that he hadn't been allowed to live; as Antonio had pointed out, Collins was a stickler for rules. He wouldn't have supported a plan such as this.

It's worse than I expected out there, Jared practically growled. *Luther had said there were so many of them in his vision – he was right. There are at least four hundred. We're totally outnumbered. The squads that were training in the rainforest are dead.*

Fear began to curdle in my stomach. *How are the vampires getting in?*

Through the tunnels that are connected to the underground bunkers in the mansion. Only the guards and the vampires in this room knew where they were.

And I would bet that Eloise got that information from the guards who she'd been shagging, and she had then given that information to Covington. Fuck.

They've been slipping into the bunkers and making their way up, taking over from the inside.

"Explain this, Covington!" demanded one of the High Masters, Ricardo. He hadn't always been my biggest fan, but I'd won him over when he came to the Binding ceremony. He then proceeded to rant at Covington. The other High Masters did the same, outraged.

"I'll explain everything," Covington vowed. "But first…Drop the shield, Sam."

"What? Are you high?" I loved Antonio, but I wouldn't risk Jared for anything or anyone. My expression pled with Antonio to understand, and his gentle smile said that he did and that, furthermore, he approved.

For the first time, I understood just how Jared had felt when he was placed in a position where he had to choose between my safety and that of his brother. It was different when the decision was placed in your own hands, when the risk was to someone you cared about and not to you. I truly adored Antonio, but Jared's safety came first to me and it always would.

Covington held the blade tighter against Antonio's throat. "*Now.*"

Jared reflexively made a move toward them, but I grabbed his arm and held him back. *Don't let him trick you into moving out of the shield. And tell Antonio I'm sorry.* Glaring at Covington, I shook my head. "Not happening."

He gazed at me curiously. "You would risk the Grand High Master's life?"

"I won't leave my mate vulnerable."

He was silent for a moment, and I realised that he truly hadn't been expecting that response. But he eventually shrugged. "No matter. Dana can deal with you."

The Pagori female beside Eloise smirked at me. "I think I'm going to enjoy this." Wow, her voice was surprisingly and painfully squeaky. She raised her arms, palms out, in a move that was very familiar. Then I felt the pull on the energy around me, causing my shield to wink out for a second. Startled, I quickly reinforced the shield.

What the fuck is she doing? demanded Jared.

Bollocks, the bitch is a Feeder. A Feeder who didn't like that her efforts weren't working as well as she'd like. But she was still a threat, because the one guaranteed way of weakening a Feeder was using another – fighting Feeder with Feeder.

"I want the shield gone," Covington snapped at her.

She was practically pouting. "I'm trying." And she really was. There was no denying that she was extremely powerful, which was a real worry. I couldn't suck in more energy without dropping the shield, and that wasn't something I was able to do. That meant I'd have to rely on the supply of hybrid energy that filled me to defend myself. But it was only really a matter of time before she'd absorbed it all and my shield fell. It wouldn't leave me physically weak, but it would mean my gift was worth shit…kind of like running on an empty tank. Still, I'd fight her efforts for as long as I could.

"Try harder," he gritted out, impatient.

"You've got what you wanted," Imani said to Covington, licking her lips nervously. "You've got me. Let them go."

It hit me then. "It was never really Paige that anyone wanted, was it?"

It was Langley who answered me. He glared at Paige as he spoke. "I sent her to retrieve Imani for me. She never returned. She completely disappeared, and I knew that she had taken Imani with her. Finding Paige would lead me to Imani."

"And now you have me," said Imani. "You don't need the others."

Covington gave her an indulgent smile. "Yes, we do have you. But it's not just about you anymore." He looked at Jared. "Eloise told me all about the conversation that you had with your brother in the infirmary. She had been lingering outside the room." He briefly glanced at the High Masters. "Samantha Parker…is a hybrid."

Shit, shit, shit.

In response to the shock and disbelief on their faces, Covington laughed. "Oh I didn't believe it myself at first. That can't be possible, right? But let's look at the facts. Here she stands with Pagori strength and Keja hypnotic beauty. And you've all seen the mercury glow to her irises that are currently glowing with anger. Who else do you know who has that? No one, no matter how powerful they are. And I'll tell you why: it's a marker – a marker that signifies that she's a hybrid." He zeroed in on me. "It's true, isn't it? Tell them."

I thought about calling him a liar, but what was the point? Seeing the fear in his eyes, it was more than obvious what he intended to do – kill me. Whether I denied it or not, he'd still do it, he'd still kill me out of blind fear. "It's true."

"Antonio lied for you."

"To protect me from people like you who are scared of what they don't understand." There was an extra hard tug on the energy constructing my shield, and Dana gasped – the hybrid energy was filling her, invigorating her. My shield was still in place, thanks to my reserves, but I knew it was weakening.

"Scared?" he scoffed. "I'm not scared, sweetheart." Oh yes he was. "I'm smart. Smart enough to know that a hybrid is a dangerous thing – many saw you duel with the vampire who Turned your mate. They know what you can do. They know exactly what any vampires you create will be able to do. They know you can't be allowed to live."

Jared made another move toward him and I again pulled him back. "You won't fucking touch her," he ground out, his irises glowing so red they were like lasers.

Covington turned suitably nervous. "Maybe you both plan to create an army. The ultimate legion." It was clear that he was planting the seed of suspicion in the minds of the High Masters, but what wasn't clear was if it was working. It couldn't be a good sign that they were still and quiet, could it?

"So you've come to kill me? You're doing this big song and dance just to destroy me? I don't think so." When he went to speak, I raised my hand. "I don't doubt that you want me dead. But what you most want is The Hollow, the position of Grand High Master. You're posing as the saviour of vampirekind to try to excuse your actions. But anyone with half a brain can see right through you." Or, at least, I hoped they could.

He snarled, "You need to die."

"And maybe I will—"

"No you fucking won't," Jared vehemently snapped.

"—but if you think there won't be repercussions, you truly haven't thought this through."

Covington didn't appear concerned. "The Hollow was considered impossible to infiltrate, and yet I am now in total control of it. Come see for yourself." Very slowly, still holding Antonio hostage, he edged toward the balcony and gestured at one of his vampires to open the doors. The sound of utter chaos filled the room. "Take a look."

When Covington's vampires moved slightly to let us pass, Jared and I cautiously moved to the balcony with my shield still encompassing us. My stomach plummeted as I glimpsed the vision below us. Buildings were on fire, people were bleeding and screaming, the bodies of dead humans dotted the ground, and the man-made beach was littered with ashes – the remains of so many dead vampires.

"Right now, all hell is breaking lose in The Hollow because of me," claimed Covington. "I've got your big, bad leader!" he declared to all the vampires below, making everyone freeze. "Not even the

Heir or his mate can help him or you. So stand down unless you want them dead!"

Oh he had to be fucking kidding.

"Stand down, and you will not be harmed! Continue to fight, and you will all die! And so will your precious leader!"

There was the briefest hesitation, and then all The Hollow's vampires surrendered. Of course they did. They would never risk Antonio being hurt because they all adored and respected him. I noticed that the squad, Evan, Alora, Ava, Cristiano, and Jude were among them. Their expressions were filled with fury, apprehension, and anguish. At least they were alive.

All those who had surrendered were instantly rounded up like sheep by Covington's men, who then surrounded them. The snickering assholes actually had guns. Vampires relied on their strength, speed, and gifts, not human weapons. This was cowardly and insulting. But it also indicated that they *knew* they were no match for the legion without the weapons.

Covington laughed. "See how they obeyed me? I am in control here. Anyone who would want to go against me would have to be very stupid." That comment was for the High Masters.

Jared snarled at him. "And anyone who would be prepared to follow you would have to be even more stupid. You didn't challenge Antonio for this position. You tried to *take* it. He welcomed you into his home, and you abused his trust. Not only that, you turned on your own High Master. I can't think of any vampire who'll follow someone who can so easily betray others."

That had Covington tensing, and I could almost see the wheels turning in his head. My shield flickered as the suction suddenly intensified, and I quickly reinforced it again. Dana was smirking, pleased with herself. Had I not been a hybrid, she would have disintegrated the shield by now. It was at moments like this when I was actually glad to be a hybrid.

"Maybe you'll kill us and keep The Hollow," said Jared. "But you're forgetting one very important thing."

"And what is that?"

"The Hollow is merely a gated community." Jared shrugged. "It isn't anything that signifies that the person residing here is a ruler. It's just something that Antonio built because he wanted to. All you've done tonight is break into someone's home. That makes you an intruder, nothing more. In other words, living here won't make you the Grand High Master vampire. It won't mean that people have to follow you. It just means that you have a new home."

Jared was absolutely right. And it was clear that now Covington knew it too.

"I'm done chatting." Covington looked at me then. "Time to make a choice, Sam."

Shit. Here it was. That all-important choice that Luther had warned me about. My anxiety and apprehension intensified.

"You see, I'm a fair person. I don't see any reason why these people here have to die purely because you need to be destroyed. In fact, I can just put them in containment cells and have someone teleport those cells out of here. I'll release Antonio and everyone here, and they can live – I give my word on that in front of all the High Masters, can show just how trustworthy I can be. But it will be *your* life in exchange for theirs."

"No, Sam!" Antonio immediately shouted while Jared growled, "Not a fucking chance."

"Do not give him what he wants," insisted Sebastian.

"We've lived very long lives," Luther told me. "It is you and Jared that are important now." Sebastian nodded his agreement, totally earnest.

Covington chuckled. "Sam might be a freak, but she's not stupid. She knows it's in everyone's best interests to agree to my deal. Every single person in The Hollow is depending on her to make the right choice in order to live."

My voice was hard, loaded with anger, as I spoke. "If I agree to your little deal, it would be killing my mate. I don't have any intention of doing that. And any vampire out there – including the High Masters that are watching intently – would understand that putting their mate first is what a vampire does."

The ugly, all-knowing smile that surfaced on his face had me tensing. "Then it's a good thing that I can solve that little matter. Or, more accurately, Imani can solve it."

I frowned, sliding my gaze briefly to a silently crying Imani.

"She didn't tell you what she can do? She didn't tell you why we want her, why Paige has been hiding her?"

Imani looked at me and confessed sadly, "My gift...I can sever blood-bonds."

Well fuck a duck. It made perfect sense for Paige to hide her. A vampire with such a gift could be a weapon – they would have the ability to detach people from their makers and separate Bound couples. Paige hadn't wanted the female to become a pawn in dangerous games like the one being played now.

"If you agree to my deal, Imani will first sever your bond with Jared. This will allow him to live after you die."

"No dice," Jared immediately spat.

Covington arched a reprimanding brow at him. "I think your mate is quite capable of making this decision all by herself. According to Eloise, she is full of opinions."

"*You* made the complaints to the Prelature, didn't you?" snickered Jared.

Covington was smug once more. "With Eloise's help, yes. I needed you all distracted, needed your morale low, needed your time to be consumed enough that you couldn't find any possible avenue of help for the tainted – that your only option would be to locate Paige. Why do you think I recommended her to you? I knew that you had the means to track her."

"There's one thing I don't understand," I said. "How did you find out all that private information about our training methods to make the complaints?"

"Quite easily, really, thanks to a human here that did a little spying for me – all I had to do was promise to Turn someone for her once I became Grand High Master. Apparently Antonio had refused to do it because the human kid she wanted Turning was only twelve. Of course your little traitor is very much dead now since she served her purpose. As I said, I'd just needed you all to be a little distracted – it was originally only Imani that I wanted. But then Eloise told me about you, Sam. I knew what I had to do for the good of all vampirekind."

I snorted. "Like people will buy that. If anything, they'll find it insulting that you expect them to believe it." Yes, that was a little reverse psychology for the High Masters, but I wasn't sure it would work.

He ignored that. "Make your choice, Sam. And choose wisely."

Luther hadn't been kidding when he said that it was a choice that would affect us all. Unless I gave my life for the lives of the people in The Hollow, they would all die and Covington would most likely rule purely because of the fear his success would induce. If others decided to battle him for the position, there would be many lives lost…and all because I wanted to save myself. Was there really a choice when so many could die? When there was no guarantee that I would come out of this alive in any case?

Sam, don't even consider it! Jared's infuriation and fear was almost palpable.

But I'd already made up my mind. "Do it, Imani."

"No!" yelled Jared, gripping my hand tight and yanking me against him.

Antonio, Sebastian, and Luther pleaded with me not to sacrifice my life for theirs, but I ignored their words because it wasn't just about them.

Jared gripped my chin and forced me to look at him. I didn't want to move my gaze from Covington, but how could I not meet my mate's pained eyes just then?

You can't do this, Sam. The desperation and determination there almost broke my heart.

I won't be the reason that you, Antonio, or anyone else here dies.

Then we fight.

Jared, as much as I hate to admit it, I'm in no position to fight anyone. The shield's weakening. I've put every ounce of energy into keeping it intact, but pretty soon there'll be nothing left and my gift will be of no use.

"Sam, do not do this!" Antonio called out. "You and Jared are the future!"

This is the only way you'll all live, Jared. You stay alive and you get revenge for me. You hunt Covington down until he's dead. I gave a sad smile. *I love you.*

Baby, please—

Taking a deep breath, I turned back to Imani, "Do it."

"Don't you fucking dare!" Jared dragged me behind him, as if it would somehow stop her. I peered around him to see that she was shaking her head, refusing to cut the bond.

"Sam agreed to the deal," Covington snarled. "Sever the bond, Imani!" But she didn't, she continued shaking her head. "Langley, I think Imani needs a little persuasion."

So Langley slapped Paige hard once, twice, three times. Imani screamed at him to stop, but instead he did it again and again, harder each time. I wished I was close enough to kill him. If it hadn't been imperative that I kept my shield intact, I'd have reshaped it into my whip and lashed him with it.

"Imani, cut it!" I shouted, coming out from behind Jared. She met my gaze then. Her own was filled with so much anguish. "It's okay."

But Jared, Antonio, Sebastian, Luther, and even Paige were ordering her not to do it. So Langley turned on Paige again, punching her this time; punching her so hard that she was on the verge of passing out.

"I'll do it!" Imani cried. "I'll do it!" With sobs wracking her body, she closed her eyes.

Jared threaded the fingers of one hand in my hair and wrapped his free arm around me, as if keeping me close would keep her out. It didn't. I felt her in my head…It was the weirdest feeling. Like having a small hand rifle through my brain. Then that hand stilled and a finger flicked something that was almost elastic – the move sent reverberations through my head and down the bond, making me wince. Then two fingers grasped it tight, pulled hard, and…and nothing. She did it again, tugging harder this time – so hard it hurt and I had to cradle my head in my hands. But, still, nothing happened.

Imani's eyes flipped open. "It's not working."

Covington's jaw clenched. "Then you're not trying hard enough. Robert, maybe Paige would like to feel—"

"No, I'll try again!"

And she did. Three more times, she tried to sever it. But she simply couldn't do it.

I could *feel* Jared's sense of self-satisfaction, but he didn't let that emotion show. *You know why she can't break it, don't you?*

No, but he'd clearly worked it out.

We had a link before we even went through the Binding, baby. It was a link that formed with no conscious effort on our part; it formed before we'd even exchanged blood the very first time. The Binding only made it stronger. She might be able to cut a bond that's born through an exchange of blood, but she can't break one that's psychic at the root. And that's what ours is.

He was right, I realised. I wasn't sure whether it was a good thing or a bad thing, since my agreement to Covington's deal was now meaningless.

"Cut it, Imani!" Covington ordered.

Fake it. We need him to believe we're vulnerable, Sam. Fake it.

Liking that idea, I doubled-over and cried out…much like I had when I'd killed my Sire and our blood-link had severed. Jared did the same, scrunching his face up in agony as we both toppled onto our sides on the floor, clutching our stomachs. All the while, Covington smirked. Imani was the image of confusion. I could only guess that Jared had assured Antonio, Luther, and Sebastian that we were faking the whole thing, because they didn't look as devastated as they should. If I hadn't known them so well, though, I might have believed they were.

Be ready, I said to Jared. *I'm going to need to drop the shield or he'll never buy that I'm truly weak. We need to be ready in case they choose that moment to attack. I don't think they will because I've agreed to his deal, but they might.*

One good thing was that since my gift was tied to my emotional state, whenever my emotions were running high – and they certainly were right now – energy seemed to envelop the surface of my entire body. Once the shield was gone, I could absorb that energy and use it to strengthen my gift. I had every intention of doing so, but I would have to be careful and discreet about it or Dana would notice and Covington would know that my agreement to his deal was bollocks.

Don't think I'm letting you die tonight, Sam. The steel there almost made me smile.

I have no intention of dying. If Imani's gift had worked, I would have given my life for the people here. But I wouldn't give Jared's life for anyone – not even for these people. If that made me cruel, so be it. I'd never pretended to be a good person.

Shoving aside my anxiety, I let the shield fade, but nobody moved to hurt us. Why would they? We were both curled up like foetuses, seemingly too weak to move. As I'd known it would, the surrounding energy very slowly began to lick across my skin – just small little wisps, since my gift was 'low on battery', but I'd take what I could get. Subtly, I used my palms to suck it inside me. Soon enough, I'd be so strong that the energy would cover me like a blanket. But right now, I was no match for the Feeder in front of me.

Dana looked at her hands; they were dripping with energy the way mine often did. Her pupils were dilated, making her look like a junkie. "I feel…so alive."

Covington didn't seem to care. "It seems your little assassin has a heart, Antonio. Who would have thought it?"

"You will not leave this place alive." Antonio's voice was strong, hard, and pure ice.

"I think you'll find that I will. Now, I'm a man of my word, so this is how it's going to work. My vampires will escort everyone other than Sam and Imani out of this room. There's no need for you to watch your mate – or should I say *ex*-mate – die, Jared."

Dana turned to Covington. "Let me kill her. Let me take the last—"

"You've had your fun, Dana. It's now my turn."

Eloise strolled over until she was standing in front of me. Then the bitch kicked me in the head. Oh she'd fucking pay for that. Jared swung his arm out to grab her, but then two of Covington's vampires came to drag him away. Ire zoomed through me, causing more of the surrounding energy to cling to me. Again, I discretely sucked it in. *Jared, don't fight them! Keep up the act!*

He let them take him, let them move him far behind me, though he cursed the entire time. Eloise chose that moment to kick my head once more. I didn't need the scent of my blood in the air to know that I was bleeding. Subtly taking in more energy, I promised myself this bitch would be nothing more than a pile of ashes soon.

"Damn, her blood smells good," someone said.

"Yes, it does," drawled Covington. "Maybe that's how she'll die. Maybe I'll drink her dry." Hearing Jared curse him, Covington laughed and looked down at me. "I don't think he likes the idea of me feeding from you." Jared flung another string of curses at him, and I heard a thud followed by a grunt of pain from Jared. The bastards who were holding him must have hit him. Still, he cursed at Covington. Why wouldn't he bloody shut up? It was so tempting to abandon the weak act and attack them all, so tempting to –

Suck it in, Sam!

That was when I realised what he was doing. He knew that hearing him get hurt was feeding my fury, causing more energy to slither over me. Smart, but I'd still like to smack him for purposely getting hurt. More wisps of energy clung to me – longer and thicker now – and I took them inside me, charging up. But this time something was different…The mix of energy within me hummed beneath the surface of my skin, pushing at me like a caged animal that wanted to be freed…almost as if it was as pissed off as I was.

Antonio winced, and I realised that Covington's knife had nicked him. A ribbon of blood flowed down his neck.

Jared growled. "I will kill you for this, Covington! You're already dead!"

Dana conjured a small energy ball and threw it at Jared, making him grunt in pain. She laughed, delighted. Oh I was *definitely* going to make sure that fucking little bitch suffered before I killed her!

An all-consuming anger surged through me; anger that intensified when Eloise once again kicked me – this time in the gut. The pain, the sight of her evil smirk, and the scent of both Jared's and Antonio's blood in the air was simply too much for me to take. Utter hatred and a white-hot rage filled me, mingling with the ice-cold fear that was already pumping through me. And I wanted nothing more than to blast them all out of the fucking room and over that balcony.

Covington spoke. "Now it's time for you all to—" He cut himself off…most likely because a gasp flew out of me and my spine locked.

The humming under my skin became more of a pulsating sensation. Then a cold draft suddenly shot through the room…just like last time. I almost smiled as a familiar silvery-blue wind built around me, swirling and swirling. *About fucking time.* Eloise wisely backed away, moving so fast that she fell on her arse. Faster and faster the wind of energy swirled, and then *bang*. The energy seemed to explode outwards, knocking everything down in its path and sending it zooming away. Some of the vampires collided hard into the walls while Covington, Eloise, Dana, and – shit – Antonio went crashing through the windows.

Jumping to my feet, I dashed over to the balcony with Jared at my heels and looked down. The four vampires were getting to their feet, confused. Antonio looked at his vampires that were still surrounded by Covington's men and yelled, "Attack!"

Once again, all hell broke loose.

CHAPTER SIXTEEN

(Sam)

Most of Covington's vampires that were below us flew back and hit the ground hard. I suspected that was thanks to Harvey's gift. Animals burst onto the scene out of absolutely nowhere – a jaguar, spider monkeys, apes, and tropical birds. No doubt Alora had summoned them. They leaped into the fray without hesitation, which was a really good thing because many of the enemies were trying to get to Antonio. To my relief, he was holding his own.

I turned to Sebastian and Luther, who were covered in pink jelly since their bubble had burst after it crashed into the wall. "You need to get down to Antonio. He's their number one target." Sebastian opened his mouth – no doubt to reprimand me for the risk I had been prepared to take – but then shook his head. Yes, there would be time to talk later. He took Luther's arm and teleported them both out of there.

"Get back here, you bastard!" a feminine voice screeched. Swerving, I saw that Paige and Imani were chasing after a retreating Langley. Covington's other vampires were scraping themselves off the floor, but Jared took each of them out with an electric bolt.

He tangled his hand in my hair and gave me a hard kiss filled with anger yet also relief. "We'll talk about the fact that you risked yourself *again* later. Right now, we fight."

I couldn't have agreed more, so I said nothing as he teleported us outside. The bottom fell out of my stomach as I took in my surroundings. The once beautiful community was such a mess that it looked more like our tactical training field. But I didn't have time to mourn that. Not now.

Instead, I held out my palms and sucked in the surrounding energy, recharging my gift until it was at full strength and I was spilling hybrid energy once more. God, it felt good. I then conjured my whip, enjoying the familiar feeling of it buzzing against my skin.

"We stay together," insisted Jared.

A quick glance at Antonio showed me that most of the mansion's guards were staying close to him, helping Sebastian and Luther protect him. But I wasn't sure he needed their help. Antonio was demonstrating just how strong an old vampire could be as he eliminated everything that came at him. A big help was that one of the guards had some kind of liquid shield in place that weirdly absorbed every bullet and weapon aimed at them.

Sure that Antonio didn't need my assistance, I sought out my squad. They were grouped together near a restaurant at the other side of The Hollow, taking cover behind what was left of the building...almost as if defending it. I had to wonder if that meant there were people inside the restaurant who needed protecting.

A whizzing sound in the air was the only warning I got. Jared and I both ducked. If I hadn't had Pagori speed, I wouldn't have managed to dodge the bullet. Instantly, I formed a large boulder in front of us. More bullets came our way, but they simply became embedded in the solid mound of earth.

Jared briefly peeked around it, moving back swiftly enough to avoid another bullet. "The bastard's lying on his stomach on the sand."

His exact location was all I needed to act. Remoulding my whip into an energy ball, I swiftly peeked around the left of the boulder and slung it at the sniper. His ashes joined the rest of those that were scattered around the sand.

"Good shot, baby," praised Jared. "Keep moving."

"Aim for the armed ones." While a large number of the vampires were engaged in combat, snipers were positioned around the place, picking people off while they were distracted during the battle. Most of them were on the rooftops while others were on the sand or stooping behind heaps of rubble. "We need them gone."

He nodded. "Then we'll teleport to the squad." They were our responsibility and it was up to us to lead them. But for now, we had to trust that they could do what they had been trained to do without us.

We proceeded to use the boulder as cover as we attacked as many of Covington's vampires as we could reach. Jared targeted them with lightning bolts while I threw energy balls, energy beams, and used my whip to snatch snipers from the roof and slam them into the ground. Knowing better than to remain in one position too long, we moved from cover to cover as we worked – heading left and going past the mansion, and then past the Guest House. I felt sick each time I came near a dead human or a badly injured vampire. Luckily, some of the guards who had the ability to teleport were appearing to take the injured to safety.

I froze when I saw that Evan, Alora, Paige, and Imani were in the middle of what had become a battlefield, trying their hardest to break through some sort of protective circle. There was a similar circle further along, but that one was much larger. I had to wonder if the smaller one was protecting Langley and the larger one was protecting Covington. In any case, I didn't like the sight of the four of them in the thick of things. "We need to help them," I told Jared. "They're trying to get to Langley."

He followed my gaze and stiffened. But then he shook his head. "This is their fight, baby. It's personal for them. Langley killed Bran, who Alora adored and who Evan automatically respected for protecting her all this time. To add to that, Langley hurt Paige and he tried to use Imani. They want him dead, just like I want Covington dead and you want the Feeder and Eloise dead. Besides, all the animals are helping to protect them. And Paige is pretty ruthless."

It was true; her gift might heal, but it was clear right then that it was indeed a weapon – she stole people's injuries and attacked others with them, and reversed any wound she was given back onto whoever had harmed her. The animals were also quite merciless in their efforts to protect. And that would have to be enough, because Jared was right – this was personal for them. No one could talk me out of going after the Feeder or Eloise or Covington. I'd be wasting my time trying to pull them away from Langley, and I'd probably also endanger them by distracting them. Plus, I had to get to the squad.

So Jared and I continued targeting the armed vampires. Our combined efforts eliminated the majority of them, but a large number of the snipers that were remaining had noticed us and been smart enough to try to quickly take us out. A worrying amount of bullets rained on the large mound of rubble that we were currently squatting behind. Some of it had crumbled on top of us, grazing our skin.

"Shit," muttered Jared. Just because we healed quickly didn't mean we felt the pain any less. He signalled for me to follow him as he slipped into the building behind us, which was the Residence Hall used by the humans.

Taking cover just inside the doorway, we narrowly missed more bullets. "They're going to come in here after us," I pointed out. "We should—" That was when I heard panicked cries coming from upstairs. "I think some humans are hiding here."

Jared cursed softly. "Then we need to lead these bastards away from here. Teleporting out of here won't help. We need to make them follow us, need to leave a scent for them to follow."

"Then let's get to the nearest balcony." Hunkering low, we stayed close to the wall. Bullets shattered the glass of the ground floor windows as we swiftly made our way to the staircase and dashed to the first floor at vampire momentum. I led the way as we barged into one of the bedrooms and made a beeline for the balcony. I released two small energy balls; one destroyed the glass doors that led to the balcony, and the other energy ball smashed the balcony doors of the neighbouring Residence Hall.

Aware that our pursuers would be in the building by now, we didn't even slightly hesitate as we leaped to the balcony opposite us and rolled to the side to take cover behind the wall. "Wait here," said Jared. "Let them follow."

Seconds later, two armed vampires landed on the balcony and darted into the bedroom. The poor bastards didn't even see it coming; before they sensed we were there, Jared attacked the first one with a high-voltage electricity bolt, and I buried a thermal energy beam in the chest of the second pursuer. Two more came, but I popped up my shield while Jared took them out.

Satisfied that no more were coming, Jared teleported us out of the building. We appeared beside Chico behind what was left of the restaurant.

He jerked in surprise at our sudden arrival and put a hand to his chest. "You scared twenty years off my life."

"That would be hard to do, considering you're immortal," snickered Harvey before returning his attention to the battle ahead, using his gift to keep as many of the attackers at bay as he could. I noticed that although the squad, Ava, Cristiano, and Jude had created one long line, the squad had stayed close to those I liked to pair them up with…although, two were missing. I tensed. "Where are Damien and Reuben?"

"Inside the building," replied Stuart.

"Why are they inside?"

"Well, because half of Damien's skull has been bashed in and, though he's okay – albeit dazed – he won't be healing any time soon. And Reuben's in some kind of catatonic state."

Shit. Paige would have been a great help right now, but I doubted I'd get her away from Langley unless the boys were actually dying. I couldn't really blame her for being so focused on getting to him. I had every intention of hunting down Dana and Eloise soon, and I certainly intended to ensure that Covington died tonight. If we were going down, he was coming with us.

A great number of Covington's vampires were attempting to reach the restaurant, coming at us from all directions. Some repeatedly took cover behind rubble while others were just boldly charging at the crumbling building. "Why are they so determined to get in here?" I asked, throwing energy balls and beams.

It was Denny who answered. "They know we're protecting people here." A sly smile curved his mouth. "Or, at least, they think we are. Harvey suggested that we make it look like we're protecting people by guarding the building; that way it would not only mean that the vampires made themselves clear targets by coming at us, but it would also draw them away from the bunker underneath the Command Centre, which seems to be the only one that wasn't infiltrated. There are a lot of people hiding in there. Fletcher, Norm, and Lucy are among them."

That truly was an excellent idea from Harvey. But…"Are they totally alone?"

"No. Two from the legion have stayed in the bunker with them, just in case someone—" He cut himself off as a large web suddenly shot toward us and engulfed Max. Oh, fuck. But before the Keja had the chance to use the web to drag Max to him, Jude was at his side with that knife of hers and slicing through it. Free, Max coughed as he jumped to his feet.

Before any of us could act, another web came and this time enveloped Stuart. But the Keja responsible had picked the wrong vampire, because Stuart simply exploded into particles and easily escaped. Before the vampire had the chance to create another web, Jared took him out.

The sight of someone shifting shape caught my attention. I watched as a Pagori changed into a buffalo. A *buffalo?* That was a new one. Realising that the buffalo was charging at an unsuspecting Chico, I screamed, "Chico, six o' clock!" Knowing better than to hesitate, he turned and exhaled a mouthful of thorns. The second they met their target, the buffalo burst into ashes. Well thank fuck for that.

Three vampires charged at Ava and Cristiano, who had together just fought off five. They had always worked well as a team. A ripple of psychic energy travelled through the air toward their attackers – a ripple that I knew was coming from Salem's psychic punch. It destroyed the vampires instantly.

Hearing a pain-filled growl, I pivoted to see Denny battling off a Pagori that was slicing at him with…claws? David cursed and then narrowed his eyes at the Pagori – a sure sign that he was using his gift. Just like that, the dick was dead. Denny jumped to his feet, thanking David, but then he staggered and blinked hard. The slices on his face and arms didn't appear to be healing well. *Poisonous claws.* Hopefully the poison wouldn't be powerful enough to do anything other than put him asleep for a while. If the poison seemed to be fatal, I'd have to get Paige's help.

"I'll put him inside the building with Damien and Reuben," said Butch as he began dragging Denny away.

Clearly taking advantage of the fact that David didn't have Butch's shield protecting him, a vampire with a sickeningly elongated, lizard-like tongue came at David. I cracked my whip at the Pagori, locked it around his waist and smashed his body into the ground so hard that plenty of bones cracked. His glowing amber eyes locked onto me and he snarled. Jared projected a bolt of lightning at him, reducing him to ashes.

I went to thank Jared, but then I was knocked to the ground by Harvey as elasticated limbs shot out to grab me. In a blink, I remoulded my whip into an energy ball and threw it at my attacker. Apparently, however, I'd missed my target because those limbs reached for me again. But before they could touch me, a cry of pain rang in the air and the limbs became nothing but ashes. I suspected Jared had been my saviour, but I wasn't sure.

I'd just bounced to my feet when something came hurtling through the air...a huge fireball. Everybody ducked, but it hit the building. I released a flow of water out of my palms that quickly killed the flames. But then came another fireball, and another, and another, and another, and no amount of water was fighting the large flames that were now engulfing the building. The vampires were obviously trying to smoke people out, unaware that the only ones inside were the three injured squad members.

I grabbed Jared's arm. "Teleport Damien, Reuben, and Denny out of there, take them to the bunker under the Command Centre. We don't have enough manpower to protect them *and* fight." It was true. We were outnumbered, and we were fighting a losing battle, but not a bloody chance would I give up.

Jared hesitated, running a hand through his hair. "Sam..."

I understood his anxiety. The last time he'd put other people before me, he'd come back to find me bitten by a tainted vampire. "This is different. I have ten people with me. Damien, Reuben, and Denny will die if you don't move them, and I can't afford to leave the fight this time."

Nodding, he gave me a hard kiss. Pulling back, he rushed into the building with me at his side. I helped a weak Denny and a clearly in pain Damien to their feet while Jared slung Reuben over his shoulder. Once Denny and Damien held tight to Jared, all four of them disappeared. Only then was I satisfied enough to leave the building – not happy to find that instead of seeking cover again, the squad had charged into the battle, trying to penetrate the large protective circle of vampires that undoubtedly shielded Covington. While Chico, Salem, Max, and Stuart worked on attacking the circle, Harvey, David, and Butch defended them – just like in training – along with Jude, Ava, and Cristiano.

Hearing a crazy laugh behind me, I realised that the restaurant was being swarmed by vampires who were clearly waiting for the people they believed were inside to finally leave. Forming a large, boiling hot fireball – the likes of which I'd never been able to create before becoming a hybrid – I launched it at the building. It instantly exploded, and so did the vampires surrounding it. Ha.

My dark amusement died a swift death when there was a loud battle cry. Twirling, I gaped as what seemed like hundreds of vampires practically stampeded onto the battlefield through the now broken security gates. *Oh fuck.* I was about to attack them, but then I made out Quentin and some of his vampires. There was also Antonio's Sire, Wes, and many from his line. In addition, there were the High Masters and their vampires…And they were all helping us destroy Covington's vampires. Relief, gratefulness, and satisfaction flooded me. I realised just then that I'd truly expected to die tonight; had expected most of us to die. Now I had hope that –

I jolted and cried out as white-hot pain pierced my chest. Shocked, I looked down to see a long, metal pole protruding out of my body. It had to be wreckage from the destruction around us, my stunned mind pointlessly deduced. Slowly turning, I found Eloise smirking smugly at me as she toyed with her mane. Oh, the mad bitch had stabbed me.

She winced in mock sympathy. "Ooh, that looks like it hurts."

It didn't hurt, it burned and throbbed and caused the most agonising pain to pound through my chest, making the rest of my body feel cold. I wanted to fall to my knees and cry out. It was sheer anger alone that kept me standing. Her smug smile only served to increase my anger. She thought she'd get away with that? She thought that she was oh so clever and had ended me? Ha. All she'd done was save me the trouble of hunting her down. The pole had narrowly missed my heart, thank God. I doubted that even a fast-healing hybrid could have come back from that.

Most likely sensing the agony blasting through me, Jared appeared in front of me. He gaped, reaching out to grab the pole. But then, as if afraid that he'd only worsen the pain, he quickly dropped his hands. At Eloise's laugh, he snarled at her. "You fucking bitch!"

"I'm so glad that you could be here for this, Jared." Eloise *tsk*ed at me. "Just because my gift to hide my scent" – well that explained why she'd thought I wouldn't sense that she had paid my apartment a little visit – "is defensive doesn't mean that I'm defence*less*, Sam. I did tell you that you would die tonight."

"And I told you," I began, slowly pulling the pole out of my chest, "that I'd kill you." With the pole finally out of my body, my skin instantly knitted together. Eloise blanched. "And I will."

CHAPTER SEVENTEEN

(Sam)

How could I not relish the utter shock on Eloise's face just then? I slung the huge pole aside. "Go help the squad, Jared. This bitch is mine."

Jared sighed at Eloise, shaking his head sadly. "You really should have known better." He then smiled at me. I could sense his amusement. "Have fun, baby."

Oh I bloody would. This waste of skin and fangs had had this coming since the evening she arrived. Jared kissed my temple, and then he was gone...and I was so, so happy because I could finally do what I'd been fantasising about doing for weeks. "Just think. If you had a better aim, someone would be laying a bunch of roses over my ashes right about now." Using the energy clinging to me, I conjured my energy whip and lashed it tauntingly at Eloise.

She jerked back, gulping. "You're going to attack someone who's unarmed?"

"Yep."

Her eyes bulged. "But that's not fair!"

"Fair? You want to talk about fair?" I lashed the whip at her legs, slicing the skin. "It wasn't fair when you tried to kill me – particularly since you slyly attacked me from behind. It wasn't fair when you spent weeks trying to make my life hell. It wasn't fair when you repeatedly flirted with Jared, *my mate*. And it really, really, really wasn't fair when you betrayed the entire Hollow and almost caused the death of everyone in it."

I slashed the whip along her chest, making her cry out. "Look at the destruction around you, Eloise. If you hadn't betrayed us by telling Covington where the tunnels were, he couldn't have invaded the place like this. And all these people wouldn't be dead. So am I going to kill you? Yes. Yes, I am. And I'm going to enjoy it." I lashed the whip again, curling it around her body and pinning her arms to her sides. That usual smug glint was absent now. "You weren't fair to us, so tell me why I should be fair to you?"

To my total shock and horror, the whip suddenly split – yes, *split* – and Eloise dropped to the ground. When the portion of the whip that was wrapped around her body faded away, she quickly scrambled to her feet. That was when I saw Dana in my peripheral vision coming towards us, holding a large energy axe. I was betting that she had been aiming for me, not the whip.

"Impressive," said Dana. That squeaky voice was annoying as shit. "The whip, I mean. I've never been able to conjure one of those. This is more my thing anyway." She waved the axe around. Smug once more, Eloise laughed in delight, though the sound was shaky.

"Two against one?" How typical of them to take advantage of the fact that I was on my own. "Fine, if that's how you want it. Novo." A red Dexter hissed as he left his tattoo form, and was now curled around my leg. Eloise and Dana stiffened. "I figure this evens out the playing field a little." I gently coaxed him to the ground. He stayed there with most of his body raised from the floor, ready to strike. He hissed at Eloise, making her gulp. Oh she knew just how badly he wanted to take a bite out of her. He'd had her in his sights for a while.

I spoke to Eloise. "So, basically, this is what will happen: if you try to attack me while I deal with dear little Dana here, Dexter will deal with *you*. If you try to run, he'll be on you before you can even retreat one step. That's why snakes of this breed are called 'Strikers'. So be a good girl and wait there nicely, and then you'll have your turn."

Dana snorted. "You don't need to run, Eloise. I can handle her."

"Now that you're hyped up on hybrid energy, you mean? It doesn't work like that. Your system's not made to take it because you're a Pagori, not a hybrid. That's why your hands are shaking and you're looking a little unsteady. I'd imagine you've got a killer headache as well."

The pain etched into the lines of her forehead told me that I was right. "It doesn't matter, freak. What matters is that you die. And now the end is near."

"And so I face the final curtain," I sang, daring her with my eyes to act.

Snarling, she charged toward me at vampire speed and swung the axe at my neck. She was fast and sharp, I'd give her that. But I'd pre-empted her. I slammed up my shield, watching in satisfaction as she collided into it and then bounced backwards, hitting the ground hard. I pursed my lips. "Not bad."

I was kind of curious as to what she could do, about how in control of her gift she was. Feeders were extremely rare, so I hadn't met many. Had the circumstances been different, we could have swapped notes. But considering that I was sure her high-pitched voice was capable of making my ears bleed, I doubted that we'd have spoken for long whatever the circumstances.

Hissing, she jumped to her feet. "Drop the shield. Or are you too scared to fight me?"

I chuckled. "Anyone who knows me would tell you that even if I was scared, I'd still challenge you – *no one* gets away with hurting my mate. You're going to suffer. And I'm going to enjoy making you suffer."

"Then let's play. We both know our power level is even right now. This will be all about who has the best techniques." She remoulded her axe into a spear and aimed it at my shield.

To my surprise, the spear actually pierced it enough to make the shield shrink like a balloon. I could have reinforced the shield, but I instead let it fade away. "Again, not bad." Before she could attack again, I blew out a long breath of energy; an air blast powerful enough to send her crashing into the tree behind her.

Pagori speed had her in front of me in a blink, aiming a hard punch at my jaw. But having the Pagori speed that came with being a hybrid, I was just as fast. I caught her fist and yanked hard, dislocating her wrist. Then I grabbed her by the throat and slammed her onto the ground. Flat on her back, she inhaled sharply, and then went into a fit of coughing. I circled her body as she slowly gathered herself. Taking a moment to check on Eloise, I saw that she was frozen in place, wide-eyed. Dexter's unblinking gaze was still locked on her.

Finally, Dana popped her wrist back into place and got to her feet. "You bitch!"

"Sorry, old habits die hard."

"Kill her, Dana!" screeched Eloise. Ooh, bloodthirsty. Of course, she soon shut up when Dexter hissed at her again.

"I'm curious; can you tap into the natural elements?" I'd always been able to do it, but I'd found that controlling them wasn't an easy feat. As an ice-cold wind whipped me up and flung me at a large piece of rubble, I cracked my head hard. "I'll take that as a yes." But the wind hadn't been able to send me very far away, I noted. Even with my hybrid energy giving her gift a boost, she hadn't coped too well with the natural elements.

Feeling the wound on my head instantly heal, I quickly got to my feet and strode towards Dana...who, I then noticed, was weirdly smirking at something behind me. I might have thought it was a trick to distract me, but I could hear footsteps in the grass.

"Looks like it's about to become three against one."

Rather than glance over my shoulder, I turned slightly, allowing me to keep my peripheral vision on both Dana and Eloise as I swiftly checked who was seemingly coming to join us. Well, fuck a duck. *Joy.* I didn't move as she approached. I'd let them all think that I was scared, let them think that my death was a sure thing, and that I was ready to admit defeat. With Dexter as back-up, there were still pretty good odds that I'd come out of this alive.

When Joy reached my side, she stopped, glaring hard. I expected an attack and inwardly braced myself for one, but instead she swerved to face the others and focused her gaze on Eloise. Joy's irises were then glowing amber as pure hatred contorted her expression. She pointed at Eloise. "I want *her.*" Joy briefly glimpsed at me as she added, "I despise you, but it would be kind of...inconvenient if you died, because Jared would die with you. But *her*...she has to die. She made him betray me."

Well, no, that wasn't quite what had happened. Jared had never been her partner, and they had never been exclusive. But Joy had never been normal, so she saw the world a little differently. "You can have her...as long as you make it painful."

Joy curled her upper lip at Eloise. "*That* I can do." Then she morphed into a man twice her size and advanced on the bitch. Huh. I hadn't seen that coming.

I shrugged at Dana. "Looks like it's just you and me now. And it's time for you to go home to Fraggle Rock."

The axe was suddenly back in Dana's hand and swinging forcefully at my head. I jerked back, wagging my finger. Conjuring my whip, I lashed it at her legs, leaving deep gouges in her flesh. Off balance, she stumbled and lost her grip on her axe, which winked out. Not giving her the chance to conjure it again, I dropped my whip – which quickly faded away – held my hands up and sent flames shooting out of my palms. Her skin sizzled and blistered, and her high-pitched scream was piercing enough to crack windows. Honestly, I was surprised that my ear drums hadn't burst. Tapping into the element of water, she did her best to put out the flames.

Hearing a cry of agony, I briefly glanced at Eloise and Joy – oh yeah, Joy was definitely putting her through some serious pain. I was pretty sure that I'd just heard Eloise's spine snap. Crap, that had to hurt like fuck.

As Dana's scream faded, I looked back to see that her flesh was half-healed and her gaze was dark and sparkling with fury. "You burned me! You fucking burned me!"

Well, yeah. Had she been expecting mercy or something? I blinked rapidly, baffled. "I thought I'd been pretty clear when I said that I'd make you suffer. Oh, you thought I was all talk?" I gave her a gentle, pitying smile. "No, luv. You're not the first person I've hurt, and you won't be the last."

Seeming a mixture of incredulous and wary, she shook her head. "You're crazy."

"A little," I allowed. "But mostly it's just that I have a violent reaction to silly little bitches like you. And like I said, *no one hurts my mate*." Then my whip was in my hand again and I slashed her face with it.

With a loud cry, she flinched away. To her credit, she recovered quickly, conjuring a large boulder to shield her. I simply sucked in the energy from the boulder, making it crumble to pieces. But apparently she'd been ready for that; her axe was back and she aimed for my legs this time. I jumped, barely dodging the weapon. She slammed her palm into my chest hard enough to send me zooming backwards. I hit a tree, making the breath whoosh out of me.

Dana smirked. "Hurts, doesn't it?"

It did, actually. Dusting off the pants of my brand new suit, which was torn, singed, and stained with blood – Fletcher was going to go ballistic – I got to my feet. Then, before the movement had time to register in her brain, I conjured a small energy ball and fired it at Dana. It caught her shoulder, and the impact knocked her to the ground once again. Of course I could have thrown an energy ball deadly enough to kill her as opposed to simply knock her down. But death by energy ball didn't seem painful enough for someone who had hurt Jared. Death by Dexter's venom, however…Yeah, that sounded much better. And he was clearly hoping to join the fun, because he was slithering around her, hissing. Eyeing him warily, she froze, obviously worried about making any sudden movements.

As I came to stand at her feet, Dexter moved his intelligent gaze to me. I knew he wanted permission to attack…so I gave it to him. At my nod, he immediately spat venom into her eyes. Crying out, she scrubbed madly at her eyes. That was when Dexter struck – in a movement that was a pure blur, he bit her upper arm. Again, she cried out, flinching away from him. But it made no difference – there was no dodging Dexter: he bit her again, this time on her leg.

"Dexter's venom is pretty cool, you know," I told her as he began to curl around my body once more. "A single bite can put a vampire through a truly ugly experience. Stage one is temporary blindness. Stage two is temporary mental disorientation. And stage three is temporary paralysis. Lucky for you, however, you'll get to escape all that…because a second bite is fatal. Yep, it causes an all-consuming, agonising pain that's swiftly followed by death. But I think you're already coming to realise that, aren't you?"

Her agonised cries told me that, yes, she was. Maybe I should have felt bad for her. Maybe I should have wanted to end her pain. But this person had thrown an energy ball at Jared and laughed at his pain. She had been part of the plan to take over The Hollow, and she had enjoyed every second of the pain that she had put me through. Furthermore, she would happily have killed me if she could have done. So there was simply no ounce of mercy in my system.

I turned away from her, and that was when I saw that Joy, now back in her own form, was standing over a pile of ashes. Eloise was dead. Fabulous. Realising that Joy was watching me rather intently, I tensed. Responding to that, Dexter – who was now twined around my waist – hissed warningly at her. Had she changed her mind about having a duel? I hoped not. A part of me felt a little sorry for her and I did kind of appreciate that she hadn't joined the other two bitches in trying to kill me. Besides, what I most wanted right then was to get to Jared.

"You're going to walk away from her?" asked Joy, sparing Dana the briefest glance. "You're not going to make sure she's dead before you go?"

"Oh she'll soon be dead, don't doubt that. Besides, if I kill her quickly, she can't suffer." And I'd promised Dana that she would. It was her fault that she hadn't listened.

"You're doing that for Jared, aren't you? It's your revenge for hurting him, isn't it?"

I nodded. "I'm not going to give him up, Joy." She needed to understand that, needed to finally accept it, because I'd really had enough of her bollocks.

Joy sighed. She looked...sad. "And he won't give you up. For him, it's only ever been you. I hate you for it." But there was no heat or threat in her words.

"I know." In her position, I wouldn't have been having warm, fuzzy feelings about her.

"No matter what I did, I couldn't make him leave you." She swallowed hard. She still seemed sad, but now she also seemed resigned. "Take care of him for me." Then, in a blink, she was gone. I supposed that was Joy's version of a truce. Although, considering the emotional rollercoaster she was constantly riding, there was every chance that she'd change her mind about it tomorrow. But for now, I'd put it out of my mind. It was time to find Jared. Time to kill Covington. Time to end all this.

(Jared)

Thanks to the appearance of our allies, the number of Covington's vampires had increasingly dwindled. Set on getting to Covington, the squad, Jude, Ava, Cristiano, and I had focused on getting through the nine circles of vampires guarding him while our allies took care of the others. Harvey and his telekinesis had been a huge help – which was exactly why a vampire with the ability to temporarily steal a gift had targeted him. *Bollocks*, as Sam would say.

At that point, we'd had to instead fight our way through them. The first six circles of vampires were now destroyed. If I could just manage to get through these other motherfuckers, I could get to the bastard. But said motherfuckers weren't making it easy.

For example, there was the Keja who kept throwing balls of ice at me – and they hurt like fuck. Then there was another Keja who was creating cracks in the ground that were wide enough and deep enough for people to fall down. Unfortunately, some had. There was also the Pagori who was covered in beetles and was throwing them at everyone; beetles that happened to bite. Worse, we also had to deal with a chameleon who was creeping up on people and snapping their necks before they even realised someone was there. He *really* had to go.

As an idea suddenly came to mind, I spoke to Denny. *I want you to find that chameleon for me. I doubt you'll get your hands on him because the son of a bitch is fast. But spray him with that ooze of yours. Then we'll be able to see him and get a clear shot.*

Denny nodded. *You got it.*

I badly wanted to contact Sam, find out if she needed me. But I was conscious that doing so could distract her – that was the last thing she'd need while she was in the middle of a duel. But I repeatedly checked on her through our link, ready to teleport to her if need be.

As another ball of ice suddenly struck my shoulder, I cursed and stumbled. It was hard to get to the little shit responsible – who bore an uncanny resemblance to Professor Snape – because he was being shielded by someone with the gift to deflect. His gift was similar to Butch's, which meant that I knew where its weaknesses lay. Of course such a gift was a substantial one, but its weakness lay in the simple fact that it didn't encompass a person's entire body. The shield would only stretch as far as the sides, leaving the person's back vulnerable. Noticing that Chico was not far behind him, I ordered, *Chico, shoot the Professor Snape lookalike.*

As the poisonous thorns embedded in his skin, 'Snape' cried out and burst into ashes. His protector swerved around in surprise…giving me the perfect opportunity. I aimed a bolt of lightning at his back, satisfied by the idea that he couldn't shield anyone else.

Harvey was suddenly at my side. "We got a problem. Stuart managed to squeeze his way through the circles by staying in particle-form. He reassembled in front of Covington, and now he's trying to take him out alone."

"*What?*"

"Stuart's got a lot of anger in him after what happened to him. Right now, he doesn't care that Covington's yours to kill."

But my real problem wasn't that. It was the knowledge that Covington was pretty powerful with his gift of enchanting objects – he could make anything deadly. The simplest object could become a weapon. "Shit."

With renewed vigour, I attacked the vampires in front of me, determined to breach the protective circle and get to Stuart. It was clear that the rest of the squad had noticed what Stuart had done, because they became just as vigorous. Soon Salem, Ava, and Cristiano had tackled the chameleon, David and Butch had dealt with the ice-ball-thrower, Max and Chico and Jude took out beetle boy, and Harvey and Denny helped me destroy the Pagori who liked to create cracks in the ground.

Trusting the squad to tackle the others, I fought through the remaining vampires in front of me and charged directly into the circle…just in time to see Stuart stabbed in the heart with the same knife that had earlier nicked Antonio's throat. *Fuck*. Torn between the urge to run to Stuart's side and the urge to attack Covington, I hesitated. Covington took advantage of that moment of hesitation, slicing at my arm with his knife. It was so unnaturally sharp that not only did it tear through my sturdy leather jacket and t-shirt, but it took away layers of skin. And I knew then that this knife could probably cut through just about anything.

"Which will it be, Jared: your revenge, or your squad member's life?" Covington's eyes were glinting with malevolence and a hint of madness. "Look at him, Jared. The life is draining out of him. I'd say he has under a minute left to live."

"Then it's a good thing that I'm here," said a new voice. *Paige*. She was with Stuart, placing her hand on his wound. At the same time, Evan appeared and slung a half-dead Langley at Covington, knocking him to the ground. Covington shoved Langley away and went to get up, but then he froze – most likely because a black panther was looming over him. Evan, Alora, and Imani watched with satisfaction as Paige walked over to the two vampires who were sprawled on the ground.

"No!" I yelled. "Covington's mine!"

Paige smiled, but it wasn't a nice sight. "Yes, but Langley's mine." Then she slapped her hand over his chest and he screamed as something seemed to ripple down her arm and onto his body – Stuart's injury. When Langley was finally nothing but a clump of ashes, Paige stood upright and released a deep, cleansing sigh.

When she didn't hit the ground crying out in sheer agony at the breaking of her blood-bond to him, I frowned. "I thought Langley was your Sire."

"He was," she replied.

"I cut their bond a long time ago," said Imani as she helped Stuart stand. He nodded in thanks at Paige.

"That was why Langley hadn't been able to track Paige," I mused. Shrugging off the matter, I returned my attention to a snarling Covington. His gaze was darting in all directions, clearly noticing what I'd already sensed. Everyone was now circling us, watching intently. The battle was over. His vampires were dead. He was the only one left…and there was absolutely no way that he was getting out of this alive.

At my signal, Alora urged the panther away from Covington. Laughing humourlessly, he got to his feet. "I guess you're very pleased with yourself, aren't you, Jared?"

"Pleased that a lot of lives were lost tonight? No, far from it."

He rolled his shoulders, preparing for a fight. "Ready for me, Jared? Think you can take me?"

Yeah, I did, but…"Whatever made you think we'd be duelling?"

His gaze narrowed and he stilled. "You want me dead."

"Sure I do. And I *will* kill you. But I never said that I'd do you the honour of duelling with you."

Covington gawked while the majority of people around us gasped.

"Ouch," said Harvey. "Now that's cold." His voice was approving.

He was right; it *was* cold to deprive someone of a duel. It said that they weren't worth the effort. "Why would I duel with someone who has no decency or integrity? You tried to *take* Antonio's position, and you tried to *take* The Hollow. You like to get things the easy way, like to cheat. So tell me why the fuck should I do you the honour of a straightforward duel, knowing that you'll cheat? What would be the point?"

My peripheral vision picked up the crowd parting, and that was when I sensed Sam coming towards me with Dexter curled around her waist. I'd known through our bond that she was fine, but *seeing* her alive and unharmed still eased my mind.

Covington's eyes found her, and he grunted. "Still alive, little hybrid? What a shame. I'd really thought that Dana and Eloise would take care of you."

She didn't answer until she reached my side. "They tried – bless their little hearts. Dana's not actually dead yet. But Dexter's venom will take care of that within the next twenty minutes or so. I'm afraid Eloise has met a sticky end, though. You can thank Joy for that."

I frowned, totally confused. "Joy?"

Sam smiled up at me. "She had a score to settle."

And that score would undoubtedly make absolutely no sense to anyone other than Joy, but whatever. *Did she attack you?*

No, we came to a truce. I have a feeling it's just temporary, though. Now, when are you going to kill this little twat?

The crowd parted again, this time allowing Antonio to come forward. But he didn't enter the circle; I realised that he was handing the matter over to Sam and me, demonstrating his trust in us for everyone to witness. He looked down his nose at Covington. "Being surrounded is not the most pleasant experience, is it? I believe that you were in fact warned that you would not leave here alive."

"They all were." Sam shook her head in wonder. "And yet they didn't just go home. I'll never understand why people insist on ignoring our warnings."

Covington's eyes danced around all the vampires circling him. "You would really back these people? You're really going to let the hybrid live?"

Sam sighed. "I have a name, you know."

"She'll Turn humans! She'll create her own line!"

"That's the thing, though, Covington," said Sam. "I have no intention of ever Turning anyone. I mean, really, do you think Jared would ever tolerate another vampire drinking from me for any reason whatsoever?"

No, I fucking wouldn't. She was mine – I didn't want anyone else touching her, let alone drinking from her. And, if I was honest, I'd be jealous of any blood-link that she had with another person. I only wanted her to be linked to me. Yeah, that was unhealthily possessive but I'd never pretended to be anything else.

"I'll have enough responsibilities with ruling alongside Jared. I don't need or want the responsibilities that come with having my own line of vampires to care about."

"That's the very same reason that I don't intend to begin my own line," I told him. The truth was that I'd never even considered beginning one. I wasn't the 'paternal' type.

"You're an abomination," Covington spat, breathing hard as he glared at Sam. "An abomination that will destroy us all!"

Sam snorted. "And why, exactly, would I do that? What, pray tell, would make me decide to rid the world of my own kind? How could that possibly benefit me in any way? You're making absolutely no sense. But then, you already know that, don't you? You're just coming up with excuses to try to justify what you did tonight. You're trying to make the High Masters here turn on me."

"If anything, her being a hybrid is a good thing," said Antonio. "Not only does it mean that she can protect our kind better than anyone else, but it means that her being so powerful will discourage vampires from beginning wars in the future."

That was true: they wouldn't want to chance what she would do to them, or what I would do to anyone who even dared to harm her. "By trying to kill her and failing miserably, all you did was demonstrate to everyone just how powerful she is. I'm not thankful for that, because too many people have died tonight. But what it means is that all this was totally fucking pointless."

"Others will come for her," growled Covington.

"Not if they want to live," I replied with a menacing smile.

From his place beside Antonio, Luther spoke. "Antonio is right. Considering that vampires would avoid committing crimes purely for fear of her response, Sam is more likely to bring peace to our kind than war – if they can let go of any ignorance they may have, that is."

"No," objected Covington, though there wasn't as much conviction in his voice this time. "They'll want her dead, just like I do."

Slowly spinning, Sam ran her gaze along everyone as she loudly called out, "Any one of you that has a problem with me, step forward and we'll deal with it right here, right now." Nothing. "Come on, if any of you have something to say, spit it the fuck out now or swallow it down forever."

I curled an arm around her shoulders, smiling. "My little breath of fresh blunt air doesn't hold back." My voice held both pride and adoration.

When nobody responded to Sam's dare, she shrugged at Covington. "I guess you were wrong."

"You're something that shouldn't exist!" he insisted.

She inclined her head. "Maybe. But it won't be me who dies tonight."

"I beg to differ." And then his knife was flying out of his hand and slicing through the air toward Sam. I expected her to pop her shield up. But she didn't. She didn't need to, because the knife froze mid-air.

"Thanks, Harv," she called out.

"No problem." His smug smile was obvious in his voice. Clearly his gift was back.

Whistling, Sam grabbed the knife by the handle and then passed it to Antonio. The next move was nothing but a blur: her whip was suddenly in her hand and it quickly snapped tightly around Covington's body until he wheezed. He struggled to free himself, but it was useless.

"Just thought it would be a good idea to keep your arms pinned to your sides," explained Sam. "We can't have you throwing anything else, can we?"

"Harvey," I called.

He stepped forward. "Yup?"

"Does this mean your gift is back and in full working order?"

His smirk was wide and excited. "Yup."

"Good. Hold this bastard up for me. I want everyone to watch." I wanted everyone to see what would happen if they considered betraying us ever again. I needed to make a point to all vampirekind that betrayal wouldn't be tolerated – that an attempt on my mate's life wouldn't be tolerated. I couldn't risk others coming for Sam. It had to be this way. There had to be a display that the people here would never forget; a story that would spread like wildfire.

Covington's eyes widened as Harvey elevated him high in the air using his gift. He struggled once more against the grip of Sam's whip, but still he couldn't get free. Eyes bulging with both fear and fury, he glowered down at me. "You won't duel with me because you know you'll lose!"

"I won't duel with you because you don't deserve the honour of one." I smiled grimly at him. "And this is the part where you'll pay for what you did – for hurting my mate, for hurting Antonio, and for bringing death and destruction to The Hollow."

Driven by a combination of fury, grief, and a need for vengeance, I held up my palm and sent a charge of electricity crashing into his brain…but not a charge high enough to kill him. No, that would be for later. What I intended to do was deliver a charge of electricity to every single vulnerable spot of his body, one by one. And I did. He screamed and repeatedly begged for me to stop, but I ignored those pleas. Then, finally, when I knew he was close to death, I delivered one last high voltage bolt to his chest. That was all it took – screaming, he exploded into ashes.

The looks on everybody's faces told me that the message I'd sent had been received, loud and clear. It was a message that would spread. And only a fucking idiot would ignore it. Sam slipped her hand into mine, and everyone bowed slightly. I had to smile when Sam groaned – she hated bowing. If there hadn't been so many deaths, the vampires here would have undoubtedly cheered at Covington's demise, but most of them were still raw with anger and pain at how many lives had been lost.

Antonio came forward, sighing at Sam. "You should not have offered your life for ours," he admonished.

No she damn well shouldn't have.

Her voice was low as she asked, "Aren't you at least a little pissed off that I would have risked so many lives to protect Jared?"

"No. I would not have expected any other response. And neither would the vampires around you have done." Murmurs of agreement spread through the crowd. He placed his hand on her shoulder. "But I do appreciate the sacrifice that you were willing to make for us all. Still, do not do it again."

"She won't." I flashed her a reprimanding look. She just rolled her eyes. That hot little ass was definitely getting spanked later. Using our bond, I sent her an image of her naked and bent over my knee with my hand raised above her ass. She gasped in outrage, turning to face me fully. "Oh it's going to happen," I assured her, my tone dark. And what did she do? She sent an image back to me…an image of Dexter biting my ear while she laughed in delight. Damn crazy bitch.

CHAPTER EIGHTEEN

(Sam)

It wasn't often that I had nightmares. Or if I did, I simply didn't remember them when I woke. But dreaming that your mate was burning alive while you were restrained and forced to watch was enough to make a girl abruptly snap awake and bolt upright in the bed.

Attuned to me, Jared was instantly awake and sitting up beside me, brushing my hair away from my face. "Bad dream?" His voice was croaky with sleep.

Still feeling choked by the agony of watching him die, I couldn't speak. Making soothing noises, he gently coaxed me to lie beside him and pulled me tight against him. The strange bed wasn't as comfortable as our bed, but as our apartment building was in a pretty bad state after the battle yesterday evening, we had taken one of the spare rooms in Antonio's mansion.

In fact, most of the people within The Hollow were sleeping in the mansion as it was the building that had suffered the least amount of damage – Covington had obviously hoped to keep it for himself. The Command Centre, the Guest House, and the Residence Halls were still standing, but other buildings had collapsed. Almost all of them had suffered from fire and smoke damage to some degree. The once beautiful place looked like a warzone.

Worse than the damage to The Hollow itself was the damage to the population within it. Six of the ten squads from the legion had been wiped out, including their commanders. Most of Antonio's many guards were dead, as were Luther's and Sebastian's consorts. Only thirty-eight humans remained, and ten of those were badly injured. There had originally been forty-three surviving humans, but seven of them had been on the verge of death and chosen to be Turned into vampires rather than die.

Thankfully, Reuben, Damien, and Denny were recovering well from their injuries – albeit slowly. Cristiano, Jude, and Sebastian had also been badly hurt, but they had almost fully recovered. The main thing was that they *would* recover. The same sadly couldn't be said for many of the other vampires that had been injured. Paige had been too exhausted to help them all – in fact, she'd passed out after a while. Our allies had also lost some of their vampires during the battle. Furthermore, those who were Bound to another vampire effectively caused the death of their mates when they died.

So many deaths. So many pointless deaths.

Unsure if the walls were vampire-soundproof and not wanting to wake anyone, I spoke quietly. "We should hold a remembrance day."

Jared's eyelids slowly opened. "A remembrance day?" His voice was also quiet.

"For all those who died last night. They deserve to have their memory and their sacrifice acknowledged and honoured."

He cupped my face, brushing his thumb over my bottom lip. "That's a good idea. We'll do it as soon as we've fixed this place up."

I sighed, knowing my eyes were glistening with tears. "There's so much damage."

"Hey, don't cry," he said gently, dabbing a kiss on my forehead. He slid his hand around to my nape and began to massage it soothingly. "Wes, Quentin, and all the High Masters have offered to help. Add their vampires to ours, and we're talking hundreds of people. I think we could have the place looking good again within a couple of weeks. It'll definitely be done in time for the Coronation."

"I'm a little surprised that not even one person has objected to us replacing Antonio due to the hybrid thing."

Releasing my nape, he combed his fingers through my hair. "I'm not. The High Masters witnessed you agree to Covington to give up your own life in exchange for the lives of everyone here." His eyes darkened with anger as he added, "And we'll be having a separate conversation about *that* very soon."

I was surprised that he hadn't already lectured me over it, considering that the anger he was feeling had been simmering close to the surface since yesterday evening.

"Plus, they would be idiots to go against someone as powerful as you, particularly considering what I'd do to anyone who even thought about it."

"No one will forget what you did to Covington." *I* wouldn't either. I had a strong stomach, but even I'd been disturbed by it all. I hadn't been disturbed by Jared, though. I'd always known that he was merciless, so I wouldn't have expected anything different. The second Covington had put a knife to Antonio's throat – the only decent paternal influence Jared had ever had – he'd signed his death warrant. It was really that simple. The fact that Covington had also wanted me dead had only made the entire thing worse.

"That was the whole idea. No one's going to forget *any* of what happened. Every vampire who wasn't there will hear the tale – it'll most likely be exaggerated ten-fold, but that can only be a good thing." Fisting his hand in my hair, Jared rested his forehead against mine. "I swear I almost died when you told Imani to cut the bond. You can't ever do anything like that again, Sam. You can't sacrifice yourself for other people – not even for me."

"You would have died," I softly pointed out, trailing the tips of my fingers up and down his back.

His smile was sad. "I wouldn't have survived the breaking of the bond, baby. Not here." He took my hand and held it over his heart. "I'd have been a fucking shell without you."

"But at least you would have been alive."

"I'd have been breathing, sure. But I'd have been dead inside." Though his voice was still low, it had turned gruff as his tightly controlled anger began to seep to the surface. "I'd have stuck around long enough to avenge what had happened to you, but that's all. You wouldn't have saved me by having Imani cut the bond. And if you think the others would have wanted you to sacrifice yourself for them, you're wrong."

I remembered the others objecting. Even Antonio, who had had a knife to his throat, had been angry with me for doing it. "You wouldn't have offered *your* life for everyone else's?"

He pinned my gaze with his. "No. Dying would have meant being without you. I can't do that. If that makes me selfish, there's not a lot I can do about it. I've told you over and over, Sam, *you come first.* I know that no one's ever put you first before so you just can't grasp that or understand it. But you come first to me."

It was bewildering, scary, and yet also sent a blaze of warmth shooting through me.

"You don't need to keep risking yourself to feel worthy of everyone's loyalty – and don't say that's not part of why you do it, I *know* you." With his eyes still holding mine, he absentmindedly began tracing my collarbone with the tip of his index finger. "You *are* worthy. You're worthy of everything that you have. The people here, the squad – they're all loyal to you because they respect you and they care for you."

"They shouldn't. I'm stubborn, sarcastic, so direct it's—"

"You're *you* – that's all it takes for people to like you and respect you. A lot of people who are straight-shooting…they're only happy to be so blunt when talking about others. They're not so upfront about who *they* are, what flaws *they* have, and what *their* issues are. But you don't hide who you are. You don't act. You don't play mind games. People always know where they stand with you." He slid both his arms around me and held me tight, lightly nipping my mouth. "It's part of what I love about you. It's what drew me to you in the first place. Of course your husky voice and your delectable body had a lot to do with it too."

I smiled against his mouth. "That's because you're a randy bastard."

"I don't hear you complaining."

"Why would I complain? I highly benefit from it."

He fell silent for a minute, studying me intently. "You know, the idea of dying hadn't really bothered me much before I met you. Don't get me wrong, I wasn't suicidal or anything, but I was fine with being rash and impulsive. The things I've done with my life since becoming a vampire – joining the legion, becoming a commander, being appointed as Antonio's Heir – I'd always thought of it as making the best out of a bad situation, out of a life I'd never wanted. That was why I was never what anyone would call 'happy'. You changed that. You made me like this life, made me want it, and made me glad to have it. You made me want *more*."

"Same here."

"Then don't even consider leaving me again. Not for any damn reason."

Wanting to calm his mood, I lightly raked my nails down his back, shooting him a teasing smile. "But if I'm a good girl all the time, you'll stop tying me up and torturing me with orgasms."

Grinning crookedly, he rolled us so that he was draped over me. "Unfortunately, I can't do that right now because I have nothing to tie you up with. But we can definitely do everything else."

I chuckled. "No, we can't. There's no way that we'll manage to keep quiet. The mansion is packed full of people and I'm not sure if the walls are vampire-soundproof."

He began slithering down my body. "Then don't forget to comment on how big my dick is."

Laughing quietly, I reached down and cuffed him over the head. Then his mouth was on me, toying with my clit, and my laugh turned into a moan.

"I love how you taste. I want more." He spread my legs wider, opening me fully to him. Then his talented tongue was doing all sorts of things – each move was sensual and teasing. Swirl. Lick. Stab. Flick. The rotation changed each time, building the friction, winding me tighter and tighter. Finally, I imploded. Of course he didn't stop. Not until he'd pulled another two orgasms from me with just his tongue and fingers.

While I was quaking with aftershocks, he crawled up my body, and rested himself on his elbows. Then he did the strangest thing. He slung the pillows and duvet on the floor and tucked the fitted bed sheet around me. "What are you doing?"

His devilish smile made my stomach quiver. "Just hold on tight."

No sooner had my arms circled his neck than there were familiar flutters in my stomach as he teleported us to...*oh.*

"I told you I was going to fuck you on the beach."

(Jared)

Almost like I was unwrapping a present, I unfolded the crème bed sheet that I'd tucked around Sam. Looking down the length of her body, I groaned. Every inch of her was beautiful, sinuous, and mine. Collaring her throat, I took her mouth – the kiss was slow but deep, and demanded everything from her. She gave as good as she got...but the sneaky little minx also tried to make the kiss her own, tried to intensify it and make me lose control. Tried to take control.

I tsked. "Uh-uh, baby. We're going to go at my pace." I skimmed my hand down her throat, between her breasts, over her flat stomach, and down to cup her possessively. She arched into my hand, moaning. I plunged a finger inside her. So damn hot and slick. "Do you know what's going to happen?" I asked, slowly pumping my finger in and out of her. "I'm going to fuck you nice and slow; I'm going to keep it like that until you can't take it anymore. Then when you beg, I'll give you more."

She narrowed her eyes, clearly not liking that plan. It wasn't often that I asked her to beg. I wasn't one of those guys who needed to constantly hear it, which was a good thing really since Sam wasn't much for begging. But hearing her tell Imani to cut our bond had hurt. Sure I knew why she'd done it, knew how her mind worked. And I knew that just because it wasn't something that I ever would have done didn't mean that she might care less for me than she had before. But still, hearing her say it...it had fucking hurt; hurt in a way that had left me feeling a little insecure in how she felt about me, about us. I needed to hear her beg now, needed to hear that she still wanted this as much as she had before, needed to see the same desperation in her eyes that I'd seen a million times before.

"You know I don't like to beg."

Withdrawing my finger, I curled my arm around her ass, tilting her hips. "But you will. Because you know how good it will be when I give you what you want." Slowly, I fed her an inch of my cock. Her muscles tightened around me, trying to pull me deeper, and it took everything I had not to slam home. Instead, I gave her another inch, watching as pleasure, need, and a hint of impatience flickered on her face. Still moving slowly, I slid deeper and deeper, groaning as her nails dug into my back. Finally, I was buried balls-deep inside her...exactly where I needed to be. Her muscles clasped me even tighter. "Fuck, baby."

"Yes, fuck," she gasped, locking her legs around my waist and bucking slightly.

I smiled. "Oh I'll fuck you all right." In a smooth, sluggish movement, I pulled almost all the way out before sliding back inside. Again and again, I did it, loving how hot and tight and slick she was around me. Knowing how sensitive her neck was, I kissed, licked, and nipped every inch of it – making her body go more and more pliant beneath mine. When I grazed my teeth over her pulse and sucked hard, she gasped my name.

Her nails cut into the skin of my back. "Do it. Bite me."

Instead, I swirled my tongue around the shell of her ear and briefly nibbled on the lobe. My thrusts were still teasingly slow, and her body was quivering with need and frustration. I spoke into her ear. "Are you ready to beg yet?" I gave her another agonisingly slow thrust and she mewled in frustration. "What is it, baby? Tell me what you want."

"You know," she bit out.

"I do, but I want to hear you say it." I licked over her pulse and nipped it gently before sucking at it once more.

She actually fucking growled at me. "I want it harder. Faster."

"Then beg. Beg me to give it to you, and I will."

She slapped my shoulder instead. "You can be such a fucking twat! You know I don't like begging!"

"And I don't like hearing my mate tell someone to cut our bond," I said softly. There was no judgment in my voice, but there was a pain I couldn't hide.

Sorrow flashed in her eyes. "You know why I did it."

"But it's not something you'll ever do again, is it?" The question was rhetorical, but she still shook her head in answer. "Good girl. Now…give me what I want, and I'll give you what *you* want."

There was a lengthy pause before she muttered, "Please."

I reared back and slammed into her, wrenching a loud groan from her. "Like that?"

"More."

"I'll give you more. And you'll take it." Without leaving her body, I sat upright, keeping her tight against me. I kissed her hard – it was too hard, too rough, but I couldn't soften it. Gripping her hips, I lifted her until only the head of my cock was lodged inside her, and then I impaled her hard. She tried to take over, but I shook my head. "All I want from you is those eyes." The second her lids flipped open and those aquamarine eyes tinted with mercury met mine, I began ruthlessly slamming her up and down on my cock.

She threaded her fingers through my hair and held tight, trusting me to give her what she needed. I bent her backwards just enough to suck a hard nipple into my mouth. She had the most perfect pair of breasts – I'd been obsessed with them since day one. I bit down on her nipple, and her blood gushed into my mouth. As I drank, I moved one hand from her hip to her other breast, zapping the nipple with my thumb. Her muscles clenched and rippled around my cock each time and, *fuck*, it felt too good.

"Jared, I'm gonna come."

That was fine with me, because I could feel the telling tingle in the bottom of my spine and I knew I wouldn't last much longer. I released her nipple and pulled her flush against me. "Tell me you'll never leave me, Sam," I demanded in a tone unintentionally harsh. "Say it."

"I won't leave."

Slipping a hand between our bodies, I sought out her clit with my thumb. "You're mine, Sam. Mine to *keep*. Remember that." A few zaps to her clit were all it took: those aquamarine eyes went blind with pleasure and her entire body tightened around me. She bit the crook of my neck and my climax thundered through me, seeming to go on and on and on.

Her whole body sagged against mine when she finally stopped drinking. "Love you," she slurred against my neck.

I dropped a kiss on her shoulder. "And I love you, baby. More than anything." And for that reason, I'd need to tell her about the vision that I'd had through Luther. There was no denying that I should have told her before we Bound, but I'd panicked that it would make her change her mind. That same sense of panic was still with me now, but it was wrong to keep this from her. She deserved to know. I just had to hope and trust that this wouldn't change anything, had to trust in *her*.

Smoothing her hair away from her face, I said, "I need to tell you something."

Lifting her head to meet my gaze, she arched a questioning brow. I sensed her sudden unease, but it wasn't visible in her expression.

"I've never told you about the vision that I had through Luther, have I?"

She blinked, her unease replaced by extreme curiosity. "No, I don't think you did."

"It was when I was made a commander within the legion that Antonio offered for me to have a vision. I was originally going to turn the offer down. I've never believed that things are pre-destined, and I didn't like the idea that I wasn't in control of my own fate. But I was curious."

Sam smiled. "It was curiosity that made me accept the offer as well."

"In my vision..." I hesitated, scared – yes, fucking scared – of how she'd react.

Sensing my fear, she tightened her hold on me and shot me a look of concern. "Jared, whatever it is, just tell me."

I took a deep breath. "In my vision, I was standing on a podium in one of Antonio's parlour rooms. And he was announcing that he would be stepping down as Grand High Master and...I *knew* in the vision that I would be replacing him, even though I didn't hear him say it. But when the vision ended, I just laughed. I hadn't believed that it would ever happen in a million years." Because no one had ever made me feel important, no one had ever made me think that I'd ever be given a role like that. "I wondered if maybe Luther's visions were more like methods of motivating people. One thing I was sure of was that it would never come true."

"But then Antonio later made you Heir."

"I almost refused. I didn't like the idea that it made me close to the fate that I'd seen in that vision. I wanted to be in control of my own path. But I also thought that that was a stupid fucking reason to turn down Antonio."

Obviously confused about where I was going with this, she pursed her lips. "So you haven't mentioned this before because...you didn't like that it was coming true?"

If only it were that fucking simple. "I didn't mention it before because...Sam, I was alone on that podium. You weren't there. Nobody was."

Her eyes widened and her mouth fell open. "Oh."

When all I sensed from her was shock and she didn't try to move away, I continued. "I wasn't alone and grieving someone, so it wasn't that I'd had you and then somehow lost you in that future that I'd seen. I was alone and I was okay with it." I watched her face carefully, searching for any sign that she would pull away. Not that I'd *let* her pull away, but I'd need to be ready to pin her down if it came to that. "I never told you about it before we Bound because I was worried that if I did, you would take it as some kind of sign that we weren't meant to be together, that our futures weren't supposed to collide or something."

Mixed in with her shock was now confusion, but there was thankfully none of the apprehension or disquiet that I'd expected. "You never thought that that was what it meant?"

I cupped her face. "The point is…I didn't care if it did. I didn't care if it meant that the only way I'd ever one day replace Antonio was if I was alone. I still don't. I'm not giving you up."

She was quiet for a minute. "What you're saying is…you knew when you Bound with me that you could very well be working against a future in which you ascended?"

"Yes, I knew it, and I didn't care. No one and nothing could have made me stay away from you. I wanted you, needed you, and I had every intention of Binding with you – even if that meant that someone else would take over from Antonio. I just wanted *you*."

She blinked, still more shocked than anything else. Again there was a short silence. "So when you say that I come first to you, you really do mean it, don't you?"

"*Finally* she gets it."

That got a smile from her, but then her expression turned speculative. "Are you sure you didn't pursue me so hard because you were fighting the idea of your fate being controlled?"

It was hard not to feel sorry for her when she came out with crap like that. "Sam, if that was the case, I wouldn't have accepted the position of Heir, would I?" My tone said 'duh'.

"And none of this ever gave you any doubts about Binding with me?" Pure and utter disbelief coated her words.

"No. Not one." I rubbed my nose against hers. "I don't know why you weren't in that vision. You told me that you'd been in Evan's vision, and I know that he had his vision around the same time that I had mine. So it couldn't have been that your future as a vampire was unsure at that time."

She shrugged one shoulder. "Maybe it was that our future together was uncertain."

"That makes no sense to me. From the second I saw you, I wanted you. Even knowing on some level that you'd turn my life upside fucking down, I was determined to have you. And after the first kiss, I was fucking hooked. Believe me when I say that I've explored every possible theory as to why you weren't in that vision and I haven't come up with squat. The important thing right now is that you aren't going to take the vision as a sign that we shouldn't be together or some stupid shit like that."

She scrutinised my face. "Why have you told me this? I can sense just how much you're panicking that I'll do a bunk. Why tell me about the vision?"

"I don't like keeping things from you. I don't want lies – not even lies of omission – between us. I don't want there to be anything that can eat away at the bond, and it didn't feel right to keep this from you. I'm trusting that you won't leave."

And that was a damn difficult thing for me to do, because my two greatest fears were that something would happen to her or that she would leave. Honestly, it was still a shock that she had given me a chance to begin with, considering that I'd been a total asshole when she first arrived at The Hollow. The fact that she Bound with me still boggled my mind because I just found it too difficult to accept that she'd always care for me. I knew my faults, knew how fucked up I was. And when your own mother couldn't love you, it made it hard to believe that anyone else would. Yet, here Sam was. And she thought I'd let her go? The crazy bitch wasn't going anywhere. If she believed differently, then she was crazier than I thought.

She stroked the tip of her finger over my bottom lip. "Thank you for trusting me. It means a lot to know that you do." She knew me well enough to know just how big it was for me to place trust in another person. "I don't care about the vision, Jared. I'm here and I'm staying."

It didn't sound like there was a 'but' coming. Still, I needed to be sure that she wasn't going to try fighting me on this. "You're not stupidly worried it means something bad?"

"No. Besides, I know that you would choose to be with me over replacing Antonio if you were made to choose. So I have nothing to worry about, do I?"

A relieved smile spread across my face. "You have absolutely nothing to worry about." I licked at the seam of her mouth, coaxing her to open for me. When she did, I plunged my tongue into her mouth, stroking her own, drinking her into me. It was a few minutes before I finally pulled back. By then, I was hard all over again. Gently, I lifted her and slowly impaled her on me once more. We both groaned. "All that other stuff means nothing if you're not with me."

She swiveled, pulling another groan from me. "I told you, I'm here and I'm staying."

I snorted, slowly impaling her again. "Like I'd have *let* you go anywhere. It just meant that I would have had to tie you to the bed for a while, keep you prisoner until you changed your mind about leaving me."

She brushed her mouth over mine, doing another swivel. "That actually sounds like it would have been fun, but it won't be necessary. I love you; I ain't going anywhere unless you're coming with me."

I flexed my cock inside her. "Oh I'll be coming." I laid her down on the sheet and then gently rolled so that she was straddling me. I let her take the lead this time; it was slow, but still deep, and I came as hard as I always did.

When the aftershocks finally subsided, she sighed. "Now take us back to bed before any sand makes its way into places it has no right being."

I chuckled, bringing her to lie flat against me. "Hold on tight." I meant more than just right then, and she knew it.

Her face softened. "Always."

CHAPTER NINETEEN

(Sam)

Where the bloody hell was Jared? As I scanned the crowded parlour room wherein soft piano music was playing and smartly-dressed vampires were standing around drinking champagne-flavoured NSTs, I was reminded of the reception of my Binding ceremony. This type of posh, formal gathering wasn't at all my thing, but it was part of the build-up to the Coronation, so there wasn't a lot I could do about it. Yep, in under an hour's time, Jared and I would be officially declared the Grand High Pair.

Note to self: When Jared and I step down from our positions, make the pre-party to the Coronation *fun*.

It had been three weeks since the attack on The Hollow, and with the help of hundreds of volunteers, the place was miraculously back to its original state – if not better. There were slight differences here and there. The main difference was that half of the mansion was now office space. When Antonio had heard that Jared and I didn't want to move into the mansion – it just wouldn't have felt right to us, it seemed too much like Antonio's home – he had insisted on minimising his 'living quarters'. He felt that us having individual work space in the very centre of the community placed significance on our role in The Hollow.

He had also insisted that the Grand High Pair couldn't live in a simple apartment. Jared and I had told him not to be daft, that we didn't care where we lived and didn't need a spacious, luxurious home. So what had Antonio done? Built us a house. I had been pissed off about his complete lack of respect for our wishes until I realised that the house was built on the beach. Antonio, the sneaky sod, knew I loved the beach and that I'd find this too hard to resist. I'd still ranted at him a little. But he'd been perfectly aware that I'd been absolutely thrilled with the house – the fact that I'd uncharacteristically kissed him on the cheek might have tipped him off.

Spotting Wes with his mate and two of the High Masters Rowan and Ricardo, I made my way over to them. Wes thought of Jared as a grandson, so he had no doubt spoken to him at some point in the past hour. Although tradition was for only a few witnesses to be present at a Coronation while everyone else watched over V-Tube, Antonio had felt that these allies who had come to us at the greatest possible hour of need and had aided us in fixing The Hollow deserved to be present if they so desired. He had a good point.

Noticing me, Wes turned away from the group. "Sam," he drawled with an affectionate smile. He placed his hands on my upper arms. "You look—"

I held up my hand. "Let me stop you right there. Compliments aren't my thing." Of course he already knew that.

"Don't tease her, Wes," his mate, Leona, gently admonished. She gave me a brief hug. "How are you feeling? Nervous?"

Nervous? Definitely. But admit that to others? Not likely. "I'm fine."

"I would be nervous in your shoes," said Ricardo.

I smiled brightly at him. "Hello, Rick."

His expression hardened in annoyance. "It is *Ricardo.*"

"Right, that's what I said."

Rowan shook his head, amused. "You cannot resist needling him, can you?"

Of course I couldn't resist.

Marcia, Rowan's mate, suddenly came to his side. She shot me a genuine smile. "It's not often that I see you alone. Where's your mate?"

"I have no idea, that's why I'm here." Turning back to Wes, I asked, "I don't suppose you've seen Jared anywhere, have you?"

Wes gestured behind him. "He was talking with your personal assistant a moment ago."

"Great, thanks." Giving each of them a brief wave, I walked to where Fletcher stood, laughing, with Norm, Ava, and Cristiano…but there was no Jared. I went to speak, but Fletcher pulled me into a hug that was tight enough to squeeze the breath from my lungs. "Can't. Breathe."

He loosened his hold. "Oh don't be so dramatic."

I could only gape at that. "This is coming from the drama queen of the century?"

Norm laughed. "Of every century," he corrected. When Fletcher scowled at him, he patted his back. "But you're *my* drama queen, aren't you?" That made Fletcher smile.

I stifled a chuckle. "Ooh, good save."

Norm winked at me. "Thanks."

Ava snatched me from Fletcher's arms and hugged me just as tightly. The tiny female was weirdly strong. "I'm so excited about the Coronation." Pulling back, she gasped. "I love this dress."

"As usual, Fletcher can take the credit." The white halter-neck was, like everything else he'd ever given me, a snug but perfect fit.

"I'm going to miss you." Ava pouted cutely.

"You don't have to leave. In fact, I'm hoping you don't. I have plans for you." She looked at me questioningly, but I simply gave her a mysterious smile. "All will be revealed shortly."

Cristiano arched a brow. "I'm guessing that invitation doesn't extend to me." Most likely in response to my 'oh shit' expression, he shook his head. "Joke. I'm eager to get back to my nest. I've been away from them for long enough. Actually, I'll be leaving straight after the Coronation."

That was good, because although Jared had grown to...tolerate Cristiano, I knew he wouldn't cope with him on a permanent basis. "Be a better leader than Victor was."

"That goes without saying." He tilted his head. "Joy left last night, you know."

"Really?" Jared had predicted that she wouldn't want to serve us directly, but..."We'd sort of reached a truce after she killed Eloise." I shrugged. "Clearly the truce is over."

"Just because someone can accept that they can't have the person they want doesn't mean that they can stand to watch that person with someone else."

The odd look on his face made me frown. "You all right?"

He nodded, swallowing hard. "You, er...take care." He looked like he wanted to say more, but instead he just smiled. It wasn't one of his usual smirks. It was an actual smile.

"I will. You, too." I nudged Fletcher. "Where did Jared go after you spoke to him?"

Fletcher frowned thoughtfully. "He said something about going to find you, but then Antonio called him over."

Knowing Antonio was near the patio doors with Lucy, Sebastian, and Luther, I said, "Okay, thanks." It wasn't until Fletcher grabbed my hands that I realised I'd been fidgeting nervously.

Fletcher kissed both of my cheeks. "You'll be fine, luv. You might want to put on a little blusher – you're white as a sheet with nerves."

"I'm not nervous." I gave him a gentle shove and then went to seek out Jared. Instead, I came face-to-face with Max, who stood with Chico, Jude, Damien, Denny, and David.

"Coach," Max greeted with a wide smile and a manly pat on the back. "Damn, you're pale – even for a vampire."

Denny cocked his head at me. "I don't think I've ever seen you nervous before. It's weird."

Jude gave him a 'Seriously?' look. "Wouldn't *you* be nervous if you were about to be crowned Queen of the Undead?"

"Queen of the Undead," drawled Chico, curling an arm around her. "I like that."

I resisted shifting from foot to foot. "I'm *not* nervous. I'm just not feeling too good."

"*Because* you're nervous," said Damien. At my scowl, he held up his hands in a gesture of innocence.

It didn't placate me. "I'll speak to you all later. I've got to find Jared."

David frowned. "I'm surprised he's left your side."

"I was late getting ready, so I told him to go on ahead of me."

"Late *because* you're nervous," Damien again insisted. So I slapped him over the head. "Ow, Coach, that was just mean."

Snorting, I advanced toward the patio doors…only to find that Antonio, Lucy, Sebastian, and Luther were no longer there. More importantly, neither was Jared. I knew through our link that he was close, but I didn't know his *exact* location. If I'd have had his gift to teleport, I could have used the link to take me immediately to him.

Inwardly growling, I still headed for the patio doors, wondering if they had wandered outside. As I neared the doors, I saw that Butch, Salem, Stuart, Reuben, Harvey, Paige, and Imani were huddled in the corner. It wasn't a surprise to find that Butch was standing a little too close to Imani, or that Stuart was teasing Paige, or that Salem had his eyes on Ava despite that she was at the other side of the room. "Any of you seen Jared?"

Harvey turned to face me. "Well hello to you too, Coach. I'm doing great, thanks."

I rolled my eyes. "Have you seen him or not?"

Paige pointed to the patio doors. "He was there a minute ago." Imani nodded.

"Wow, Coach, you're kind of…pale," said Stuart with a wince.

Reuben grimaced. "Seriously pale."

"I'm a vampire. I'm hardly going to have a bloody tan, am I?"

Butch snickered. "I think Jared might have gone outside."

"Thanks." I went to walk away, but then I noticed that Salem's heated look had morphed into a scowl. Tracking his gaze, I saw that Damien was flirting with Ava. "You know, you could just go over there and *talk* to her."

Salem frowned down at me. "I talk to her."

"But you also blow hot and cold with her."

He sighed. "She's…"

"What?"

"Good…and I'm not."

He flinched when I slapped his arm. "Hey, what was that for?"

"None of us are particularly 'good', Salem, or we'd be crap at our job. But we're not 'bad'."

He sighed again. "She's leaving with her brother tonight anyway."

"Don't be too sure of that." I didn't respond to his arched brow. Instead, I turned away and headed outside. My vampire night vision enabled me to easily spot Antonio, Lucy, Sebastian, and Luther at the other side of the pool…but no Jared. I was starting to wonder if he was deliberately avoiding me, if maybe he was having second thoughts about the Coronation. I could pick up through our link that he was slightly nervous, but he was also excited. If he was having doubts, he was doing an extremely good job of hiding them from me.

Confused and frustrated, I went to Antonio and the others. He gave me a beaming smile. "Sam, you look…" – his smile faltered – "annoyed."

"My mate seems to be avoiding me."

Lucy shook her head. "He said he was going to find you, but then Evan came and took him aside." She pointed to where the brothers were standing on the fringe of the beach. *Finally.*

Sebastian studied my face. "Aside from annoyed, how are you feeling?"

I shrugged nonchalantly. "Fine."

Luther twisted his mouth. "You're rather…pale."

I was getting sick of people commenting on that, even though it was true. I gave him a sardonic smile. "You're good for the ego, Gandalf." He just grinned.

Antonio curved an arm around my shoulders. "It is okay to be nervous. It does not make you weak."

Lucy nodded. "It happens to us all." Currently, it was happening to her. She had every right to be nervous. The plan was for Antonio to Turn her later tonight. She had actually confessed her worries about being a Keja to him. Antonio had offered to have a Sventé Turn her – he really was too sweet. But she had changed her mind, not wanting to be linked to anyone other than him. I knew that had relieved Antonio.

If Jared and I had been in that situation, he wouldn't have given me the option of being Turned by another, he would have hounded me until I changed my mind. Jared wasn't the 'sweet' type, but that was fine with me. If I had a 'sweet' person, I'd make them cry sooner or later.

"You should go and get Jared," Antonio told me. "It is almost time for the Coronation."

Nodding, I moved out of his hold and made my way to the brothers. When they sensed my approach, they both turned. I halted. "Am I interrupting anything?"

"No," Evan assured me, gesturing for me to come closer.

Jared held out his hand. "Get over here, baby."

Walking to him, I slipped my hand in his, allowing him to tug me to his side. When he frowned at my expression, I pointed hard at him. "Tell me I look pale and I'll—"

His mouth landed on mine, giving me a hard but sensual kiss. The second the stiffness left my body, he broke the kiss and briefly sucked on my bottom lip. "Better?"

Yes, actually. Weirdly, his kisses had a way of calming my nerves. Relaxing against Jared, I looked at Evan. "Where's Alora?"

"Chatting to a bird," he replied dryly.

Not what I'd expected to hear.

"I was just telling Jared that I asked her to Bind with me in a few months' time."

"Really?"

"She said no." Strangely, he didn't sound guttered. In fact, he'd used the same tone that one might use when referring to a confused toddler...like it was kind of cute that she thought she had a choice. Yeah, well, Evan's determined streak wouldn't allow him to ever accept a 'no' from Alora. He'd been waiting too long to find her.

"You can hardly blame her," I said gently. "I mean, she's only just got out of one Binding. It makes sense for her not to want to throw herself into another one straight away. Give her some time."

Evan smiled. "They were almost her exact words. I'm just happy that she's no longer joined to that prick. It means we *can* have that one day, when she's ready – thanks to Imani. I owe that girl more than she can ever realise." Imani had used her gift to sever the bond between Alora and Gregory. I was guessing that the bloke hadn't taken it very well, but fuck him. Alora belonged with Evan – anyone could see it.

Jared cocked his head at Evan. "Ironic how much I panicked about bringing Paige here. If she hadn't come, I'd have lost Sam and you for sure. And if Paige had never requested refuge for her and Imani, we would never have realised that Imani is your only chance to be able to Bind with Alora one day."

Evan nodded. "It seems like sometimes we have to go the long way round before getting to the place we need to be – if that even makes any sense." Seeing Alora approaching, he raised his arm invitingly. She melted against him, smiling. "Did the bird have anything interesting to say?"

She gave him a playfully impatient look. "So, what have I missed?"

"We were just talking about Imani and Paige." Evan looked at me then. "I heard that Paige was having second thoughts about staying here, worried that people would be told how she'd healed me, you, Max, and Stuart. She didn't want to become someone's tool that was put away until the next time The Call surfaced." Which was totally understandable.

"Antonio doesn't need to tell anyone anything. The only people who knew that some of the people here had been tainted were Bran, Covington, Langley, Collins, Eloise, and Quentin. The first five are dead, and because Quentin was so grateful for all Antonio's help and for us rescuing his brother from the humans, he agreed to let Ryder wipe what had happened to us from his memory." The Pagori had a psychic hand that could search a person's mind and even steal specific memories, though he couldn't wipe away years of memory.

"So she and Imani might stay here permanently?" asked Alora.

"I hope so." I had plans for them.

Able to read me well, Jared narrowed his eyes. "Something I should know, baby?"

"Nah."

He chuckled. "Fine. I guess as long as it's not that you're planning to run, it doesn't matter for now. Besides, Evan…we have something to ask you."

Evan stiffened, but his smile remained in place. "What?"

"Sam and I would like to ask you…if you'll accept the position of Heir."

Shock painted Evan's features as his mouth started bopping open and closed like a landed fish.

Jared pinned him with his gaze. "This isn't because you're my brother – I need you to know that. It's because you're the one person we trust to do the best for all vampirekind and to protect those who need it. I know it's not something you originally would have wanted, so I understand if—" Evan's abrupt, solid, one-armed hug cut Jared off. "Is that a yes?"

Releasing his twin, Evan cleared his throat and nodded, doing his best to look cool about it all. "It's a yes." Evan turned to Alora. "Oh, but I—"

She put her index finger against his lips. "This doesn't change anything. I still want to be with you. It's a scary thought to one day rule, but I have a perfectly good role model in Sam."

Me a role model? I inwardly snorted.

"You're fidgeting," Jared noted, tucking my hair behind my ear. That was when I realised that I'd been clasping and unclasping my hands. I instantly relaxed them, blanking my expression. Cupping my chin, he turned me to fully face him. "You don't have to put on an act for me. It's perfectly normal to be nervous right now. Hell, even *I* am. I don't think this is something anyone can ever really be totally ready for – not even me, and I've had a hell of a lot longer to get used to the idea than you have. If you need more time—"

I squeezed his hand, shaking my head as much as his grip would allow. "Stop worrying about me. I'm as ready for this as I'm ever going to be." And that was all I could really ask of myself.

Hearing someone delicately clear their throat, we all swerved to find Antonio. He smiled. "It is time."

(Jared)

Five minutes later, Sam and I were standing hand-in-hand on the man-made podium of the parlour room while Antonio, who was in front of it with the Prelate, gestured for silence. It was the same Prelate that had performed the Binding ceremony. I hadn't been kidding when I told Sam I was nervous, but luckily they were good nerves. Still, having all these people about to witness our Coronation and knowing that the whole thing was being shown live on V-Tube…it was a little unnerving.

"I realise that it is unusual for so many to be present at a Coronation," began Antonio, addressing those witnessing over V-Tube. "But I think we can all agree that it was unusual circumstances that brought these vampires here. Their aid and support will never be forgotten. And neither will the actions of the pair you see here – Samantha Parker and Jared Michaels."

Sensing Sam's anxiety intensify, I comfortingly rubbed my thumb along her knuckles.

"I am sure you have all already heard the story of how she was willing to not only give up her bond with her mate but to sacrifice her own life for the lives of so many. I am sure you have also heard of how Jared defended his mate, avenged the harm that she and everyone here had suffered. These are people who will risk themselves for those who are under their protection, who will fight to the death if need be, who will avenge those that have suffered. I do not believe there is a bonded pair who would be better suited to rule and protect vampirekind."

Antonio looked around the room then, addressing everyone. "And so I hope you will all follow and support them as I step down from my position and they rise as the Grand High Pair." Sam's hand tightened on mine as both Antonio and the Prelate joined us on the podium. They each laid a hand over our clasped ones, smiling.

The Prelate spoke then. "With everyone here as witness, do you, Antonio, relinquish your position as Grand High Master?"

"I do."

"Samantha, Jared — will you both agree to lead in his stead?"

"We will," she and I both said in unison.

"Do you accept their pledge, Antonio?"

Antonio smiled widely, proudly. "I do."

The Prelate then recited a string of Latin and lifted our raised hands. And it was no more complicated than that.

Antonio's smile widened as he stepped down from the podium and bowed. Everyone followed suit, including the Prelate.

Oh God, they're bowing again! Sam was totally freaked out.

It's all part of the formality.

When we step down, it's going to be fun, not stiff and…weird.

Stifling a smile, I brushed my thumb over her knuckles again. When Antonio gestured for me to speak, I turned my attention to our audience. "Before I say anything else, I have to thank all of the people who came and joined us against Harry Covington. I also have to thank all of you for accepting Sam's hybrid status. It was a change that was forced upon her, and she didn't deserve to be punished for something that she'd never wanted by being hunted or targeted."

To come after Sam would be to face the wrath of every single resident of The Hollow. Whether she realised it or not, they were as much her protectors as she was theirs.

"With regards to replacing Antonio, I'm torn about the whole thing. On the one hand, this position is an honour and it's one that I'll enjoy. But on the other hand, I'll miss having Antonio as our Grand High Master. I'll also miss my life as it is now…which is why Sam and I have decided that some changes should be made."

The Prelate looked horrified by the prospect.

I squeezed her hand. "Want to take the floor, baby?"

She didn't, I could sense, but I knew that she wouldn't back out. We'd discussed in advance how this would go, and this was as important to Sam as it was to me. Taking a deep breath, she announced, "Jared and I won't be isolating ourselves the way that rulers have done before us. It's not in our nature to sit back and dish out orders while everyone else takes the risks. We like to be in the thick of things. That's why, although we'll no longer be Commanders within the legion, we'll still be personally commanding the squad we have trained."

Since I was watching all ten of the guys closely, I saw the effect that this emotionally had on them. Hell, not even the mostly emotionless Butch had been untouched by that, though he tried to cover it quickly by bowing his head.

Jokingly, Sam added, "I mean, really, how could we – in good conscience – hand over those awkward sods to another Commander?" The guys just laughed. "They'll be thought of as the personal squad of the Grand High Pair. Oh and Fletcher, you'll be remaining our PA."

Unreal as it was, Fletcher was actually crying and dabbing his eyes with a tissue, while an amused Norm was patting his shoulder.

Sam continued. "The next few matters are kind of close to my heart. There will be no consorts within The Hollow from this night forward – anyone who knows me will no doubt find this amusing, but I don't care." And they *did* find it amusing; the entire room was laughing. "Bonk as much as you want, but if you want exclusivity, you give those girls – or blokes, in some cases – a better title than 'consort'; that's all I'm saying. I hope this will become a trend worldwide, but that's up to you.

"As for anyone who doesn't want their maker at the Binding ceremony, they don't have to have them there – sod their rights. Also, the act of Turning humans against their will is punishable by death from this night onwards. Hey, if you're going to take someone's human life, why shouldn't I take your vampire life?" And that was a pretty good point. It was a point a lot of people would agree with, since almost half of the population hadn't chosen this life for themselves.

"And lastly…"

Lastly? She should have been done by now.

"As part of rebuilding the legion, I'll be introducing an all-female squad."

Smiling, I groaned. I shouldn't have been at all surprised.

"My hope is that the females in this room by the names of Alora, Jude, Ava, Paige, and Imani will accept a place in that squad – you have all earned it." Going by their pleased expressions, they intended to accept her offer. "Sebastian has agreed to help me scout for other additions to the legion as a whole. So if there's anyone out there –

male or female, Pagori or Keja or Sventé – who thinks they have what it takes, I look forward to meeting you. For now, though, I'm going to say goodbye so I can go spend some time with my mate."

As everyone clapped and cheers rang out, I turned to face her. "An all-female squad, huh? I should have seen that coming."

She smoothed out the collar of my shirt. "It will make things interesting."

Before I had the chance to agree, Luther and Sebastian joined us on the podium, bowing – and, thus, freaking Sam out again.

"The bowing is not necessary," she assured them.

Sebastian smiled at her fondly. "We just want you to understand that we have pledged our loyalty to you."

"A few words of explanation could have cleared that up just fine," she told him.

"We will serve you as we have served Antonio," vowed Luther…who was just the person that I wanted to speak to.

While Sebastian chatted with Sam, I took Luther aside. "I wanted to ask you something. Your visions…do they always come true?"

My question clearly surprised him. "No. Most of them do, and most of them are extremely accurate, but not all. I have come to think of them as warnings rather than glimpses of what is coming."

"What do you mean?"

"Well, if what I see is something bad, it gives me the ability to find some way to prevent it from happening. That would suggest that the future is not set in stone. We *can* change it." He studied my expression for moment. "Your vision did not come true," he guessed. Although Luther could help a person have a vision, he never saw that vision for himself.

I jiggled my head. "Part of it did. The thing is…I was happy in the vision. No, not happy. I was content. So the vision wasn't *bad*, although I'm happier and more content with the way things are now."

He thought on that for a few seconds. "Then maybe the vision was a warning. A warning that if you remained on the path that you were then on, the future ahead of you would not be one of total fulfillment."

That *would* make sense. Back then, I hadn't believed that I was built for relationships or that there was any point to them. I'd been fine with being mostly alone, with only having consorts. Maybe I would have been reasonably content if I had continued that way because I wouldn't have known what I was missing. Now though, I couldn't even imagine being without Sam. It was her who had changed my perceptions on relationships. "In other words, it was a warning to get my shit together?"

Luther chuckled. "Yes, I would say so. I have had my fair share of those."

Feeling better, lighter, I smiled and patted his upper arm. "Thanks, Luther."

"You do not need to thank me. I am your Advisor now."

"Just don't think that means you need to be a constant companion for Sam and me. It's obvious that you and Sebastian spend so much time with Antonio because he's a close friend. You should continue to do that. I can teleport to you if I need your advice – which will probably be often, but you know what I'm getting at."

"You are telling me to ensure that I live my own life and not to allow my position to dictate who I am."

"I once made that mistake. I don't want you to do the same."

He nodded. "Then I will take your advice, as you will take mine. Now go and rescue your mate from Sebastian – he is teasing her about how her initial doubts to attend the try-outs could have led to her missing out on all that she has now. She is not impressed."

Glancing at her, I realised that no, she wasn't impressed at all. I smoothly came to her side. "Thanks for keeping her company, Sebastian."

Taking the hint, he nodded and walked away, seeming extremely too amused for Sam's liking.

She gave me a grateful look. "I have to wonder if he's curious about how much my whip hurts. Surely common sense told him that this is not the right time to wind me up."

Cupping her neck, I searched her gaze. "You sure you're okay? I mean, this probably wouldn't have been something you'd have taken on if it wasn't for me being Heir. And yet you Bound yourself to me anyway."

"Why wouldn't I? You're good in bed. You get rid of unwelcome creepy crawlies. You don't leave the toilet seat up. And, being nice and tall, you can reach all those places that I can't reach. I reckon I got a good deal."

Laughing, I pulled her flush against me. "Maybe you *think* you got a good deal. The truth is that you could have done better. But no one else would have loved you like I do." I kissed her gently, meaning every word. "Tell me you know that even though we have all these huge responsibilities now, you'll still always come first to me."

"I know."

That was easy. I arched a brow, surprised by the confidence in her response. "You do?"

"It's kind of hard not to believe you when you won't stop harping on about it."

"I don't harp."

"Yes, you do." She slid her arms around my neck. "And, for the record, I *did* in fact get a good deal. I love you in spite of the harping, and the overprotectiveness, and the fact that you're *squeezing my arse* in front of all these people and while anyone watching over V-Tube can see."

"Can't help it." I gave it another squeeze. "Do you remember what you said to me the first night we met?"

"Now who's the pretty girl?" she offered, referring to the time we had duelled and she had put me on my ass.

I scowled. "No, after that. You said you could improve the squad's control of their gifts within five nights—"

"Actually, I think you'll find that I originally said 'seven' nights."

"—and I proposed a bet: that if you didn't manage to do it within five nights, I'd get to taste you. But we both know that no one can get you to do anything that you don't want to do. So the question is: would you have let me bite you if I'd won the bet?"

She pursed her lips. "Using the excuse that I was just honouring the bet...yes. But I'd have wanted you to do it – although hell would have frozen over before I admitted that."

"I wouldn't have done it, you know." I could see that I'd surprised her. "I didn't want to taste you until I knew for sure that you wanted it. Of course I strongly suspected that you did, but the fact that you enjoyed whipping me and causing me physical pain didn't instil me with confidence."

"I'm all about the tough love."

"You fought me and fought me back then. Fought me on every level...but I wanted you too much, and I was too determined to have you. And now you're mine." Not even Imani's gift could sever our bond; it was solid and untouchable.

Her arms tightened around my neck as she kissed me lightly. "And you're mine as well."

"Baby, I've been yours since you put me on my ass and called me a pretty girl."

She laughed. "We should thank Antonio for playing cupid. I've got some matchmaking games of my own to plan." Her smile was impish. "Want to play?"

"What did you have in mind? Or should I say, who?"

ACKNOWLEDGMENTS

I want to say a big massive thank you to my husband for being so supportive and for helping me with – okay, doing all of – the housework to give me that alone time I need. And thank you to my fabulous children just for being them.

I must say a huge thank you to my Beta reader, Andrea Ashby – what would I do without you, lady? She's the extra eye I need and is always there when I need her advice and help.

I also wish to thank Ruby José – once again, she did an amazing cover for the book and I absolutely adore her.

Finally, thank you to all my readers. Without your support, this may never have become a series so I'm eternally grateful to you.

If for any reason you would like to contact me, whether it's about the book or you're considering self-publishing and have any questions, feel free to e-mail me at: suzanne_e_wright@live.co.uk

Take care,

Suzanne Wright, Author

Website: http://www.suzannewright.co.uk

Blog: http://www.suzannewrightsblog.blogspot.co.uk

Twitter: https://twitter.com/suz_wright

Facebook: https://www.facebook.com/pages/Suzanne-Wright/1392617144284756

ABOUT THE AUTHOR

Suzanne Wright lives in England with her husband and her two children. When she's not spending time with her family, she's writing, reading, or doing her version of housework – sweeping the house with a look.

TITLES BY SUZANNE WRIGHT:

The Deep in Your Veins Series

Here Be Sexist Vampires
The Bite That Binds
Taste of Torment

The Phoenix Pack Series

Feral Sins
Wicked Cravings
Carnal Secrets

From Rags

Made in the USA
Lexington, KY
03 January 2017